A DANGEROUS KIND OF LADY

MIA VINCY

Inner Ballad Press

A Dangerous Kind of Lady

E-book ISBN: 978-1-925882-04-9

Print ISBN: 978-1-925882-05-6

Cover: Studio Bukovero

∾

CONTENT NOTES: *Male character (secondary) physically assaults female character; past death of a child by illness (main character's sibling); death by fire; controlling parent (now deceased)*

A DANGEROUS KIND
OF LADY

Wit is the most dangerous talent you can possess. It must be guarded with great discretion and good-nature, otherwise it will create you many enemies. ...

Be even cautious in displaying your good sense. It will be thought you assume a superiority over the rest of the company.— But if you happen to have any learning, keep it a profound secret, especially from the men, who generally look with a jealous and malignant eye on a woman of great parts, and a cultivated understanding.

A man of real genius and candour is far superior to this meanness. But such a one will seldom fall in your way...

A Father's Legacy to his Daughters
Dr. John Gregory
London, 1808 edition

CHAPTER 1

Fifteen minutes into the Prince Regent's costume party, and Arabella was reaching the conclusion that she would not make a very good spy.

Which was unfortunate, as "become a spy" topped her list of things to do if her father disinherited her. For the most part, she surely qualified for the job—she excelled at knowing things she ought not know, at dissembling, and at guessing others' misdeeds before they'd even had a chance to commit them—but she now suspected that being a spy required patience, and patience had never been her forte.

Already her patience had reached its limits. If only she could order people to arrange themselves as she pleased! But no, she had to conceal her vexation beneath polite greetings and gracious nods, as she drifted through the crush of guests spilling out into the gardens.

It was a fine, fresh evening, the late-summer sky as clear as one could hope for in London, and the expansive lawns were ablaze with flaming torches and hanging lanterns. If the party's organizers had intended an atmosphere of carnivalesque chaos, they had succeeded: Colorfully dressed acrobats cartwheeled among the costumed guests, fire-eaters breathed out flames, troubadours sang and jugglers juggled and tightrope dancers leaped and twirled.

A dazzling spectacle, certainly, but it rather frustrated Arabella's secret, simultaneous missions: hunting Lord Hardbury, avoiding Lord Sculthorpe, dodging Mama, scaring away the fortune hunters who had multiplied after Hardbury jilted her, and pointedly eyeing every other Minerva so they maintained an appropriate distance.

Arabella had ordered the Minerva costume—comprising a draped Roman-style robe and red-plumed helmet—knowing it was not unique, but, as she had said to Mama, "If one must face society's scorn at a costume party with the Prince Regent and three thousand of his closest friends, one ought to do it dressed as a warrior goddess."

"It is not like you to exaggerate, Arabella," Mama had scolded in her serene way. "Lord Hardbury has not actually jilted you. He was correct in saying that an agreement between your fathers when you were infants is not a binding engagement, and everyone knows that. No one will mention it."

True, no one was mentioning it. In every conversation, Arabella could *hear* them Not Mentioning it. How dreadful people were, the way they went around Not Mentioning things.

If only someone would mention it! What a relief if someone were to say, "Well, Miss Larke, Guy Roth has finally returned to claim the title of Marquess of Hardbury, after an absence so long some feared he was dead, and his first announcement is that he will not marry you. Tell me, Miss Larke," this wonderful person would say, "how fares your famous pride now? Shall we prepare a poultice for it, fetch it some bandages, or is it time to send for the vicar?"

Arabella would look down her nose at them, in the imperious manner she had perfected by age twelve, and say, "Pray, do not trouble yourself. It will take more than a set-down by Lord Hardbury to finish off *my* pride."

Yes, her blessed pride, her most loyal companion these twenty-three years. Always stepping in to save her, taking control of her mouth, and making her say things she didn't mean. It was a wonder she could stay upright under the weight of all that pride, though sometimes she doubted she would stay upright without it.

And now her pride had brought her to this: After a lifetime of boasting that she would become the Marchioness of Hardbury, while secretly praying she would never actually have to marry that detestable Guy Roth, she needed to ask him a favor.

That Arabella Larke asked a favor of anyone was enough to make the sky crack and tremble. That she was asking it of Guy Roth would surely make the heavens collapse onto their heads.

But ask it she must, when the alternative was—

Lord Sculthorpe.

Arabella froze.

The Baron Sculthorpe stood not five yards away, conversing in a small group, his face mercifully turned away. He was dressed as an old-fashioned highwayman, in a tricorne hat, black cape, and lacy cuffs. The costume made him look every inch the dashing, athletic war hero that society so admired. He was approaching thirty-six, but that didn't matter, not for a man as hale and hearty as he.

A few more steps and he might have seen her. Under her helmet, Arabella's scalp prickled, her heart pounding from the close call. *Don't be ridiculous*, she scolded herself, and glanced around to assess her avenues of escape.

Sidling toward Sculthorpe's group were a pair of jesters, their medieval costumes a riot of red and yellow, from their three-pointed fool's hats to their long-toed shoes. They danced close to Sculthorpe and the matron at his side, grabbed their wrists, and briskly tied man and woman to each other with a length of pink ribbon.

Arabella could not hear the words over the crowd's merriment, but she knew this game, slightly risqué but not uncommon at such gatherings: The jesters announced his lordship had only to kiss the fair lady to be released. Sculthorpe clutched at his heart with exaggerated delight, bestowed a peck on the lady's round cheek, then made a show of fanning himself, as their little audience cheered. The jesters cut the ribbon and skipped away, and the group resumed their chatter, enlivened by the interlude.

What a performance! What charm! No wonder wealthy, handsome Lord Sculthorpe was one of the most eligible bachelors in the land.

And lucky Arabella, she was the one he had chosen.

That was how Papa had put it, when he announced that, after Lord Hardbury had written to confirm that he would not marry her, Lord Sculthorpe had written to confirm that he would. Arabella did not feel lucky. This past spring, when Sculthorpe first displayed an interest in her, she had realized within three conversations that she could not bear to be his wife. With society speculating about Guy's return, she had insisted on waiting for him instead. She had counted on Guy not returning, at least not before Sculthorpe married someone else. Wrong on both counts.

"You're fortunate Sculthorpe still wants you, so don't spoil this too," Papa had said to Arabella, his eyes on his beloved Queenie as he stroked her bright-green feathers, while the portrait of her dead brother Oliver smirked from its prize position on the wall.

"If Lord Sculthorpe is so eager to marry me, Papa, I don't see how I could spoil it."

"Heiress to a grand estate, yet men fall over themselves to avoid marrying you. Lord Luxborough jilted you, and now Lord Hardbury has jilted you, so make sure Lord Sculthorpe doesn't jilt you too."

"A wiser course would be to dispense altogether with this tiresome parade of lords," she had argued.

"Are you saying you refuse to marry Sculthorpe?"

"I told you, I have a viable alternative, if you would only wait. I have written to—"

"I am tired of waiting! No more talking. I've been patient with you, my girl, but it's past time you married and provided me with grandsons." Then Papa had concluded with a definitive statement: "When you come back from the Prince Regent's party, you will be engaged."

"Or?"

"Or you need not bother coming back at all."

Once more unto the breach, Arabella thought, and melted into the crowd before Sculthorpe could see her. A juggler, hands a blur, winked at her as she slipped past. She felt like a juggler herself, juggling potential husbands. Of course she had a plan to avoid marrying Sculthorpe—Arabella always had a plan—but it would take months to come to fruition, and with Papa stubbornly issuing ultimatums, she needed to buy time. Her resolve hardened. If her only way to avoid losing everything was to get engaged tonight, then get engaged she would.

For which she must find Guy.

~

How was Arabella to identify Guy Roth, Marquess of Hardbury, in a crowd this size, after an absence of nearly eight years, with everyone in costumes?

Easy: Look for the cloud of sycophants buzzing like gnats around a useless, self-satisfied dandy.

He would be preening at their flattery, no doubt, failing to see, as always, that he would be nothing if not for his money and name. As children, on those all-too-frequent occasions when their families had gathered at the same country house, Arabella would watch, amazed, as the other boys let Guy win whatever game they played, and he was too conceited to realize it. Arabella was the exception, of course; she never let anyone win.

To be fair, Guy had been a gracious winner. He never boasted, but he never needed to: There were always toadies eager to do the boasting for him. Neither was he a sore loser when Arabella defeated him. Publicly, he would congratulate her and laugh off jibes about being beaten by a girl, especially the one he was meant to marry, but they both knew. Privately, he would say, "I'll defeat you next time, *Arabella*," to which she would retort, "You'll never defeat me, *Guy*," and they'd exchange glares and not speak again.

He was dazzling society years before Arabella made her come-out, and she had to suffer through glowing reports of how he had won this footrace and that debate, how he danced so elegantly and wore the latest fashions to perfection. Then the final reports, of course: that he had fallen in love with a lady who spurned him, and so, when he didn't get his own way for the first time in his life, he had run away from England for an eight-year sulk.

Yet it was one thing for him to go missing for years; it was quite another—and vexingly inconvenient—to go missing at the party held to celebrate his return. Arabella worked her way through the crowd, exchanging nods and gliding on, inspecting and dismissing a man dressed as a bear, a knight, a hangman. Then an acrobat back-flipped across her path; Arabella swerved just as a fire-eater blew flames into the air.

When her vision cleared, she found herself blinking at a tall man dressed as Caesar, with a red cape thrown over a leather breastplate and knee-length skirt. A small space surrounded him, for even in this crowd his imperial presence kept others at a respectful distance, save for the middle-aged man chattering at his side. Arabella let her eyes drift over Caesar's bare arms, and was absently examining the pteruges that ended inches above his boots when she remembered herself and pivoted away.

Mid-turn, her legs stopped; a heartbeat later, her mind caught up.

No. Surely not.

And yet...

Twisting, Arabella looked over her shoulder. Then turned her whole body. And blinked again.

For while the man dressed as Caesar was definitely Guy, he was not Guy as she knew him.

This version of Guy seemed... Well... He had... Guy was...

Good grief.

Guy had grown up.

He was bigger than she remembered, broader, more solid. He had always been athletic, but only in relation to gentlemanly pursuits; if this man were a stranger, she would not take him for a gentleman, let alone a lord. Perhaps it was the way he was weathered, as no English lord ought to be, with the ends of his thick hair turned nearly gold by the sun and his complexion unfashionably tanned. His narrow nose bore a bump; perhaps that imperfection was what unsettled her. Once upon a time, no person in England would dare break that lordling's nose. Indeed, nothing about his features was smooth. The hollows in his cheeks provided a counterpoint to the sharp definition of his jaw, and he had a furrow in his brow, as though the world posed too much of a conundrum to give him a moment's peace.

But it was something more that arrested her, something about the way he held himself. As a youth, Guy had strutted unseeingly through the world, secure in the belief that no harm would come to him. Now, an alertness thrummed beneath his confident ease, as if he anticipated an attack.

Where have you been, Guy? Arabella wondered. *What have you been doing, to make you like that?*

Yet despite his watchfulness, he had not seen her, and she let her eyes travel over him again. More pteruges hung over his shoulders, the leather strips caressing the muscular lines of his bare upper arms. His forearms, too, were bare, the tanned skin stretched over corded muscles and veins.

Really, Guy. Arabella's gaze lingered on his forearms. *What have you been doing, to make you like* that?

The way his eyes roamed, it was only a matter of time before he saw her. Arabella felt unusually ill prepared. The Guy of the past would have been easy to manage, but this man... This man was someone new.

As she watched, his eyes drifted over a trio of young gentlemen who loitered nearby. Their attitudes sharpened, their smiles beckoned—but his eyes kept traveling as if they were not there. Had he made eye contact, that would have been the cut. As it was, it barely skated over politeness. The gentlemen knew it too, for they stiffened and launched into an animated discussion as if they had never sought Guy's attention.

Arabella slipped back into the crowd. If Guy did that to her—and given their history of mutual antagonism, there was a good chance he would—others would be sure to notice. The humiliating gossip would never end. Curse him. He could too easily dismiss her without even hearing her proposition, while she stood like a petitioner begging an audience with a king. How society would snicker at her, for Arabella was prideful and outspoken, and everyone loved to mock a woman who thought too much of herself.

Then she must find a way to approach him without risking her pride. If her plan failed, her pride would be all that remained.

As she considered her options, she again spied the jesters with their pink ribbons. She thought of Guy's bare, muscular forearm and the contents of her reticule.

Within a minute, Arabella had a plan.

YET ANOTHER FELLOW was babbling at Guy about something, another of his late father's cronies hoping the son would pick up where the father had left off. How adorable they were, the way they clucked at him about their corrupt schemes, like so many eager hens. And how amusing, the way their clucking grew more insistent the longer that Guy acted obtuse.

But at least while this chap clucked on, no one else approached, so Guy let him talk while he scanned the carnival party for Freddie, hoping he would recognize her; there would be a big difference between the eleven-year-old girl he had left behind and the nineteen-year-old lady she would have become. Fiendishly clever of them, to put everyone in costumes, thus making the game of Find-My-Sister-In-A-Crowd-Of-Thousands that bit trickier.

"Does that not strike you as ridiculous, my lord?" the man was saying, with a chortle.

Guy glanced at him. Speaking of ridiculous: The fellow, a

politician of some description, had inexplicably chosen to wear a badger costume, although, to be fair, it went nicely with his thick white hair. His deceptively boyish face was bright with conspiratorial glee, as if certain of Guy's agreement.

"What strikes me as ridiculous is your conviction that I wish to pass this evening discussing your petty politics," Guy replied.

"Ha ha, how droll you are! Quite right, quite right." The politician nodded enthusiastically, apparently undeterred. "Let's discuss it next week at my club. Over a bottle of the finest Burgundy."

This bit of nonsense made Guy snort. "Even six bottles of the finest Burgundy would not make your notions appealing."

"Please, my lord. Have you no interest in the fate of our nation?"

"In the fate of our nation, yes. In the fate of your corrupt schemes, no."

"I would not call them that!"

"Of course you wouldn't, you naughty little rascal. But I would."

His companion's mouth opened and closed as he spluttered his outrage. Guy couldn't help laughing. Never had he expected politics to be such fun.

The man rallied fast, although if he wanted to appear dignified, he really should not have dressed as a badger.

"This scheme benefits you too, my lord," he hissed. "I would expect you to appreciate my assistance, given that your late father bequeathed to your sisters every bit of property that wasn't entailed. Why, I hear he did not even make you their guardian, so you haven't the benefit of managing their trusts."

No, indeed. That "benefit" went to Sir Walter Treadgold, an obscure knight whose sister had married Guy's father a few years earlier. The law stood firmly on the side of his father's will; according to Guy's solicitors, the Court of Chancery would overturn the will only if Sir Walter was found to be mismanaging his wards' trusts. Evidence of that should be easy to find: Any intimate of the late marquess was almost certainly corrupt.

"Your concern is touching, dear sir," Guy said lightly. "But fortunately for me, the entailed property generates enough income to provide all I desire from life, namely several pairs of comfortable boots and a supply of hot buttered toast." His gaze snagged on a pair of young ladies dressed as flowers, heads together in intimate conversation. Their bright eyes and fond smiles aroused a pang of nostalgia for something he had never had. "Oh, and a bride."

"Is it true, my lord, that your bride will not be Arabella Larke? An alliance with Miss Larke would bring you considerable wealth."

An alliance with Arabella would also bring him considerable indigestion, if she was still the bossy, quarrelsome know-it-all that he recalled.

"True," he conceded. "But Miss Larke was my father's choice, and it's so much more sporting to choose one's own wife, don't you think?"

The man steepled his fingers. "Now you mention it, I recall that I have a niece."

Guy laughed. Heads turned. Among them, he spied a pair of jesters, pink ribbons dangling menacingly from their hands. The young ladies dressed as flowers exchanged a mischievous glance and drew closer. A tempting diversion, but Guy could not be distracted by a merry game of courtship tonight; first he must find Freddie, before Sir Walter played another of his tricks and whisked her away again.

He casually sidled away from the jesters, his latest hen clucking along beside him.

"Of course you have a niece," Guy said, still searching the crowd. "And if you didn't have a niece, you'd have a daughter or a sister or a cousin. During my absence, everyone in Britain has developed a female relative of marriageable age." He spread his arms expansively, taking in the hubbub of the costumed, perfumed crowd. "May everyone send them all my way, and let the games begin."

"If I might be so bold, my lord, my wife is planning a dinner party. You could meet my niece and we could discuss—"

Guy clapped the man on the shoulder. "I admire your persistence, old chap, but you have nothing else to recommend you. Here's an idea: Come up with an honest scheme, one that doesn't involve lining your pockets at the expense of the good people of Britain, and I shall happily attend all your dinner parties and meet everyone's nieces. But for now, do me a kindness and toddle off. Go. Begone. Shoo."

With that, Guy wheeled about.

Only to nearly collide with a Minerva.

Instinctively, he stepped back, excusing himself, already looking past her at the crowd. But the Minerva made no effort to move aside or apologize. Indeed, she did not betray any surprise at all.

Now he was paying attention, it dawned on him that this particular Minerva was tall for a woman. That the dark curls artfully arranged under the elegant helmet did little to soften her pale, angular features. That her gaze was as blue and unflinching as the desert sky. That her lips naturally curved upward at the corners, in the promise of a smile that would never come.

And when her eyebrows arched ever so slightly, wielded with as much control and skill as an orchestra conductor wielded his baton, Guy reached the dismaying conclusion that this was not any Minerva.

This was Arabella Larke.

Arabella Larke, matured from a gangling, scowling brat to a poised, haughty woman. Her unfashionable height was increased by the warrior's helmet, whose mane of red feathers cascaded down her back. The drapes of her long Roman robe were fastened at one shoulder with an owl-shaped brooch, a reticule resembling a shield dangled from one wrist, and her pale arms were bare but for a silver snake coiled around her upper right arm.

His thoughts shattered. Arabella had somehow transformed into a compelling woman, and the sight crashed against his memories of her as a child. He shook off the sensation. Seeing people after a lengthy absence was always strange; that was all. He had last seen her when she was fifteen or sixteen; it was only natural that she had matured. Besides, judging by her demeanor, quite unlike the obvious amiability of the young ladies he had admired, she had not otherwise changed.

So Guy saw no need to change his typical greeting.

"Oh no, not you," he said. "And I was having such a lovely evening."

"So it's true: You're not dead." Her drawl was as imperious as ever, but her voice had developed an appealing huskiness. "The government was in quite a state over your absence."

"So touching to know they cared."

"Oh, I shouldn't take it personally. It just doesn't look good for the country, to go around misplacing its marquesses." She eyed him with some perplexity. "How astonishing that no one did kill you."

"Many tried. None succeeded."

"Perhaps one did succeed but the Devil spat you out again."

"He sends you his regards."

Was that—a smile? No, not from Arabella. She had never been one to give smiles away easily.

Then she flinched, and a strong hand gripped Guy's wrist.

Instinct had him jerking away, spinning, arm raised, ready to strike. Only to freeze— It was a jester who had grabbed him. Stars above, Guy had nearly hit the jester, and he felt sick to see that same knowledge reflected in the other man's eyes.

With a resigned nod, Guy forced himself to relax; Arabella had distracted him, and it was too late to escape. He had to suffer through it, suffer through the two jesters pressing his bare forearm against hers, suffer through them deftly wrapping their joined arms with an ungodly length of ribbon. Her skin was soft and warm. What a surprise: She was not made of marble. He thought he caught a matching surprise in her eyes, but her eyelids lowered before he could be sure.

A greater surprise was that she did not object to being manhandled in this way. How disappointing, if the years had turned Arabella docile. Her ferocity had been one of her few charms.

"Three thousand guests are attending this party," Guy said. "What are the odds that I'd get tied to you, of all people?"

"Rather better odds than if I'd not paid for it to happen, I suspect."

"Huh. You bribed them," he said, nodding. She must have guessed he would refuse to talk to her, so she went to these extremes to get her way. But then, Arabella always had cared more about winning than about trivial things like rules. "I ought to have guessed."

"Do calm down. I'm not the only one who had the idea of thus securing an audience with you."

"But you're the only one with no scruples about doing it."

"I beg to differ. It was a very scrupulous bribe."

"A bribe, by definition, cannot be scrupulous."

She lifted one silk-clad shoulder in a nonchalant shrug. "I factored in the risk these men would take to assist me, and offered an exceedingly generous payment accordingly. Which makes this bribe scrupulous, wouldn't you agree?"

"I agree," said one of the jesters.

"As do I," said the other.

"There," Arabella said. "Everyone is content with this arrangement."

"Except me."

She made a dismissive "hm" sound in her throat, indicating that Guy's approval was of no concern.

Their arms had been pressed together long enough that it was no longer clear where his skin ended and hers began. Guy tried to keep his shoulder as far from Arabella's as he could, but the hint of her orange-blossom scent attempted to lure him near.

The jesters triple-tied their final knot and skipped back to admire their work. Around them, other guests were pausing to watch—naturally. Guy couldn't scratch his chin without attracting comment, and Arabella would never pass anywhere unnoticed; given their history, the sight of them tied together would have the satirists composing lines.

But Guy was marquess now, only one rank below duke, and being one of the highest-ranking men in the land had to be good for something.

"You've had your entertainment," he said to the jesters. "Release us."

A waste of breath: England had a long tradition in which jesters alone could say what they pleased with impunity, and these two jesters did not relinquish that ancient right.

Instead, grinning, they recited a rhyme in unison. "We bring a gift from Cupid above: a bucketful of mischief, a cartload of love."

"No love here," Guy muttered. "This is all mischief."

One produced a dagger out of thin air; with a sleight of hand, it vanished again. "If you wish to be freed from this—you need but give the lady a kiss."

"Kiss Arabella Larke?" Guy glanced at those curved lips. "Not a bloody chance in hell."

CHAPTER 2

The jesters skipped off into the crowd, and Arabella was alone with a large, displeased marquess tied to her arm.

Alone but for the other three thousand people, that was, at least two thousand of whom were watching.

"All this for a kiss." Guy waved his free arm. "Well, well, well. I expected England to change during my absence, but I never dreamed that quarrelsome Arabella Larke would grow up into an enticing adventuress who flirts with danger."

Arabella blinked at him. She'd never flirted with anything in her life.

"Danger?" she repeated mockingly. "Why, is mighty, muscular Lord Hardbury frightened of a little kiss?" She had not considered he might actually kiss her. That would ruin everything. "Do calm down," she hastened to add. "I wish only to talk."

"But I don't want to do that either."

"Hence the ribbon."

He shook his head, still so annoyingly pleased with himself.

"By the age of twelve they were calling you accomplished, but clearly you have yet to master the art of charm, if your only means of engaging people in conversation is to tie them up."

"If you must know, my preferred method is to whack them over the head. But that seemed impolitic, given that you are the guest of honor."

"I thank you for your restraint," he said dryly.

Shooting her a glance—his eyes were green; she had forgotten that—Guy bent his head and picked at the knot with his free hand. The light from a flaming torch caught the gold in his hair, licked the angle of his jaw, and cast shadows over the other side of his face. Arabella tried to ignore his closeness, his biceps inches from her own.

"I suppose you wish to discuss my letter to your father," Guy added, without looking up.

"Indeed. Quite a way with words you have. 'I am not responsible for my father's promises,'" she quoted. "'It is ludicrously medieval to expect an agreement concerning infants to be binding.' And, my personal favorite, 'Nothing on this Earth will induce me to marry Arabella Larke.'"

"I thought you'd like that one."

"I was almost inspired to embroider it on a cushion."

He flashed her a smile and returned to his task, the hand teasing those ribbons tanned and callused as no English lord's hand should be.

"Those jesters of yours have tied a fiendishly excellent knot," he muttered. "But, hmm, if I can simply..."

He twisted at the waist to examine the knot from another angle, before attacking it anew. That, too, she had forgotten: his appetite for a challenge. Whether crossing a swollen river or solving a rhyming riddle, Guy always threw himself into challenges with energy and fearlessness. He had thrived on the thrill of a chase, the excitement of a dare, always treading just this side of danger with a glint in his eyes and a smile on his face.

With the benefit of age and hindsight, Arabella suddenly realized it was likely his ebullience that had made him the leader as a boy, not merely his title and size.

This new understanding was...unsettling; how else had she been wrong? She was silently rewording her proposition when he spoke again, eyes on his task.

"I was surprised to learn you were not already married and making some poor man's life an utter misery," he said.

Arabella shrugged. "Well, there are so many men who deserve to have their lives made a misery, it's difficult to choose just one."

"Why only one? A woman with your talent and resources, you could have run through five or six husbands by now."

"A wasted opportunity, I suppose. I would make a very fetching widow."

"And whomever you marry would be happy to oblige you in that ambition. But that man is not me."

Guy released the knot and let his arm fall; hers had to drop too. They stood so close that her fingers brushed his leather-clad hip, and his knuckles bumped her through the silk of her gown. He didn't seem to notice. He was searching the surrounding carnival for inspiration or assistance. He'd find a solution soon. She had to stop wasting time.

"But really, Guy, I'm afraid you didn't think this matter through," she said. "If you had, you would recognize that an engagement would benefit us both."

His expression was incredulous. "I don't need to think it through. A lifetime of knowing you, Arabella, is enough to be sure."

"Oh, you great men, you are always so *sure*. One day you are sure of one thing, and the next day you are equally sure of its opposite."

"Direct that wit elsewhere. I know my own mind."

"Nonsense. How can you possibly know your own mind when I have not yet explained it to you?"

A chuckle burst out of him, though not, she thought, because he recognized that as one of her little jokes.

"Ah, Arabella, you've not changed one bit." His gaze rippled over her, flicked away. "Still as arrogant and ambitious as ever. First it's my father insisting I marry you, then it's your father, and now you make demands, proving, true to form"—he indicated their bound arms—"that you'll stop at nothing to get your way. You always said you wanted to marry me."

She sniffed. "No, I always said I wanted to be a marchioness and that you would merely be an unfortunate appurtenance."

"I do remember you saying that." Galling laughter warmed his voice. "I was impressed that a ten-year-old knew a word like 'appurtenance'. Was that the day I threw you in a snowdrift? You came up spluttering like an outraged cat with snow coming out of your nostrils."

"Yes, I recall you found that amusing. Right until I threw a snowball smack in your laughing mouth."

"I remember the summer when we stole your oars and left you stranded on the water."

The years melted away; they were behaving like children again, tumbling into their familiar pattern of competing to defeat each other. Oh, but he was as maddening as ever! The way everything had always come so easily to him. The way everyone had told her to behave nicely with him, because, "Oh, he'll be your husband one day!" It had only strengthened her resolve to bring him down.

"Was that the same summer when you boys were playing war games on the lake and I destroyed your boat?" she said coolly.

His eyes narrowed. "You weren't even playing, and I was about to win."

"And there we have it: the reason boys hate playing with girls. Because they know the girls will get the better of them."

"Ha! Do not imagine you'll ever get the better of me."

"Says the man dangling off my wrist like a reticule."

He held her gaze a heartbeat longer, then shook his head with another small laugh. "Why did they imagine it was a good idea for us to marry? All we ever did was quarrel, compete, or ignore each other."

"Sounds ideal for a modern marriage."

"That is not what I want from my marriage."

It wasn't what she wanted either. She uttered such lines out of habit, for her own amusement, if nobody else's. She could hardly admit to anyone—especially not to Guy—what she truly wanted from marriage.

She forced her attention back to her mission. This conversation had fallen so far off track, it was in a ditch spinning its wheels. Time to change her strategy.

"Speaking of marriage, namely your past failed attempt at it, have you renewed your acquaintance with Clare Ivory?" she asked. "No doubt someone has already told you that, after throwing you over for Lord Sculthorpe, she went on to become one of London's most expensive and sought-after courtesans. And Lord Sculthorpe is now a greatly admired war hero." She suppressed a shudder. "He mentioned that when you challenged him over Miss Ivory all those years ago, he dealt you a beating, after which you ran away."

There: Surely that reminder would prime Guy for revenge and make him listen to her proposition.

But he only shrugged and went back to fiddling with the knot.

"Any young man who reaches his majority without embarrassing himself over drink, cards, or a woman is a disgrace to young men everywhere. Doing foolish things in public is the whole point of being a young man. An exciting youth serves as our only redeeming feature when we turn into crashing old bores." He flicked her a glance. "A word of advice, Arabella: This is not the way to get a man to marry you."

"Do pay attention. I never said a word about marrying you."

He kept picking at the ribbons. "You said—"

"I said an *engagement* would benefit us both. If you tell my father you mean to marry me and—"

"No."

"We announce our betrothal—"

"No."

"After sufficient time has elapsed—"

"No, Arabella." Once more, he let their arms drop, his expression hard. "No, no, no."

"If you would just listen. If not, I must—"

"No. I have spent my entire life being ordered to marry you, if only because my father was determined to make me obey. Whatever your schemes and ambitions, leave me out of it. After your behavior tonight, I am more certain than ever that you are the last woman I would marry."

Curse him. He was set against her so stubbornly that he would not even listen to her proposition, let alone consider it. Her solution to her marriage problem was so obvious she had berated herself for not thinking of it sooner: a marriage of convenience with her neighbor's heir, Hadrian Bell. She had written to him, but Hadrian held a diplomatic post in Prussia and would not return for months. All she needed Guy to do was act as a placeholder until then—and he would not even listen!

What must she do next? Beg? If only she knew how! Tell him about Papa's ultimatum and how Sculthorpe repelled her? Most likely, he would mock her fear, say she and Sculthorpe were well matched. If she didn't salvage her pride now, for the rest of their lives Guy would regard her with scorn.

He must be getting desperate to escape her: He raised their hands to his mouth and tore at the knot with his teeth. His lips brushed her skin, sending warm shivers up her arm.

"Take care, Guy." Her tone was sharper than usual. "Your slobber would not go with my costume."

"If only my costume came with a sword," he muttered. "Or if I could use that sharp tongue of yours to cut this ribbon."

It was useless. He would never understand her precarious situation. He would never understand this gnawing hollow in her gut, this sick feeling of dread at her looming fate.

But she still had her pride and a lifetime's practice in hiding her feelings. She arranged her expression into disdain.

"That sounds almost lewd," she drawled. "At any rate, scissors would be more effective."

"A dagger, a sword, an army—all would be more effective."

"Yes, but I don't have any of those in my reticule, do I?"

His eyes dropped to the shield-shaped bag dangling from her free wrist and bounced back up again.

"This whole time, you had scissors in your reticule?"

She raised an eyebrow coolly. "You don't imagine I would submit to being tied to you if I did not have an escape plan?"

"You are diabolical."

"Thank you."

"Not a compliment."

"Hm."

He reached across her for the reticule. She tried to whisk her arm behind her back, but he moved like lightning; his fingers wrapped around her wrist, warm and implacable. She held herself steady, even as the studded leather strips over his skirt knocked her thighs, even as his throat loomed before her. His scent of leather and spice warred with her own orange blossom, and she ran her gaze up the length of his neck, over his jaw and cheek, to meet his eyes, unamused and hard. They were close enough now to kiss, after all.

"Guy, first, hear me out."

"No."

He looked down, and those long fingers deftly loosened the tie of her reticule. When she let the little bag slide from her wrist, he clasped it like a prize.

"I'll cut myself free of you, Arabella, and I'll not hear another word."

THE LADY'S scissors were so tiny that Guy feared his fingers would get stuck. The blades were designed for nothing more arduous than snipping threads—because heaven forbid perfect Arabella might have a loose thread—and he felt he was sawing away at the ribbon clumsily. He tried to focus on the ribbon, but he could not ignore Arabella's pale skin, with its network of blue veins and scent of orange blossom, the memory of its heady silkiness lingering on his lips.

"We are attracting interest," Arabella said softly.

"I'm trying not to hurt you," he muttered.

"Do you think me so delicate?"

"You, no. Your skin, yes."

Finally, the last of the ribbon fell away and he returned the scissors. Guy rolled his wrist, his skin tingling with her absence.

Pink indents crisscrossed her forearm; Guy brushed them with his thumb, as if to soothe them, though heaven knew she did not deserve soothing.

He hastily stepped away, but she made no comment, as she sheathed the scissors and slipped them into her reticule. The fading light accentuated her sharp cheekbones, her aristocratic jaw. She had grown into her angles and height; her face would only become more interesting with age.

"You've grown up," he said irrelevantly.

Her eyelids flickered. "As have you."

"It's curious, really. Through no fault of your own, you have been a presence shaping my life, but in the end, we are strangers."

"If I were a stranger, you would listen to my request."

"If you were a stranger, you would not ask."

They would never be strangers. They would exist forever on the edges of each other's lives, moving in the same circles, passing each other at dinner parties and balls. They would be polite and remote, starting now.

"Thank you for this exciting adventure," he said. "And now I bid you good evening."

Her eyes narrowed. "We have not finished talking."

"As flattering as it is to receive your marriage proposal—"

"That was not a proposal—"

"—I have more important things on my mind than your marital status. Pray, excuse me, Miss Larke."

He turned away.

"Winning custody of your sisters, I suppose," she said from behind him. "Although Freddie doesn't seem bothered by it, one way or another."

Guy turned back. "You've spoken to Freddie?"

"She is here tonight."

"As are three thousand other people, and I daresay she's changed in eight years."

"Do you mean to say you have not seen Freddie since your return?" She drew her head back. "Have you even met Ursula?"

Ah, the mysterious infant Ursula. Guy had not even known Ursula existed until his return, when he learned that his widowed father had married Caroline Treadgold, who had borne him a daughter before passing away.

Now, little Ursula was in the care of Sir Walter and Lady Treadgold. They were her uncle and aunt, but Guy was her brother; it was only right that he become her guardian, regardless of his father's will. Father must have gone to his grave crowing at having thwarted Guy, but no longer would Guy allow the old man to dictate his life. He would marry a pleasant, amiable lady, bring both Freddie and Ursula into their loving home, and rebuild the family he and his father had destroyed. Then he would feel at peace and know he had come home.

"Once I solve the tricky little puzzle of where Sir Walter Treadgold stashes my sisters, I shall see them both," Guy said.

Arabella raised her eyebrows in a silent question.

"Sir Walter has a cunning talent for always leaving a place hours before I arrive," he explained. "I was hoping to see Freddie here tonight, but the party organizers have not made it easy for me."

"I imagine not. Come along, then."

Arabella pivoted and glided away, with the graceful fluidity to which all ladies aspired, but only some actually attained. Beneath the mane of red feathers from her helmet, he glimpsed a trio of glossy dark ringlets.

After a few steps, she twisted and shot him an expectant look.

"Arabella, I am not a dog that you take for a walk."

"Do you want to see Freddie or not?"

Without waiting for a response, she resumed walking along the lawn, the white silk of her gown swaying around her long, hidden legs. Immediately, other people began to press forward. Cursing under his breath, Guy fell into step with her. His would-be audience subsided.

"I hear your father's will left Freddie and Ursula wealthier than you," Arabella remarked as they cut through the crowd. "One can only hope they still have that wealth when they come of age. Sir Walter Treadgold has bought himself a fancy new coach-and-four, but of course your father left him a generous bequest, too."

"How the deuce do you know all this?" he asked.

"I keep abreast of all that happens in society. Including your stated intention to marry as soon as possible. An engagement may bolster your case in Chancery, and an heiress would remedy your financial situation."

Guy chuckled. She was relentless! But her wealth would never sway him, not given the evidence of how unscrupulous she would be in chasing her ambition to become a marchioness. He knew exactly what he wanted in a wife, having spent years daydreaming of his ideal bride, as he wandered the world in his self-imposed exile.

"My income is still sufficient that I need not consider wealth a criterion for a suitable bride."

"Ah yes, a suitable bride for Guy Roth. What would she be like?"

"Whomever I marry will have a talent for making a peaceful, comfortable home for our family. She will be gentle, pleasant, and..." Guy caught Arabella's arch, sideways look. "And," he repeated emphatically, "she would never plot or scheme or even consider offering bribes."

"But of course." She waved one hand regally. "Someone eternally cheerful and undemanding, who will engage you in diverting conversation and never bother you with what she is truly thinking. As a result, you will assume that her thoughts are the same as your own, and you will congratulate yourself on choosing a bride who is so well matched. She will be agreeable, amenable, and amiable, and when you find yourself thinking that your wife is a little dull, you will assume that is her fault and never realize it is your own."

"You have a low opinion of your sex."

"I have an extremely high opinion of my sex. My low opinion is reserved for men who see only what they want to see and then blame women for being the lack." She shot him a look. "I have never met anyone who relished a challenge as much as you do. You'll bore yourself with a bride like that, and make the poor girl miserable too."

Guy stopped short, Arabella pausing at his side.

"Ah, so you would nobly rescue me from a lifetime of boredom by offering yourself instead," he said, his tone mocking. "A lady too clever for her own good, a lady who pays bribes and makes demands and seeks to embroil me in some scheme to satisfy her own ambitions." He stepped closer, but she did not yield an inch, her stance rigid, her glare fierce. "For both our sakes, Arabella, find someone else to command and leave me be. No doubt other men grovel wherever you go, but you're wasting your time if you think you'll ever make me fall to my knees."

Those eyebrows lifted. "Good grief, Guy, what use would you be on your knees? No— I should put a ring through your nose like a bull. I'll tie a ribbon to it and use it to lead you around."

Her voice dripped with scorn, yet a lost look flashed across her face—a startling, naked vulnerability, come and gone like lightning. But perhaps it was a trick of the light, for the next moment, she was giving him her aloof profile. A mole graced her high cheekbone and a single dark curl caressed her ear.

She jerked her chin. "There," she said.

Guy followed her gaze, which led him to a three-tiered fountain. On the low stone wall encircling the fountain sat a pair of matching shepherdesses; one had reddish-blonde ringlets and a blue dress, and the other was a brunette in pink.

"Freddie is the shepherdess in blue," Arabella went on. "She is something of a wallflower, if only because of her indifference to others' opinions and her marvelously original views. The pink shepherdess is Miss Matilda Treadgold, Sir Walter Treadgold's niece. She has been his ward since she was a small child. She is not a wallflower, by any means. The fact that she is with Freddie now, rather than surrounded by besotted gentlemen, suggests that Freddie is the bait and you are the prey."

"Do you think all women are schemers like you?"

"Only the admirable ones, and I admire Miss Treadgold immensely. She has little in the way of wealth or connections, but as you don't require those, she fits your notion of an ideal wife very nicely."

Even from afar, Guy could not deny Miss Treadgold's appeal, but he kept his eyes on his sister. The ringlets and profusion of blue flounces and ribbons did not suit her, but he'd know that face anywhere: the slightly upturned nose and wide mouth, big eyes and fierce brows, a face that could appear mischievous and elfin one moment, and sullen and mutinous the next.

On his visits home from school and, later, university, she used to run from the schoolroom to throw herself into his arms, and he'd swing her around while she squealed. She would have to marry soon, but perhaps not for another year; they'd have time to get to know each other as adults, rebuild their family first.

He glanced back at Arabella. "I would never have found her myself. Thank you."

"In terms of an engagement, I'm only talking—"

"No talking. No engagement. Enough."

She inhaled through her nose, audibly, and flicked a glance over his shoulder. "Freddie needs your protection. I suspect that Sir Walter may be scheming—"

"Of course he is. Arabella. Desist."

He closed the gap between them. Again she did not budge, as yielding as a marble pillar.

"You are not part of my family, and never will be," he said. "Do not tell me whom to marry, or how to manage Sir Walter, or what my sisters or I need."

"I'm saying this for Freddie's sake, not for yours."

"You are meddling."

"Don't be absurd. I never meddle. I simply fix other people's problems for them."

"I do not need you to fix my problems."

He did not need her at all. Their fathers' agreement was not her fault, any more than it was his, but damned if he would sacrifice himself for anything, whether his dead father's persistent tyranny or Arabella's persistent ambitions.

Besides, they were not children playing war games on the lake. They were adults, both unmarried, and matters had a way of getting confused. Their entire relationship had been characterized by mutual resentment and the desire to defeat each other; that, at least, had not changed.

Time for their final farewell, though Guy felt an urge to make a truce first. "I truly regret that you have spent these years awaiting my return, only to be disappointed now."

"Disappointed," she repeated dryly.

"But you are an accomplished, attractive lady with excellent connections, breeding, and wealth. You will have no trouble finding a husband."

Unexpectedly, amusement glimmered over her face. "You have no idea," she murmured.

"Good night, Arabella."

Guy spun around and strode toward Freddie. He fancied he felt Arabella's gaze searing into his back, and he quashed his impulse to retrace his steps and ask her what she meant.

CHAPTER 3

Arabella watched Guy stride off toward Freddie and Miss Treadgold, his red cape swirling around his booted legs. Once he had reached them, she turned around to consider her next move.

No need: Her next move was already decided. For there stood Lord Sculthorpe, black tricorne tilted back, studying her with a faint smile. Society called him handsome, though surely a wealthy, heroic peer could never be called anything else. Certainly, all his features were present and correct and arranged in the usual way. The overall effect might be described as strong and square: quite unobjectionable. But then, Arabella's objections had never been about his face.

As their eyes met, his smile broadened and he headed toward her.

"No trouble finding a husband," she murmured ruefully to herself. "It seems my husband has found me."

Her sole gambit had failed. Now Sculthorpe would propose,

and if Arabella refused, her father would cut her off and cast her out.

Proud and haughty, they called her. The lady who had everything, they said. Well, the lady who had everything would lose the lot in the next ten minutes if she did not take care.

Lord Sculthorpe was still smiling as he reached her. "Good evening, Miss Larke, or should I say Minerva? You make a fitting goddess."

"And you, my lord, make a dashing outlaw."

"Ridiculous costume, is it not?" Chuckling amiably, he flipped one lacy cuff. "I always wonder whether other people are sending a message with their costumes or if, like me, they simply put on whatever their valet laid out. I am terrified of upsetting my valet, in case I find myself one day dressed as the back end of a horse."

Ah, that self-deprecating wit. How charming he was. And how commanding and courteous, for he had summoned a footman, bearing drinks. Sculthorpe swept up two glasses of wine and handed her one. Between his fingers was one of his thin cigars, a habit he had picked up while fighting in Spain during the Peninsular Wars and which he never allowed etiquette to restrain. Another servant appeared at his side, proffering a flame. With a wave of his lit cigar, the servants disappeared.

"And, if you do not mind my saying so," he added, in a more intimate tone, smoke puffing out the side of his mouth, "you will also make an excellent baroness."

I'll make an even better widow, Arabella didn't say.

No. She did not have the luxury of speaking her mind. She must parrot the right words, or lose everything. One did not vex the man who held one's future in his hands.

"You are too kind," she did say.

Over his shoulder, Arabella spied her mother, ostensibly in

conversation with a friend, but one eye on Arabella and Sculthorpe.

Dear Mama, so lovely in her ermine-trimmed Queen of Hearts costume, her face serene under the red-and-gold turban perched on her dark hair. Arabella didn't want to disappoint her parents, or scheme and manipulate and lie. She didn't want to stay unmarried. She asked only to be granted her birthright, and to choose her own husband, someone who respected her for what she was, in contrast to those who criticized her for what she was not.

Then she would pretend, she decided. She would pretend that Sculthorpe was not Papa's choice. And as for Sculthorpe's whisper during a waltz a few months ago, those words that made her skin crawl so she could scarcely bear to think of them? Perhaps she had misheard or misunderstood. It was one thing to pride herself on solving her own problems; it was quite another to invent problems that were not there.

"You were speaking with Lord Hardbury," Sculthorpe said. "You know that he and I do not get along."

"I am aware," Arabella replied. "But it seemed preferable that Lord Hardbury and I deal with our history immediately, that we might leave it in the past."

"Admirable," he said. "You are a very admirable..."

He paused, as though seeking the right word. Arabella's breath caught. *Don't say it, don't say it.*

"...lady," he finished.

He hadn't said it. She was mistaken.

"Your mother was telling me that your hobby is producing books," Sculthorpe went on amiably. "A publisher here in London prints them at your commission."

"It is very satisfying. I began by creating my father's ornithology journals when I was sixteen."

"As she said. Every bird-fancier in the world is familiar with your father's journals, but I had not realized it was you who edits and compiles the convention papers. You truly are an accomplished..."

Don't say it.

"Lady," he finished. "What are you working on now?"

"My first color book: *An Illustrated Guide to the Vindale Aviaries.* Papa's aviaries have become famous, and we receive many visitors and requests for information." After a pause, she added, "I have a fondness for reading essays, and mean to commission writers on a variety of topics for future books. It is my belief that every lady should engage in a worthwhile pastime."

"I agree. I look forward to whatever books you publish in the future."

There. Sculthorpe would not be an interfering husband. She studied her wineglass, turning it between her fingers. Her forearm still bore traces from the ribbon, the lingering sensation of Guy's callused thumb soothing the pink lines.

Something caught her eye: the end of Sculthorpe's cigar, falling to the grass. He ground it out under one boot heel. When she lifted her head, she found herself looking right into his eyes, blue-gray and flicking back and forth.

"Miss Larke, you will forgive my directness, but I am a direct man, and you are a practical lady, and neither of us is given to foolish sentiments. I am too modest to make a scene in public, and too impatient to wait until we can be alone. Might I ask if my hopes are to be realized, and you will do me the honor of becoming my wife?"

As proposals went, it was what she might have expected. She did not want him, but neither did she want to lose everything. So, ignoring the sick hollow in her gut, Arabella looked her fate right in the eye, and said, "Of course, my lord."

He lifted her knuckles to his lips. Arabella let him do it. She did not throw her wine in his face, or smash her glass over his head, or punch him in the jaw. She was doing very well.

Without releasing her, he twisted toward Mama, who looked at him right away.

Lord Sculthorpe bowed to Mama.

Mama glanced at Arabella.

Arabella nodded at Mama.

Then Mama nodded at Sculthorpe.

And like that, it was done.

Arabella was engaged.

"You are not pleased?" Sculthorpe still held her hand, a small smile playing around his lips.

"I am excessively pleased."

"You don't smile."

This was true: She did not smile.

His own smile broadened. He really was very handsome. More handsome than Guy. Lucky her: a handsome husband.

"How proud you are," he murmured, each word slinking from his mouth, and that lewd gleam she recalled—it slithered into his eyes, and he was not handsome, not anymore. Arabella tugged at her hand, but he clasped it tight, slid a fingertip over her palm. If only she had worn gloves, but Roman goddess costumes did not come with gloves. If only her skin did not crawl. If only the silver snake on her arm could come to life and tear out his throat.

No. She was being melodramatic. That was foolish. Arabella was never melodramatic. Or foolish.

But that look did not leave Sculthorpe's eye, as, at his leisure, he dropped her hand.

"Such a proud..."

Don't say it.

"Fierce..."

No. Stop.

"Willful..."

Don't say it.

"Virgin."

He said it. The same word he had murmured months earlier, during a waltz.

It's a harmless word, she told herself, but her prickly body ignored her, for the unease came not from his words but from his eyes, from that knowing, possessive leer that crawled over her, as if her bracelet truly had come alive, a real snake coiled around her arm, its cold-blooded scales slithering over her skin and down her spine and into her swirling gut.

Around her, the party grew oppressively loud. Arabella escaped Sculthorpe's leer by looking into the crowd, where flames rose in hellish columns and an acrobat cartwheeled past, his grinning face a mask of horror. A pair of female rope dancers leaped up—high—so high—too far—they'd fall. Her breath caught, awaiting disaster. No disaster: They landed on the rope, their feet sure.

Arabella breathed. The noise receded. The snake bracelet was just a bracelet, and the crowd was just a crowd, and Sculthorpe was just a man. She had not eaten enough; that would account for the nausea.

If Lord Sculthorpe had noticed her reaction, he gave no sign as Mama joined them.

"Lady Belinda, I do hope that you and my betrothed will not run straight back to the countryside," he said. "It would be my great pleasure to escort the pair of you to the military review next week. Miss Larke will enjoy watching the soldiers, as she is about to marry one."

"Of course, my lord," Mama said.

"I shall send 'round a note."

With a gallant bow and a "Good evening, ladies," he left them.

Arabella did not watch him go. Instead, she sipped her wine. The nausea eased. Perhaps she would take up drinking. Something to look forward to.

"That wasn't so hard, was it?" Mama said.

Arabella sipped more wine. "No."

"Lord Sculthorpe assured me that he will never interfere with your interests or movements. No ladies report ill of him. The exception is that matter with Lord Hardbury all those years ago—though neither of them had their titles back then—but the woman in question was a courtesan, and she entered into a contract with Lord Sculthorpe of her own will."

"Thank you, Mama."

Papa would have checked his finances. Mama was checking his social standing. Sculthorpe would not mistreat her.

And it was only a word. Arabella *was* a virgin, and had always expected to remain so until marriage. Sculthorpe would be her husband; therefore, her virginity was for him. Technically, he was not wrong in calling her *his* virgin.

Yet he spoke as if the fact of her virginity excited him, as nothing else about her did.

Guy had looked at her lips and she had looked at his, and she had enjoyed his closeness, though the Spanish Inquisition could not impel her to admit it. Guy had insulted her, and she had insulted him in return, and not once had she felt diminished or demeaned.

Yet one true word from Sculthorpe left her unsettled. How could she allow a man to exercise such power over her that a single look could make her sick with fear? Surely, she should be able to laugh him off, deliver a set-down, put him in his place, as she had done to so many other men over the years. Her rational mind told her this, but it seemed another, less rational part lurked inside her. Her rational mind could insist that Sculthorpe was honorable, charming, and heroic; this secret part of her stepped out of the shadows to insist that he was not. What was this hidden part of her mind, and how did it know things that the rest of her did not?

The wine was no longer helping, so Arabella handed the glass to a passing servant and willed herself to touch the bracelet on her arm. Her eyes drifted back to the rope dancers, their feet on the ground, resting after their finale.

"Arabella?" Mama said, seeing too much. "Lord Sculthorpe has not given you cause for alarm?"

"He seems to display an interest in my...virtue."

Mama frowned, considering. "Of course a peer requires virtue in his bride to be sure his sons are his own, but I am surprised he would insult you by questioning it."

"He did not question it. He rather took it for granted."

"If a man describes a lady as virtuous, that is a compliment. I would not expect him to mention it directly, but Lord Sculthorpe is a directly spoken man and he admires your practical nature."

"Yes, he said that too."

Arabella didn't know what else to say. No doubt she was overreacting, some childish trick of her fancy because she resented not having her own choice. Perhaps these were the small intimacies that developed between husband and wife. She had educated herself in the mechanics of intercourse, but she knew nothing of intimacy or desire. She hated not knowing. She hated that Sculthorpe knew something about her that she did not. She hated that no book would provide an explanation.

"Lord Sculthorpe is a good match," Mama said. "Had you formed an attachment to another man, it might have been different, but you have only ever insisted that you were promised to Lord Hardbury, although your mutual animosity was clear from a young age. And just think," Mama added, a radiant glow stealing over her face, "the sooner you and Lord Sculthorpe marry, the sooner you could be a mother. I would be a grandmother."

Arabella liked the idea of having children, of watching her mother with them. "Yes, Mama."

Mama squeezed her hand and returned to her friends. Arabella moved inside, in search of her own friend, but first, she slid the silver snake off her arm and presented it to the rope dancers as a gift.

NEITHER FREDDIE nor Miss Treadgold seemed to notice Guy approaching the fountain where they were seated.

Miss Treadgold was chatting, apparently to herself, for Freddie was staring at nothing. Her expression was reassuringly familiar: odd, dreamy Freddie, the child who rarely listened and was always wandering off. Sometimes, she would forget to wander back, and they had to search for her. Once, they had found her up a tree, and Guy needed all his ingenuity to get her down again; when he had asked her how she got up there, she shrugged and said she didn't know.

Fondness swelled his chest. She was a young woman now, true, and a stranger of sorts, yet undeniably his little sister. Freed from their father's tyranny, they'd be a proper family at last.

Miss Treadgold noticed him first. Her big brown eyes widened in her pretty, heart-shaped face and she fell silent, her lips forming an O. When Guy bowed, she jumped to her feet and curtsied, her cheeks turning a becoming shade of pink, her brown ringlets bouncing.

Courtesy out of the way, Guy turned to his sister. "Freddie."

She didn't respond.

He tried again, more loudly, arms wide, ready for her to grin, to squeal and launch herself into his arms. "Freddie?"

"Yes?" Freddie turned toward him, smiling vaguely. "Oh, good evening, Guy," she said, and went back to her thoughts.

Guy let his arms fall. Well. No embrace then. Right. He nodded, managed something like a laugh.

"Lord Hardbury, we are honored that you joined us," Miss Treadgold said. "Lady Frederica has been so looking forward to seeing you again."

"Yes," he agreed dryly. "Her enthusiasm is evident in the way she greeted me as if we last saw each other at breakfast this morning."

"She does tend to daydream, and we always— Oh, but we've not been introduced!"

She slapped a hand over her mouth, looking as mortified as if she had stumbled into his bedchamber at night.

"It hardly matters." Guy leaned toward her and added in a conspiratorial tone, "Let's pretend."

"But the rules of etiquette, my lord! Whatever must you think of me?"

"What I think, Miss Treadgold, is that your aunt married my father, so we do not need an introduction. I also think you are very becoming."

Even her coquetry was becoming. Perhaps it was simply her pleasant sweetness in contrast to Arabella, so vibrant and demanding and ruthless. He was uncomfortably aware that

Arabella was right: Miss Treadgold nicely matched his image of the ideal bride.

She blinked her long lashes. "My lord, you and Lady Frederica have much to discuss, after so many years apart. I shall leave you together."

Bobbing another curtsy, Miss Treadgold left. Guy twisted to watch her go, but through the crowd, his eyes landed on Arabella, talking to... Hell, was that Sculthorpe? He turned back to Freddie, who was studying a pair of acrobats.

"Do you prefer to be called Frederica now?" he asked her.

"Lady Treadgold prefers to call me Frederica. *Lady* Frederica," she said absently. "Freddie is a man's name and not becoming on a lady, Lady Treadgold says."

"You can choose what people call you," Guy said. "You don't have to do everything they say."

Freddie said nothing. An indifferent stranger. Perhaps he could have done things differently, but as a confused, angry twenty-year-old, leaving England had seemed his only choice.

Guy dropped onto the wall beside her, the mist from the fountain cooling his neck and arms. He absently arranged his skirt over his knees, watching the partygoers, picking out familiar faces, reminding himself of names.

With every hour back in England, the years of his exile became more removed, his adventures as remote as if he had read them in another man's journal. Despite everything, he had enjoyed his adventures, relished the freedom he could never know in England. Upon his return to London, he had worn out his comfortable boots rediscovering the city on foot. As for the time spent chasing Sir Walter from one country house to another— For all Guy's complaints, it had felt good to ride through the familiar countryside. It had felt good to stop in a village inn for a pie and a pint and a chat about the crops.

It felt good to be home.

Yet still a restlessness plagued him, with his big houses holding nothing but memories of Father and a keen awareness of the emptiness of his life.

"How have you been?" he asked Freddie.

Her fierce brows drew together. "Would you like me to summarize eight years in one word, or may I have a whole sentence?"

"Good point." A new riddle: how to converse with one's sister when she had become a surly stranger. "Did you know our father well?"

"Indeed," she said. "The descriptions in the newspapers were very informative."

"Do Sir Walter and Lady Treadgold treat you and Ursula well?"

"We are family now, they say."

"What is Ursula like?"

"She is two years old."

"What was our stepmother like? Ursula's mother."

Freddie shrugged, her eyes on a pair of acrobats performing, one balanced on the other's shoulders. "She was bored. She'd spend hours dressing or paying calls or playing cards, being bored. I think that's why she died. Life was too boring for her to bother staying alive."

"Who are your friends?"

"Everyone."

"Everyone?"

"Oh yes. What with Father's will making me rich and your return making me sister to England's most eligible bachelor, I have become the most sought-after lady in the land." She stood. "I'm going to ask the acrobats how they do that."

Guy grabbed Freddie's hand. "Sit down."

She sat. He released her and drummed his fingers on the cool stone wall between them. She studied the crowd as if he wasn't there, as if his eight-year absence had turned him into a ghost, and not a particularly interesting one.

"Listen. I mean to gain custody of you and Ursula. It isn't right that Father made Sir Walter your guardian. I'll marry as soon as possible, make us a proper family home."

Freddie made no response.

"Freddie? Are you listening?"

"Not really. Did you say something interesting?"

"I said I hope to marry soon."

"I like Miss Larke. She doesn't simply repeat the same boring things everyone else says. And gentlemen are scared of her set-downs."

Guy didn't mind Arabella's set-downs. He did mind her attempts to bend him to her will. After a lifetime of commands from his unscrupulous father, he was hardly going to sign up for a lifetime of commands from an unscrupulous wife.

"I shan't marry Miss Larke. She was Father's choice and I'll choose my own wife. And you can choose your own husband."

"Thank you."

Her bland politeness irked him. Surely she would rather live with him than with the Treadgolds?

"But Freddie— Are you listening?"

"Yes, Guy."

"If I am to gain custody of you and Ursula, I must prove that Sir Walter is mismanaging your trusts. Embezzling, for example. Have you noticed anything that might help? Any detail that seems suspicious. Something about Sir Walter's behavior, or his spending."

No answer.

"Freddie?"

"I don't know."

"You don't know what?"

"Whatever you were saying." She smiled dreamily. "I wasn't listening."

"I am talking about your future."

"Everyone is always talking about my future. I will live in Sir Walter's house, or your house, or my faceless future husband's house. Install me wherever you please; I'll be a good doll. How does the acrobat do that? I think I'll ask."

This time, Guy let her rise and drift away. He should have anticipated her response. Once he was her guardian, they could start anew.

Which meant he must deal with Sir Walter.

When he stood, heads turned, people still loitering in the hope of talking to him. As much as he appreciated the honor shown him by the Prince Regent in throwing this party, and the opportunity to renew acquaintances and strike up new ones, it was Sir Walter he needed to meet. Scanning the crowd for someone to help him identify Sir Walter, he only realized he was looking for Arabella when he didn't see her.

Guy rubbed his eyes and tilted his head to study the sky. No stars here, just London's habitual smoke. During his travels, he had become fascinated with stars. Perhaps he would buy himself a great big telescope and study astronomy. Another thing to help him rebuild his life.

An exuberant voice drew his attention away from the heavens.

"My dear Lord Hardbury! I am excessively delighted by your return!"

Marvelous. Another of Guy's would-be bosom friends. This time, it was an average-sized man around fifty, with a pink bald patch, neat goatee, and wide smile that revealed a gold-capped tooth.

"We have so much to discuss, my lord," the newcomer added, beaming.

Guy put the pieces together. "Sir Walter Treadgold, I presume. I was just looking for you. Thank you for making it easy."

"Always your servant, my lord."

This bit of nonsense made Guy laugh. "If only that were so, my dear sir! You might have bothered to reply to my letters. In the meantime, your solicitors have surely advised you that I am filing a petition to gain legal custody of my sisters." He leaned toward him. "I trust you are excessively delighted by that too?"

Not for a heartbeat did Sir Walter's smile slip, as he rubbed his hands together and nodded agreeably. "Let us not spoil this lovely evening by discussing tedious legal affairs. My greatest wish is that you and I might be friends."

"And my greatest wish is that I become my sisters' legal guardian."

Sir Walter sighed in apparent commiseration. "If only it were that easy! A man's will is a powerful legal document. If the Court of Chancery will not overturn your late father's will, there is nothing I can do."

"Yet if the court finds you are mismanaging their trusts..."

"My lord!" Sir Walter's jaw dropped. "Whatever can you mean to imply? Why, your father trusted me to take care of things as he did."

"Precisely my concern, given my father's habitual corruption."

The insult had no effect. Sir Walter merely scratched his chin thoughtfully. "Actually, my lord, I might be able to offer a solution to our little problem."

"It's *our* problem, now, is it?"

"You've met our Matilda, I believe?"

"Who? Oh, Miss Treadgold. The frilly one."

"She is my niece, by way of my dear departed brother, but she is like our daughter, just as Lady Frederica is now. Our Matilda is most charming and impeccably behaved."

"Is she?"

"She has been tireless in assisting with my numerous charitable institutions."

"Has she?"

"And she plays pianoforte beautifully."

"Does she?"

Sir Walter's expression was entirely without guile. "I hear you are seeking a bride. Permit me to remind you that your late father's will names three properties that will become yours if you marry Miss Larke, and mine if you marry anyone else. If you were to marry our Matilda, I would include those properties in her dowry. I would also assist you to become guardian of your sisters."

"So my sisters would also form part of your niece's dowry."

Sir Walter stopped short, then spluttered and laughed and spluttered some more. "You mistake my meaning, my lord."

"Oh, I don't think I am at all mistaken. What did you get your knighthood for, Sir Walter? Not for subtlety, clearly."

And so it went. If Guy married Miss Treadgold, he'd get what he wanted—and become this man's puppet instead of his father's.

"You will require friends, my lord," Sir Walter said, unperturbed. "I am willing to be a friend to you."

"You and everyone else in Britain."

"And my son, Humphrey, is a fine young gentleman. Why, he could be like a brother to you! Perhaps you could put in a word for him, sponsor him at your club."

Guy had to laugh. He almost missed Arabella. She made demands too, but did not do it under the guise of friendship or love.

"My dear, dear Sir Walter, listen: You are up to something, you little scamp, and I mean to find out what. If you want us to be friends, allow me to see my sisters."

Sir Walter threw up his hands. "My lord, whatever can you mean? You can see your sisters any time you like. When you call on Matilda or take her for a drive, then—"

"Sounds like a jolly game, you scallywag, but I don't want to play," Guy said, and walked off into the crowd.

CHAPTER 4

The military review was sheer perfection. Thousands of red-coated soldiers marched in exquisitely straight columns, their uniforms matching right down to the gleam of their brass buttons, their boots and muskets clacking in harmony.

It was the most peaceful sight Arabella had ever seen.

The columns of ten thousand soldiers would stretch a mile or more, Lord Sculthorpe had earlier informed Arabella and Mama, as he competently maneuvered his carriage through the crowd gathering on Wimbledon Common to watch the Duke of York present the regiments. The promise of a fine day and a grand spectacle—complete with a military band, cavalry charge, and a glimpse of the Royal Family—had drawn some hundred thousand people to the massive Common. All sorts were in attendance, from workers to bankers to aristocrats: a boisterous, cacophonous mass of humanity, in the midst of which Arabella finally found a moment alone.

It had been a trying week of social gatherings, as Arabella was besieged by felicitations on her engagement. "Congratulations," everyone said, as though she had accomplished something more onerous than simply living to adulthood and saying the word "yes." For bonus agony, Lord Sculthorpe would appear at her side, charming, affable, and never missing an opportunity to drop a light touch somewhere on her person, say something affectionate, and sicken her with a leer. Arabella had to bear it, along with the stream of good-natured comments about his lordship's devotion.

Just as she had to bear his solicitous inquiries about her well-being this morning, when they relinquished his open carriage to Mama and her friends and took a stroll through the crowd.

"You look tired, Miss Larke, if you'll forgive my blunt speech," he had remarked. Saying nothing of nights spent staring into darkness, she had offered the standard complaints about London's weather, at which dashing Lord Sculthorpe dashed off to find her a drink. For such were her mighty powers: Sculthorpe would take her property, own her body, and control her behavior, but never mind that, because she could send him to fetch a glass of lemonade.

But she still had this: the ability to forget her plight in the thrilling exactness of military maneuvers.

Only when the soldiers came to a perfectly timed stop did Arabella drag her gaze away—to find herself looking at Guy, who was studying her with an expression of puzzled amusement.

He stood with one booted leg slightly in front of the other, hands clasped behind his back, broad shoulders straight in his blue coat, hat tipped back on his head. Even the insouciant ease of his stance could not mask his bold vitality.

When their eyes met, a slow smile spread over his face. Arabella fired off the kind of withering look that sent other men scuttling for the drinks trolley. So what did Guy do, but saunter to her side.

The sunlight revealed faint lines around the corners of his

eyes, which were as green as summer, with an intriguing depth. He displayed a lean hardness at odds with his easy smiles: a man prepared to tackle any challenge and enjoy himself while he did it.

"You appear to delight in the regiments," he said. "Your expression is nothing less than rapt."

Because it was Guy and she didn't care what he thought, Arabella replied with the truth. "It is very soothing."

He laughed, a fearless chuckle that danced down her spine. "Only you could find the presence of ten thousand armed men soothing."

Still smiling, his eyes whisked over her. Naturally, she had honored the occasion with a stylish, military-inspired outfit. It was blue, with epaulets, frogging, and braids, topped by a tall-crowned hat like a shako. The ornamentation was quite useless, of course, but it made a good impression; in Arabella's world, that was half the battle.

"It pains me to admit it," Guy said, looking remarkably unpained, "but military-style attire suits you. I wonder why they have not yet made you commander-in-chief."

"I wonder that myself. If only I had all these soldiers at my command, marching in unison." She shifted her parasol to her other shoulder, all the better to shoot him a look. "Do suggest it to the Duke of York when you see him next. I would happily take his place."

"Perhaps your betrothed would mention it, given that he is a war hero."

And there went her blessed peace. Curse him.

"You sound bitter, Guy. Surely you are not jealous that Lord Sculthorpe did something useful while you were off sulking over your lost sweetheart."

Guy merely shook his head. He was vexingly difficult to provoke. "On the one hand, I think you and Sculthorpe are a good match. On the other, men must be lining up to marry you and I cannot imagine why the deuce you would choose a man like that."

A man like what? she longed to ask. *What does he mean when he calls me his virgin? Why does it repel me so? What will he do to me? Will you tell me? Will someone please just tell me?!*

But she could never say that. She could never show anyone her fear, especially not Guy.

Irritation surged through her. Her hands gripped her parasol, tightening with a furious impulse to tear at him—tear at his golden skin and smiling eyes and broad chest—because she had attempted to ask for help and he had refused to listen, because she had no right to anger, because he owed her nothing. It wasn't Guy's fault she had to marry Sculthorpe, but it was his fault he was so cheerful and confident and attractive, and that, surely, was sufficient grounds for a grudge.

He didn't seem to notice. Of course not: She had a lifetime's training in hiding her thoughts, and she drew on it now to quash the emotion. Emotions were useless and pointless.

Just like Guy, really.

"Come now, Lord Sculthorpe is adorable," she drawled. "He puts me in mind of a lapdog. I'm inclined to teach him to do tricks."

"If there is any woman who can make a man jump through hoops, it is you."

"Thank you."

"Not a compliment."

"Hm."

A rifle salute drew her attention back to the soldiers. Inexplicably, Guy lingered.

"If you did have all those guns under your control, what would you do?" he asked.

"You would be the first against the wall," she said automatically.

That was untrue. Sculthorpe would be the first against the wall. Guy would be the second. Or she could make them face the firing squad together and save on bullets. What a fiscally responsible commander-in-chief she would be.

"Careful." Guy sounded cheerful despite her death threat. "You wouldn't want your betrothed to catch you flirting with me."

She stared at him. "Flirting? I threatened to have you shot."

"Which coming from you surely counts as flirting. Such sweet nothings! I'm very flattered."

"You're very annoying. Did you come here solely to provoke me?"

"Pretty much." His eyes narrowed as he studied her, shaking his head slightly. "But why *Sculthorpe*? Although I must admire your efficiency, snaring him minutes after I turned you down. You couldn't be a marchioness so you settled on becoming a baroness. Does he know he was your second choice?"

Sculthorpe was so far down her list of choices, he didn't appear on it at all. If only Guy had listened to her, then she could have bought time until Hadrian Bell returned, and now it was too late.

"You have it the wrong way around," she said, haughtily turning away from him to study the crowd. "You were merely practice, to be sure I got it right when it actually mattered."

Through the crowd, a flamboyant emerald-green bonnet snagged her eye, the headdress of a woman who wanted to be seen. It was Clare Ivory—renowned for her wit, her beauty, and for the fact that she had once been respectable, a gentleman's daughter whom Guy Roth had wanted to marry, until she threw it all away by having an affair with Lord Sculthorpe and becoming a courtesan.

Guy was standing so close that Arabella sensed his new tension.

"I had to encounter her sooner or later, I suppose," he murmured.

"The woman who broke your heart and made you run away," Arabella said. "Did it never strike you as a trifle extreme, leaving the country for eight years? You do realize that the standard cure for heartbreak in a young man is overindulgence in poetry and drink."

"I was no good at it."

"At drinking or at writing bad poetry?"

"Either." He sighed. "Alas, I was an utter failure as a tormented youth. I was rather looking forward to becoming brooding and pale. I even fancied I might become a rake." He glanced at her sideways. "Women would have found me irresistible, of course."

"Of course. The poor darlings could not have withstood the lure of your tortured soul."

"Naturally I'd have broken their hearts."

"For which they would adore you all the more."

"Unfortunately for me, I have a debilitating fondness for daylight, company, and physical activity. Besides, the world has so many interesting things to see and people to meet that I kept forgetting to be heartbroken and miserable."

Arabella suspected that Guy was telling partial truths to conceal his true feelings, but she said nothing. The conversation was surprisingly enjoyable; besides, a truce presented a chance to discuss Freddie.

"Is Freddie here?" she ventured. "I have not seen her."

"I don't know. Blasted Sir Walter is still playing his game of hide-and-seek."

A chill shivered over her. "Guy, this isn't a game. You must take care of Freddie. I might be able to find them but—"

"So now you are a Bow Street Runner."

"Sir Walter is not an honest man. If he is—"

"Embezzling from their trusts? Yes, Arabella, I know." His flippant manner had vanished, replaced with a hard seriousness. "I have several men investigating that possibility, and Sir Walter knows it, which is why he has disappeared. He is playing an excessively delightful little game, but I am adequate for the task without you meddling."

"If it concerned only you, I'd happily abandon you to your misguided arrogance, but it is Freddie who will pay the price."

"You don't know everything, Arabella."

"Neither do you."

Somehow, in their quarrel, they had turned to each other, their faces so close that the fringe on Arabella's parasol cocooned them both. If only she could grab his ears and force him to listen. Arabella had not been able to save herself, but she could still protect Freddie.

Yet she had nothing more than suspicions about Sir Walter's plans for Freddie. If only she could investigate Sir Walter and find proof. Perhaps Mama might be persuaded to invite the Treadgolds to Vindale Court? Sir Walter would imagine himself safe there, because Papa would not receive Guy now, and once the Treadgold family was at Arabella's house, she could—

Guy's laughter disrupted her thoughts. Startled, she saw that he had stepped back to study her. Something about his easy gusto was irritating.

"What?" she snapped.

"There are thousands of people here, an army, and a military band, and yet still I can hear your brain whirring with schemes. I remember how you used to..."

He trailed off, his gaze sailing past her. His amusement faded. Arabella did not have to turn to understand the cause. All her effort went into preparing herself, so as not to flinch when Lord Sculthorpe laid a hand on her sleeve.

Guy's eyes flicked to where Sculthorpe's gloved hand rested on Arabella's arm. Remembering herself, she slipped her hand into the crook of Sculthorpe's elbow. Maybe after their marriage, her skin wouldn't crawl with revulsion, but it would warm and tingle as it had when pressed against Guy.

"There you are, my dear," Sculthorpe said, not looking at her. "Hardbury."

Without a word, Guy pivoted and walked away.

Lord Sculthorpe chuckled, apparently tickled by Guy's reaction. "His lordship just gave me the cut direct. He does have his petticoats in a tangle." His voice dripped with scorn. "Look at him now: still drooling over that whore."

Arabella said nothing, not interested in Sculthorpe's nonsense. Much more intriguing was the unfolding encounter between Guy and Miss Ivory: They froze mid-step like a pair of warring tomcats, until Miss Ivory whirled away in a swish of jewel-green skirts, and Guy escaped in the opposite direction.

What a jolly little cotillion this was, with the four dancers that they were: Guy had been promised to Arabella as a child, but he threw her over so he could marry Clare Ivory, who threw him over when she was seduced by Sculthorpe, who was now marrying Arabella. Then Miss Ivory went off to be a courtesan, and Sculthorpe went off to war, and Guy went off to tour the world, and Arabella stayed right where she was. It sounded like a nursery rhyme. Maybe Arabella would compose one. It would give her something to think about in her marriage bed, while Sculthorpe was engaged in the onerous business of relieving her of her virginity.

"Ah, I have shocked you, Miss Larke," Sculthorpe said.

Arabella turned. *Shocked, am I?* she didn't say. *Do tell me what I am feeling. You seem to know it so well.*

He offered the glass of lemonade, so Arabella took it and sipped. It was unpleasantly weak and tepid, but it kept her safe from speaking her mind. Perhaps that was why she had enjoyed chatting with Guy: His opinion meant nothing to her, so she could say what she pleased.

"You will forgive me," Sculthorpe went on. "My language is not always appropriate for the company of a lady. But you are marrying a military man, and I am plainspoken and direct. I call a spade a spade. And a whore a whore."

And a virgin a virgin, Arabella didn't say.

"But you are a practical woman, and I am grateful I need not guard my tongue with you. This is why we are such a good match. We have that in common."

What we have in common is that we both wish to own me, Arabella didn't say.

He was looking at her expectantly, so she offered a small nod that seemed to please him. Not that her response mattered; he would interpret it as he wished anyway.

"I trust you are not exhausting yourself with the wedding preparations," he said. "You must take care of yourself, until I can take care of you."

"Our wedding is not until spring. We have plenty of time to make the arrangements."

"Did your father not write to you about our change in plans? I am to follow you to Vindale Court, where your parents will host a betrothal ball. The banns will be called in the following weeks, and we'll be wed soon after Michaelmas."

Arabella thought irrelevantly of the Michaelmas goose, fattened and roasted and laid out on every table in England that could afford it, with a blackberry pie to follow. September was one of her favorite months, when they trooped out under blue skies and orange leaves to pick blackberries and nuts, ahead of Michaelmas at the month's end. She and Mama always prepared a feast for the tenants and villagers, before the winter began. She wondered if they would manage that this year, with a wedding as well.

"I thought we had agreed on a spring wedding, here in London, during the Season next year," she said.

"I changed my mind." He leaned in, the sun glinting on the medals on his chest. "I am keen for us to begin our life together. I fear my patience grows thinner, every time I look at you."

Then do us both a favor and stop looking at me, she didn't say.

Really, she deserved a medal too, for all the times she held her tongue. Was this how it would be the rest of her life?

"Perhaps I might be plain spoken with you too, my lord," she ventured.

He pitched his voice to a low, intimate tone. "I hope you will, my fierce, sharp-tongued virgin."

Tightening her belly to restrain her shudder, she sought a casual tone. "You use that word a lot. With me."

Something flickered in his eyes. "It is true, though."

"Of course," she said hastily. "I merely wonder at your anticipation of something that you will dispense with more quickly than you smoke a cigar."

He crept so close that his tobacco-flavored breath crawled over her ear. "The anticipation *is* the pleasure. You feel it too, don't you, my own Miss Larke?"

Holding very still, Arabella forced herself to look at him, and adopted a cajoling tone that sounded distastefully false to her own ears. "But if I may, my lord, I do not belong to you."

He lashed out, swift as an adder, seized the stick of her parasol, nearly knocking it from her hand. His eyes were hard; his square jaw clenched. A jolt shuddered down her arm and into her suddenly tight chest.

Then just as quickly, the harshness vanished, leaving nothing but affection and smiles. His fingers slithered down the stick, to find and briefly squeeze her hand.

"I see you're one of those ladies with a taste for games, my dear," he said chidingly, fondly. "But I can feel your little shivers of delight when I speak of our anticipation. You need not be ashamed; I will be your husband and your excitement pleases me." He dropped his hand. "You are right, of course: You do not belong to me *yet*, but you will. On our wedding night, I shall claim you fully, after which you will be mine and no one else's. Oh yes, I see you can hardly breathe at the thought."

Finally, Sculthorpe had something right: Arabella could hardly breathe. She shifted to stare past him, at the soothing, flawless columns of soldiers.

"And then?" Her voice came out strangely hoarse.

"Then what?"

"After our honeymoon. After you have..." The soldiers marched, marched, marched. At some unseen signal, they stopped. "Claimed me fully."

Stepping away, he pulled out his silver cigar case and signaled to a boy with a lantern to bring him a light.

"Then you will be the mother of my children," he said calmly. "Once our sons are born and our second son is named heir of your father's estate, you may live there independently with him. I can put that in the marriage settlement, if you wish."

A month before their wedding and they were negotiating separate lives. It was not the worst offer. This marriage would secure her dream: Vindale Court, her home. A wife could not turn her husband away from her bed, not if he insisted on claiming his rights, but she need only suffer his attentions until she had borne him two sons, and then she would be free.

"You are pleased," he said.

"I am...overcome. I think I need some air," she added, foolishly, for they were already outside.

"I understand," he murmured. "We truly understand each other. I watched you and knew you would be perfect for me."

"I am honored, my lord," she managed to say, before thrusting her glass into his hands and making her escape.

Unseeingly, Arabella pushed through the crowd. She had crossed the limits of propriety in speaking thus to Sculthorpe, driven by her need to know, but the knowledge left her feeling even more helpless. Perhaps all men had thoughts like that, but they hid them under bad poetry and good manners, and Sculthorpe only revealed himself because of their engagement.

She might have walked aimlessly for miles, until that elaborate green bonnet once more caught her eye.

Clare Ivory, also alone, was heading toward a copse of trees. Without knowing her own intention, Arabella casually adjusted her direction to follow the other woman.

No sooner had Arabella reached the trees than Clare Ivory whirled around.

Under the bonnet, her pale face was a perfect oval. Her pink lips were uncommonly plump, her large eyes a silvery-blue. The whole was framed by hair so fair it was almost white. Clare Ivory had the face of a seductive angel, they said; no wonder she was a successful courtesan.

"Are you following me, Miss Larke? I wonder that a lady of your station would even acknowledge me."

Arabella closed her parasol with a snap. She must not be seen anywhere near Miss Ivory, but the trees sheltered them, and for now they were alone but for some boys playing dice and a pie seller taking a break.

"Yet we have much in common," Arabella said. "We were both once thought to be engaged to Guy Roth, and Lord Sculthorpe was the first man to bed you, as he will be for me."

Miss Ivory's eyes widened. "You show a surprising lack of delicacy, not to mention care for your reputation. What would the world say if you were seen with me?"

"For one, they could make a marvelous portrait of us. The title suggests itself."

"'The virgin and the whore.'" For a woman with an angel's face, Miss Ivory could employ a tone as dry and sharp as Arabella's. "Do you think yourself daring?"

"Curious, rather."

Fear, anger, and desperation combined to create a certain daring, Arabella supposed. Her only recourse was to learn about what frightened her.

"You could have become Guy's marchioness," she said.

"But I did not want to." Miss Ivory raised her chin in a challenge. "Did you follow me here to speak of Guy?"

Arabella absently untangled the fringe on her parasol. "Guy is of no interest. It is Lord Sculthorpe I wish to inquire about."

"Oh dear, Miss Larke. The things I can tell you about Lord Sculthorpe are not things a lady should know about her husband."

"I beg to differ. A lady should know as much as possible about everything that affects her. I wish to understand his preferences. His...tastes." The other woman averted her face, but not before Arabella caught her mocking smile. "This amuses you, Miss Ivory?" she said sharply.

"I suspect this is not a typical conversation for you, Miss Larke. Are you finding it enjoyable?"

"I am finding it excruciating. And you?"

"Equally."

"Then let this be finished quickly."

"Every harlot's prayer," Miss Ivory said dryly.

"And every wife's?"

That riposte earned her a laugh; their eyes met with an unexpected sense of alliance.

"Is Lord Sculthorpe feared?" Arabella asked.

"He is not known for cruelty, no."

Arabella hazarded a guess. "But is he known for visiting harlots in search of virgins?"

"You do know more than you ought. Such knowledge is dangerous for a fine lady like yourself."

Arabella ignored her. It remained a mystery why people insisted it was dangerous for ladies to know things; surely ignorance was much more dangerous. If only information were not so difficult to obtain!

"They must be a rare delicacy, virgins," she speculated. "Are they difficult to procure? Or are they simply very...young?"

"His lordship prefers his women to be mature—and willing, to his credit. They are not cheap but he is happy to pay the premium. He takes particular pleasure in winning an auction. They are, as you say, a rare delicacy, and he is willing to indulge only when they become available."

"Because the anticipation is the pleasure." Arabella caught the other woman's expression and looked away, through the trees. The risk to her reputation increased the longer she spent here, but she had to know. "What does a man seek, with this preference for virgins?"

"Possession, I believe. Planting his flag, as it were, and

conquering the territory. The belief that a part of the woman will always belong to him. The more virgins he beds, the more women he owns."

"Like bagging grouse."

"Quite."

"Then it is about defeating other men," Arabella mused. "Not about his pleasure, or even about the woman."

"The amusing part is that such men cannot infallibly determine whether or not a woman is a virgin, although they persist in believing they can, and refuse to listen to the midwives, wise women, and courtesans who say differently."

A strange thrill of excitement streaked through Arabella's veins. "Is that so?" she said, her mouth shaping the words carefully. "I was always made to believe that a woman's virtue can be physically proven."

Miss Ivory shook her head, ever so meaningfully. "I always believed that too. Before I... Well. Before."

"Then a cunning woman might sell her virginity several times over."

"It is a good business, albeit a short-term one. A man expects blood and some barrier to break through. One can learn a trick for producing blood, and the rest is performance." Miss Ivory laughed softly. "In some respects, the practiced harlot makes a more satisfying virgin than an actual innocent does."

From somewhere came a volley of musket fire. Arabella had stayed too long. She opened her parasol, her hands unusually clumsy.

"Thank you, Miss Ivory. Your knowledge and experience are invaluable."

Another topic for Arabella to commission from writers, if she could publish it discreetly. Perhaps she could conceal the information amid frivolously feminine subjects where men would never venture.

"A baroness is not as impressive as a marchioness," Miss Ivory said, a shrewd look in her eyes, "but after your marriage you will wield considerable influence, I daresay. Certainly, your reputation precedes you."

Arabella heard the invitation. "I would not be averse to continuing our acquaintance, albeit with discretion."

"I would like that."

Miss Ivory extended one hand in an elaborately embroidered glove. Without hesitation, Arabella shook it.

"An unexpected pleasure, Miss Ivory."

"Indeed. I have caught glimpses of you over the years and wondered why Guy was so opposed to marrying you."

"We never got along, though we were promised to each other as children."

"Perhaps you would have got along better had you not been promised to each other as children."

"Perhaps."

With a nod of farewell, Arabella headed out of the trees and back through the crowd toward Mama and Sculthorpe, her thoughts racing.

The main question was whether she would marry Sculthorpe —and that was no question at all. He repelled her, but for ladies of her station, repellent husbands were merely an unpleasant fact of life, like one's monthly courses, and boiled fish for dinner, and that odd little toenail that always caught in her stocking. Like her mother and grandmother and aunts, she was a lady born to wealth and privilege, and this was the price she paid.

If she refused? She would lose everything and then what use would she be? As a baroness, she would have the power to help others. How foolish to give that up, simply because she didn't like the way he looked at her.

She had to marry Sculthorpe. She had to become his in law. She did not have to become his in spirit. She did not have to give any more of herself than necessary. She did not have to go to his bed a virgin.

Arabella stopped walking so abruptly someone jostled her with an explosion of curses. At her look, the curses changed to apologies, but she hardly heard those either.

The notion was shocking. Impossible. Utterly unthinkable. Yet she had thought it. And there, among the chaotic crowd and orderly soldiers, the thought hardened inside her like a shield.

The law declared that a man owned his wife, but Arabella had little respect for the law, because she knew the men who made it. Let Sculthorpe think what he pleased. She would prove to herself he did not own her, and never feel weak beside him again.

Suddenly, she felt revived. That panicked, unknown part of her mind relaxed; the sense of helplessness melted. She would be a baroness. She would raise sons and daughters, and love them equally. She would use her social position to influence politics and help those in need, while her husband bought his virgin whores and left her in peace.

Arabella moved on again, her limbs deliciously light.

The main obstacle, of course, was that she had not the faintest idea how to get seduced. Men never so much as flirted with her. Even the wickedest of rakes took one look at her and scurried off in search of easier prey.

Were there such things as male harlots? Perhaps Clare Ivory could find her one.

But no— Something this important could never be entrusted to a stranger. She intended to marry Sculthorpe, and did not want to spend the rest of her life looking over her shoulder. The ideal man was someone whose discretion was assured.

She was still considering her options when Mama emerged from the crowd.

"You're looking very bright-eyed, all of a sudden," Mama said.

"The soldiers are terrifically invigorating. I say, let's invite Sir Walter and Lady Treadgold and their family to Vindale Court. Apparently, they have left town, but if anyone can find them, you can."

Mama said nothing, questions in her eyes.

"I have taken an interest in Miss Matilda Treadgold," Arabella explained airily. "And of course I adore Freddie."

"Very well. Young ladies are always a welcome addition to a party."

Arabella started to walk on, only to falter at a flash of green. Clare Ivory. Mama looked at her and said nothing. As always, there was no withstanding Mama's silence.

"I was only talking to her," Arabella said.

"Take care, my dear."

"Yes, Mama."

"Take very good care."

CHAPTER 5

A clandestine meeting was actually rather diverting, Guy was pleased to realize, as he prowled around the drawing room in his deserted house at midnight, glass of wine in hand.

It was not the thrill that had induced him to accept Clare's request for a meeting, though; it was curiosity. Clare's note had surprised him, when it arrived the day after the military review. They should talk, she wrote. She would make no demands or trouble, she promised. No one must ever know; she would come at night and he should send all the servants away.

The secrecy struck Guy as unnecessarily dramatic, but he was intrigued and amused enough to play along.

Curious, too, because years later, Guy still didn't understand what had happened, and almost nobody dared mention Clare Ivory in his presence.

Mainly he was embarrassed by his youthful foolishness. How smitten he had been, from the first moment he saw Clare. How ardent, in his youthful declarations of love. And how fervent, after that final, dreadful fight with his father, when he had traveled all night to beg Clare to elope, only for her to confess that Sculthorpe had seduced her and left her to her ruin.

Still, he had offered to marry her; still, she had refused. He had left without asking why, because he had been young and proud and feared he might weep, and he could not bear for the woman who broke his heart to see him weep. Instead, he had challenged Sculthorpe, earned a beating for his trouble, then boarded the first ship out of England, barely able to see through his swollen eyes.

When he heard the sounds of the front door opening and the sole servant murmuring, Guy's roaming had brought him to the writing desk. He set down his glass, arranged the green silk banyan over his shirt, and leaned back against the wall to await Clare's entrance.

A light knock sounded. The door opened silently. A person glided in and shut the door without a sound.

The person was not Clare. A shapeless cloak disguised the intruder's figure, its hood shadowing the face, but Guy did not need to see the face. Clare was smaller and rounder, with a bounce in her step. This figure moved like water and was tall enough to be a man.

Well, well, well. It seemed Clare was still playing games, and Guy had walked into a trap.

He eased a letter opener off the desk, as the figure turned her —his?—head. In a bound, Guy had the blade pressed to the intruder's chest.

"You seem to be lost, my friend," he said. "What are you: assassin or thief?"

"Worse."

The figure threw back the hood. It was indeed worse.

It was Arabella.

She was without adornment, without expression, regarding him as coolly as if they were in a daytime crowd. As if it were not unacceptable—indeed, *unthinkable*—for an unaccompanied lady to call on a gentleman at any time, let alone at night.

"Good grief, Guy," she drawled. "I had no idea you had such a penchant for drama."

"What the deuce are you doing here? I might have stabbed you."

"Which would have been awkward for us both, I agree."

She lowered her eyes pointedly to the blade still aimed at her breastbone. Guy stepped back. He thought he had faced everything during his adventures, but nothing could have prepared him for the sight of Arabella, in his house alone at night, calmly removing her gloves and whisking off her cloak to reveal a dowdy gray gown better suited to a governess.

"Is this another of your schemes, some attempt to trap me into marriage?" He waved the letter opener at the door. "Will your mother come bursting in and scream about honor and ruin?"

"I sincerely hope not. But if she does, please refrain from stabbing her. I'm very fond of my mother."

Guy had to laugh, though from absurdity or horror he could not say. He tossed the letter opener onto the desk and reclaimed his wineglass. It seemed he might need it.

"What have you done with Clare? I recognized her handwriting. Was it hers, or have you added forgery to your accomplishments?"

"Not yet, but that's an excellent suggestion." Arabella swept across the room like a diva taking center stage. "Miss Ivory penned the note at my request."

"How do you even know her?"

"I know everyone."

She poured herself some wine and gulped it down in an incongruously unladylike manner.

"I am here," she announced to the room at large, "because I have something for you."

"You have nothing I want."

"An opportunity for revenge."

"Against whom?"

"Lord Sculthorpe, of course."

Her glass hit the table with a thud. Guy waited but she only aligned the glass with the carafe. She straightened a fork. Nudged a cup.

"Revenge against Sculthorpe for what?" he finally prompted.

She frowned at him. "You have to ask?"

"Certainly, he beat me up years ago, but..." Guy shrugged. "He was a trained soldier, and I didn't know how to fight. The past is the past. I have no interest in revenge." He carried his wineglass back to the fire and flung himself into his chair. "Now get out before I throw you over my shoulder and hurl you into the mews."

"You're not much of a strategist, are you?" She moved only to perch on the chair opposite him. "You intended to marry Clare Ivory, but Sculthorpe seduced her. Now Sculthorpe intends to marry me, but you can seduce me first."

Guy spluttered, sending his mouthful of wine up his nose and into other places wine had no business being. He coughed, eyes watering, glass slamming onto the table. Unperturbed, Arabella handed him a serviette.

"I can *what*?" he managed to say.

"Revenge," she repeated impatiently. "Doesn't that sound like something you might want to do?"

"No. It sounds like something Sculthorpe might want to do, but I'm not Sculthorpe." He wiped away his last tears and tossed the serviette onto the table. "Have you completely lost your reason?"

She appeared to consider this. "No."

"If you don't want to marry Sculthorpe, don't. None of this involves me."

"Oh, I'll definitely marry Sculthorpe. You may calm yourself on that point. Now, shall we repair to the bedroom? I haven't much time."

She stood and looked down at him, her face unreadable in the golden candlelight. Even unadorned, in that plain dress and her dark hair in a simple knot, she made a compelling sight. Guy couldn't help running his eyes over the promising, intriguing curves and shadows of her figure. His daft body stirred. If they were strangers... If it were a different time and place... If—

Too many ifs. This was Arabella, and *if* she didn't leave immediately, he'd toss her out the window.

He lurched to his feet. A mistake: Now their faces were close. Her hand drifted up, hovered perilously close to his chest, which was shielded only by a linen shirt.

He caught her fingers. "What is this madness?" he murmured.

Her head jerked up, and in a single move, she yanked her hand from his, spun around, and glided away. Finally, she was leaving! But no— As though dancing with herself, she whirled back around.

"The fact is, I have not had enough adventures in my life." Her words came out unusually loud and fast. "I am sure neither you nor Sculthorpe are virgins. Why shouldn't I, too, have a chance to sow my wild oats?"

What a load of nonsense! But Arabella clearly had no intention of explaining, so Guy didn't waste his breath pressing for more.

Instead, he said, "Women don't have oats to sow. Women are the field, so to speak, in which the oats are sown."

She did not sigh, but she gave the impression of having sighed. "Let us not debate metaphors. You understand my point. But speaking of that, you will take care to avoid sowing any oats in this field."

"There will be no oats."

"If you say so. So long as the plow enters the field, I am unconcerned as to whether there are any oats. Only that if there are oats, they do not, in fact, enter the field."

Guy hardly knew whether to laugh or groan. "Arabella, you and I have never been friends, but I have always respected your abilities. So please understand that I speak with the utmost respect when I say: You are dreadful at seduction."

"Then it is as well that I am not seducing you, but rather demanding that you seduce me, which is an entirely different matter."

"You're serious about this."

"I would hardly risk my future for a joke."

He wandered over to her, carefully keeping his eyes off the long, intriguing lines of her body. "You seriously think that we should take off all our clothes and pretend to like each other long enough for me to bed you, and then you'll merrily go on your way."

"That sounds right. Although we needn't take off all our clothes. Or pretend to like each other."

"This is absurd. Get out."

She turned her head away, but her jaw clenched. He studied her profile as she pressed her lips together, the column of her throat as she swallowed nothing, the rise of her breasts as she took a deep breath.

"I will go through with this," she whispered to the wall.

Unsettled, Guy reached a hand to her straight back, let it drop. "What is going on? If you need help..."

She said nothing. None of this made sense. Arabella had never been a model of feminine sweetness and docility, but her conduct had always been beyond reproach. That a young woman might succumb to lust or seek to explore her sensual side was something he could understand. But that *Arabella* might? She avoided his touch and barely looked at him, let alone betrayed any sign of actual desire. The only rational explanation was that this was a scheme to trap him into marriage, following her failure at the costume party, but her approach was decidedly odd.

"You'll ruin your reputation if anyone learns you were here," he said.

"I have been very careful, and your discretion is assured, is it not?"

Guy snorted. "Of course. If anyone knew you were here, they'd either shoot me or march me to the altar. The last thing I want is to wind up married to you." He considered. "Being shot doesn't appeal much either."

"No one need ever know."

"Not even Sculthorpe?"

"Especially not Sculthorpe."

"But won't he—"

"I did not come here to discuss Sculthorpe. Now, if you have dispensed with your maidenly sensibilities?" Her eyebrows raised. "Given the amount of effort that men expend trying to gain access to women's bodies, and the corresponding effort women expend trying to deny them, you should be grateful I am making it so easy for you."

Her expression remained imperious, but her gaze flickered and veered away. A tiny tell. Guy considered his options. He could carry her out and dump her on the street. Pull on his clothes and leave the house. Simply ignore her, or lock himself in his bedroom. She held no power over him, not physical, not financial, not social—and definitely not sexual, whatever her passing, puzzling allure.

Arabella could not make him do anything he did not want to do.

And, quite frankly, Guy wanted her to admit that. To explicitly concede defeat. The nerve of the woman: to conspire with Clare, to lie her way into his house, disturb his evening, and jeopardize his future. Sending her away would be easy—but too easy. How much more satisfying to make her give in, just as he had at the costume party. And Guy knew exactly how to win: Mockery had always been her downfall.

"Well, well, well. Flawless, frosty Arabella Larke, turned adventuress. This might have seemed like a grand idea inside that head of yours, but the reality..." He inhaled with a hiss, making an exaggerated grimace. "Naked bodies. Skin on skin. Limbs getting in the way. Me touching you in places you probably cannot even name. And the bodily fluids! Ugh."

"Thank you for the warning. Shall we proceed?"

Somehow, the gap between them had shrunk, yet still she refused to yield an inch. She had no idea. She might know the facts—Arabella always knew the facts—but as for the actual experience of tupping? The awkwardness alone would horrify her. Not to mention the mess.

"Proceed?" he scoffed. "You would not even have the courage to kiss me."

Her eyes narrowed. "Do you think this is a game?"

"It is now."

YEARS BEFORE, Guy had witnessed Arabella practicing archery. From the moment she nocked the arrow, she might have been alone in the world. Every inch of her body had been directed toward the target, her limbs steady as she drew back the bowstring. Her eyes had flicked to consider the wind, then returned to aim. To loose the arrow. To hit that target at its center and coolly claim the prize.

He felt like that target now.

Arabella hesitated, but only for a heartbeat, before lowering her gaze to examine his mouth. Her curved lips twitched; Guy tore his eyes away. He would not think about kissing her.

Yet clearly her focus was on kissing him. He tried to laugh at her, but his laughter choked under the intensity of her gaze. An intensity that was growing perilously erotic.

Would she peck his cheek? Firm, brisk, cold? No, he decided. Arabella would kiss him to win. No hesitation, no half measures.

And if he were to kiss her—he wouldn't, of course—but if he did... How would proud, poised Arabella react to the intimate brush of cheek against cheek, to the mingling of breaths, to the sensual slide of fingertips over her skin?

First, he would soften her: run his thumb over her mouth, wait for the catch of her breath, part her lips, and then—

And then he realized she was closing the space between them, her long lashes lowered as she targeted his mouth. She pursed her lips slightly, her tongue darting out; Guy's own mouth was a little dry.

Don't disappoint me, a voice whispered in his head, his last coherent thought before her hand drifted onto his jaw and cheek, a delicate touch that brushed his skin like smoke and coiled hotly in his stomach.

She leaned into him, and for one baffling heartbeat, he was looking into her eyes, then her lids fluttered closed, and her scent engulfed his brain, and his own eyelids lowered as her lips captured his.

Soft. Warm. Open mouthed. Lingering.

Sweet-hot desire shot to his groin like an arrow. She persisted with the kiss, infused it with a beguiling mix of hunger and tenderness. As if intoxicated, Guy cupped her neck, to hold her in place as he touched his tongue to hers. She flinched under his hand, tried to retreat, but he deepened the kiss, and back she came; a heartbeat later, her tongue stroked against his, and heat washed over him like steam.

Bloody hell. He released her and staggered back. What the devil was he doing? Giving her *lessons*? His aim was to chase her away! But perhaps he was succeeding, for her posture had grown stiff, her face turned aside, her hands balled into fists.

Here was his advantage: his experience with desire. He knew how to control it and when to unleash it. Arabella did not. She was proud, and desire and pride could not coexist. Desire was the great leveler, turning emperors into beggars and paupers into kings.

Arabella in the grip of desire would be easy to overcome.

"That's done," she said, in a fine semblance of composure. "Now, if we can stop dithering?"

"What? No flowers? No poetry?" He managed a light tone, hoping she did not notice the rasp in his voice. "How to make a man feel cheap! You'll steal a kiss and offer nothing in return?"

She glared at him. "I weary of your games, Guy."

"Unfortunately for you, we've barely begun." He knuckled her chin; her breath caught. "You are too direct, sweetheart. A man wants to be wooed. Seduction succeeds when you entice your companion to want it too. Whisper sweet nothings, flatter and coax, feather them with light touches and kisses until you set their desire ablaze."

"Surely you have enough imagination to pretend I've flattered and coaxed? The end result is the same."

"That won't do at all, I'm afraid. If you want me, earn me."

With an exasperated sigh, she marched across the room, yanked the bunch of flowers from their vase, and marched back to shove them into his hands. Their stems were slimy, and cold water trickled down his wrists.

"There. Flowers." She wiped her hands on a serviette. "And poetry. Ah... Shall I compare thee to a summer's day? Your eyes are nothing like the sun. All coaxed and flattered? May we begin?"

Her briskness betrayed her. Whatever her true objective, she did not seek intimacy. Then—aha! Intimacy would scare her away. That kiss had not been his best idea. Time for a new approach.

"No, no, no. You need to make me feel special." He separated a small red zinnia from the bouquet, pinched off its wet end, and dried his hands. "Like this." He brushed the petals over her cheek and tucked the flower behind her ear. "Oh yes, very pretty. Suits you."

"You are making fun of me."

"Not at all. I am generously tutoring you in the finer points of seduction. If you don't wish to know, well, you might as well leave."

With daggers in her eyes, she went to remove the flower. Catching her hand, he tutted. "Leave that pretty flower in your hair, while I charm you with poetry."

"No need for charm or poetry."

Yet she shifted, betraying discomfort.

Encouraged, Guy entwined his fingers with hers. Desire continued to coil inside him. Ignoring it, he recited softly: "*She walks in beauty, like the night, Of cloudless climes and starry skies.*"

Uncertainty danced across her face. She looked young, vulnerable. This closeness unsettled her. Good.

"And all that's best of dark and bright, Meet in her aspect and her eyes."

Guy had an image, suddenly, of the desert of Anatolia, where the night sky stretched forever and the stars were bright and fat, as if he was that much closer to heaven. Under that fathomless blanket of stars, he had melted into insignificance yet expanded to become part of something magnificent, the splendor of the heavens filling him with both peace and awe.

He blinked away the image and focused on Arabella, her eyes dark and unsure. This was a dangerous game he was playing. He would never become intimate with her—of course he wouldn't— but for all her flaws, Arabella was a compelling woman, standing very close, and he was a man who responded to compelling women who stood very close.

He had to teach her not to make demands of him.

"That poem goes on," he added. He caught one of the silken dark curls tumbling about her face and ran it through his fingers. "Something about raven tresses and sweet thoughts and winning smiles. Why, Byron might have written it for you. The raven tresses part, anyway. Certainly not the sweet thoughts or winning smiles."

She spun away, yanked the flower from her ear, and flung it to the floor. "Have you quite finished?" she snapped. "Let's dispense with this tedium, pretend we've whispered nonsense at each other, and get on with it, shall we?"

Her confidence was a façade; it had to be. Arabella and her famous pride, refusing to admit when she was out of her depth. It would be interesting to see what made that façade crumble.

"You really think I'm going to do this," he said.

"I never start things that I do not intend to finish."

"Very well, then. Take off your clothes. All of them."

She stiffened, turned to marble. Oh, she would not hold up at all! Soon she would concede that she hadn't the courage for this outrageous scheme, whatever it was, and she would leave him in peace. He would defeat her, as he had when they were children.

Folding his arms, Guy lounged back against the wall.

Then her chin lifted. Her limbs relaxed.

Arabella began to undress.

CHAPTER 6

G uy's mirth faltered. Arabella was actually doing this.
She slipped off her shoes and arranged them neatly, then unfastened her gown.

"Are you going to stand there and watch?" she demanded.

"Yes. I think I shall. If you don't like it, you can leave."

A frustrated sound escaped her throat, which was much more arousing than it should have been. In the circumstances, he should not be getting aroused at all.

She undressed efficiently and entirely without self-consciousness, as if his opinion mattered as little as a chair's. Once naked, she made no attempt to conceal herself, but stood tall and straight. Bloody hell. Arabella, naked in his drawing room. Her body was a breathtaking gallery of angles and curves, light and shadow, with the candlelight gilding the dark curls between her thighs, her pink nipples, the moles scattered over her skin like stars. His daft body responded helplessly. He had to remember to swallow, to breathe, to unclench his greedy, eager fists. And as for his cock... Well. He was in close proximity to a naked woman; no surprises there.

She perched on the edge of the oversized daybed, hands folded as if waiting for tea. "Now what?"

Good question.

"Take down your hair," he ordered her.

"It is too difficult to pin up again. I must leave here looking as I did when I arrived."

"You should leave now."

"I shall leave when we have concluded this business."

Bloody hell. What did a man do with an attractive and apparently willing woman, when his only aim was to make her admit she was wrong? He would not go through with this; of course he would not. But neither would he give in first. *That* was what mattered most: to watch her famous composure crumble, to compel her to scuttle away and never make demands of him again.

He was on the right track: Her shoulders were stiff, her muscles tense.

If her own nudity did not frighten her, then surely his would.

"Have you ever seen a naked man, Arabella, a virile young man? You may find it a fearsome sight to behold."

"I shall make every effort to be impressed."

Chuckling at her nonsense, watching her watching him, Guy slowly slipped his dressing gown off his shoulders, the silk and velvet pooling on the floor. Next was his shirt, tugged over his head and tossed at her. Impatiently, she flung it aside, and watched as he dispensed with his remaining clothes and presented himself.

Her gaze roamed over him; he fancied it a hot blue like the center of a flame, singeing his chest, his waist, his hips. With surprising boldness, her eyes lingered on his cock, which preened under the attention. Desire spread helplessly through his blood. He was vain enough to hope he impressed her, with this body forged by years of adventure, long marches and short skirmishes and heavy lifting. He had worked his body hard, and it had served him well, and if any women enjoyed the result, he would not object.

"You're all muscle." Her breathiness rippled over his skin.

"That's not what I call it," he said, and, with deliberate crudeness, wrapped one hand around his eager, upright cock.

A small mewl escaped her mouth. He took one step toward her, and another. Her eyes widened. Her lips parted. Her breath caught.

She was troubled, unquiet. Good.

"Lie down," he said.

She didn't move.

"So you'll be leaving, then."

Her shoulders flinched, and she slid up the daybed with sinuous grace. Guy placed his knees on either side of hers and crawled over her length until their faces were level. He moved slowly, to give her time to escape. Time, too, for her scent and warmth to curl over his skin and take possession of his senses. Stars above, but she was lovely, her body a carnival of angles and curves that his fingers and mouth longed to explore.

He would not. He could see to himself later, after she had fled.

"Now," he murmured, his mouth inches from her own, "are you ready to be ravished?"

One of her legs knocked against his own and bounced away. She would not last long, if she could not bear to be touched.

"No need for a ravishing." Breathiness undermined her attempt at hauteur. "If you would simply proceed to—"

"Oh, Arabella, sweetheart, have you learned nothing about seduction? No, no, no."

Shifting his weight to one arm, he splayed his other hand over her chest. His fingers nudged her collarbones, and the heel of his hand savored the warm swell of her breasts. The incongruous sight of his rough, tanned fingers against her delicate skin and fine bones was unexpectedly arousing, and he fought the urge to traverse those few desperate inches and palm her soft breasts. She trailed her eyes along the length of this arm. He shifted so his cock brushed against her. She gasped, jerked, lay still. He nipped her ear; again she jerked and gasped.

"I don't think you're ready yet." He traced lazy patterns over the no-man's land between her throat and breasts. "Whatever shall I do?"

She reared up slightly. "You can stop toying with me, for one."

"You started it," he growled. Fighting his own desire became harder with every second he hovered over her. "You came here to play with me, but this is a dangerous game—a game you are guaranteed to lose. Admit you were wrong, that this was a mistake, and go."

A rueful expression crossed her face, chased away by what he might have called amusement, were it not for her lack of mirth.

Then she sighed, sounding impatient and bored. "I had not expected this to involve so much talking. Do hurry up, Guy. I don't have all night."

A fine performance, but her muscles were tight and her heart pounded under his hand. Any moment now, she would realize her mistake and flee, proving to them both that she could not make him obey.

Speaking of obeying...

"Touch me," he ordered.

Her eyes roamed over him, burning his skin.

"Your shoulders..." she murmured. "They're very..."

Her expression was fleeting, but he saw it: hunger. Arabella, who had been trained to show no enthusiasm or passion, suffered not from anxiety but desire. The knowledge acted like oil on the fire of his lust. Damn her. He did not need another aphrodisiac.

He had misjudged. He should stop this. Now.

And give in before Arabella admitted defeat? Never!

Soon. She would find an excuse to go soon, spout some nonsense to salvage her pride.

Her hand fluttered onto his upper arm, danced upward to his shoulder. Guy turned his head and watched, as she reverently traced the indent between his muscles.

Yet she had flinched under his touch; touch would be her undoing.

He shifted beside her on the daybed. Barely leashing his lust, he trailed his hands over her: along her throat, into the dip above her collarbone, across her shoulders and down her arms, over her belly, her waist, lingering on the crests of her hips. He stroked her thighs to her knees and back again, his eyes seeking her reactions. She withheld them all.

He was determined to coax them from her.

Where his fingers failed, his mouth would succeed. He nibbled the smooth, warm curves of her shoulder, dragged his lips back to her throat, nipped at her ear, and then—

She moaned. The sound shot straight to his groin. He jerked up as she slapped a hand over her traitorous mouth. Aha! She was embarrassed. Almost there.

"What on earth are you doing?" she said. "Why don't you..."

Laughing raggedly at this self-inflicted agony, Guy tangled his fingers in hers and pressed her hand over her head. She licked her lips. Swallowed hard. Breathed out. Their eyes met, hers as potent as the desert sky. Fierce, unbounded, bold.

He fell. He fell into those fathomless eyes, until some part of him was lost, as if in the desert, as if under the night sky. This woman's fierceness and vastness and vulnerability—they merged and mingled, like a heavenly blanket woven around him. The sensation was humbling and inspiring, diminishing and enlarging. He tried to shake it off, because he knew—he knew!— he was just a man and she was just a woman and this act was nothing extraordinary and yet— It possessed him, this fantastic conviction that there was so much more, that she held infinite possibilities, this maddening, demanding, vibrant woman.

And something new entered her eyes, a touch of confusion, but something more, something beautiful and vivifying. Her free hand feathered over his face, as if checking he was real. He was real. Never had he been more real.

No longer could he bear to look at her, for fear he might see the heavens, so he closed his eyes and kissed her lips, because it seemed the only thing left to do.

When their mouths met, delight struck him like a dizzy spell. Like a goddess she rose into him, pushed her mouth fiercely into his, dueled with his tongue. She wound an arm around his neck, melded him to her as she crushed her breasts to his chest. A soft sound escaped her; he tried to capture it with his tongue, plundering her mouth as she plundered his. He planted a knee between her thighs, and she wrapped a leg around him like a vine.

A wild fury simmered deep inside her; he vowed to unleash it. That was her façade crumbling. Yes, yes! *That* was what he sought.

He wrenched his mouth from hers, dragged his hungry lips along her throat, tasting and teasing her skin. And her tantalizing breasts: He tormented them too, rewarded by her heel pounding his buttocks, by her fingers gripping the muscles in his back, by the animal sounds issuing from her perfect mouth.

Finally, he slipped his fingers between her thighs, his brain melting from her scent as he teased her. Her eyes were indigo and wild, her breathing ragged, and every mewl and gasp further heated his blood.

With a growl she grabbed his head and kissed him, savage and demanding, always demanding. Still he stroked her, relentlessly, even as her hips bucked, as her fingernails tore his skin, as her mouth devoured him. Exhilarated, undeterred, he pushed his fingers inside her; she besieged him with teeth and lips and every limb, hammering, squeezing, clutching. She was not gentle; he did not want her to be. He ignored the roar of his own desire as he dedicated himself to the delicious compulsion to pleasure this passionate creature.

"Make it stop now!" she cried and slapped his bicep, but when he tried to pull away, she gripped him hard, hissing, "I need you to touch me more. Curse you. You must touch me more!"

Exhilaration made him light-headed, laughing, yet still his fingers worked, so that finally—

She cried out and shuddered and gasped. Sensations visibly rippled over her, distorting her face. He was stunned: What ferocious beauty!

Then she lay still and breathed. "Guy," she sighed.

Finally, a victory. It dimly occurred to him that was not the victory he had originally sought, but the thought dissolved when confusion entered her eyes.

"Please..." She glared at him. "Do it, curse you."

Lust stole his last resistance. He moved over her, arranged her limbs, and thrust inside her on a wave of pleasure and relief. She released a long sound like the wind on the moors; too late, he remembered it was her first time. He stilled. Her closed eyelids quivered, but if she felt any pain, she betrayed no sign. He waited, trembling, testing his strength, until she took a deep, shuddering breath.

When she opened her eyes, they were dark, wild. Her legs were tempestuous around his waist, her palms were savage on his back, and his name catapulted off her lips like a command. "Guy."

And he was lost. Every thrust of his hips unleashed her passionate fury all over again. He could not be gentle, for she fought to get closer, to take control of something she didn't understand. It was like being buffeted by a gale, being enveloped from beneath, and he held on fiercely, taking his pleasure with an intensity he could not fight. Her nails dug into his back; her muscles gripped his cock. Bliss almost blinded him, and he barely managed to pull out and spend his seed onto his abandoned shirt.

He collapsed, aiming for the cushions, mostly hitting them; they thundered with the echoes of his heart, pleasure still swirling through him like a typhoon. The air shivered over the sweat on his skin. He had just enough strength left in his tortured limbs to slide his arms around her and gather her up, to hold her against him, hold her close.

THE AIR on her skin was cool; Guy's dozing body was hot. Arabella stared at the ceiling moldings, traced the patterns, counted Guy's breaths. Anything to silence her screaming mind and distract herself so she would not weep.

She never wept, and she must not weep here, now. She must not relax against him, curl into him, revel in the feeling of his hot, hard body, in the comfort of his heartbeat, in the musky smell of sex.

She could do none of that. She must rise, dress, walk the few streets home.

Carry on.

She eased away from him in inches, hoping to dress and escape while he slept. She rolled off the daybed, dropped onto the floor, hesitated, dizzy, fearing her astonished limbs were drained of strength. Somehow, she climbed to her feet, tiptoed to her gown, found her kerchief, and pressed the linen against her still-pulsing quim. It came away with a tiny dark smear, nothing she would call blood. It had not been particularly painful either; uncomfortable at first, certainly. Not... Well. She had expected something surgical at best, sordid at worst. But instead, it had been...

Oh so help her, never had she imagined that—that—whatever that was. The glory of his touch, of his mouth, of his body joining to hers. The way his touch skimmed over her skin and into her veins, stripping her of everything but sensation and fury. And his body! Its hard muscle and hot skin and heavy weight, its maddening, magnificent immovability, the roughness of his palms, of the hairs on his legs. And oh! the relentless pleasure that his fingers dealt. And that hunger that exploded inside her, that fierce, wild, desperate hunger to possess.

Now she ached, not in her body, but in another of those concealed parts of herself. As though something deep inside of her had crashed open, an iron gate to a secret garden, and she could not close it again. That was where the ache lay, and with it this terrible urge to weep.

She balled the kerchief in her hand, squeezed her eyes shut. Her legs threatened to fail her; she gripped the edge of a table to keep herself upright and tilted her face to the indifferent heavens. She must pull herself together. She must stop feeling this.

What had he done to her? What on earth had he *done*?

A sound. Startled like a deer, she turned. Guy was awake, watching her, carelessly, indolently naked. He was frowning, his expression soft.

Soft with worry. With tenderness. With *pity*.

"Arabella?" He reared up in a single movement. "Are you all right?"

He had seen. Curse him. He had witnessed her moment of

weakness, of despair. Realization lashed her, like a whip at her heart: He saw past her façade to the hidden parts of herself, to that shrouded, panicked part that knew to fear Sculthorpe, that secret, wondrous part that exulted in Guy.

In a few minutes, she would walk home. In a month or so, she would marry Sculthorpe. Her life would go on, with Guy always on the edges; Guy, who had seen her, furious and passionate, raw and weak, helpless and alone.

Her heart wanted to say: *When you held me in your arms, I did not feel alone.* Her heart wanted to say: *Please help me. There is no one else and I am afraid.*

She opened her mouth to speak her heart, to the caring in his eyes and the concern on his face. *But no*, her pride screamed, *he will mock you, pity you, and you will never recover from that.*

So her blasted pride took control of her mouth and spoke other words instead.

"You must be engaged to me now," she said coldly. "I was a virgin and now I am not."

His features hardened and the traces of compassion vanished, like a delicate songbird chased away by the ferocious, snarling bulldog of her pride.

"So that was your scheme, after all," he growled.

Lip curled with scorn, he threw himself back against the cushions, naked, decadent, uncaring. Red marks marred his golden skin. She had put them there.

"Because honor demands I marry you? So you would use my honor as a weapon against me." He laughed, rough and mirthless. "A baron isn't good enough for you, then? Still you angle for a marquess. If only you had some principles to go with your ambition! To think I was worried about you. Stars above, but I'm a fool."

She could not bear to look at his face, so she whipped up his banyan and tossed it over his head. He slapped at it, shrugged it on, and fell back onto the daybed to watch her dress, insolent, impassive, irate. In her haste, she missed buttons, but whirled her cloak over them; it was barely two minutes' walk home. Every item of clothing strengthened her like a suit of armor, helped her wrestle those unruly emotions back where they belonged.

"Did Clare know your plans for me?" Guy asked. "How are you two even acquainted? Do you take tea together and discuss your betrothed, the man who forced her into a life as a courtesan?"

"You don't know," she said with wonder. "Oh Guy, you and your honor."

He snorted. "You adore my honor. In case you aren't clear, I'll never marry you. This—" He waved an arm at the daybed. "This means nothing. I owe you nothing."

Arabella shook her head. He would never understand, he who swam in power like a fish in water. She had chosen him deliberately, used him ruthlessly: the one man certain not to be cruel, the one man whose discretion was assured, because if this became public, they would have to marry, and he was the one man certain to never marry her.

"I suppose no one has told you the truth about Clare Ivory." She fumbled for coins to buy his servant's silence. "But then, no one ever tells you things you don't want to hear. Sculthorpe did not seduce and ruin Miss Ivory. They had a contract. She sold her virginity to him for three hundred pounds. She *chose* to be a courtesan."

He sat up slowly. "Impossible. As my wife, she'd have received a lot more than three hundred pounds."

"Oh, Guy. You lack sense at times, but one could never accuse you of lacking a heart."

His eyes were shadowed and unreadable. Her own heart whispered again, begged her to stop fighting, to negotiate a truce.

Once more, tears began to choke her. How he would taunt her if he knew!

He must never know. This ended here. From now on, they would be Lord Hardbury and Lady Sculthorpe, haunted by a lifetime of petty squabbles and an hour of furious sex. He would always know her secret, and she would always hate him for that. It was preferable that he despised her, for anything was better than his pity.

"What did you truly hope to achieve tonight?" he asked. "Your first time..."

"Was quite satisfactory."

And then, because that didn't feel like enough, she turned a shilling in her fingers and flipped it to him. He caught it one-handed.

"For services rendered," she said, and swept out before he could reply.

Then she used every last shred of discipline to get herself home, without anyone seeing her, without shedding a single tear.

CHAPTER 7

The best thing about the approaching wedding was that Arabella always had something to blame.

Shadows under her eyes? Wedding. Fidgeting the entire two-day journey from London to Warwickshire? Wedding. Snappy and short-tempered? Why, blame the wedding.

And if her body tingled and throbbed with the memory of Guy's touch, if her heart keened for what it had lost, if Mama had to recall her attention several times, because she was staring at the passing scenery and seeing nothing but Guy's anger and scorn? Just blame the blasted wedding.

Her first measure of peace came when they arrived at their parish of Longhope Abbey, as the road turned at the ancient, twisted oak and there— Perched on a hill, golden in the afternoon sun, were the famous ruins of the abbey, run centuries earlier by the Abbess Avicia, who had ruled over this part of Mercia like a queen. How Arabella longed to ride up there, give her horse its head while the wind whipped her face and the beauty of her home soothed her.

Surely that would dispel these emotions roiling inside her, unfamiliar, unwelcome, uncontrolled. It was as though she had always believed herself to be a mountain, only to discover she was instead a volcano, full of fire and molten rock that she had not known existed until Guy's stirring touch. Now, ugly, messy emotions were pouring out of her like so much hot, stinking mud, and it took all her willpower to keep them tamped down.

By the time they climbed out of the carriage, it was all Arabella could do not to run for the stables, now that she was home.

Not for long. Soon, this would not be her home anymore.

As they entered the front door of Vindale Court—hardly cozy, this massive pile of white arches and spires, but then, neither was she—Ramsay welcomed them.

"Your father wishes to see you," Ramsay added in his glum manner, as if bearing bad news. Glumness was his way of achieving the solemnity fit for a butler. At heart he was as boisterous as ever—everyone had overheard him flirting with Mrs. Ramsay when they thought no one was listening—but that was beneath his dignity now.

There, another sharp pang of wretched emotion: When Arabella married Sculthorpe, she would leave Ramsay and all the staff, who tended to stay for years out of devoted loyalty to Mama. Ramsay had been a boisterous footman when Arabella was a child. She had a memory of him pulling her and Oliver in a little yellow wagon. The twins had been tucked side by side, holding hands, grinning at each other, cheering while Ramsay spun them around the yard.

She had no idea, now, why a footman had been pulling the children in a wagon. Perhaps the memory wasn't even real. She wasn't sure how many, if any, of her memories of Oliver were real.

Still in her carriage dress, she went to Papa's study, where

Queenie announced her arrival in the usual way, by flapping her huge green wings and crying "What a day! What a day!"

Papa hauled himself out of his armchair and took the few steps to the parrot's perch. Pleasingly, he had regained weight while she and Mama were in London, though his coat was still loose on his tall frame. He soothed Queenie and ignored Arabella, though she could feel all the other eyes on her. Forty-seven other eyes, belonging to the twenty-four stuffed birds that perched throughout the room, an unforgiving jury that heard and judged her many failings. She knew them all: the green woodpecker, the cockatoo, the jay of Bengal. The falcon on the center table had only one eye. She called it Pirate. They got along quite well.

Forty-nine eyes, if she counted the portrait of Oliver dominating one wall, that perpetual eight-year-old angel with his rosy cheeks and fine dark curls.

What is it this time? she silently asked the little boy, who smirked at her. *Smug little worm. If you'd lived long enough, you would have disappointed him too.*

Finally, Papa deigned to acknowledge her, studying her with eyes so like her own.

"Congratulations. You have managed to stay engaged to Lord Sculthorpe for more than one day. I should have let him have you back in the spring. But oh no, you insisted on waiting for Guy Roth. You misjudged that one, my girl." Papa lifted one thin hand; Queenie rubbed her beak against his finger and made that little purring sound in her throat. "But you've done well this time. With that illness last winter, I truly feared I would die without a grandson. I'm nicely recovered now, but I refuse to let you waste more time." He shot her a sharp look. "I daresay marrying you off would have been easier had you grown up to be sweet and demure."

Arabella clasped her hands. "I am exceedingly sweet and

demure. And if anyone says otherwise, I shall strike them with my crop."

"You and your jokes." Papa shook his head wearily. "This betrothal to Sculthorpe had better not be a joke."

The door opened and shut with a swish of skirts and air of fragrant calm. Papa continued as though Mama had not arrived.

"Sculthorpe arrives here tomorrow, I understand, and will stay until the betrothal ball. The sooner you marry, the sooner you'll have sons. Your second boy will come here to live with us."

Well. She had not yet birthed any children, and already they were being taken from her. Up on the wall, Oliver sang, *At least you'll be useful for something!*

Oh go jump off a cloud, you tiresome cherub, she snapped at him. *My only crime was to live when you did not.*

"And let me tell you, my girl, if you don't get Sculthorpe to the altar, I will cut you off and give the whole lot to Archibald Larke. You will not botch this. No excuses."

"The wedding will take place, Papa."

He lowered himself into his chair. His winter illness had worried them all. There were so many things Arabella still wanted to say to her father, so many words she still wanted to hear. In a month, she would leave this home for her loveless marriage.

Yet her parents had cooperated well together for a quarter century in their appropriate, cordial arrangement: wealthy Mr. Larke, cousin to a duke and renowned ornithologist, and Lady Belinda Misson, beautiful, unflappable daughter of the Earl of Keyworth.

"Papa, Mama, perhaps..."

Two faces turned toward her expectantly. Arabella's heart lurched in her chest. Wretched, stinking emotions.

"Why don't we spend some time together? The three of us. We could perhaps—"

"What for?" Papa looked truly baffled. "I already have many demands on my time, as do you both."

"You have not yet seen my work on *The Illustrated Guide to the Vindale Aviaries*."

"That can wait. More important that you plan the wedding and prepare for your new home."

High on the wall, Oliver was gloating. *Next time, just ask for a slap in the face*, he chirped.

Shut up, you pestilent putto. I hope the angels molt their feathers into your tea.

"I understand you invited Sir Walter Treadgold and his family," Papa said. "Which means the Roth girls will be here. I don't want Guy Roth—Lord Hardbury, I mean. He had better not show his face. He broke his father's promise that he'd marry you, and that's not something I can forgive or forget."

No, Papa never did forget. Arabella touched Pirate's beak so she wouldn't look at Oliver.

"It is highly unlikely that Lord Hardbury will even learn they are here," she said. "Even if he does, he will surely stay away, given all the bad blood. He has feuds not only with you, but also with Sir Walter, Lord Sculthorpe, and me."

"Lord Hardbury is a marquess now," Mama broke in gently. "If he does show up, I can hardly turn him away, but must offer him every hospitality."

Mama met Arabella's look serenely. How odd. The Russian Tsar could show up with an army and if Mama didn't want him here, she'd find a way to make him leave.

Papa waved a hand irritably. "Yes, yes, I suppose so. But I'll allow him only the barest of civilities should he choose to stay under my roof."

"He won't show up," Arabella repeated, and yet another pang stabbed her, at the punishing memory of Guy's gentle, generous hands, of the loathing and disgust in his eyes. Guy would never come near Arabella again.

Guy's vague restlessness had intensified into a desperate inability to sit still by the time he arrived at Swann's to meet his old schoolfriend Leo Halton, now the Duke of Dammerton.

He had little wish to revisit the upscale St. James gaming house. Swann's had been his primary haunt in his youth, but by default, not choice: It was one of the few London establishments that had merited his father's approval, which made it one of the few that would let Guy in.

The gaming house appeared to be prospering, though it had changed little in the past eight years: the same soft-spoken doorman murmuring the same bland greeting, the same elegant rooms hung with gold-colored satin and furnished with comfortable chairs. In the hushed intensity of the gaming room, where a faro bank was in full swing, Guy's arrival turned heads, but he swung directly into the livelier adjoining saloon.

Dammerton was already there in one of his colorfully embroidered waistcoats, sprawled in an oversized armchair and nursing a snifter of brandy. Guy envied the duke's apparent ease; days after that encounter with Arabella, he still felt as rumpled as his bed after a particularly poor night's sleep.

Guy dropped into the chair beside Dammerton and was served within a minute. Still the best service and refreshments, hence Father's approval. Guy had not minded Swann's particularly; what he minded was the humiliation of being turned away from most London establishments like a blacklisted scoundrel, because everyone was too scared to disobey his father. Friends had suggested Guy offer bribes or attempt a disguise, but he refused to deploy such tricks.

"Well, Hardbury? How was my information?" Dammerton asked lazily, looking half asleep. Guy wasn't fooled; lions usually looked half asleep too. "Did it lead you to Sir Walter?"

"Almost. I missed him by an hour and have no idea which road he took. He could be anywhere in England by now." Guy stretched out his horse-weary legs and groaned. "The man's like a bloody rabbit in a warren, diving down one hole and popping up somewhere else."

"How does he even know to hop away? Surely your solicitors didn't tell him of your investigations."

"It was me," Guy confessed. "I told him."

Dammerton chuckled. "Ah, Guy the Impulsive. You never were any good at diplomacy."

Guy had also confessed this to his solicitor, whose mouth had tightened before he said, "No doubt the right thing to do, my lord."

Ah, what blather. No one dared tell a marquess he had erred. Once upon a time, Guy would have taken those words at face value, assured that he was right. Such were the benefits of maturity: All his life he had been a fool, but now he had the dubious wisdom of knowing it.

As proven by that whole debacle with Arabella.

What the devil had he been thinking? Well, he hadn't been thinking, had he? Every step had seemed like a grand idea at the time; stars above, the lies he had told himself! She had stated directly what she wanted, then made a supremely inept attempt at getting it. How easy it would have been for him to kick her out! But no— He had to be an arrogant, deluded fool and turn it into a game, a game in which he was hopelessly outmatched.

Bloody hell. Guy was hardly a rake, but neither was he an

innocent. Yet look at him: seduced like a naive virgin. Seduced *by* a naive virgin.

Virgin, at least; Arabella was about as naive as Mephistopheles.

"Ah," Dammerton said, his tone suddenly alert. He gestured with his glass as if toasting someone across the room. Before Guy even turned, he knew what he would see: a fair-haired woman in a gown as blue as sapphires, disappearing through the French doors. A scandal sheet had mentioned that Clare Ivory always wore jewel colors; it was her signature, much as her fellow courtesan Harriette Wilson was known for wearing only white.

He twisted back. "Seriously, Dammerton? You knew she'd be here?"

"She never comes here. That's why I suggested this place."

Guy sat back, but a moment later, he was cursing and standing and striding toward the terrace, his friend's chuckle floating in his wake.

Out on the balcony, Clare was in conversation with a man and woman. All three fell silent as he joined them, but he had eyes only for Clare. Ah, that angel's face of hers, that had so tormented his youthful body and heart.

"Leave us," Guy said to the couple.

"We are in the midst of a negotiation, my lord," Clare said. "Perhaps—"

"Leave us."

The two left.

Clare slapped her fan into one bejeweled hand. "I am a businesswoman and I will make a substantial commission from facilitating their contract. If you wanted to talk to me, you should have made an appointment."

He lounged back against the balustrade. "I thought we had an appointment the other night, but instead I found myself entertaining Arabella Larke."

Entertaining? That was one word for it. Days later, he could not dispel the image of her gripping the table, face turned up as if pleading with the heavens. In that moment, compassion had conquered him, so he was ready to do anything to protect her—until she revealed it was a manipulative, cold-blooded scheme.

Honor be damned. He owed her nothing. But the very idea that Arabella Larke, of all people, had slipped under his skin!

Damn near literally.

Every time he undressed, he twisted before the mirror to inspect the scratches she had left. Over and over he'd relive her passion like a fever dream, and was sorry to watch those scratches fade.

He forced his attention back to Clare. "You will tell no one I met her," he added.

She laughed, a melodious sound that had once delighted him, and now meant nothing. "Of course not, though for her sake, not yours. Miss Larke is my newest ally. Besides, no one would believe it; her reputation is impeccable." Clare shook her head. "For my part, I thought you'd never agree to the proposed meeting, but she said you like to solve puzzles and play risky games. It seems she was right, and she knows you better than I ever did."

Heat prickled under his suddenly too-tight cravat. He already knew that Arabella made observations, considered matters from every angle, drew shrewd conclusions. Everyone knew of her flawless appearance, her proud manner, her sharp wit, but did others guess at the vast expanses behind those eyes?

"What a curious pair you and Miss Larke make," Clare mused. "You both seek me out to talk about each other."

"I didn't seek you out to discuss Arabella."

"How interesting. She said much the same thing about you."

Guy studied her, that angel's face, those knowing eyes. He had feared that meeting Clare again would transform him back into the besotted clown he'd been at twenty and lead once more to a broken heart. No such fear. All that remained was a vague sorrow for his younger self, for having squandered his innocent, fervent love.

"Explain why you chose to become a courtesan," he said. It had shocked him, Arabella's revelation about Clare. "You knew I wanted to marry you. I even gave you my mother's jewels as proof of my sincerity, and you *sold* them."

A faint flush stained her cheeks. "They were mine to do with as I wished."

"You could have had more than jewels, had you married me. You could have had everything."

"Like you did?" Her tone was dry, her smile kind. "You had everything: title, status, and a father who controlled your every move like he controlled most of London. As I see it, you had nothing but what he let you have. Had I had married you, I'd have become a prisoner in a gilded cage."

"And your life as a courtesan— Is that not a cage?"

She spread her hands. "If so, then it is a cage whose door is always open. I make my own choices, am beholden to no one, and have secured enough lucrative contracts that I never need work again."

Past her, the bright rooms seemed as distant as his youthful self. Father's arrangements had allowed Guy to gamble here, but only on an account; he could never walk away with so much as a coin. Every avenue to earning his own income had been barred; even the Army and Navy had refused to take him.

"Why didn't you tell me this at the time?"

"Oh Guy, I tried, but you did not listen." She touched his shoulder. "You were so preoccupied with breaking free from your father. I wondered if you even saw me, or if I had simply become a symbol of your freedom from him, the way Miss Larke became a symbol of his control."

Guy spread his hands over the smooth stone of the balustrade, stared into the shadowy garden below, recalling that final bitter fight with his father, over Clare Ivory and Arabella Larke and Guy's determination to choose his own life.

"I loved you," he said.

"And how freely you expressed your feelings." Her soft smile was rueful. "But the more you told me you loved me, the more trapped I felt. I treated you poorly, and I regret that. My only excuse is that I was young and confused. I didn't have the courage to refuse you to your face, so I took the easy way out."

Not once had he questioned Clare's feelings for him. He had loved her; therefore, by the logic of a young man born to wealth and privilege, she must naturally love him. She had been a beacon of hope, his promise of freedom, his escape.

"Regret nothing," he said. "I am grateful now that you turned me down. I enjoyed my adventures and my years of freedom. They enabled me to become the man I am."

He straightened, ready to leave her behind, along with his past, when she said, "I hear you are having troubles with Sir Walter Treadgold."

"Bloody hell. Does everyone know everything?"

"We talk. We listen. One of the York sisters has plans for Sir Walter's son. Humphrey Treadgold was always extremely generous with us courtesans, but we lost him when he took a position in Ireland. Apparently his father has called him back."

"Why should I care about Treadgold's son?"

"You could use such information against him."

A little blackmail here, a touch of extortion there. Bribes and favors and whispers in the dark. That was how Guy's father had operated, how he had expected Guy to operate.

He shook his head. "No wonder you get along with Arabella. You are each as unprincipled as the other."

"Just because someone does not share your principles does not mean they are without them." Again, she laughed. "I take it you are not invited to her wedding."

"I wouldn't attend even if I were invited. If you see either her or Sculthorpe, be sure to wish them every joy of each other."

"Perhaps your sister can relay your message at the wedding."

"Freddie? At Arabella's wedding?"

"I presume so. Sir Walter and his whole family are already at Vindale Court, ahead of Miss Larke's betrothal ball." Her head drew back. "Did you not know?"

Guy laughed, a loud, mirthless sound that flew out into the thick night air. He'd been interrogating people across the south of England, and the whole time, Clare knew. And Arabella was three steps ahead of him again.

Guy was still shaking his head as he rejoined the duke. Well played, Sir Walter, to hide in the one place in England where Guy was most emphatically not welcome. And well played, Arabella, to redouble her efforts to trap him into marriage by using Freddie and Ursula as bait.

Let Arabella scheme in vain. Guy would not go to Vindale Court.

CHAPTER 8

The victory was more complicated and costly than Arabella had anticipated, but it was a victory nonetheless.

"A nice haul, my clever virgin," Lord Sculthorpe murmured, indicating Arabella's basket of freshly picked nuts with a wave of a cigar-laden hand, as their party tramped through the woods.

And Arabella felt nothing but smug satisfaction and serene superiority.

Indeed, in the week since Lord Sculthorpe had joined the house party at Vindale Court, ahead of their betrothal ball and wedding, not one word or act from him had bothered her in the slightest.

With her desperate, dangerous, immoral deed, she had claimed herself first. She had calmed that unknown part of herself. She had won.

And if thoughts of Guy whirled inside her like a howling gale, that hardly signified. During the day, the multitude of guests kept her busy, and at night, when the memories crowded her— Well, it concerned no one but herself, what she did alone in her bed.

"Yet I fear Miss Treadgold has outdone you," he added.

Matilda Treadgold had outdone everyone. Arabella was impressed, not because Miss Treadgold's basket held so many nuts, but because she had not picked a single one herself. The quartet of visiting gentlemen who had joined their nutting expedition—a pair of German ornithologists, a botany student from Sierra Leone, and someone's distant cousin—had all dedicated themselves to her service. Petite Miss Treadgold had only to gaze longingly at a nut for them to rush to pick it. Throughout it all, she remained unfailingly amiable and warm-hearted, the kind of lady who brightened a room with her presence and whom everyone enjoyed having near.

Exactly what Guy would seek in his bride.

Freddie's basket was full too, but her treasures included stones, a feather, and an orange mushroom. Arabella's neighbors and friends, Mrs. Cassandra DeWitt and Miss Juno Bell, had apparently abandoned nutting in favor of blackberries. Both were caught in the brambles, helpless with laughter as they tried to free each other, only to get further ensnared.

Past them, little Ursula's nanny stayed busy trying to stop the toddler from putting things in her mouth, and Miss Norton, the efficient young governess supervising three children from other visiting families, did an admirable job of keeping her charges entertained.

"Miss Treadgold is welcome to the prize," Arabella said to Sculthorpe.

"You do not compete?"

"Why should I compete when I have already won?"

He preened because he thought she meant him. Now she no longer feared him, he was even easier to manage than she had hoped.

Then a squeal came from Miss Treadgold.

"Oh, it's dead! How horrific!" she cried, poking a dead squirrel with a stick.

Belatedly, she dropped the stick and jumped backward, mouth covered, eyes wide. Her retinue nobly gathered close.

"You poor girl, how do you tolerate staying in Vindale Court?" asked one of the ornithologists. "Mr. Larke's stuffed birds are mounted everywhere."

"Oh, they are hideous, those dead birds! They give me such nightmares." Miss Treadgold shuddered dramatically, and the men soothed her with meaningless words.

Freddie had drifted over to peer at the dead squirrel. The children clamored to get near, but their governess held them back.

At Arabella's side, Sculthorpe laughed indulgently. She studied him carefully, but there was nothing untoward in his expression when he looked at Freddie and Miss Treadgold, so no call to protect them from him; only Arabella merited his secret smiles and leers.

But as she watched, his gaze shifted. That repellent light entered his eyes, and his lips twisted in a scornful but hungry curl. Arabella followed his gaze.

He was looking at the governess.

His nostrils flared slightly, and he audibly blew out a spiral of smoke. Then he glanced at the sky, sucked on his cigar, and, avuncular smile back in place, returned his attention to the group.

It was over in a few heartbeats; Arabella was thankful to have witnessed it.

"I must say," she said casually, "Miss Norton excels at managing those young tearaways."

"Who?" He glanced at the governess, looked away. "Oh, the governess."

Arabella adopted a light tone as she continued her secret

interrogation. "I imagine you must have been such a young tearaway yourself once. A torment to your governess."

Something flashed in his eyes but he laughed in his charmingly self-deprecating manner. "I'll own she was a torment to me. My sister's governess, that is."

"Was she very terrible?"

"On the contrary. She was sheer perfection and I was infatuated." He shook his head. "I daresay I am not the first boy to decide I am madly in love with a governess, pining over her prim dress and bossy manner."

"I suppose if you were to meet her now, you'd see she is merely another woman and the shine would come off her."

He made a derisive sound. "The shine came off long ago, when I learned the truth about her. I— You will forgive me for speaking plainly."

"Always, my lord."

"Indeed. We understand each other. The truth is, my elder brother seduced her. I saw them in the act in her bedroom."

Sculthorpe did not explain why he had been spying on the governess in her bedroom, and Arabella did not waste her breath asking.

"But that was Kenneth for you," he went on. "The heir, the eldest, who already had everything. He knew about my infatuation but he took her anyway. She was mine and he took her. He never cared how much that hurt me." His expression hardened, followed by another self-mocking laugh. "Such are the foolish, futile passions of a boy. But we never do forget our first." He glanced at her. "It is inappropriate to tell you such things, but you are a practical lady and we are shortly to be wed."

"I am glad you tell me these things," Arabella said honestly. "Very, very glad."

Because now she was prepared to protect her future employees too. When the time came to hire a governess, she must select one who had been widowed three times, could chop wood with her bare hands, and would help Arabella hide a corpse.

Sculthorpe's look was lingering. "You still don't smile. On our wedding night, you will smile for me."

"Of course I shall."

Hopefully, she would remember to do so at the appropriate point. Perhaps she should practice smiling, the way she practiced producing a smear of blood for her second deflowering.

Freddie's voice intruded. "We should burn it," she said, her eyes on the dead squirrel.

Sculthorpe moved away. "Your wish is my command, Lady Frederica."

Using the side of his boot, Sculthorpe piled dead leaves over the little cadaver and dropped the smoldering end of his cigar onto them. A wisp of smoke curled over the leaves.

Arabella took the opportunity to walk on alone. How she loved these woods in autumn. In spring, winter, summer. How she would miss the seasons and the people who had been the fabric of her life.

No need to be maudlin, she scolded herself. One day, she would live here again. In the meantime, her marital home sounded perfectly pleasant. The Sculthorpe seat was in Norfolk, by the sea. Arabella thought she might enjoy living by the sea. All those cliffs for her husband to fall off.

Before long, the sun-dappled path left her at the edge of the roadway, across from a field that was half gold with stubble, half brown from the plow. She lingered, breathing in the crisp autumn air, the smell of freshly turned soil.

Until a movement drew her eyes along the road, to where a lone horse and rider approached.

The rider's features were obscured, but she knew who it was.

She knew from the confident ease of his posture, from his greatcoat and hat, from the hot electricity jolting through her limbs.

Guy had come. She had been sure he would not. But he had.

She stood her ground throughout his approach, until he reined in his horse and stared down at her from his great mounted height. Despite herself, her eyes tracked over his shoulders, his thighs, along his arms to his gloved hands expertly holding the reins. Every inch of their skin was covered except their faces, but she warmed as if they were naked again.

And in his eyes... She dared herself to meet their challenging, amused stare and saw—nothing. Nothing in his look made her recoil. He knew things about her that she had not even known herself, yet he betrayed no sign of gloating or possession, no superiority or scorn.

"I am joining your house party," Guy announced cheerfully. "Perhaps I'll even stay for your betrothal ball. You'll save me a dance, I hope. I promise not to step on your feet more than twice."

She glared at him. She had been so sure he would not come. "You weren't invited."

"Oh, I think we both know that you invited me when you invited my sisters."

"At least I was able to locate them. You seemed to be having a little trouble with that."

"After which you used them to lure me here. Very Machiavellian of you."

"Thank you."

"Not a compliment."

"Hm." She ran her fingers through the nuts in her basket, letting them soothe her. "Be warned: Papa has declared that you are not welcome in his house."

"I don't care what your father says. And you, surely, are not surprised to see me. In the circumstances."

Her heart leaped with— What? Hope? Joy? That he had wanted to see her and... *Don't be ridiculous*, she scolded herself. He despised her, and it was better that way. He made her feel weak, but her pride kept her strong.

"Which circumstances might those be?" she made herself ask.

Before he could speak, a twig snapped and leaves crunched. The hardening of Guy's features told her who had emerged from the woods.

"My sisters being here," Guy said coolly. He inclined his head. "Sculthorpe."

Lord Sculthorpe planted himself at Arabella's side and pressed his fingers to the small of her back. She didn't cringe or shudder. She supposed she should feel embarrassed, for this was the most awkward situation she had ever been in, but she didn't feel that either. All she felt was that smug relief at taking back control from Sculthorpe, and her lingering, confused regret over Guy.

"Hardbury. Didn't know you were invited."

Guy didn't answer, as Miss Treadgold came darting out of the woods, her followers crowding in her wake. A warm smile lit Guy's face. Everyone smiled warmly when they looked at Miss Treadgold, as though the mere sight of her made them happy.

No one ever smiled at Arabella like that. She had never even known she wanted them to. But now it struck her as the most marvelous thing in the world.

"Lord Hardbury!" Miss Treadgold bobbed a curtsy. "What a splendid surprise!"

"The country air agrees with you, Miss Treadgold." Guy made no effort to hide his admiration. "You make a pleasant sight for a weary traveler."

"You are too kind, my lord. Lady Frederica is here. You must be longing to talk to her."

"Of course." Guy's smile broadened. "I trust I shall have an opportunity to talk to you too."

"Oh." She lowered her lashes and blushed.

So. That was how the wind blew. Again, Arabella ran her fingers through the nuts. Perhaps she should pelt them at him.

Guy had seen; his expression suggested he had guessed her thoughts. Then he dug in a pocket and flipped something at her: a coin that glinted in the sunlight as it tumbled through the air.

Arabella caught it neatly.

"What is that?" Sculthorpe asked.

She turned the coin in her fingers. She didn't need to look at it to know it was a shilling. Perhaps the exact same shilling she had flipped to Guy that night in London.

"Miss Larke," Sculthorpe said sharply. "Why did Lord Hardbury toss you a shilling?"

Arabella kept her eyes on Guy. "Oh, just a token from some silly moment in our past. Something silly and foolish that meant nothing at all."

The horse tossed its head and danced sideways. Guy half laughed, dug in his heels, and rode on.

GUY HAD VOWED to avoid Arabella during his stay at her family's house, but watching her with Sculthorpe in the drawing room after dinner that first night, he itched to make trouble.

He had already received several subtle admonitions to behave, from Lady Belinda ("I trust you will enjoy a *harmonious* stay with us, my lord"), Mr. Larke ("That girl will marry Sculthorpe, so don't you foul that up, Hardbury"), and Sir Walter ("How excessively delightful that we can be friends—nay, family!—my lord.").

But Guy was growing restless, and of course—*of course*—Arabella was the cause, so provokingly poised and haughty, from the top of her flawlessly coiled hair to the hem of her glacier-blue gown.

It was her manner toward Sculthorpe that irked Guy. She displayed the sort of familiar forbearance one would expect in a woman two decades after her wedding, not a month before. Sculthorpe chatted freely and did not seem to notice that Arabella did nothing more animated than nod.

How wrong it was that Arabella, vibrant, vexing Arabella, was muted. No wonder Guy wanted to stir her up. Bloody hell. What *was* this compulsion to tease her? It was proving as dangerous as the obsession that summoned other men back to the tables even after their last penny had been gambled away.

Yet when Sculthorpe brandished his silver cigar case and excused himself to step outside, and Arabella crossed to show Miss Treadgold the sheet music, Guy wandered toward the pianoforte too, only for Arabella to drift away. Guy helped Miss Treadgold choose some music and relinquished the right to turn pages to another man, by which point Arabella was conversing with Freddie. Guy sauntered that way, yet by the time he reached his sister's side, Arabella was with her mother. Guy sidled toward Lady Belinda...as Arabella glided to the tea tray.

Better he stop now, before anyone noticed that he was chasing Arabella around the drawing room. But when she lifted the teapot, he crossed to her side, creating a small world where they stood apart from the others.

Arabella glanced about, apparently saw no escape, and resigned herself to pouring him a cup of tea he didn't want. The square bodice of her gown revealed her sharp collarbones. Guy could still feel those collarbones under his fingers, still see his hand splayed over her chest. He tore his eyes away.

"Are you avoiding me, Arabella?" he asked in low tones, so no one overheard.

"Don't be absurd. I never avoid anyone. I'm merely discerning in my choice of company."

She turned the teacup's handle to align its pattern with the saucer, and passed it to him with steady hands.

"What are you up to, Arabella? What do you want from me?"

One eyebrow lifted. "What on earth could I possibly want from you? You have already served your purpose. Or had you forgotten so soon?"

Her bold gaze was like a whirlpool, sucking him in. Memories swarmed between them: their bodies, their mouths, their exhilarating passion, and this infernal longing for more.

If only he could whisk them both away to the desert and lay her down under the endless night sky. But they were in a drawing room, amidst chatter, candles, music, tea. He despised her. He wanted her. She was dangerous. He was mad.

"I am not here for you," he managed to say through gritted teeth, and plunked down his teacup before he crushed it in his rough, hungry hands.

She nudged the abandoned cup on its saucer to align their patterns, but she overshot.

"I am not here for you," he repeated, as again and again she tried and failed to align that saucer and cup.

Finally, scowling at the recalcitrant china, she clasped her hands in front of her and opened her mouth to speak. Nothing came out. Another attempt, and still she had no words. Her eyes darted around the room, landing on Freddie.

"You..." She cleared her throat. "You are here for your sisters, no doubt. And you seem to be friends with Sir Walter suddenly."

Sweet relief: She had mercifully salvaged the conversation.

"Have you discovered the power of subterfuge?" she went on.

"Diplomacy," he corrected. "I am exercising admirable restraint. I even refrained from calling him a brazen and corrupt hypocrite to his face."

It was not to his taste, pretending to like someone he despised. When Sir Walter casually inquired as to the purpose of his lordship's visit, Guy had murmured something vague about Vindale Court having multiple attractions and let his eyes rest on Matilda Treadgold. That set Sir Walter's face aglow, and he had promptly arranged for his niece to lead Guy to little Ursula. His infant sister turned out to be a delightful doll-like creature, with feathery blonde curls, a sweet smile, and a stream of incomprehensible babble.

"Congratulations," Arabella said dryly. "But I do wish you would listen to me about Freddie. You must find out—"

"No." He raised one hand. "You do not tell me what I must or must not do. Let that be the first rule."

Her eyes widened. "Oh, are we to have rules? How adorable. Next you will expect me to obey them."

"I'm not such a fool as that. But I do not need your help to gain custody of my sisters and rebuild my family."

"If you care so much, I wonder you let something as trivial as a broken heart drive you away."

"I didn't leave because Clare Ivory broke my heart."

"Why did you leave?"

Leaving had been the only possible end to a decade of struggle for control—over Guy. That struggle culminated in that final, bitter fight, when Guy insisted on marrying Clare, at which his father, using his bulk to loom over him, threatened to lock him in the cellar until he agreed to marry Arabella.

"You cannot make me!" Guy had yelled, with the fervor of youth. "I will never be your puppet."

Father had been scornful. "You've not enough sense to make your own decisions. You'll do as I say, until you learn to be the man you should be."

"A corrupt tyrant like you?"

"This is my country," Father had replied coldly. "And you will do as you are told as long as you breathe my country's air."

So they had divided up the world: Father had won tyranny in Britain, and Guy had won freedom everywhere else.

Arabella was eyeing him expectantly.

"It was about principles," he finally said.

"Principles?"

"Yes. Have you heard of them?"

She shrugged. "My governess might have mentioned them, but then she told tales of fairies, unicorns, and honorable gentlemen, so I never paid her much mind."

He laughed despite himself. "My father was certainly not honorable. His favorite game was finding ways to milk money and power from his position, and he expected me to do the same. His explanations for his unethical behavior always sounded so reasonable. I was a terrible disappointment to him, what with my ethics and all."

"Terrible affliction, ethics. Rather like a rash, I imagine."

"I can see why he approved of you. In every letter I wrote, I promised to return if I could earn an income and marry as I wished, to which he declared I would behave as he saw fit and marry you."

Finally, he had shocked her enough for it to show. "You cannot mean you spent all those years arguing over me? That's preposterous. Britain has other heiresses, and our fathers were never that devoted."

"You became the symbol of my obedience."

"No wonder you were so adamant against marrying me."

He shrugged. "Your ruthless, quarrelsome nature was a factor too."

"Oh dear. And here I thought that was my chief charm."

The world tilted. Was Arabella *laughing* at herself? Impossible.

"And so you seek your perfect bride," she continued, cynical to the bone. "She'll gaze at you with wide, adoring eyes and once more the great man will tumble headlong into love."

"I'm looking forward to it," he said cheerfully, refusing to be riled. "I enjoyed being in love. It makes one feel more alive, not unlike drinking and gambling, but better for one's health. And when I meet a lady both adoring and adorable, pleasant and pleasing— Believe me, Arabella, I shall fall so fast I get a concussion."

Something flickered in her expression, like a soft wistfulness, chased away by the sardonic hoist of a perfectly arched brow.

"Can it be thus arranged? Does one order one's sweetheart like a new coat, specially tailored and cut to size? Who knew love was so convenient?" Her gaze traveled pointedly to Miss Treadgold, finishing up at the pianoforte. "But of course, what his lordship orders, his lordship gets. Sir Walter informed me at dinner that you are here to court his niece."

"Any man would happily choose Miss Treadgold over every other lady in the room."

Her eyes widened. "Even over *me*? Good grief. I cannot imagine why."

"Ha! Because men prefer a woman who nurtures her young to one who eats them."

"Don't be absurd. I haven't eaten any babies in years."

Surprised laughter burst out of him. No mistaking it this time: Arabella was definitely making fun of herself. Another revelation: Her lips might not curve, but her eyes smiled and laughed.

Stars above, had she always been laughing at herself? Were her outrageously arrogant declarations in fact jokes at her own expense?

Once more, Arabella was rendered new and strange, like the night sky on the other side of the world, where the stars were arranged differently, fascinatingly familiar yet forever changed.

He had to remember where they were. Who she was. What she had done.

To remind them both, he said, "Sculthorpe must be pleased about that."

Her eyelids barely flickered in response. "Was it he who broke your nose?"

"No. That happened when I was away. I was this big brash Englishman, expecting everyone to leap to my command. My face practically invited other men to hit it."

"Because in England, everyone always let you win."

He shifted uncomfortably. He had only discovered that upon venturing into the world without the protection of his name. Yet Arabella, years younger than he, had noticed. But then, when he was a boy, she was the only person who ever challenged him.

"Let you win what, Hardbury?"

It was Sculthorpe, come back inside, awash in tobacco smoke.

Arabella's face went blank. "Lord Hardbury was telling me about his travels," she said smoothly, pitching her voice to carry across the room. "Italy, among other places."

How easily she lied. And how steady her hands, when she poured tea for her cuckolded betrothed.

The fine china cup and saucer looked delicate in Sculthorpe's big hands. His eyes met Guy's. Perhaps they were both remembering that day when Guy issued his challenge and

Sculthorpe's big hands had formed big fists, and beaten twenty-year-old Guy for his insolence.

"I spent some time in Italy during the war," Sculthorpe said. "What were you doing there?"

Lady Treadgold's voice sailed across the room. "Oh, Lord Hardbury, Matilda and I are simply *dying* to hear more of your travels in Italy. Aren't we, Matilda?"

Miss Treadgold did seem bright-eyed. "I hear one can see dead bodies left by an ancient volcano."

"Matilda," Lady Treadgold admonished softly.

Her face fell with becoming distress. "But Aunt Frances, it sounds so horrible. Those poor people."

"Your tender heart does you credit. Doesn't it, Lord Hardbury?"

"Indeed."

Guy looked back at Arabella and Sculthorpe. Stars above, this whole situation was too absurd for words. Why the devil had he changed his mind and come here?

Shaking his head, he crossed to Lady Treadgold, who said, "Tell us about Venice. They do such wonderful things with glass."

And Miss Treadgold, sweet, pretty, unchallenging, smiled shyly. Guy set about making himself agreeable, and not once did he look back across the room to where Arabella calmly conversed with Lord Sculthorpe and the botany student as though nothing untoward had ever passed at all.

CHAPTER 9

The wind seemed to blow right through Arabella as she climbed the hill to the abbey ruins. Normally, she would ride, but if she had taken a horse, Lord Sculthorpe could have learned that she was gone.

Not that she was hiding from Sculthorpe, of course. She simply chose to be out of the house while he was in it.

What a nuisance. Every other day, Sculthorpe had occupied himself with shooting or fishing, yet on this sunny, windy afternoon—ideal weather for a man to be outside killing things—he had declared his intention to haunt the house.

So Arabella had fabricated an errand and stepped outside, and kept on stepping until she ended up here.

The abbey ruins looked philosophical in the autumn light, the remaining arches and ivy-clad walls indifferent to time. Odd how some walls stood for centuries, while others crumbled and fell. She had always admired the persistence of Longhope Abbey, which had stood so long it gave the parish its name. *You'll not get rid of* me, it said.

She stripped off her gloves and trailed her fingers over the stone. She and Oliver used to play here, clambering over the rocks and daring each other to visit the crypt. And picking blackberries, of course, grinning at each other with purple mouths.

One autumn, the year after they lost Oliver, the visiting children had competed to see who could pick the most. Arabella had won, but at a cost: stained fingers, messy hair, torn dress. Mama had sent her to tidy herself, sternly reminding her she was a lady, saying Papa must not see her like that. But Papa had seen her. His lip had curled with disgust, as he looked her over and said, "Call yourself my daughter. Unnatural child. What a disgrace."

So she had perfected the art of picking blackberries without getting snagged or scratched or stained. She did not harvest very many, but moderation was prized in a lady, whereas winning was not.

And here was a blackberry bush that still held fruit, plump, purple, and glossy in the sun. They would all have to be picked by Michaelmas. According to lore, that was the day the Archangel Michael had cast Lucifer from heaven, and Lucifer landed on a thorny blackberry bush, spat on it, and cursed.

Identifying a suitable berry—one not quite ripe, to spare her the messy juice—Arabella snaked her hand through the brambles and tugged off the fruit. Closing her eyes, she popped the berry into her mouth. Its early sweetness pleased her tongue, even as its tartness radiated along her jaw.

She swallowed. Savored the moment. Opened her eyes.

Guy.

He was watching her, impervious to the wind whipping his greatcoat around his boots. The sunlight hit him sideways, and thrushes fluttered in the orange leaves behind his head.

In the days since his arrival, they had not spoken again; she had not so much as looked at him directly. Now, she could not look away. Nor could she move, not with every inch of her skin feeling more than it ought, as if the wind and sun themselves were stealing under her clothes and into her blood.

No matter: He would walk away. He would hasten to avoid her, as he had every other day of the past week.

He didn't.

Instead, he advanced, stopping too close.

"Poaching blackberries?" he said.

She swallowed away the dryness in her mouth, the lingering taste of sour and sweet. "You?"

"Guilty as charged."

He held up a hand, his fingers stained purple. Then that hand seized hers, his fingers warm despite the wind. He took her other hand and examined them both.

"Remarkable," he said. "I witnessed you picking and eating a berry, yet your skin carries nary a mark. Unless you only eat unripe blackberries. You prefer the sour ones?"

"I am already sufficiently sweet."

He laughed, the sound reminiscent of his hands skimming over her body: fearless, playful, and with an exhilarating edge.

"I could think of a thousand words to describe you, Arabella, and 'sweet' would not be one of them."

"And you prefer the sweet ones."

"The sweet, amiable ones," he agreed.

"The ones who flatter you with their adoration and warm you with their smiles."

"The ones who do not scheme and manipulate and play games."

Their hands were still linked; they seemed to realize it at the same time. He did not resist when she turned his hands over to examine his palms. She pressed a thumb into the muscle. The calluses were fraying, and the blackberry-stained fingers bore fresh scratches, not enough to draw blood, just to chafe the skin. The hands of a man who lived boldly, an adventurer, sensual and sure.

How had these hands so transformed her? How had they reached inside her, to rouse those messy emotions that she had not even known were there?

"Your calluses are peeling away." She ran a thumb over them. "Soon your hands will not be so rough."

"I've yet to receive any complaints."

A shiver rippled over her, as surely as if he had trailed one of those fingers down her spine.

She had to look at him then. Had to hold his summer-green gaze, had to bear the roiling emotions and sensual memories, until he tugged his hands free and shoved them in his pockets.

"I still do not understand what happened that night in London," he said. "I had vowed never to speak of it, to never speak to you at all, but that night, it..."

Beyond him lay the autumn patchwork of orange woodlands and fields in green, gold, and brown. "It doesn't matter," she said to the landscape. "It is over and finished now."

"Is it?"

She had no reply. Silence fell but for the wind in the leaves, the fluty song of a mistle thrush. From the corner of her eye, she saw him slide a hand from his pocket. As if called, she turned back to him. He raised that hand and brushed her lips.

"Do you ever think about that night?" he asked. "The way we touched each other? What we did?"

It was a pointless question with only one conceivable answer.

"No," Arabella lied. "Never."

He edged closer. If she stepped away, she would be in the brambles. She did not mind. His closeness thrilled her. How easy it would be, to twine her arms around his neck. Lower his mouth to hers, crush her aching chest to his. She could imagine it as easily as if she had done it a thousand times.

In her mind, she already had.

"You must think of it occasionally," he murmured, so close a strong gust of wind could push them into each other's arms. "Not even alone in your bed at night, remembering how your body felt against mine? Reliving my touch, perhaps?"

Heat coursed through her, stirring up that now familiar pulse between her thighs, that molten pressure in her belly. He could not know what she did alone in her bed at night.

"You're giving yourself away, Hardbury," she managed to drawl. "You might spend your nights dreaming of me, but I can hardly remember it."

"You're right, I confess. I do remember it." His voice was lower now, its rough edge plucking at her. She let her body remember as his words caressed her, his eyes holding hers fast. "I remember every curve and angle of your body. I remember the taste of your skin. I remember how you responded to my touch, so wild, so furious, so demanding. It was splendid. *You* were splendid."

Her breath caught. "Do not mock me."

"I don't." The words were simple, sincere. "It was like standing in the middle of a storm. It's thrilling and dangerous and leaves one feeling intensely alive. I cannot stop wondering what else lies behind those eyes."

No response to that: She herself no longer knew. But he did not wait for a reply.

Lazily, he looked sideways and lifted one arm away from her. The movement swept his coat against her legs, and even that touch of fabric beguiled her sensitive skin. She watched—as if in a dream, as if this were a lazy summer afternoon and not a fresh day in autumn, as if they were only a man and a woman and not Guy and Arabella—as he extended one long arm toward the blackberry bush, toward a plump, ripe berry she could never touch, for fear of its messy juice.

Mesmerized, she watched him catch that berry between two fingers. It tumbled eagerly into his embrace and he carried it back between them. But then his hand drew too close to see, so she looked at his face instead. His eyes were on her mouth, his lowered lashes thick and dark, his expression mesmerized too, as she felt the press of that soft fruit against her lips. She parted her lips, and he pushed the berry between them. She took it into her mouth, let her tongue dart forward to claim it, let her tongue linger on his finger, which lingered in her mouth, desire a bittersweet jolt in her loins. His finger slid away. She closed her mouth and bit down on the blackberry, reveled in the sweet juice flooding over her tongue and filling her mouth and conquering her senses. Never had a berry tasted so good, or been so perfect and so dissatisfying. She swallowed and licked her lips, inviting another look from his heated, hooded eyes.

He was going to kiss her.

How she wanted him to. How she wanted to kiss him.

She touched his face. A mistake: It broke the spell.

He stepped back with a "No," and pivoted and strode away, greatcoat flapping, head shaking, while she stood there, foolishly poised for their forbidden kiss.

ARABELLA HEARD voices carrying on the wind, and shook herself out of her reverie.

How careless, that even for five minutes she had forgotten that this estate was large but teeming with people. Had anyone spied that intimate interlude, gossip would spread and everything would be lost.

But Guy had disappeared, and the intruders had not seen her. She slipped away.

She hardly remembered arriving at the gardens, rushing with her desperate need for the solitude of her room, where she could pull herself together, before she came undone.

But her way through the gardens was blocked: Sculthorpe was patrolling the paths. She could not face him. Of all the people in the world, he was the one she could not bear to see.

She veered off the path into a walled garden, and stood with her back to the wall, next to trellises covered in pink clematis blooms. She closed her eyes, listened to the birds, to the tinkling of the fountain, to her own deep breaths.

The birds fell silent. She did not open her eyes. But she knew she was no longer alone.

"There you are." Sculthorpe's voice was light and intimate. "Playing hide-and-seek with me."

No. Please, no. Let a thunderstorm strike, a gale, an earthquake, a plague of blood and locusts and frogs. Let it be anything but Sculthorpe, catching her alone, that repulsive smile slithering through his voice.

The world never did obey her wishes. And now, still reeling from Guy's touch, even her own body and thoughts were not hers to command.

Oh, why had she ever imagined she could control anything? Had she learned nothing? All her life she had tried to bring the world under control; every day it resisted.

Curse you, Guy Roth. Curse you, Sculthorpe. Curse you, Papa, and Oliver, and everyone who ever trod this misbegotten earth.

"I was looking for you. Miss Larke?"

His tone was sharper now. Vexed.

She opened her eyes. Sculthorpe stood inside the entrance to the walled garden, paused mid-step, hat in hand and expression pinched. His gaze was sharp enough to pin her to the wall.

"My lord. I was enjoying the birdsong."

He relaxed visibly. With a jaunty flip of his wrist, he tossed his hat onto the bench. "A pretty place to find a pretty virgin."

"We have no chaperone, my lord."

Her voice sounded shaky. Good grief. Arabella Larke, turned into a trembling ninny! Who needed an earthquake or plague of frogs? Clearly the end of the world was already nigh!

"We are engaged. No one will mind."

I mind, you repellent lecher!

Smiling, he strolled toward her. There was something new in his expression, not only the stomach-turning possessive leer, but something sharper, harder. A predatory gleam.

An unfamiliar sensation spread through her, which she belatedly identified as panic.

She had gone too far. It had all gone too far.

Not taking her eyes off him for a heartbeat, Arabella forced herself to breathe through the tightness in her chest, the peculiar lightness of her limbs. She let the anger come. How dare he prey upon her, and frighten her, and try to take more from her when he already had so much.

"I have decided to kiss you," Sculthorpe announced.

Arabella pressed her back into the cold wall, silently reciting the reasons she had agreed to this: Vindale Court, the patchwork fields, playing with Oliver, her happy childhood before he died.

"You said you intended to wait," she managed to say.

"Just one kiss," Sculthorpe murmured, as if to a skittish horse. "A single kiss to whet our appetites. You do not quiver and tremble with desire for me as you used to do. I miss that."

He was not touching her, yet she shuddered all the same. He

laughed, low and horrid. She would scream or kick him or vomit on him, she didn't much care what, so long as he moved away.

He came closer.

"There it is, your desire, that helpless frisson," he said. "You wanted more, didn't you? For a virgin, you are turning out to be very hungry."

She couldn't do this. Yet she had agreed to it; she had *agreed*. This was the choice she had made, though she had no other choice, and was it a choice if she had no other choice? She had not won, after all. It wasn't fair. She had defeated Guy, she had defeated Sculthorpe, but still they had defeated her.

Curse them both. They should be the ones against the wall, Guy and Sculthorpe. She would dispense with a firing squad and shoot them both herself.

"Just look at you, so prim and proper and bossy. Perfect for me. How I treasure you. Yes, I shall kiss you."

He was looking at her mouth, licking his lips, speaking to himself, really, but she had never deluded herself that his desires had anything to do with her.

She tried to will herself away, back to the abbey ruins, to the wind whipping her skirts and Guy's safe, solid heat, to Guy calling her splendid, sliding that blackberry between her lips.

"Kiss my own virgin before I claim her."

"Oh, for heaven's sake, I am not your virgin," she snapped.

He went as cold and still as the stone at her back. Her limbs unlocked and she slipped past him, but she had taken barely two steps when he lunged. Fast as a snake, his arm lashed out. His hand gripped her forearm, his fingers digging into her flesh through her sleeves.

"You are not— What?" he snarled. "You are mine! Are you not?"

"I am not—"

His fingers squeezed harder, as if to crush the bone. She cried out, a horrid sound like a trapped animal.

"Unhand me, sir!" she managed to say. "You are hurting me."

"*I* am hurting *you*? What of the pain you cause me?"

She swung her other hand to strike him, but he caught that arm too. She tried to pull away, but he gripped both her forearms, leaning too close, forcing her to arch her back.

"Your innocence was for me, and me alone!" His once-handsome face was feral with rage. "What man took what is *mine*? You were my perfect, precious dream, a fine lady, untouched but prim and bossy as a governess. I treasured you, and you—*betrayed* me?"

In vain she struggled against the vise of his grip. She kicked at her skirts, tried to kick him, and abruptly he released her, shoving her away. He was shoving, and she was kicking, and then she was falling toward the grass, her legs confused, her body twisting instinctively, so she landed hard on her shoulder, jarring her stunned bones and emptying her tortured lungs of air.

She had barely sucked in a breath when his boot slammed into her side. Dreamlike, as if watching herself from the outside, she pictured her body slowly rise with the force of his kick, and just as slowly fall.

She braced herself for more. But nothing. He was tearing the trellis off the wall, sobbing and ranting about betrayal, and his dead brother Kenneth, and the unbearable pain when others took what was his.

Before her eyes, the stubby blades of grass were growing every which way. A brown beetle was tromping through them, the blades big to it like oak trees were to her. A brave little beetle, which cared nothing for her troubles. It did not care about Sculthorpe and his governess-stealing brother, or what happened to Arabella Larke. It cared only about making its way through these chaotic, disordered blades of grass.

A bitter taste flooded her mouth, but behind it lay the sweet taste of a blackberry, juicy and plump and ripe. If she concentrated, that would be all she tasted, all she knew, all she felt. The touch of Guy's fingers on her lips, the autumn wind, the rustling leaves. And Guy. Hating her, wanting her, teasing her, touching her. If Guy were here now, would he smash Sculthorpe's head against the wall? She didn't know. She would never know. She would have to smash his head herself.

Tentatively, she rolled over and rose, testing her limbs. They did not fail her. She smoothed her skirts and wriggled her toes. Her arms throbbed. Her side throbbed. She ignored them; now was no time to feel pain.

Sculthorpe stopped destroying the trellis, his mouth distorted, his face red, and he swiped at his tears furiously like a little boy. He *cried*? He had kicked her, yet she did not cry. How dare this vicious brute cry!

"We will not marry," Arabella said, her voice as cold and hard as the stone wall that had witnessed her weakness and shame.

"Of course not," he sneered. "I would not marry a soiled, disgusting, traitorous—"

"Silence. How dare you mistreat a woman thus."

"You made me do it." He clenched his fists. Gripping her skirts, she readied her feet to run, but he did not come near. "You let another man take what was mine. I shall tell your father of this!"

"I shall tell him that you kicked me."

"And I shall tell all of England why you deserved it."

After which, Papa would disinherit her. No excuses, he had said. She would have to keep fighting. How she wearied of fighting.

But she had fight in her yet.

This would not be her defeat.

Her mind and body felt icy and numb, but her pride would never let her down. Her pride knew what to say.

"You will go directly to my father and inform him that you have received a letter," her pride ordered coldly. "The letter was from a lady whom you had once hoped to marry, and now she is available and willing. You begged me to release you from our engagement so that you might marry your former sweetheart."

"What utter rot."

She ignored him. "I agreed because I felt it would be wrong to wed a man who longed for another. You will assure my father that my behavior was impeccable and had no bearing on your decision."

"Your behavior! I will tell your father—the world!—about your behavior."

"And I will tell them that on the strength of a passing comment I made, a misunderstanding—"

"A misunderstanding!"

"—You attacked my person. What kind of lord and gentleman do you claim to be? The famed war hero, who beats a woman."

His mouth twisted with disgust as he ran his eyes over her. "Everyone will understand why. You yourself said you let another man fuck you first."

She swallowed away her own disgust. "I don't even know what that word means, so no one would believe I said it."

"It will be your word against mine. You have no evidence. Who would believe a soiled, lying—"

"Oh dear, my lord," she drawled. "Perhaps you are in the habit of only striking horses and dogs, so you cannot see the bruises on their skin."

He went still. Completely still, but for his eyes, shifting to study her concealed arms. He could not know, but she knew her body. She would not think of it. First, one fought the battle; later, one wept.

"I should—"

He advanced on her but she held her ground.

"What? Add more bruises to my collection? Murder me, perhaps? I think people might notice, don't you?"

He jumped back, wringing his hands. "I've never done that before. You made me do it."

"If you give my father cause to suspect that I have misbehaved in any way, I will spread the word faster than you can blink. When everyone learns what you did, not one person in Britain will allow you near any ladies, let alone a precious daughter."

"Is this meant to be some kind of blackmail?"

So now she was a blackmailer too. She had never asked for this. All she had asked was to exercise a little control over her own life. They had built the maze and dropped her into it; she was only trying to find her way out.

"I must protect myself, my lord, since clearly you will not." She gestured at the garden entrance. "The days grow shorter. You should leave soon, if you are to cover a good distance before nightfall. Ride ahead. The servants will send your belongings after you."

"And when this sweetheart does not appear?"

"Alas, the course of true love never did run smooth."

His mouth worked as he stared at her, his red-rimmed eyes poisonous with loathing.

"Very well," he finally said. "You say nothing, and neither will I."

"Go." Gathering her courage, Arabella turned her back on him. "You will be gone before I return to the house."

CHAPTER 10

Arabella entered Vindale Court through the front door, with a secret sense of ceremony. Perhaps this would be her final entrance. Perhaps the next time she left this house, it would be for good.

Ramsay was in the foyer. He sent away the other servants as she peeled off her gloves.

"Lord Sculthorpe?" she prompted. She unpinned her hat and dropped it onto the table, ignoring the protest of her tender ribs. A chunk of hair tumbled onto her face. She pushed it back. It fell again. She must fix that before Papa saw her.

"He is gone and we are packing his belongings. Your father wishes to see you."

"I don't doubt it. Is he in a terrible temper?"

Ramsay's lips thinned. The mirror confirmed that her walking dress betrayed no signs of misadventure, though her eyes seemed unnaturally bright. And she really must fix her hair, but she took a sudden perverse delight in it. That her coiffure was coming undone seemed fitting right now.

This time, when Arabella entered her father's study, Queenie was silent and Papa was already on his feet.

"A fortnight," Papa said. "You managed to keep a man for two whole weeks."

Arabella stared at the horizon like a soldier. She ignored Queenie, ignored the stuffed birds, ignored Oliver's smirk.

Mama slipped through the door. Papa did not pause in his tirade.

"Sculthorpe was staying in the very house his son would inherit, yet a letter comes from someone he's not seen in years and he cannot get away fast enough."

Arabella fixed her eyes on the wall. Sculthorpe had obeyed her. He feared her, then, a little.

"Look at you, this disgraceful mess." Papa sneered at her loose hair, which, to be fair, was irritating Arabella now too. "That I was robbed of my son and cursed to have only one living child, and that child is you!"

"Peter! Enough!" Mama said sharply.

Papa wiped a hand over his face. Arabella's eyes went helplessly to Oliver, who crowed, *You know he wishes it were you up here and me down there!*

Oh, go break your head against a rainbow, you irksome brat.

Silence blanketed them. Arabella could think of a thousand things to say, but she would only make matters worse.

"We have a houseful of guests and a betrothal ball in three nights," Mama said, ever practical. "We must cancel it."

"No, make her attend the ball. Let everyone see her shame. A betrothal ball and no betrothal."

Finally, Arabella spoke. "You could put me in stocks in the middle of the ballroom and provide the guests with rotten fruit to throw."

"Don't tempt me."

Of course she had to face the world. Why not at her own betrothal ball? She would glide through that ball in her elegant new evening gown, long gloves hiding the marks already blooming on her arms, flawlessly coiffured head held high. No one would know how her engagement ended; no one would guess how weak and helpless she had been.

"The morning after the ball, you will leave," Papa continued. "I don't want you in this house unless you bring a legitimate son by an acceptable husband. Until then, I am changing my will."

"Peter, please consider whether that is necessary," Mama said. "This isn't Arabella's fault. If Lord Sculthorpe loves someone else—"

"I'm tired of you defending this hoyden, Belinda. It *is* her fault. If Sculthorpe *loves* someone else, it's because our daughter is a woman whom no man can love."

"Do not say that," Mama said quietly. "Never say that."

His mouth twisted sourly. "Consider that Treadgold girl. Three minutes with a man and he's wrapped around her finger. Yet Hardbury has known Arabella most of his life and he can hardly bear to be in the same room as her. Sculthorpe should have procured a special license in London and married her on the spot." He collapsed into his chair. "Now get out of my sight."

It was no surprise that Mama followed Arabella to her room and sat.

"Tell me what happened," she said. "Surely you did not let Sculthorpe go without a fight?"

Arabella said nothing. Mama had always been on her side, even when it didn't feel like it, pushing her harder, trying to mold

Arabella into the best version of herself. Yet still she had turned into a woman whom no one could love.

She released the four buttons on her left sleeve, fumbling a little, and slid the fabric up her arm. It was tight, and resisted, but she yanked and did not care when a seam tore.

Red welts bloomed over her pale forearm. One did not need much imagination to picture the fingers that had left them.

The loose lock of hair fell past her face as she bent her head and ran her fingers over them. The tender flesh was slightly swollen and hot with indignation.

She kept her head bowed through the whisper of skirts, the comforting fragrance, and then Mama was taking her forearm, turning it gently to study the marks, her palms dry and cool.

"Oh my darling. Why didn't you say?"

Mama's fingers were brisk, but not nimble, as she released the buttons on the other sleeve and pushed back the fabric to reveal the other set of marks. Mama had never been tender, and Arabella was glad of that now.

"I was wrong about Lord Sculthorpe," her mother said.

"You didn't know, Mama."

"I should have." She ran her fingers over the mottled skin. "You didn't tell your father."

"Papa would have blamed me for provoking him." She looked up. "I did provoke him."

"And you would have continued to provoke him every day of your married life." Mama tweaked the loose lock of hair, tucked it behind her ear. "I truly believed Sculthorpe was not threatened by your strong character."

"I said something."

"I don't care." Mama's eyes flashed. "Whatever you said or did, no man does this to my daughter. By heaven, I'll shoot him myself. The shame is his, not yours, do you hear me? If you had discovered his true nature after your marriage, you would never have escaped him and it would only have grown worse."

"You must tell people, Mama. I promised to say nothing, but you must. Whisper it to the other ladies, so that no one ever lets Sculthorpe near another woman. Let him die a miserable old bachelor and never know why."

So what if she double-crossed Sculthorpe? He did not deserve her honor. She was disinherited anyway, and she would be disinherited a thousand times over before she let him do this to another bride. She wasn't good for much, in the end, but she could be good for that. It was excruciating for society to know of her weakness, but of course, they would Not Mention it, and her pride would suffer in silence.

"Is this all?" Mama asked.

The image of that little beetle swam before her eyes, the memory of the jarring thud. She could not admit to such helplessness, not even to Mama. She could hardly admit it to herself.

"Isn't that enough?"

Mama slid the sleeves back down and set about unfastening all of Arabella's dress. The help made her feel young and weak, and she hated that too. Yet she longed to have someone's arms around her. Mama never hugged her; that was not their way.

"And so I am cast out."

Arabella clutched her unfastened gown to keep it from falling down. Falling to the grass. Fallen lady.

"We will find a solution. Have a bath now. Take your supper in your room. Tomorrow, you must face the world with your head held high and let everyone say what they please."

"I suppose I should be grateful Papa left me that."

Mama considered. "After the ball, you can go home with my

parents. They'll help you find someone suitable to marry. When you have a son, your father will relent."

Arabella already knew of someone suitable to marry, but no doubt that plan too would fail. Perhaps when Hadrian Bell had received her letter, her proposition had made him roll laughing on the floor.

"Is there a man left who would take me? The promise of a great inheritance and dowry covers a multitude of sins, but now those sins are all I have."

"Do not become bitter, Arabella. I have raised you to be stronger than that."

Then she was failing her mother too. Only to be expected, of a woman whom no one could love.

"I am tired, Mama."

"Rest now. We will discuss this tomorrow."

Alone again, Arabella stripped off all her clothes and twisted before the large mirror to inspect the purple mark blossoming over her ribs.

This was meant to be her body, but only in small moments could she experience it as her own: during a hot bath in winter, a cool bath in summer, riding her horse, sliding between clean linens, donning a silk petticoat, an intimate touch.

When she was younger and her attitude unformed, gentlemen took it upon themselves to comment. "You're too tall, Miss Larke," they would say, as if being short were something she could accomplish, if only she practiced more. A woman should not be that tall, they said. But she was this tall and she was a woman, so surely she was exactly as she ought to be, the same as every other woman was exactly as she ought to be, simply because she was how she was.

Sculthorpe thought her body had belonged to him. When

Arabella had tried to claim it for her own, he sought to destroy it in response.

But with Guy, it was different. By some odd alchemy, when she gave him her body, he gave it right back to her.

She provoked Guy too. Their entire relationship consisted of them provoking each other. He did not seem to mind; an eager glint entered his eye. For her part, she rather enjoyed it when he provoked her. It made her feel more alive, more herself.

The door opened and Holly came in. Arabella did not move, watching the maid's approach in the mirror. Her eyes were on Arabella's ribs, which were beginning to throb.

"Oh, miss," Holly said. "Her ladyship never said about your side. And him a war hero too."

"Please don't tell her about that one."

Holly bustled about, mercifully unsentimental. "We'll pretend it was a horse that did this. You've had worse from a horse, you recall, and you survived that."

Arabella would rather have been kicked by a horse. A horse was not malicious. It did not seek to own or diminish or control.

"We've a fresh batch of your orange-blossom water for your bath, and how about some nice hot chocolate with a bit of orange grated in, you like that. And some supper."

"I'm not hungry."

"A quick egg and some hot buttered toast."

Holly's practical busy-ness was soothing. Arabella sought something else to think about, to force her mind off the ache starting in her muscles, as though they had just received news of their own abuse and wished to lodge a complaint.

"How fares the search of Sir Walter's room?" she asked.

"Slowly, miss. It has to be Joan or Ernest, because they read well enough to pick anything with Lady Frederica's name. They can only search a bit each time. If he's got something, he's hidden it well."

So either Sir Walter knew he was up to no good, or Arabella was seeing schemes where there were none.

"Tell them to keep searching. And reassure them they'll suffer no consequences if caught. But we must look after Freddie."

"You can't be worrying about Lady Frederica right now," Holly said.

"Don't be absurd. I never worry. I merely plan for every possible outcome."

"Right you do. Worrying about Liza when her babe came, and old Mr. Niles when they tried to take his house, and the head gardener's boys when their ma was sick. You stop worrying about others and let someone look after you."

Arabella was too tired to pretend anymore, so she let herself be coddled and bathed and fed until finally, finally, she was allowed to slide into bed and close her eyes on the world.

THE NEXT MORNING, after a maid lit the fire and opened the curtains, Arabella rose to use the chamber pot and wash, but then she stood in the middle of her bedroom and could not think of anything to do.

Outside the windows, the world had dissolved into nothing but gray fog. Perhaps her room was floating in the middle of nowhere. Perhaps her room no longer existed. Perhaps *she* no longer existed. Maybe Sculthorpe had murdered her after all, but she was too proud to admit it.

She opened a drawer for a kerchief, but her fingers fell on her miniature of Oliver. She traced the frame, recalling one of their squabbles, when he had pushed her and she'd landed on her rump, only to trip him so he fell too. They'd wrestled, then, until someone had intervened. Only Arabella had received a scolding, because she was a girl, but Oliver had insisted on sharing the punishment.

She shoved the miniature back in the drawer, closed the curtains on the fog, and went back to bed.

Mama came in and sat on the side of Arabella's bed. Mama knew Arabella was not ill. She never was. The last time she was ill, she had risen from her sickbed to learn that Oliver had died, leaving a hole inside her and their family forever changed. Better to not get ill again.

"Do you need help with the guests?" Arabella asked, though she did not care. She meant to stay in her floating room forever. "The final preparations for the ball."

"Mrs. DeWitt has agreed to help."

Her neighbor at Sunne Park, amiable Cassandra DeWitt. Cassandra would be kind to Arabella, and Arabella did not know if she could bear that. Her pride would take over, make her mouth say horrid things; she would be unkind to Cassandra, who was the kindest person she knew. Arabella would hate herself for that, but Cassandra would never hate her, and that would make it even worse.

"You will not tell her," Arabella said. "Everyone must know, but not yet."

"Of course not." Mama squeezed her hand and stood. "You must pull yourself together, Arabella. It was ghastly, I know, but you cannot indulge your misery forever. We fall over and then we get back up and face the world as though nothing is amiss."

"I shall be better tomorrow."

She slept all day as if she truly were ill. At one point, she awoke and lay staring at nothing, her mind also invaded by gray fog. Eventually, she realized someone was sitting by the fire.

Arabella propped herself up on her elbows. "Freddie?"

Freddie looked up. "You don't mind I'm here?"

"Not at all. Why are you here?"

"They won't look for me here. If they find me, they'll take away my sewing."

Arabella sat up further. A mass of teal fabric was spread over Freddie's lap. "What are you sewing?"

"One of the German ornithologists described the Turkish trousers his niece wears to ride *en cavalier*." Freddie stood and shook them out. "You see, they are a kind of pantaloon, which means I can ride astride, but because they billow, they are modest. He told me it is not uncommon for ladies on the Continent to ride *en cavalier*. But Lady Treadgold insists it is not becoming."

"That is an excellent solution. I recall a portrait of Marie Antoinette dressed and mounted thus."

"Indeed!" Freddie dropped back into her chair and arranged her sewing over her lap. "I told Lady Treadgold that, but she pointed out that Marie Antoinette was guillotined."

"It is safe to say that the reasons for her beheading were more complex than the way she rode a horse."

"I don't know," Freddie said glumly. "I feel that I shall be beheaded if I do not behave as they say I should."

Arabella had no response to that. She was hardly in a position to offer reassurances. How abhorrent to think that dreamy, original Freddie might face a similar dilemma to her own! Not if she could prevent it.

"Do you know if Sir Walter has found someone for you to marry?" she asked.

Freddie resumed sewing. She was silent so long Arabella wondered if she had forgotten their conversation.

"I'm nineteen," Freddie finally said. "Lady Treadgold says it's time now we're out of mourning. She says I'm an heiress and my brother is a marquess, so it doesn't matter that I'm not pretty or good with people."

"But have they suggested any names?" Arabella persisted. "Held parties with suitable gentlemen? Made a point of introducing anyone to you?"

"No, I don't think so."

That was suspicious. One would expect Sir Walter and Lady Treadgold to be seeking a suitable husband for their ward. Sir Walter would not miss an opportunity to forge new connections by parading the wealthy sister of a marquess about like a prize ewe.

The fact that they were not encouraging Freddie to wed strengthened Arabella's theory about their scheme. If only she—or rather, the servants—could find the proof.

"What about spring?" she asked. "Are they planning to take you to London for the Season?"

"No. I mean, they said they might. I don't know. I don't care. It isn't as though anyone will ever court me properly. Men like Matilda. They like my money." She stared at the ceiling. "I wonder what it is like, to be admired and flattered, to have a man whisper sweet nothings and make one feel special."

"I wouldn't know. Men never whisper sweet nothings to me."

Except Guy, mocking her, that night in London, tenderly tucking a flower behind her ear, his eyes intent, her surprised lips still tingling from their first kiss. *She walks in beauty like the night...*

Longing throbbed through her. Immediately after their lovemaking, when her body was still trembling with erotic sensations, he had wrapped his arms around her and held her against his hot skin, his fast-beating heart. By some miracle, that had made her feel complete. As though in gathering her to him, he had gathered her together, merging her familiar parts with those parts she kept secret, even from herself.

Don't be ridiculous, she scolded herself. After the pain and indignity she had suffered at the hands of one man, how could she possibly crave the embrace of another? Maybe it wasn't about Guy. Maybe she simply longed to feel someone's arms around her again.

"I imagine it would depend on whether he meant the words and whether he values you," Arabella added. "I shouldn't be in a hurry for it."

"I just wonder what it would be like, that's all."

Arabella had no answer for that either, so she dropped back onto the pillows and once more closed her eyes.

CHAPTER 11

The female voices coming from the hallway bore that tense, overly controlled quality of women engaging in polite argument when at least one of them longed to scream.

"You can have them back when we return home," said one of the women; Guy identified the voice as belonging to Lady Treadgold. "You may ride astride in the privacy of our estate, not here amid this fine company."

Bouncing a chortling Ursula on his hip, Guy rounded the corner to see Lady Treadgold with Freddie, who wore a green riding habit and a mutinous glare.

"Why," Lady Treadgold added, her tone brightening, "whatever will your brother the marquess think?"

Freddie flicked him a scornful glance. "I don't care what he thinks."

"What I think about what?" Guy asked, absently unhooking Ursula's fingers from his cravat before she choked him.

"I was making Turkish trousers so I could ride astride, but Lady Treadgold took them away."

"Not in this company," Lady Treadgold repeated. "Riding astride is not becoming in a fine English lady."

"I'm a good rider and I want to ride fast." Freddie turned her scowl on Guy. "You remember. You let me go fast before."

At first, he had no idea what she meant. Then a memory arose, of tobogganing through the snow with little Freddie between his knees as they sped down a hill. Freddie had shrieked with delight and demanded they go faster; Guy had happily obliged.

"But you were a child then," he said. "You oughtn't behave like that now, should she, Ursula?"

Ursula's lively response sounded like "Marcus Aurelius would not approve," but probably wasn't. At first, her babble left Guy feeling awkward. He could barely decipher one word in five, and his interpretations were impossible. But in the end, her words didn't matter nearly as much as their games.

"Arabella doesn't care," Freddie argued. "She thought it a brilliant idea."

"You've seen Arabella? How is she?"

Ignoring him, Freddie pushed into the front hall to grab her gloves and hat. "Never mind, I'll wear this," she muttered, and marched out the door.

Lady Treadgold also left before Guy could offload Ursula, so he carried her outside and fell into step beside Freddie, as they headed for the stables. If Freddie had spoken to Arabella, he needed to know more.

Guy had not seen Arabella since the afternoon before, at the abbey ruins, when the wind had swept away his vows to avoid her, and he'd fed her a blackberry and nearly kissed her again. When he had finally come back to the house, it was to learn that Sculthorpe had ridden off in a rush, the engagement was over, and Arabella was nowhere to be seen.

Freddie set a brisk pace, but Ursula seemed to enjoy it, judging by the way she squealed and slapped Guy's bare head.

"What are you doing with Ursula?" Freddie asked.

"We were about to visit the aviaries. Look, I tied this ribbon in her hair," he added proudly.

Freddie rolled her eyes and kept walking.

"Have you talked to Arabella? Since yesterday?" Guy asked.

"Yes."

He waited. She added nothing more. "And what did she say?"

"Who?"

"Arabella."

"I don't know."

What the devil had happened with Sculthorpe? Perhaps Sculthorpe had learned about London, but if the truth had emerged, Guy would have suffered a close encounter with the pointy end of a gun.

And why was Arabella in hiding? Surely her pride, at least, would demand she show her face. If Arabella wasn't sweeping through the world and glaring it into submission, then something had to be wrong.

"Yes, but how was she?" he tried again. "Freddie?"

"Who?"

Guy gritted his teeth. "Arabella."

"Same as usual. She kept asking questions. But she was... You know."

Freddie jumped over a stone and skipped on.

"No, Freddie, I don't know. She was what?"

"In bed."

Bloody hell. Getting information out of Freddie was like getting a dragonfly to play chess, and no one else would say anything at all.

A courteous inquiry of Lady Belinda had resulted in "How

thoughtful of you to ask, my lord. She has simply overtired herself, with the ball."

And Lady Belinda kept loyal servants, every one of whom had given the same bland response of "Miss Arabella is merely tired."

And Mrs. DeWitt and Miss Bell, the neighbors who'd arrived to take over Arabella's duties, had brightly said, "She's worn herself out. She does so much. Look, it took two of us to replace her!"

Vibrant, demanding Arabella? Tired? Not a chance.

Half the night he'd lain awake debating whether to sneak into her room, to make sure she was all right, wondering whether he should offer to marry her after all, if he was the cause of the rift. Only to punch the pillow and remind himself that he owed her nothing.

"So she is ill," he said, as they arrived at the stables and waited for the groom to finish saddling Freddie's horse.

"When Matilda was ill, men sent her flowers," Freddie volunteered. "Of course, they send her flowers when she's not ill, too."

"I can't give Arabella flowers."

Everyone would talk, and she would mock him horribly. Tempting, actually. He would present her with a bouquet and she would deliver some sharp set-down that would make him laugh. Perhaps he would even compose a poem for her. It would be terrible, naturally, and he would tease lines out of her so outrageously arrogant that even she would have to laugh.

She had not laughed in London, when he slid that flower behind her ear and likened her beauty to starry skies. Even that feigned intimacy and tenderness had unsettled her. She was not as invincible as she wanted to appear.

How disconcerting, to think of Arabella that way.

"But at least you can marry her now," Freddie said abruptly.

You must get engaged to me, she had said in London. *I was a virgin and now I am not.*

"I'm not marrying Arabella."

"Father wanted you to."

"I will choose my own spouse. As will you."

"What if I never get married?"

"Of course you'll get married. But you choose to whom." He shifted Ursula to his other arm, as the groom finished his task and stood back. "I want a home, a proper home and family, such as we never had. My wife will be someone pleasant and amiable, who—"

Freddie snorted, derisively, and her mare gave an answering huff. Pointing one chubby finger, Ursula launched into a lengthy discourse on the nature of horses.

"What's wrong with wanting that?" Guy asked over her chatter.

"Nothing, for most men. Just not for you," Freddie went on, suddenly as chatty as a bloody magpie, as she went to greet her horse. "Consider Father. No one ever dared to disagree with him and look how he turned out."

"I am not like Father."

"A tyrant."

"Nothing like Father."

"A great big tyrant."

"You don't know me," he snapped, sounding childish.

Freddie, indifferent, patted the horse's neck. "You don't know me."

"Father controlled every facet of my life," Guy said. "I won't marry Arabella because he demanded it. I won't let Sir Walter ruin your life because of Father's rules."

"It sounds like he's still controlling you." She kissed the horse's nose, shot a look at Ursula, and nodded at the groom. "Why bother with me and Ursula and a perfect bride, Guy? Tying a ribbon in her hair! If you want to play with dolls, get a dollhouse. Much less trouble that way."

With the groom's aid, his perplexing sister mounted her horse and rode away.

Ursula watched them go, saying something that sounded peculiarly, and improbably, like "Man is born free but he is everywhere in chains." Having apparently quoted Rousseau, she yanked the ribbon from her hair and smashed it onto Guy's head.

"Bloody hell," Guy muttered, reaching for the ribbon.

"Bloody hell," Ursula repeated, and burst into wild laughter.

Guy had to laugh too. "Ursula means 'little bear,' did you know that? Like Ursa Minor, a constellation I'll show you one night. You were well named," he added. "No one would ever mistake you for a doll."

It was after midnight when Guy finally saw Arabella again.

She had not appeared at dinner, and further queries yielded nothing. Her mother and friends appeared unconcerned, but Guy could not dispel his unease that he might have contributed to the broken engagement and should help put things right.

Which was absurd. Did he think he had to rescue her? More likely, someone would need to be rescued from her.

Devil knew he did.

His restlessness made him wretched company, even for himself. To avoid going to bed, he sat up late in the Reading Room, a cozy book-lined parlor adjoining the library. Everyone else had long since retired by the time he ceased staring into the embers and headed to his room.

Only to see Arabella hovering outside his door.

At the sight of him, she froze, looking young and haunted. Her bare feet were visible under the hem of her long-sleeved nightgown, and her hair fell in a single braid. The glow of her candle softened her features, turned her eyes large and dark. She set the candle on the small hall table, turned it, picked it up, put it back down.

Around them, the sleeping house was quiet.

"What are you doing here?" he asked softly.

"I shouldn't be here."

"Are you all right?"

"I am fine. Nothing is amiss."

Go into your room and shut the door, Guy ordered himself, only to catch one of her hands in his. "You are chilled."

"I lied," she said.

"That doesn't surprise me."

She shook her head, impatiently. "I told you I never think of it, but I do. London."

He didn't need the clarification. "Was that why...? Your engagement."

Again, that impatient shake of her head. "Sculthorpe doesn't know about London. No one does. You are safe. It was badly done of me."

"What happened with Sculthorpe? Do you need help?"

"Oh, will you be quiet about that beast? You, I mean. It was badly done of me. In London, to put you in that situation. To use you like that. To... You know."

"Seduce me?"

"Yes."

Guy stepped closer, amused. "I say, Arabella, that sounded suspiciously like an apology."

"Don't be absurd. I never..." She sighed. "Just accept the wretched apology, would you?"

"I am a grown man. I could have kicked you out at any point."

It was dark, and she was in her nightwear, and he still held her hand; it would be disastrous if anyone discovered them like this. But no one was around, not at this hour. He moved only to put his candle down beside hers.

"Do you regret it?" he asked. "London?"

"Do you?" she countered.

He had no answer. He regretted his own folly at impulsively playing a game that he had lost. Yet the astonishing experience of knowing her like that... He could no longer imagine his life without that experience in it.

She withdrew her hand from his. "No one must ever know," she whispered. "You will choose a bride soon, I think. You must choose a woman who will make you happy, a woman whom you can love."

"Now you're worrying me," he said. "If there are consequences from London, you will tell me."

"There are no consequences."

Her eyes dropped to his chest. As if in a dream, Guy watched as she placed one palm against him, flat and firm and scorching. She eased closer. Her hand traveled over his ribs, to his waist.

"Put your arms around me." Her whisper was half command, half plea. "I'm all right. I just want..."

Without thinking, he wrapped his arms around her, welcoming the feel of her pressed against him. She ducked her head, rested her cheek on his shoulder.

A sound. A door. A footstep.

Guy dropped his arms. Arabella held on. He pulled away, forcing her to let him go and transfer her hug to her own belly.

Suddenly, Guy recognized the impulsive words riding unspoken on his lips: to offer to marry her if she needed it. And how clear they became, the steps of her plan, laid out like a game of chess, a dozen moves in advance. She was ambitious and she had explicitly declared her desire to be a marchioness. She had tried to persuade him to marry her and paid bribes to make him listen. Following her engagement to Sculthorpe, she had come to Guy at night in a bid to trap him into marriage. She had used Freddie and Ursula to lure Guy to Vindale Court. Now, after getting rid of Sculthorpe, she stood outside his door, in her nightgown, in a house full of guests. Everyone knew this age-old scheme to catch a husband.

Regret rolled through him. If only this was no plot or ploy. If only he could simply hold her, and kiss her, and take her into his room.

Bloody hell. He was in a bad way. He needed to escape this house and this woman as quickly as he could.

"Yet another scheme," he hissed. "Who had you intended to see us?"

The softness in her expression melted like mist. Once more, she stood straight and proud, and replied in her usual imperious drawl.

"Good grief, Guy. As if I would employ such a tired ruse as that. Grant me a little credit."

Without another word, she picked up her candle and swept away.

ARABELLA SLEPT LATE, and awoke with her eyes gritty and dry. She lay in bed and probed her body. Her side was tender, and the marks on her forearms had turned an interesting shade of purple. All of her still felt Guy's solid, comforting warmth.

Fool.

Sunlight seemed to lurk behind the curtains, so she opened them to see if the world had reappeared.

It had.

The autumn sun shone down on the familiar, beloved view: the hill with the abbey ruins, the patchwork of woodlands and fields. Below her window, the lush green lawn offered a pleasant scene. Several gentlemen were engaged in a game of bowls, supervised by Miss Treadgold. Arabella's eyes went straight to Guy, who was dancing with Ursula, or trying to anyway: Ursula was doing a dance all of her own, ignoring Guy's efforts to show her where to put her feet.

Arabella touched the cold glass. Last night's encounter with Guy had felt like a dream from the moment she slipped out of bed, driven by a fierce urge to feel his embrace. How glorious those seconds in his arms—before he accused her again.

Fair enough. It did look bad, loitering outside his door late at night in her nightgown. Although every country house needed a young lady wandering around in her nightgown seeking trouble.

Below her on the lawn, a dispute seemed to have broken out among the bowls players, but then Miss Treadgold must have made some sound, for the three gentlemen turned.

Just as something fluttered to the grass at Miss Treadgold's feet.

A canary-yellow ribbon.

One of the gentlemen stooped, hand outstretched toward the ribbon. A heartbeat later, a second one lunged for it, knocking aside the first man, and while they gesticulated at each other, the third made his move. In disbelief, Arabella watched as three grown men scrambled to seize Miss Treadgold's fallen ribbon.

Only Guy did not move, his expression bemused.

Well, Arabella thought. Clearly, she had been approaching life completely wrong, given those men's response to a dropped ribbon!

When Arabella dropped a ribbon—

But Arabella never did drop a ribbon. She never dropped anything at all. In fact, Arabella was immensely talented at not dropping things. Which was just as well, because if Arabella were to drop a ribbon and a gentleman noticed, he would say, "Miss Larke, your ribbon has fallen," then dash off to Miss Treadgold in case she did something adorable, like sneeze.

Oh, for powers like that! If Miss Treadgold ever needed anything, she wouldn't have to scheme and lie and bribe and steal and blackmail, nor tolerate insults and injury. She'd simply drop a ribbon and men would knock themselves out in their scramble to obey.

All except Guy. Yet when Miss Treadgold turned to him, he smiled warmly.

With a sigh, Arabella turned away from the window. In the duller novels, this was the part of the story where the woman realized what a sinner she was, reformed her ways, and lived tediously ever after. But it seemed premature to reform. After all, Arabella wasn't much of a villainess. She hadn't even murdered anyone. Yet.

But neither was she ready to face them, so she climbed back into bed.

Today, Mama delegated to Cassandra and Juno. They crept in with the hushed eagerness of any sickroom visit, eyes wide as they tiptoed toward her. Cassandra held a bunch of flowers so big Arabella could see nothing but the top of her chocolate-brown hair and her hazel eyes peering through the stems. Juno carried a portfolio, her round cheeks pink and blonde curls bouncing as she laughed at Arabella's expression.

Cassandra set the vase on the bedside table and arranged the blooms, their fragrance floating over Arabella in a soothing cloud.

"Everyone has been asking after you," Cassandra said.

"Including Lord Hardbury. He has made polite inquiries several times."

"Today?" Arabella asked.

"Yesterday."

Before that misjudged encounter last night.

"He wished to know if you needed anything," Juno chimed in from across the room, where she was opening her portfolio of drawings on a table.

Tell him I need him to hold me. Tell him I need help, even if I don't know how to ask. Tell him to pretend to be engaged to me, so I can buy time and not be cast out.

"What could I possibly need from Guy?" she asked.

She climbed out of bed and checked her appearance in the mirror. Even now, she was tidy. Her plait was neat, her blue bed-jacket smooth. How decadent she was, to entertain guests in her nightwear.

"It seems I have mastered the art of lying in bed," she said.

She caught Cassandra and Juno exchanging a glance and regretted her admission. She was meant to be ill, not languishing in sorrow.

Cassandra, predictably, was kind. "You are being very brave. I was devastated after I was jilted. But I found someone else to marry."

And in the two years since the day Cassandra Lightwell both met and married Joshua DeWitt, he had not visited her once. Indeed, as far as anyone was aware, Mr. and Mrs. DeWitt had not even communicated since their wedding day, and Cassandra preferred that everyone Not Mention her marriage. Cassandra had married a stranger purely to save her inheritance, and she did not mope about in her bed.

Then there was Juno, who had sacrificed all hope of respectability to become a professional artist with her own studio in London, and neither did she complain. Arabella thought herself so strong, but clearly they were stronger.

"What is your concern, Cassandra?" She turned away from the mirror. "That my famously cold heart is broken or my famously enormous pride is dented?"

"At least I needn't worry about your famously acerbic tongue. Anyway, that is all rot. I believe you are a warm, loving woman like any of us."

"Yes, but you also believe that you can reason with your mother's goat and that your sister Lucy will not end up as a courtesan."

"You *are* feeling better then." Smiling, Cassandra laid a hand on Arabella's arm. "If you ever need help, you will ask us, won't you?"

"I never need help."

"Of course not. But I need to offer help. So please indulge me."

Cassandra did not fool Arabella, but clearly Arabella did not fool her friend either.

"Very well," Arabella said. "If it makes you feel better, I will come to you if I need help."

"It does. Because you always help others, even when you pretend not to."

Juno looked up from arranging her illustrations. "I remember when I was... That is, when my body matured earlier than most girls. Some village boys were teasing me, until you ordered them to stop. You hit one with a stick."

"I don't remember that."

Cassandra laughed. "Probably just another day for you. You're always fighting about something."

"For which I shall not apologize," Arabella said.

"Of course not," Juno teased. "First you would have to learn how to apologize."

"Why on earth should I learn how to apologize when I never do anything that merits an apology?"

Cassandra and Juno only laughed; they had known her too long to be fooled.

Ignoring them, Arabella joined Juno to study the bird illustrations she had commissioned.

"These drawings are excellent." She touched an exquisitely rendered nightingale and glanced at Juno, who beamed proudly. "Your studio will soon be flourishing."

Arabella would take these drawings with her to her grandparents' house, where she would complete *The Illustrated Guide to the Vindale Aviaries*, and send several copies to Papa. The ornithology journal had not interested him at first, either. All alone, she had gathered the papers from his convention, edited, translated, and compiled them, solicited subscribers, negotiated with a London printer, and organized distribution. Now he was involved every step of the way.

"I should also like to commission *An Illustrated Guide to the Longhope Abbey*, if you have time," Arabella said, moving to the window to view the famous ruins. Too late, she remembered that Papa had cast her out; after the ball, this would no longer be her home.

Juno joined her at the window. "I shall make time. Which reminds me, I must thank you. I secured a lucrative job illustrating a book on wildflowers, thanks to your recommendation."

"I have no hesitation in recommending someone with your talent and professionalism."

There: Arabella was not entirely useless. She had helped her friend Thea publish a pamphlet and Juno build her career, and she made Cassandra feel needed, and perhaps she would save Freddie from Sir Walter Treadgold's schemes. She could be of some use to the world, for all that the sight of her made no one smile and she could not drop a ribbon to save her life.

Just as well. How annoying it would be, to have men always underfoot picking up her ribbons.

"I would provide my artistic services for free if you commissioned an Illustrated Guide to *that*," Juno said, as Cassandra joined them. Juno pointed at Guy. He had taken off his coat and was lounging on the grass, as he had lounged naked on the daybed. "Lord Hardbury has become quite magnificent. Speaking purely as an artist, of course."

"Of course."

"Would you like to hear a shocking secret?" Juno added.

"They are the only sort worth hearing."

"When I was studying in Florence, a group of us women artists started secret life-drawing sessions with laborers who needed extra coin. You may think me lewd, ladies, but a muscular male body is a work of art in itself. His lordship puts me more in mind of those laborers than nearly any other peer I've seen." She sighed dramatically. "I suppose I have little chance of persuading a marquess to pose for me nude."

Arabella could not take her eyes off him. "I doubt you could find a canvas large enough to hold a portrait of him *and* his immense presence."

"Oh, it's not his immense *presence* I'd be concerned about."

Juno chuckled and Cassandra's blush was almost audible, but Arabella could not smile.

They left soon afterward, her room and spirits transformed.

"You will be better for the ball, I trust," Cassandra said, turning in the doorway.

"Of course," Arabella said. "A ball is a medical miracle. The mere mention of a ball can make an ill person suddenly well or a well person suddenly ill."

A few minutes later, Holly darted in and said, in a dramatic whisper, "Miss, that thing you wanted... We think we found it." With a furtive glance, in case any spies lurked in the corners of Arabella's bedchamber, she offered a piece of paper.

It was exactly what Arabella had suspected: a special license, authorizing the marriage of Lady Frederica Roth to Mr. Humphrey Treadgold, Sir Walter's son, who was due to arrive at Vindale Court the following week.

"Do we need to put it back?" Holly asked. "Joan said she found it tucked away."

"Lord Hardbury must see this," Arabella said. "Hopefully Sir Walter won't notice it's gone, as he won't need it until his son arrives."

Guy would have to listen to *this*. Arabella had lost everything, but at least she could save Freddie. Now, she needed only to get through the ball, and then see what she could salvage from the debris of her life.

"I am not worthless and I shall not apologize," she muttered.

"Pardon, miss?" Holly asked.

"I think I shall go for a ride."

CHAPTER 12

Guy chose to watch the dancing like a wallflower, while he waited for Arabella to arrive at her betrothal-ball-with-no-betrothal. For one thing, he had forgotten half the dance steps; for another, the ball made him feel like a foreigner in his own land.

There was something so quintessentially *English* about this kind of ball. Lemonade and supper, flowers and foliage, orchestra and gleaming chandeliers. White gowns, white gloves.

And an old bore rattling away at his side.

"...our Humphrey has distinguished himself in Ireland, so you'll find him of value..." Sir Walter was saying.

No doubt it was Guy's fate to spend his life with some self-important chap attached to his side, spouting obsequious opinions and unsolicited advice. Not unlike Mr. Larke and his parrot.

Maybe Guy should get a parrot. More stimulating conversation, at least.

"I'm returning to London tomorrow," he interrupted.

The morning after that midnight encounter, Guy had ordered

his valet to pack—until a startling realization had compelled him to stay. *Freddie* needed protection, Arabella had warned; not Ursula, only Freddie.

Now he stood in this merry, musical crowd only so he could seek Arabella's explanation while in a public place, not because he wanted to hear Sir Walter blather on about how they were family or soon would be or some nonsense like that.

Damn. What a failure of strategy, giving the impression he was courting Matilda. It had not tempted Sir Walter to confess any sins. Quite frankly, diplomacy and subterfuge were a waste of time.

Guy would leave the next day.

Arabella would leave the next day too, he had heard, to travel to her grandparents' house. Only to be expected, the guests agreed, best for a lady after such a disappointment.

A disappointment? Whatever Arabella had experienced with Sculthorpe, Guy was sure it was not a disappointment.

Perhaps he would ask her, when he spoke to her. He would exorcise the feel of her in his arms and leave tomorrow with a clear head.

"...and our Matilda has saved the waltz for you, my lord. Lady Treadgold says the dance is not quite proper, but—"

"I don't know how to waltz. England didn't waltz when I was last here."

"If only you had said! Our Matilda would have been happy to..."

But Guy never heard his next words, because Arabella had arrived. She drew every eye. Guy drifted away from Sir Walter, drawn into her orbit.

How had he ever imagined she might need help? Most likely, Sculthorpe had realized how much there was to her, her splendor and strength, her intelligence and complexity, and done the smart thing and run away.

Guy would do the smart thing and run too—he would not surrender to this infatuation; he would not allow this woman to manipulate him—but first he had to look at her.

Just...look at her.

Her gown was the pale blue of a summer twilight, dotted with crystals that reflected the candlelight like stars. More crystals glittered in her pile of dark hair. White gloves stretched to her elbows, and a fan dangled from one wrist.

She was a mass of contradictions; perhaps that was her appeal. He never could resist a challenge, or a riddle that needed to be solved. But resist it he must: this urge to take her in his arms, to offer to move the Earth, that she might have whatever she asked.

He imagined her pursing her lips to think, then tapping him with her fan.

"Now you mention it," she'd say, "I am in need of a titled husband. Marry me. Oh, and bring me the king's head on a silver platter while you're at it."

Not a chance.

Yet he could not tear his eyes from her, as she glided through the crowd toward him, snapped open her fan, and regarded him with her desert-sky eyes.

"I wish to talk to you," she said shortly, already turning away. "Meet me on the terrace."

He disciplined his feet, which were much too eager to obey. "What are you scheming now?"

She turned back. "If you meet me on the terrace, I can tell you without us being overheard. It is a private matter."

"No."

"Everyone will be able to see us."

"Precisely."

"Good grief, Guy. You behave like a coy virgin being coaxed into debauchery by a wicked rake. What on earth do you imagine I intend to do? Tear off your cravat and ravish you right there on the terrace? And force us both into a marriage that neither of us wants?"

Except she did want that marriage. She had been angling for it ever since his return. Yet her haunted look the other night... All these pieces of her did not add up.

"I must show you something," she added briskly. "I am leaving tomorrow, as are you, and we must speak first."

"I do not trust you," he said. "You are unscrupulous and hungry for power."

Emotion flashed in her eyes; he would swear it was hurt. He hated that he hurt her, but if he did not protect himself, he would be inviting her to hurt him.

A snap sounded, like something breaking, and her face shuttered, cold and aloof.

"Never mind. I shall send a servant. I need some air. This conversation is tedious. 'Tis as well we need never speak again."

He reached for her hand. She jerked away and instead he caught the fan looped around her wrist. For three ridiculous bars of the waltz, they formed a comical statue, until she let the fan slip from her wrist as he let it slip from his fingers. It clattered to the floor between them. She glanced at it disdainfully. She would not stoop to pick it up. A lady never did.

"Running away, Arabella?" he said.

"Don't be absurd. I never run away. I simply make a timely exit."

And exit she did, sweeping across the ballroom and out onto the terrace.

A footman scooped up the fan and dropped it onto Guy's

outstretched palm. The fan looked fragile. One delicately carved stick was broken.

Careful of the fracture, he eased the fan open; the silk was painted like twilight to match her gown. He closed it again, gently, as much as the broken stick allowed. When he glanced up, guests were gawking at him; his glower made them look away. Speculation must be rife, with Arabella's broken engagement, and Guy, the big, brash marquess who had already spurned her, now acting like a slavering, devoted swain.

After tonight, they would not see each other again, not for months or even years. He would attend house parties over autumn and winter, and if that did not find him a bride, he'd find one when society gathered in London in the spring. The next time he saw Arabella, he would be engaged or even married; she would look right through him, but by then this mad infatuation would have passed and he would not care.

After everything, they needed a farewell. He was not doing her bidding. He was simply returning her fan, and bidding her *adieu*.

ARABELLA DID NOT ACKNOWLEDGE Guy when he joined her on the terrace. She was studying the night sky as intently as if it had flaws and she was personally appointed to fix them. Gooseflesh gathered on her upper arms, on the inches of bare skin between her long gloves and short sleeves. If she were Matilda Treadgold, she would shiver pointedly and he would offer his coat, an intimate offering she would demurely accept. But this was Arabella Larke, and she stood tall and tense and ignored the cold. He was of a mind to offer his coat anyway, just to make her snarl.

"Your fan," he said.

She unfurled a gloved hand. Without touching her, he laid the fan across her palm.

"It's broken," he added.

She made that dismissive sound in the back of her throat and returned to studying the sky. Before, it had been overcast, but she had frightened the sky into a picturesque scene, with ribbons of silvery cloud floating around the bright three-quarter moon.

He would not take back his unkind, ungracious words, because they were true; Arabella was those things, but he could tell her she was other things too. Things he could not yet imagine. That behind her eyes lay a whole solar system, to be discovered by the man who was brave enough or foolish enough to look.

Before he could speak, a footman arrived and handed Arabella a piece of paper. She thanked him, and once they were alone again, she held out the paper to Guy.

"This was taken from Sir Walter's belongings. He is not yet aware it is gone."

"You are stealing now too."

"I am always seeking new skills."

Unfolding the paper, he found enough light to read it by. The meaning was clear on the first read, but still he read it twice more: a special license permitting the immediate marriage of Freddie to Sir Walter's son, Humphrey.

"Freddie knows nothing of this," Arabella was saying. "But it explains why Sir Walter has hastily recalled his son, and why they make no effort to find her a husband. You were seeking his scheme; that is it."

"How did you know?"

"If I were Sir Walter and I wanted to get my hands on your sister's wealth, that's what I would have done." She raised one brow. "Those of us who are *unscrupulous* think like that."

Guy slipped the license into a pocket. "We have evidence that he embezzled from his charitable organizations. We were seeking embezzling."

"Why steal Freddie's wealth when he can get it legally by marrying her off to his son? I wasn't certain until we found that. Had you listened to me in London, you could have asked the archbishop directly, as I cannot, and I would not have had to take up stealing."

"Do you want an apology?"

"Guy, the list of impossible things I want is so long there is no room for anymore. Just make sure that Freddie is not forced into a match against her will for someone else's benefit."

He shook his head in frustration. "But I have no legal power to stop the marriage while Sir Walter is her guardian. The only way I can gain custody is to prove mismanagement."

"Which this is." She rapped his chest hard with her fan, her own frustration clear. "There have been numerous court cases in which Chancery removed guardians for arranging an unequal and improper marriage for their wards. Your solicitors were negligent in failing to mention them. Humphrey Treadgold is Freddie's inferior in every way, in status, wealth, connections. This, you numbskull, *is* evidence of mismanagement, because Sir Walter is using his guardianship for his son's benefit and to Freddie's disadvantage."

"How do you know the case law?"

"I read it. I can read. Or is that a crime now too?"

"You're irritable."

"I'm always irritable."

"No. This is different. What is the matter?"

"That is none of your concern. You have made your opinion of me perfectly clear." Her speech was fast, her manner hard. "Use this, Guy. Stop being honorable and think like a criminal instead. Practice being *unscrupulous*, if you can."

Suddenly, belatedly, he understood. "There are discrepancies in Ursula's trust but the accountants couldn't see where the items had gone. He's likely funneling Ursula's wealth to Freddie, so that his son might take it all."

His brain raced. The archbishop's office would have a record of this license. Tomorrow, he would write to his solicitors, or directly to the Vice Chancellor.

"That's why you invited Sir Walter and his family here: to seek proof," he said. "I accused you of using them as bait to lure me. Why didn't you correct me?"

"You seemed so pleased with yourself, I hated to disillusion you."

She never did defend herself, he realized. Every accusation he made, she accepted the charge, even if it wasn't true. That pride of hers would be her undoing.

"Please accept my apologies. I should have listened to you." He thumped the balustrade. "Damn it. I'm meant to protect Freddie and I got it wrong."

Her tone was unusually gentle as she said, "You did not see your sister as a piece of property to be passed around or used as a pawn in marriage. That does you credit. It is nothing to regret." After a pause, she added, "But perhaps next time, you will listen to me."

"Listen? You were trying to get me to marry you."

"I never wanted to marry you."

"Ever since you were a child—"

"I boasted, yes. When I was nine, Miranda Olivares Lightwell —Cassandra DeWitt's half sister, if you recall—she declared that I was too tall and skinny, so I retorted that at least I was going to be a marchioness one day, which was more than anyone could say for Miranda or anyone else. Then I kept saying it. Did you never make empty boasts when you were a child?"

"At the Prince Regent's party. You said you wanted us to get married. You bribed the jesters and tied me to you. Then at my house—"

"You never heard a word I said, did you?"

"Well, if you would stop speaking nonsense."

She stared at him, her eyes burning. He thought again of the broken fan, that little snap. For all her restraint, Arabella was not without feeling, but she had learned to bury her emotions so deeply they erupted with fury whenever they had a chance.

"I'm listening," he said.

"*Engaged*, you blockhead!" she snapped. "I asked you to tell my father you *meant* to marry me. I never said anything about actually doing it. An engagement could have benefited us both. If you had listened, I would have explained that I meant a temporary arrangement so I could avoid marrying Sculthorpe and you could demonstrate to the court your ability to provide a stable home for your sisters. But never mind, Sculthorpe is gone and you never needed me to stand in for a bride."

Guy tried to remember what she had said, but he only recalled what he had heard. Until this moment, he had believed those to be the same.

"But..." He struggled to pull the pieces together. "Why did you come to me that night in London?"

She shook her head and said nothing.

He tried another tack. "An engagement generally precedes a wedding."

"But a wedding need not follow an engagement. An engagement indicates a commitment, but it can be broken relatively easily, and it is socially acceptable for a lady to do so. Once or twice, anyway. My connections, reputation, and wealth are such that I could weather a more ferocious scandal than most."

"What is the point of feigning an engagement?"

She consulted the sky, giving him the angle of her jaw, the length of her throat, the curls around her ear.

"Because after you announced you would not marry me, after I spent years avoiding marrying Papa's other choices by insisting I wait for you, he threatened to cut me off if I did not wed immediately, and he refused to wait until I presented a man of whom we both approve."

"You exaggerate. Your father would never disinherit you."

"It's already done," she said softly. When she turned back to him, her expression was unreadable. "Almost. His new will has only to be signed and notarized. And as for my famous dowry, which has fortune hunters across the world drooling... Well." She waved her hand dismissively. "Do you think I am leaving tomorrow because my grandmother wants company? I am being cast out. I stand here only because Papa wanted me to face my shame at my *betrothal* ball. Pride goeth and all that."

Guy steadied himself with a hand on the balustrade, the stone cold through his glove. He stared at the gardens until the lights from the hanging lanterns blurred.

Arabella's position had seemed as stable and enduring as this stately family home in which they stood. She claimed her place in the world with such self-assurance that he had never even considered it might be precarious.

Clare had been right: Arabella had indeed become the defining symbol of Guy's struggle to free himself from his father's control. Then, what with Mr. Larke writing to insist Guy marry her, and Arabella bribing the jesters to force Guy into conversation...

He had made assumptions and leaped to conclusions, unable to hear her message over his own determination to never do anyone's bidding again. He had failed to see how she was being controlled too.

This explained— He rubbed his temples. Still the pieces did not add up. Marriage to Sculthorpe would have secured her future. Why the devil would she have risked everything by coming to Guy that night in London? And why insist that same night that Guy get engaged to her, when she was already betrothed? What the hell had Sculthorpe done?

Before he could ask, her eyes skewered him once more. "Vindale Court is my birthright, as Roth Hall and the marquessate are yours. Had my brother survived, it would have been his. But he did not survive, and I am tired of being punished for that." She briefly considered her broken fan before continuing. "There is no legal reason I should not inherit, and Papa intended to bequeath me everything, so the family legacy would pass to his grandsons. But now I am old and he is desperate, and he would rather leave the estate to a stranger than to his own daughter." She shook her head. "Of course you think I exaggerate. When you fight with your father and disappear for eight years, you can resume your position as if nothing ever happened, because your birthright is enshrined in law. You cannot imagine knowing that you might lose everything simply because you are not as they think you ought to be. Yes, I have behaved badly," Arabella added. "But when the alternative is being pushed around like a pawn? I may be 'unscrupulous' and 'power hungry,' but curse you, I am no one's martyr."

He had no idea what she saw in his face, but she must have misread it because she looked almost disgusted.

"Oh for heaven's sake, Guy, don't you dare feel sorry for me now. It is none of your concern. And never fear, I'll not importune you again. I can manage by myself. I always have and I always will."

She whirled about, only to pause in the door to the ballroom. Her shoulders rose and fell as she took a deep, slow breath. Then she glided into the ballroom. Something fearsome must have shown in her demeanor, for everyone moved aside to let her through.

Guy kept staring long after the crowd had swallowed her, still seeing the angle of her jaw, the set of those shoulders, the tilt of her head.

He had never seen anyone look so alone.

WHEN GUY'S feet finally carried him back into the ballroom, the crowd parted for him too. As if they were all co-conspirators, they parted to lead him right to where Arabella stood, on the edges of a conversation between Mrs. DeWitt and Miss Bell, as elegantly aloof as if nothing had happened and nothing was amiss.

Everything was amiss.

Guy planted himself in front of her and held out his hand.

"Come, Miss Larke," he said loudly. "We must tell your father of our engagement."

Her face went blank, and she stared at his outstretched hand as if she had never seen anything like it before in her life. He looked at his hand too: It appeared foreign in its white glove but was mercifully steady. He did not feel steady. What he felt was the floor beneath his feet and his blood galloping under his skin and a million eyes watching the show.

Still she didn't move and a thought struck him: that she might take her revenge and publicly spurn him as he had spurned her. What an impulsive fool he was, yet again duped by sentiment and desire.

But then he looked at her face, and her eyes traveled up to meet his.

And something wondrous happened.

Arabella Larke smiled.

The smile started with a gentle curve of her lips, but it grew to take over her whole face, her whole body, the whole world.

It was a moment of splendor, a moment of hope. The moment in a gloomy cathedral when the sun broke through the stained-glass windows and lit up the cold stone with a thousand dancing colors and patterns, a carnival of light that dazzled the eye and emboldened the heart.

She had been so taut and tired. He had thought that was simply her nature, but she had carried a weight, which he had lifted.

And so dazzling was the effect of her smile that when she placed her gloved hand in his, he entwined his fingers with hers.

Guy ignored the eyes following them, as did Arabella, and hand in hand they walked through the over-loud murmurs and the over-bright candlelight and the over-scented air.

Arabella's parents stood together near the supper table, and turned to watch their approach. When they came to a stop, Guy released Arabella's hand and bowed.

"Mr. Larke, Lady Belinda. Miss Larke and I are engaged to be married. I trust we have your blessing."

Lady Belinda smiled graciously, held out her hand in congratulations. Larke looked from one to the other, features twisted with suspicion.

"What's going on, Hardbury?" he said. "You said you wouldn't have her."

"You seem to be under the impression this is a discussion. It is not."

"And you'll marry her soon?"

"Plan the wedding for London in the springtime, that every lord, lady, and gentleman in the country might bear witness." Guy could feel Arabella vibrating beside him but he didn't look at her. "Now seems as good a time as any to make the announcement," he continued. "Would you like to do it, Mr. Larke, or shall I?"

Larke grinned. "You've realized what a gem Vindale Court is, eh?"

"Your estate is of little interest to me."

"What's your reason for the betrothal, then?"

Guy laughed. This was almost too absurd for words.

"Because we are in love," he said. "What other reason could there possibly be?"

CHAPTER 13

Yellow wagtail. Short-eared owl. Red macaw.

Arabella drummed her fingers on the smooth oak of the massive library table as she considered Juno's illustrations, laid out in rows as if she were playing a game of Patience.

Patience? Absurd name for a solitary card game, given she had absolutely none.

The illustrated birds might have been alive, the way they flittered under her hands. Or perhaps in the excitement of the impromptu betrothal celebrations last night, which had offered no opportunity to speak privately to Guy, her brain had been replaced with that of a goldfinch. It was certainly chattering like a goldfinch —like a whole charm of goldfinches: *Need a plan. Must talk to Guy. Why did Guy do it? Doesn't matter. Don't care. Must make a plan. Guy doesn't even like me. What was he thinking? Doesn't matter. Don't care. Need a plan. Must talk to—*

Good grief! Those poor little birds must be exhausted!

In addition, her birdbrain had her hopping like a finch every time one of the library doors opened—but every time it was only a guest, wandering in to join the others lounging around in a post-ball haze.

Until the door opened for the hundredth time, finally revealing Guy.

He paused in the doorway to study her, as if struck by something unexpected. She resisted the unfamiliar urge to smooth out the skirt of her striped morning dress and adjust its long sleeves.

He was frowning, of course. Still no "happy to see you" smile for her! Then he was moving again, charging at her across the library, as he had charged across the ballroom last night: as though she were a dreadful accident about to happen and it was up to him to stop it.

She lowered her eyes to the illustration of a chiffchaff—a confusion of chiffchaffs!—but all she saw was Guy, shoulders broad in his tailored riding coat, buckskins hugging his long, booted legs, Guy coming closer and closer, bigger and bigger, setting a gale blowing through the room as the huge library shrank to a cave.

Until he was there, by her side, infuriatingly untouchable. He took up too much space and carried the elements with him: his hair tossed by the wind, his cheeks warmed by the sun, his eyes bright like leaves after rain.

Her skin burning like fire.

"You were out riding," she said.

"Keeping track of my whereabouts already?"

"I had little choice in the matter. The standard greeting used to be 'Good morning, Miss Larke,' but today everyone greeted me with 'Oh, Miss Larke, Lord Hardbury is out riding.' One would think our engagement were a matter of such consuming importance that I could not possibly have an interest in anything else."

A glance around the library showed a few guests eyeing them with idle curiosity, but a room this size allowed for private conversations. Nevertheless, she lowered her voice.

"I did not get a chance to thank you last night, for agreeing to... help me." He watched her steadily; his expression gave away nothing. "I will not pretend to understand the reason you changed your mind, and I do not intend to inquire too closely, in case you change it again."

As if already bored, he shrugged and turned away, his eyes on the pages spread out on the table. "You went to considerable trouble and risk to help Freddie. It seemed a fair exchange."

"I didn't help Freddie to secure an exchange," she said. "She needed helping and I was in a position to do it."

"I know."

"Have you confronted Sir Walter?"

"No, and I don't intend to. This morning, I called on Sir Gordon Bell, and with his legal advice and assistance, have written express to request an urgent hearing in Chancery."

Arabella fingered the corner of a turtledove. A pitying of turtledoves. "And Miss Treadgold?"

"What about Miss Treadgold?"

"You appeared to be courting her."

"When our engagement is over, I shall choose a bride."

"Someone sweet and amiable. Of course," she murmured, and busied herself with moving the peacock. A pride of peacocks.

"What are these drawings for?" he asked.

"*The Illustrated Guide to the Vindale Aviaries,* a book I am making. This is to decide the final page order."

He picked up a drawing: a heron. A siege of herons. "These

illustrations are excellent. There is joy in every line of these birds. You count writing and drawing among your talents too?"

"Good grief, no. My talent is for issuing orders; other people do the actual work. Juno Bell drew the illustrations, and Livia Bell wrote the text."

"How do you make these into a book?"

He put down the heron—crookedly!—and picked up a page of writing. Arabella took her time straightening the heron illustration while she tried to form a reply. The world had gone mad: She and Guy were making harmless, civilized small talk. They should be fighting. If they were not fighting, then they were...what?

"I send the pages with my instructions to a publisher in London, who organizes the engraver and colorist for the illustrations, and sets the type. When the galley-proofs are ready, I check them, and when I am satisfied, they print and bind them. This will be my first attempt at full color, because of the cost."

"But you've made books before."

"I began by creating an ornithology journal based on Papa's conventions."

He replaced the page of writing and scowled at the table. She scowled too, as she straightened the page.

"You make *books*," he said.

"I do have some respectable interests. It cannot be all skulduggery, you know."

He nudged the corner of another page. Apparently, he did not even *care* that he had made it crooked. She straightened it irritably.

"Do you even like birds?" he asked.

"I don't dislike birds." She considered his question. *Did* she like birds? "I like the way the hawk circles and dives, all that speed and precision. I like how magpies use tools, and how crows recognize faces, and how blue tits chatter at each other like friends. I like that so many birds mate for life and that when they migrate, they know unerringly where and when to fly."

He said nothing, but regarded her as though she herself were a new species of bird.

"Why are you looking at me like that?"

A hint of a smile touched his lips. "I found that charming. I am not accustomed to thinking of you as charming."

"Indeed. You made your opinion of me very clear last night."

"Ah. Those words were unkind and uncalled for. I apologize. I hurt your feelings."

"Don't be absurd. I have no feelings. My enormous pride swallowed them up years ago."

Still smiling, his eyes searched her face, and clearly she had become bird-brained, because she thought she read in them some tenderness, even affection, and that could not be right.

Then he propped himself against the table, legs outstretched, losing enough height to bring their faces level. He was so close that her skin anticipated his touch.

The door opened. Mama came in and joined a trio of ladies. From a distance came music: Someone in the drawing room played the pianoforte.

"You ought not stand so close," she said. "People will think we're..."

"In love?" he finished easily.

"Yes. That."

"That's what we want them to think."

"You ought not have said that last night. About us being..."

"In love?"

"Yes. That. You should have given a rational reason. My property, your title."

"If I gave a rational reason, people would feel entitled to ask rational questions and demand rational answers. If we say we are in love, no one will expect us to be rational ever again."

She couldn't help but laugh, but that made him regard her oddly again.

"You laugh now," he said. "You smile. I do not think I have ever seen you laugh or smile before."

She pressed her fingers into the table. "At any rate, it's ridiculous. The very notion of us being..."

"In love?"

"Yes. That. No one will ever believe it."

"They will if we pretend."

"How on earth do we do that?"

"It's easy. For example, every now and then I shall comment loudly on how pretty your eyes are and how sweet you smell."

"How I *smell*?"

"Yes. It's very romantic. You try."

"You smell like horse."

This time it was he who laughed. She liked the way his laugh rumbled through him and danced over her skin, the way his eyes lit up and deep furrows formed alongside his mouth.

"Do you mean to say that you have never been in love?" he asked.

There had been those giddy feelings last night, when Guy had gifted her with hope, then tangled his fingers with hers and led her to Papa. The fluttering in her chest that she'd carried to her bed like a souvenir. But that was merely...what? Gratitude, no doubt. Relief.

"I have liked some gentlemen, but they think that..." She shrugged. "You will agree that I am not that kind of lady."

"Do you mean never to marry?"

"I have always hoped to marry. Married women have more

freedom, and I would like a family. When I made my come-out, I imagined marrying a man who..."

No. She would not confess that childish, long-buried daydream of a love match. If he knew, he would always be able to hurt her. Weeks or months or years from now, when they were married to other people, he would know her deepest desires and dreams, and she could not bear to be in the same room with anyone who knew such things as that.

"When a woman marries, she gives everything to her husband —her property, her body, her very safety. If I must give so much power to a man, I should prefer one who will not abuse it. Who respects me for who I am and takes me as an equal partner."

"He would need to be brave, too."

She shot him a look. "True. Terrifying men is one of my more notable talents."

"Maybe you should not try so hard to terrify them."

"I do not try at all. I achieve it with the greatest ease."

Idly, she adjusted an illustration of a parrot. A pandemonium of parrots. The morning before, the long-awaited letter from Hadrian Bell had arrived; yes, he had written, he would indeed be interested in discussing marriage when he returned to England in the new year. Now was the perfect moment to mention that to Guy.

But the words did not come. Instead she said, her tone brisk and bright, "So you see, the question is whether my ideal husband even exists."

"Ah, quite a conundrum." He made a show of studying her. "It would take a very particular kind of man, I think. Obviously, he must not be terrified of you, but any man who is not terrified of you is a fool, and he must not be a fool."

"Then, by your own reasoning, he cannot exist."

"But he can exist, if he wants you so much that he does not let his terror deter him. He must be clever too. Perhaps even as clever as you, which means he is clever enough never to let you know he is as clever as you. And he must be a man who..."

His words trailed off, and although his eyes were roaming over her face, one would think his mind was somewhere else and he did not see her at all.

"Who what?" she prompted.

His eyes stilled, met hers. She knew those eyes, she knew them from that night in London, when his hands were sliding over her body, when he swooped to claim her mouth in a kiss.

"He must be a man who knows how to unleash your passion."

Guy stood so near, and there was so much of him, all shoulders and chest and arms and legs, that if she dared close the space between them, she could discover herself in him again.

Her rational parts wanted to hide behind words, say *how to know whether a man can do that, are we to conduct interviews and tests*, but the words dissolved, crowded out by images and sensations from that hour when their bodies were entwined.

A bang released her, as the nearest library door crashed open.

Startled, Arabella hopped away like a wren. Guy rose lazily to his feet. He had set more pages in disarray, but she could not straighten them, for she was struck by the sight of Papa in the doorway, with Queenie perched on his arm and an unprecedentedly broad smile on his face.

It seemed Guy's move last night had brought a plague of smiles to the Larke family.

But Papa's smile was not for Arabella.

"Excellent news, Hardbury," he said. "I've just now spoken to the vicar. Your wedding will take place in sixteen days."

SILENCE STRETCHED OVER THE LIBRARY. At Guy's side, Arabella whispered, "Sixteen days," her horror plain.

Despite everything, Guy had to laugh.

All morning, as he went about his business with Sir Gordon, he had been second-guessing his impulse of the night before, assuring himself that he had misunderstood Arabella, that he had the situation in hand.

Yet their engagement was not a day old and already he had lost control, with a gambit from Mr. Larke.

What a game this was turning out to be.

At least he and Arabella were playing on the same side for once. She did not appear remotely threatening, just another genteel lady in an elegant morning gown. And surprisingly charming, the way she kept straightening the pages to align their edges with the table, so that Guy could not resist setting them crooked. They had eased into conversation as if they had not been battling each other their entire lives. He had teased her, as if he was not playing with fire.

Arabella elbowed him. "You laugh?" she hissed.

"You must admit, it is a little funny," he said softly.

"Sixteen days," she repeated with a shake of her head.

She truly did not want to marry him. Well. Good. Of course, he didn't want to marry her, regardless of this infatuation, but it seemed he was just conceited enough to feel a trifle stung.

Lady Belinda, her serene gaze on her daughter, had joined Larke, who was looking pleased with himself.

"Explain yourself, Mr. Larke," Guy said. "How is a wedding in sixteen days even possible?"

"Simple," Larke said. "The vicar will read the first of the three banns in church tomorrow. Two more Sundays, and the wedding will be the day after that."

"I'll tell you what is simple," Guy said. "Arabella is my

betrothed, so I decide when and where the wedding will take place. We would prefer to wed in London in spring."

The parrot muttered something incomprehensible and Larke squinted suspiciously. "Why the delay? You already know each other. We can settle the paperwork now. You'll get her dowry and your second son will inherit my estate, if that's your concern."

"That isn't my concern," Guy said. "A London wedding will be witnessed by all society."

"Bah, because you're in *love*." Larke shook his head. "All the more reason to marry her quickly. She won't keep your attention for long, judging by her history with other men."

Beside him, Arabella stood as still and straight as a soldier, her expression impassive, while her father openly declared that she could not be loved.

Guy was not amused anymore.

The night before, he had realized how poorly he understood her. Now, suddenly, he wondered if she even understood herself: this proud woman who insisted on fighting her battles alone, but smiled as radiantly as an angel when someone took her side. She fought for her inheritance, she had claimed, but Guy suspected the fight was actually for her father's affection.

He took her hand. She twitched, then settled. He longed to pull her close and push her far away, this impossible woman whose hand felt so right in his. This was not his fight, but he could not leave her to fight alone in a battle he wasn't sure even she fully understood.

Larke was talking about their unborn children. "I've waited years for another boy. If you two marry now, I could have a grandson by spring."

"Summer," Guy corrected absently.

Lady Belinda pressed two fingers to her forehead, as if she had a headache coming on.

Larke frowned. "Is there a problem with that?"

"Regardless of the wedding date, there can be no son before early summer," Guy said. "Arabella is highly accomplished, but even she cannot produce a child in less than the usual time. Not that I would object if we started early, but even—"

Guy's words were interrupted by a well-timed coughing fit from Lady Belinda.

Beside him, Arabella smoothed out her frown and adopted an expression of reason. "Papa, I fear a wedding so soon cannot be convenient for his lordship. He has important lordship business in London. He was just now telling me that the Prince Regent wishes to see him," she lied.

Guy squeezed her hand, willing her not to quarrel.

"The Prince Regent can wait another three weeks," Larke said. "Or invite him to the wedding."

"But Papa—"

"Curse you, girl! You'll not argue with me on this." Larke looked from one to the other, squinting with suspicion. "Why are you two so set on dragging your feet?"

Arabella fought because she was used to fighting. It was simply her nature to command, but she was an unmarried woman, so the world refused to obey. Still she kept fighting, battling on alone.

"Papa—"

"Your father makes a good point, Arabella."

Guy squeezed her hand, harder this time. She dug her nails into his palm.

"He does?" she said.

"It would not do for the Prince Regent to think I am at his beck and call."

"You *are* at his beck and call. He is the ruler of the land."

"And you are the ruler of my heart."

"Oh, good grief."

Guy grinned. "Besides, you are prettier than he is, and only slightly more tyrannical."

This bit of nonsense made Lady Belinda smile and Larke chuckle, and Guy chuckled too as Arabella looked around in uncharacteristic confusion, as if someone had redesigned the world when she wasn't looking.

Between them, he and Arabella could make this work, to ensure she did not lose everything, while also avoiding a marriage that neither of them wanted. Guy had no solution yet, but Arabella would surely think of something.

"Let us discuss the paperwork shortly, Larke," Guy said. "For now, my betrothed and I shall take a turn by the lake to discuss our future."

That seemed to satisfy her parents, but while Arabella left to dress for the outdoors, someone entered who was definitely not satisfied: Sir Walter, looking cross.

He'd be even more cross when he learned of the letter Guy had sent that morning.

"What are you all so happy about?" Sir Walter asked.

Mr. Larke released another broad grin. "More celebration, for my daughter's wedding will take place in sixteen days."

Sir Walter's mouth pinched sourly. "You were here to court our Matilda, my lord."

"I'm afraid I got distracted."

"After the care I have taken of your sisters, this is the thanks I get?"

"Oh my dear, dear Sir Walter," Guy said. "I promise, you will shortly get all the thanks you deserve."

"Easy now, Sir Walter." Mr. Larke slapped that man's shoulder. The movement upset his parrot, who muttered her complaint. "Lord Hardbury was promised to my daughter when he was still in petticoats. Your Matilda is a fine girl, but she doesn't offer what we can. Put that aside and join us in celebration."

Sir Walter wriggled away from his host's arm. "I shall seek my refreshments at the village inn," he grizzled. "The company is better there."

CHAPTER 14

Ten thousand times Arabella had walked the path toward the lake, but this was the time she'd remember: when her life unraveled, when her half-baked plan crumbled.

Beside her, Guy was restless, like a horse on a windy day. He shoved his gloves into his pockets and, with his bare hands, tore a branch from a tree, stripped off its twigs and leaves, and whacked at things as they walked.

"You wanted me to be silent," she said.

"It's clear you and your father don't get along, and arguing only makes matters worse. You were trying to take control and for you that means starting a quarrel."

Arabella had no response to that. Guy knew things about her now that he had not known before.

"Do you always attempt everything on your own?" he asked. "You're really not used to having someone on your side, are you?"

She had a sudden memory of herself and Oliver hiding from their tutor, smothering their giggles as they huddled together under Papa's desk. As soon as the chance came, they had burst out into the garden and run away—only to run right into Papa. But he hadn't been cross. When they confessed their naughtiness, he had laughed, then taken them each by the hand and guided them through the garden to show them an owl's nest.

Papa laughing and taking her by the hand? Impossible. That memory must be fabricated too.

Guy did not seem to expect an answer, and he did not speak again until they turned onto the white gravel path that circled the lake.

Well?" he demanded. "What is your clever scheme?"

"What makes you think I have a scheme?"

"You always have a scheme."

"I always have a *plan*, which is an entirely different matter."

He whacked a shrub and kept walking. He would have to end this now. If only they could suspend the decision and simply take a stroll together as two people without a history, not as two people with decades of being forced together against their will.

"But I suppose my plans don't matter," she said. "As we shall have to end the engagement."

He said nothing.

"If that's what you want," she added.

"Is that what you want?"

"I asked if that's what you want."

"And I asked if that's what you want."

"What I want is to..."

Alongside them, the lake's surface was choppy. A leaf tumbled through the air, tossed and turned by the wind, which dropped it onto the lake to be tossed and turned by the water.

"To stop feeling like that," Arabella finished, pointing at the leaf.

Guy reached out his stick to snare it, but the wind rippled along the surface and the leaf skittered away.

Walking on, they turned onto a straight stretch of path, sheltered by a towering hedge and lined with statues of Greek gods.

"This is not what you agreed to," she said, as they passed Poseidon with his beard and trident. "It was kind of you to step in, but this is hardly fair."

"You said you are no martyr."

"No, but I imagine you are not one either. No need for us both to be miserable."

He huffed out air. "Arabella, speak directly. I haven't your subtlety or complexity of thought."

"It seems you have become a rare beast: You hold noble principles and you live by them. That is something to be honored, not exploited. It is time I faced the fact that Papa will never accept me on my own terms. You never meant it to go this far, did you?"

"No." He trailed the stick in the gravel. "And you'll— What? Simply walk away?"

"Perhaps I should have done so years ago."

"Your father will cut you off. You'll lose everything."

Perhaps it had never been hers to lose, and her biggest mistake was thinking it could be.

"I'll figure something out," she said. "I always do. It is my problem, not yours."

There: She had released him. But he did not answer. Instead, he pulled off his hat and balanced it on the end of his stick as they walked, spinning it, throwing it into the air, and catching it again.

Good grief. The man was a marquess, yet he behaved like a playful child. And she— *Oh, be honest.* She was as much a child. She could gather her skirts and leap for that hat. Knock it off the stick and grab it and run. He'd catch her easily, and they'd tumble onto the grass and—

Not like children, then.

Finally, Guy threw his hat into the air, jumped to seize it in his free hand before the wind stole it, and stopped beside the next statue. Apollo, with sculpted muscles, long curls, and a lyre.

"I refuse to surrender until we have exhausted all options," he said. "We have a whole sixteen days to fix this. I cannot believe you are giving in."

"Don't be absurd. I never give in. I am merely changing my strategy."

Finally her brain caught up with her ears. She stared at him. A smile hovered over his lips.

"I don't need you to rescue me," said her pride, which did not know how to thank him.

"Don't be absurd. I'm not rescuing you," he said, mimicking her. "I'm helping you rescue yourself."

The look she gave him should have sliced him like the wind, but he only grinned and turned to study Apollo.

"I'll not be forced to marry you, Arabella," he said to the statue. "But I find it despicable, the way your father uses the promise of your inheritance to control you. Do you have any idea how thoroughly my father controlled me? I could not even choose how the tailor cut my coat, or how my valet cut my hair. Duty and one's place in society are all very well, but to deny our personal choices is to erode our very selves. So we must secure your inheritance without your choices being taken away."

Guy finished this speech by placing his hat on Apollo's head. He tilted it to a rakish angle and stepped back to admire the effect.

Arabella stared at the statue too, yet while her eyes saw the weathered stone, she was aware only of Guy. Strong, powerful Guy, who owed her nothing, who despised her, who would help her anyway.

And all was right in the world.

Except—

She stepped forward and straightened Apollo's hat, so it sat evenly on his head. There. *Now* all was right in the world. Nodding with satisfaction, she prepared to walk on when Guy brushed past her, touched his fingers to the brim, and set the hat crooked again.

His face was the picture of innocence. She glared at him, but when he did not rectify his error, she used both hands to once more straighten the hat.

He waited until she had stepped back, and then, with a lazy tap of his knuckles, tipped it again.

Again, Arabella straightened it.

Again, Guy set it askew.

She curled her fingers into her palms. She was not going to play his games. And look! One thing he knew about her—one harmless foible—and he used it to torment her. This was what happened when people knew you cared about something.

With a haughty toss of her head, she continued along the path. He fell into step beside her.

One step. Two steps. Three. Four.

Curse it.

She dashed back and straightened the hat, and he laughed, looking carefree and rumpled, with the smile in his eyes and the wind in his hair.

When he extended his elbow, she returned to him and slipped her fingers into the crook. They walked on, like a typical engaged couple, shoulders bumping, her wine-red pelisse flirting with his greatcoat.

"Are you already married?" she asked, oddly breathless for such a short dash.

"Not that I'm aware of."

"Using a false name?"

"No."

"Underage?"

"Hardly."

"Insane?"

"Only around you."

"Impotent?"

He whirled about. Her hand slipped from his arm. His eyes glinted with that heated intensity so familiar from that night in London.

"What do *you* think?" His growl was rough with promise. "You have some experience in the matter of my...potency."

"Things might have changed."

"Would you like a demonstration? To check everything still works as it ought?"

He lowered his gaze to her mouth, and then over her body, his look inflaming her skin, as though his hands were touching her again. In his eyes, amusement mingled with that heat, an infectious mix that rippled through her blood in delicious ways and, that, oh yes, she remembered that from London too.

That night when she had ruined everything, with her fears and pride and carelessness, long before it had occurred to her that there might be anything precious to ruin. All those years of despising him, only to learn too late there was nothing to despise. Caring nothing for his good opinion of her, until that good opinion was irrevocably lost. And what heartrending cruelty, to discover this longing for him, after all she had done to ensure he would never want her.

Maybe it was not too late. Maybe she could grab his head and make him listen. Make him understand that sometimes she got frightened, and fear turned her stupid, and her pride concealed it so no one would know. Even then, what was the point? Perhaps he would understand, perhaps even forgive. But it would not make him want her.

He thought her unscrupulous and arrogant and power-hungry,

and a good, honorable man did not want a woman like that. She had made enough mistakes already; she would not mistake his fleeting desire and essential decency for anything other than what they were.

"I'll take your word for it," she managed to say.

His eyes held hers a moment longer, then he turned back to the path, his boots crunching on the gravel, and he trailed his stick in the water as though nothing had happened.

Because nothing had.

"Those questions relate to marriage, I take it?" he asked.

"Legal impediments. There are none. The other option is to delay the wedding."

He raised his eyebrows. "I daresay you have some ideas."

"For the marriage to be valid, the vicar must read the banns three Sundays in a row, in the parish church in which the wedding is to take place," she recited. "If there are no objections, the ceremony must take place within three months of the third banns, witnessed by at least two people. If there is any disruption or delay, it must start all over again from the first banns."

"How do you know all this?"

"I like knowing things. It makes me feel…"

"Less like a leaf on the lake."

Curse it. Another thing she had revealed.

She pressed on. "Therefore, to delay or prevent the wedding, we simply remove one or more of the essential elements, namely: the vicar, the church, the witnesses, the bride, or the groom."

"I'm sure you have a suggestion."

"It's obvious, isn't it? We kidnap the vicar."

GUY WHIRLED TO A STOP. Kidnap the vicar? *This* was her solution? Bloody hell. Why did he keep forgetting this about her? When would he learn that she was—

Joking. Of course she was. Laughter danced in her eyes, along with a touch of defiance as if she knew his first thought.

"We should do it immediately before the third banns," she continued. "Perhaps the Saturday night, so there is no time for the curate to stand in."

Guy tried to look stern. "Arabella, we are not kidnapping the vicar."

"We wouldn't hurt him. He might even enjoy it." Her face brightened. "We could take him to the seaside."

"No," he said, but he was laughing.

"I suppose you won't let me burn down the church either."

"Not if we can avoid it."

She sighed dramatically. "You never let me do what I want."

"You're just trying to make me laugh."

"I like it when you laugh. You become appealing."

"And the rest of the time I am not?"

"The rest of the time you have that furrow."

She touched her thumb to the spot between his brows, and he wasn't laughing now. Her gloved hand was a blur before his eyes, the caress of soft, cool leather like a benediction that made him want to drop to his knees and—

He flung the stick aside, shoved his fists into his pockets, and when she lowered her hand, he was seeing her again, her smiling eyes, her mocking brows, her temptingly parted lips.

"As though you are always annoyed at the world generally," she added.

"Not always. Sometimes I am annoyed at the world specifically."

"But when you smile and laugh, you get these deep furrows

here, beside your mouth, as if your smile is so important that everything else must make way for it."

Then she was touching him again, both hands cupping his face. The pale sunlight caressed every enticing detail of her dark brows, her thick lashes, her soft skin, her curved lips. If only she had removed her gloves; he craved her naked touch.

"I cannot decide if you are handsome or not," she went on. "Your features are too bold, and you let your complexion become weathered, and you have these faint lines, under your eyes, here, from squinting at the wind and sun."

"Did you not notice that I'm brown on my torso too?" he said without thinking. "This summer, I stopped on my way back to England to work in an orchard in Valencia, and when it was hot, we took off our shirts."

"I suppose the señoritas did not object."

"Their grandmothers did not either."

She laughed, the breathless sound carried by the wind, and he wanted to capture her sudden bright beauty. When she dropped her hands, the cold wind rushed through him. He did not move away. Neither did she.

"But it will all fade," she said. "Disappear like those calluses on your hand."

"Indeed. I shall become soft and pink, and fit for nothing but eating roast beef and lecturing on topics I know nothing about."

"Your hair will darken too, once you wear a hat and stay only in the English sun." She caught a few strands of his windblown hair, then set them free. "Juno Bell used to wash her hair in lemon juice to make it golden like this."

"I shall suggest it to my valet."

Again she laughed. And before he knew what he was doing, his hands were out of his pockets and tugging at the bow of her bonnet.

"What on earth are you doing?" she asked, as the untied ribbons fluttered wildly.

"I have not seen your hair in the sunlight."

"It is only hair. It looks the same at any time."

He slipped off her bonnet and she grabbed it from him, but made no attempt to hide. Within the glossy, dark mass, a tiny comb winked at him. He tugged at it, claiming it—

"Don't!" she cried. "It will get messy."

—and a thick lock of hair tumbled alongside her face, then rose and waved in the wind. He tucked the comb into his pocket and curled her hair around his fingers, letting the silken strands slide over his skin.

"You are appealing when you smile too," he added softly.

"I'm not smiling now."

"You smile with your eyes. It is enough. Besides, your lips are always slightly curved, in the promise of a smile."

He touched his thumbs to each corner of her mouth. It occurred to him, suddenly, that they had never kissed merely for the sake of kissing. They had kissed as a dare, a dangerous game between nemeses, after which they had been naked and in the middle of their—whatever that was. They had it all upside down and back to front. Even if he kissed her now, they could never start again, because everything between them would always be wrong.

The thought gave him the strength to drop his hands, to pivot, to put several yards between them. *Keep walking*, he told himself. *Walk away, walk away!* But his body disobeyed; he needed to see her again.

She stood motionless by the lake's edge, worshiped by a weak beam of sunlight, while the wind tormented her wine-red skirts and her bonnet danced at the end of its ribbons. The loose hair whipped about her face, and Guy fancied he saw her as she truly was: magnificently proud, heartbreakingly vulnerable, standing in defiance of the elements themselves.

He had to walk away. Walk away from the temptation to kiss her, from this risk to his plans. Walk away from her unexpected charm and her secret nobility, and her strength, that splendid strength that rendered him weak.

"Walk away," Guy said out loud, but the wind swallowed his words and spun him around and pushed him back toward her.

CHAPTER 15

Arabella was staring at Guy's back, but then it was not his back. He spun on his heel. He strode back toward her. A thrill pulsed through her with every step of those long, powerful legs.

His greatcoat streamed out behind him, as he charged at her, eyes fierce, face scowling, heated, furious, intent.

She could not move. There was nowhere to go, nothing but him and his approach, shrinking the world and thinning the air and heating her blood, so that it rushed through her veins and swirled and pooled and throbbed.

He hardly slowed even when he reached her. Still moving, he caught her face in one hand, her waist in the other. Their bodies slammed into each other, and she was reaching into him, gripping him, her hungry mouth meeting his. His lips were hot and demanding, and she answered with demands of her own. She twisted one hand in his hair and the other in his waistcoat, and she must have dropped her bonnet, but who cared, she had a million bonnets and only one chance to kiss him. Only one chance to own his lips, to claim his mouth, to taste, to explore, but —curse him!—his tongue was in the way, and she had to battle it with her own, until he made a noise in his throat— Was that laughter? Did he dare *laugh* while he kissed her?

But oh, so help her, she needed more.

As if sharing her urgency, his hand curved under her buttocks and hauled her against him, the whole hard hot length of him, their chests, their hips, and there, yes, *there*, she could almost feel him. If she could just press closer, deepen this kiss—

He was feverish too, his hands roaming, finding her waist, her breasts, as their tongues tangled, and her hands roamed too, under his coat, hunting his heat and promise, and he kissed her so she was full of him, his taste, his scent, his touch, and yet not full enough, never enough. She needed more. Why did he not touch her more?

Oh, she wanted to laugh too, from the sheer exhilaration! This was everything she remembered. The fever in her blood and under her skin, spreading through her like wildfire, smashing everything open, everything she had learned to keep locked away, and all these feelings—these feelings she had buried so deep— once more they burst free.

Splendid, he had said. *Splendid*.

They broke off the kiss to gulp at air, but still his arms clutched her, and his lips burned a trail along her jaw, her cheek, her ear. Every inch of her yearned for those lips. Her lips yearned for every inch of him.

"Oh Arabella, you annihilate me," he muttered. "I can't not... I can't not touch you. Oh hell. I don't care. Whatever the consequences, I don't care."

Arabella froze. She heard herself breathing, hard and heavy like a winded horse.

"The consequences?" she repeated.

He released her so abruptly she staggered. He spun away, laughing mirthlessly, his hands raking his hair, as if he had so much energy coursing through him the only way to dispel it was to move.

Arabella did not move. She stood very, very still.

"I'll end up married to you after all. How Father must be laughing in his grave right now! All these years I insisted I would not do his bidding." His back was still to her, as he shook his head. "Your reputation."

"By all means, let us consider my reputation."

Still he did not turn. "I do not owe you for what happened in London. But if anyone reported seeing *that*, I would definitely have to marry you. Honor would demand it."

His face was hidden, but his bitter tone told her everything she needed to know.

Thankfully, her pride was the one part of her not obliterated by his kiss.

"How inconvenient it must be to have honor," she drawled. "I am eternally grateful I do not suffer from that particular flaw."

He nodded, as though she had confirmed what he already suspected. Then he threw up his hands and started to pace.

"That night in London. I still don't understand why you came to me that night. And Sculthorpe. What happened with Sculthorpe?"

Memories and thoughts and possibilities pounded through her, as if she had a dozen hearts and every one of them was working double time.

She could tell him everything. Tell him about her fear and loathing, about Sculthorpe's obsession. Admit why she had misused Guy.

He had tried to outdo her that night in London, but in the end he had done her bidding. That made him hate himself, and hate her, and that—well, she understood that. She understood that he could kiss her and laugh with her and stand by her side, while hating a part of her too. That was the trouble with feelings; they were complex and messy and contradictory, and, oh, if only she could pack them neatly into boxes, tied with colorful ribbons.

If she told him what Sculthorpe had done? Mama had started whispers at the ball. Over time, the news would circulate, and by springtime everyone would know. But for now...

If she pulled back her sleeves to reveal her fading bruises? How that would offend Guy's blessed principles! Honorable and impulsive, he would hare off to challenge Sculthorpe. If any blood were shed, Arabella would always know it was her fault, because she had known the power of her words, because she understood Guy's character and how his principles would make him wade into a fight.

"Once more, I apologize for how I treated you in London," she said, sounding stiff to her own ears.

"I sought an explanation, not another apology."

"There is nothing to tell. I have said I will release you."

For long moments, he stared out over the lake. She picked up her bonnet and tried to smooth out its crumpled ribbons, as if she could smooth out all the wrinkles in her past, all her missteps and mistakes.

"Tell me honestly, Arabella," he finally said, as though he truly believed that every other word she spoke was a lie. "What is your scheme? I confess I haven't the wits to keep up with you. I have only my principles to guide me, and my desire for you so addles my mind I hardly know what to think." He pinned her with his direct, honest stare. "Speak plainly. Do you mean for us to marry in the end?"

What a thing for him to admit! How easily he revealed his weaknesses, so sure of his strength that it diminished him not at all to reveal his flaws. How marvelous it must feel, to live like that. How freeing.

Yet she could use his weaknesses against him. If she chose the right words, in a few weeks, she would be a marchioness, and her position in society, future, and inheritance would be secure.

She could have it all—including a husband who despised her. Guy deserved better than that. He deserved better than to spend the rest of his life trapped with a woman he loathed. Just imagine: a lifetime tied to Guy, craving his good opinion, but receiving only resentment.

"Honestly, no," she said. "That would be the worst thing in the world."

He nodded in agreement, and added, "For your father to disinherit you in these circumstances would be an injustice. I abhor lying to everyone, but allowing that injustice would be worse. Let us make a plan. I wish to play this out. It need only be until spring."

Papa would say the injustice was that Oliver had died, that his wife had not borne him more sons, that his daughter was a hoyden and a scold. Arabella would say the injustice was that she did not have the same rights as men, that her brother's death hung over her like a curse.

"I promise I shall never try to make you do something you don't want to do," she said.

It was meant as a sincere promise, but this, too, made him laugh, and she wondered what she had misunderstood. He turned, their eyes met, and it seemed they would both break ranks, close the space, start kissing again.

But instead, he spoke. "How do you plan to find a husband? You have a plan, of course."

"Of course." She turned to watch the waterfowl surfing the

choppy waters of the lake. "I am corresponding with Hadrian Bell. Sir Gordon's son. You remember him?"

"I hear he's at the embassy in Potsdam." He stilled. "You mean to marry Hadrian?"

"He is interested in discussing it. Their estate neighbors ours, so our marriage would combine our estates. That will ensure Papa's agreement." Turning back, she lifted her chin. "So you see, all I ever needed was time."

"Because you have a plan." He nodded and nodded and kept on nodding. "Right. Yes. Hadrian Bell. Good match for him. He always was ambitious. Well played."

Ambitious. Because, of course, no one would want to marry her for any other reason.

"You must go away, to delay the wedding," she made herself say. "We cannot remove the vicar, the church, or the witnesses. And I cannot go anywhere, so that leaves you." She shoved back her loose hair, pulled on her bonnet, and briskly set about tying the ribbons. "If we are not married within three months of the third banns, it has to start again. Tell Papa you have urgent business and will return for the wedding. But you get caught up in business and stay away for three months, writing frequently..." She dropped her hands. "It's a lot of trouble for you. You didn't ask for this."

"I have to go to London anyway, deal with this matter in Chancery." He shoved his hands back into his pockets. "If others make demands on my time, an invitation from a peer, perhaps an order from the Crown, the weather could turn. Staying away is not unreasonable. We'll call your father's bluff. He cannot truly mean to will his estate away from his direct line, when there's still a chance of a grandson."

Side by side, they watched the waterfowl.

"We shall proceed like this," Guy said. "Over the next week or so, we do whatever is necessary to make everyone believe this engagement is real, and that we are indeed in love, and if that sometimes means..." He glanced at her mouth, shook his head with a rueful smile, and looked away. "We are sensible adults, in full control of ourselves."

"Indeed."

She thought of Mama, caught in this decades-long struggle between Arabella and her father. She thought of herself being cast out. "I wish I didn't have to do this," she said.

"No, but I cannot stand by and allow an injustice, when I might help put it right. I've come through trickier situations."

In silence, they walked back along the path. Guy retrieved his hat from the statue's head and pulled his gloves back on.

As they neared the lawn, a quartet of workers' boys dashed past, yelling greetings, clutching little boats.

Guy paused to watch them run. "I remember Oliver designed the fastest boats. He was something of a prodigy."

"Yes, I suppose he was."

"Do you ever think about him?"

"We were very young and it was all so long ago."

"I still think of my brother sometimes, though of course he was older than Oliver when we lost him."

How easily he spoke of loss and love, and he didn't collapse in a heap or cause the sky to fall on their heads. Perhaps she should try it.

"I think of Oliver sometimes, I suppose," she ventured.

He nodded. "They never quite go away, though, do they?"

No. Oliver would never leave her, always an empty space at her side, a palpable void in their house.

By the water, the boys finished negotiating the rules of racing and lowered their boats.

"The tall boy is John, grandson of our head gardener,"

Arabella said. "John won a purse in the midsummer footraces this year, and he gave it to his sister Eliza, so she could marry the baker's boy and set up house. His little brother there, Paul, he adores dogs, but the head gardener has been feuding with the kennel master since last century, so I must help him sneak into the kennels in secret."

"They matter to you." His words came out like an accusation. "It's not simply about besting your father or getting an inheritance. The people here matter."

The wind devoured her rueful laugh. "You have a very poor opinion of me, don't you?"

"Honestly, Arabella, I have no idea what to think of you. You hide behind that aloof façade, and make outrageously arrogant statements that you do not mean, and you never defend yourself from accusations, yet your schemes are as undeniable as your ruthlessness in carrying them out." He stepped closer, his eyes intent, as he brushed a hand over her jaw, to rest on her shoulder as lightly as a bird. "Yet you fight for others' well-being, and use your cleverness to help and protect them, and your splendor... Your splendor cannot be denied."

Her heart leaped at his words, at his light, reassuring touch as his fingers skimmed down her arm to catch her hand.

Voices carried toward them on the wind. Papa and the ornithologists were crossing the lawn.

"You're standing very close." She didn't move away.

"I am only holding your hand. We'll do nothing to harm your reputation, while convincing everyone we like each other." He flashed one of his smiles. She wondered if his cheer served to conceal his true thoughts. "I'll flirt with you madly, pay lavish compliments, and every chance I get, I shall..." His eyes dropped, lingered on her lips. "I shall make you blush."

"I don't blush."

"We'll see about that."

His gaze was warm and intent, a lover's bold gaze, to go with his flattery and easy smiles. They were only pretending, for the sake of the witnesses, but it unsettled her nonetheless.

"You're very good at it," she managed to say. "But I don't know how to flirt."

"Then heaven help me if you ever learn."

With a shake of his head, he released her hand and turned aside.

You could teach me, she wanted to say.

But her mouth was dry and her throat was tight, and besides, he had already strolled away.

CHAPTER 16

Sunday being fine, several of the remaining guests decided to walk the mile to church. The small party was mingling on the front steps when Arabella emerged, bonnet in hand, unfamiliar tightness in her chest.

Today, in church, the vicar would call the first banns.

Her eyes went straight to Guy, towering over a chatty, bright-eyed Miss Treadgold. The sun lit the tips of his hair under his hat, and the brass buttons on his blue coat, and the shiny pink ribbons on Miss Treadgold's bonnet.

Look at me and smile, Arabella willed him, *as if the mere sight of me brings you joy.*

But instead, when he saw her, he spread his arms wide in a parody of delight.

"Miss Larke, good morning!" he called. Silence fell, heads swiveled. "I trust you slept well?"

In his eyes lurked a knowing glint, as if he knew she had lain awake half the night, her body heated with the persistent memory of their kiss, and her mind racing to find the words to put things right, before remembering there was no right. She had lost his good opinion before she even realized it mattered.

"I had pleasant dreams," she replied.

"So did I, for they were all of you."

Everyone laughed like they were actors in a comedy at Drury Lane, and Arabella had to perform her role, though it felt wrong to perform in a play where someone else wrote the script.

To make matters worse, Guy crossed to take her hand and lifted her knuckles to his lips.

"A touch excessive, wouldn't you say, Hardbury?" she muttered.

"Not nearly enough," he murmured, then added, more loudly, "Let me help you with your bonnet, oh wondrous fair."

As if this was all they had been waiting for, the group moved off down the laneway in the haphazard manner of such groups, while Guy took her bonnet and positioned it on her head.

"I am perfectly capable of dressing myself," she said, and did not step away.

"I don't doubt it." He tilted his head, frowning, as if the task of positioning her bonnet were a grave responsibility. "But to convince the world that we are besotted, I must offer assistance and you must accept it."

"You mean, I pretend to be weak and helpless to allow you to feel important."

"If you wish, though asking for help does not make one helpless."

"It's only a bonnet, Hardbury."

"And a lovely bonnet it is too."

He took his time tying the ribbons, carelessly brushing her throat and jaw, and when he stepped back to admire his handiwork, she immediately missed his summery scent. She touched her bonnet: perfectly straight.

"Teasing you is excellent sport," he said. "You take on this confused expression, as if no one has ever teased you before and you don't know what to do."

"Of course people have teased me. But they're all rather dead now."

"As I said, excellent sport." He flicked a glance at the door. "While we wait for Freddie, smile at my dazzling charm and do everything in your considerable power to demonstrate your adoration."

Arabella briskly pulled on her gloves. Perhaps flirting with him would indeed be excellent sport, but she hadn't a clue how to flirt and would not make a cake of herself trying.

"Do you require me to recite nonsense too, to nourish your self-regard?" she asked.

"My self-regard requires only that you bat your eyelashes."

"I wouldn't know how."

"Spare me a blush."

"Not on your life."

"And declare yourself devoted to my every pleasure."

"I haven't the faintest notion what your pleasures even are."

He shrugged. "They're very simple. Comfortable boots, hot buttered toast, and the fragrant silk of your unbound hair sweeping over my naked skin."

She made a strange sound, like a baby crow's call.

"Oh dear," he said. "Seems I won that round."

Before she could retort, Freddie came striding out, in her green riding habit and hat, Lady Treadgold at her heels.

"Freddie!" Guy called. "Walk with us?"

Freddie hardly glanced at him as she said, "I'm going riding," and walked in the opposite direction.

"Ah." Guy stopped short. He nodded at his sister's retreating back, a hurt half smile twisting his lips. Without thinking,

Arabella slipped her hand into the crook of his elbow and squeezed his arm.

Lady Treadgold appeared crestfallen. "I am sorry, my lord. But Lady Frederica has been in such a mood recently, I thought one missed Sunday would not matter. She'll take a groom, of course."

"Of course."

Miss Treadgold, who had been waiting nearby, stepped forward. "She received a note."

"Hush, Matilda."

Guy's head whipped around. "What do you mean, a note?"

"I saw her—"

"That note was from me," Lady Treadgold inserted smoothly. "Saying she could go riding instead of attending church today. Now, stop your pouting, Matilda, and let us enjoy this walk."

The pair of them hastened after the rest of the party. Guy stared in the direction Freddie had gone.

"She is an excellent rider and loves horses," Arabella ventured. Offering comfort: another skill she had failed to learn. What might someone kind like Cassandra say?

"Freddie's life has undergone many changes in recent years, and she is trying to find her footing," she tried. "At that age... Recall, you were only a year or so older when you ran away."

"True."

Her hand still curled around his arm, they walked down the laneway. The hedgerows were colorful with autumn fruits: red rose hips and clusters of purple sloe berries. A blue tit bounced among the berries and fluttered away.

Guy yanked off his gloves. She had to let her arm slip from his.

"I suppose it was too much to expect Freddie to care about seeing me again," he said abruptly. "Before, she would run to greet me and we'd head off on some adventure. It was my favorite part of going home." He grabbed some berries, jostled them in his palm. "She was too young to take with me, and I couldn't have stayed."

"You could have written."

"I did. Father never passed on the letters." One by one, he pelted the berries over the hedge into the field. "I wrote to her as soon as I arrived in Naples."

"Why Naples? Did you have friends there?"

"No, I boarded the first boat I could find. But the locals in Naples proved to be very friendly and kind." His expression was wry. "They gave me a few friendly punches and kindly relieved me of my purse and boots."

"How did you survive?"

"Labor, in exchange for food and bed from an elderly couple, and boots from a local cobbler."

Again, he reached into the hedgerow but immediately jerked his hand back with an "ow." He sucked his finger, but, undaunted, once more reached to pick a rose hip.

"After that?"

"Whatever work I could get. Protected caravans in Anatolia as a private guard, joined expeditions in Peru, picked oranges in Spain. That sort of thing."

Arabella studied his profile: the broken nose, the weathered complexion, the hollow cheeks. And as for his body—like a laborer's, according to Juno, who had some experience in the matter of men's bodies. As a youth, Guy had seemed so pleased with himself, so accustomed to having everything his way, that Arabella never dreamed he would even tolerate hardship, let alone welcome it.

"You could have come home at any time, or been welcome in any great house in Europe," she pointed out. "Most people would fall over themselves to assist a future English peer."

"I know, but... That first night in Naples, I walked out of town. I had no money, no shoes, and no idea what to do. I lay down in a field to pass the night and... It was clear, no moon, but millions of stars. And for the first time in my life, I felt free. On nights like that, the sky goes on forever and one's soul expands. It's..." He threw the rose hip at an oak tree. "I felt free."

Arabella navigated a puddle. "So when you said your father would not let you choose your own haircut, you were not exaggerating."

"He hired my staff, decided which shops and establishments I could frequent, and pulled strings to prevent me from getting any employment. Such was his influence that even the Navy wouldn't take me. If anyone else served me, they would suffer for it. So I learned not to stray."

"Good grief. He was obsessed."

"Yes—with turning me into his puppet. The worst of it is, I still miss him at times." He clasped his hands behind his back, but a few steps later was once more plundering the hedge. "I enjoyed my travels. Being challenged, learning what I could do without my money and name. In England..." He glanced at her. "You were the only one whoever challenged me."

"No wonder you despised me."

"But in recent years, I came to miss having a place to come back to. A home, connections, friendships: That's what Father took from me. That's what I want now."

And that was why he wanted a peaceful, amiable bride, someone as unlike Arabella as could be.

"I hope you get what you want," she said sincerely. "One's home should be one's heart and soul."

She could feel his gaze hitting the side of her face. She walked on in silence, her muscles tense.

"You take an interest in my heart and soul?" he finally asked.

"Don't be absurd." She tossed her head haughtily. "The only part of you I find remotely interesting is your body."

Guy stopped short, his jaw dropped. Shooting him a cool look, Arabella continued on toward the bustling churchyard.

His laughter chased her. "Take care, Miss Larke. You'll make *me* blush."

"Oh dear," she called over her shoulder. "Seems I won that round."

A moment later, he fell into step beside her again. "What I truly adore," he said cheerfully, "is how you can say that and still sound prickly."

Well, that was no compliment. Just more of his teasing, his excellent sport at her expense.

"Are you being romantic again?" she drawled. "Do you mean to torture me with dreadful poetry about roses and their thorns?"

"Rose? No, no, no, Arabella, you in no way resemble a rose." He caught her hand, bringing them both to a stop. As he spoke, his bare fingers found the gap between her glove and sleeve, and made slow circles on the sensitive skin of her wrist. "You are prickly like a blackberry bush. Like a tangle of whips and leaves covered in sharp thorns. But among those thorns dangle delicious berries, fruit so enticing that the mere promise of a taste is worth being scratched and snared."

His eyes, playful and warm, possessed hers, as he took her unresisting wrist in both hands, parted the fabric with rough thumbs, and brushed his lips over her skin.

Then he straightened and muttered, "Shouldn't have done that." He shook his head at the people milling about in the churchyard. "I am now feeling decidedly sinful."

"The vicar's drone will soon put us to rights."

She bit her lip at the "us" but he didn't seem to notice.

"Either that or lightning will strike the church," he said.

"Which would solve the problem of our wedding, at least."

"Yes."

Abruptly, he released her. Arabella smoothed her sleeve over her wrist, pressing her other palm against it as if she could burn the feeling of him into her skin like a brand.

A flock of swallows were clustered on the church roof, welcoming churchgoers with their low warble. The flocks were getting larger now; soon they would all fly away.

"Have you given any thought to your departure?" she asked.

Guy took his time answering, pulling on his gloves. "I shall return to London next Monday," he finally said.

In eight days, he would be gone.

He flashed one of his smiles and extended his elbow.

"Now, let's see what happens when the vicar tells everyone we are to be wed. Ten pounds says someone laughs."

THE FOLLOWING EVENING, Lady Belinda made a rare mistake with the table settings and sat Guy and Arabella together.

It was the first time Guy had seen her that day. An army of dressmakers had invaded and taken Arabella prisoner, closely guarded by her friends, Mrs. DeWitt and Miss Bell. Heavy rain trapped everyone inside, except Freddie, apparently, who once more demonstrated her talent for escape. Guy spent the day playing with Ursula.

But now he sat beside his intended at dinner. For the sake of politeness, and their sanity perhaps, they ignored each other and the closeness of their legs under the tablecloth.

Fortunately, he was quickly engrossed in a debate among the ornithologists about whether they had spotted a jack snipe, newly arrived for winter.

"Where do birds go when the seasons change?" Guy asked. "And how do they know?"

Mr. Larke wagged a finger at him. "That, my lord, is one of the marvelous mysteries of migrating birds. Aristotle suggested that birds changed species from season to season. Others said they hibernate, and one fanciful chap even insisted they flew to the moon." He laughed. "We are now certain they stay on Earth, but we are yet to determine where they fly to and from."

"But they are instinctively compelled," one of the others chimed in. "One sees the signs in caged birds. *Zugunruhe*, we call it in German: the restlessness in migratory birds when it is time for them to fly home."

Zugunruhe. It sounded like the restlessness that had plagued Guy during his exile. Except his restlessness persisted, even now he was home.

"If you want to know more, Arabella can point you to the relevant journal. I say," Mr. Larke added. "I'll need to hire someone to make those journals, now my girl will be married and producing sons instead." He grinned at the others. "Little men of science like their grandfather."

"Or a woman of science," Guy felt impelled to say.

Larke laughed again. "Do you truly believe such a thing is possible, Hardbury? Or are you merely trying to charm my daughter?"

"I don't need to charm her. The poor darling is already utterly besotted with me."

Arabella kicked him under the table. An erotic thrill shot up his leg. He pressed his foot against hers and carried on.

"If I am ever fortunate enough to have a daughter, I hope she proves as talented and resourceful as my betrothed."

"Yes, well." Mr. Larke returned to his roast lamb. "You just concentrate on producing these famous children, and we'll see."

Before Guy could loudly express his enthusiasm, Lady Belinda had one of her fortuitously timed coughing fits. This one was so violent she knocked over a glass of water, and the conversation was forgotten in the ensuing fuss.

A distraction plus a tablecloth equaled an opportunity: Guy planted his hand on Arabella's thigh. Her fork jerked and a pea jumped onto the white linen between them. She glared at it.

Such behavior was dangerous, but he could not tear his hand away, not when her thigh felt so perfect through the silk-net of her gown. The gown was a rose color, with little white flowers unfairly embroidered along the edge of her bodice. She shifted under his hand, but not to escape him, he thought. Perhaps to relieve discomfort. Excellent.

"If I were to squish that pea into the cloth, leaving a green, mucky stain, would that make you scream or only swoon?" he asked.

"It would make me gut you with my butter knife."

"But that would create a mess."

"I would gut you very neatly."

He removed his hand to flick the pea toward the flower arrangement, where it hid under the ivy.

"I have saved you from the pea," he said.

"It's still there," she muttered, and he chuckled, and he and his burning hand made it through the rest of dinner without touching her again.

Neither did he look at her, not even when the ladies abandoned the gentlemen to their cigars and port. But upon rejoining the ladies in the drawing room, Guy sought Arabella automatically, as she turned her head and looked right at him. He would swear an understanding passed between them, something as tangible as a silken thread slung across the room between their eyes.

Before he could interrogate the fanciful thought, someone clapped him on the shoulder with impudent familiarity.

It was Sir Walter, miraculously cured of his previously sour mood.

"Felicitations on your engagement, my lord," he said jovially. "I assure you I bear you no hard feelings for breaking our agreement, none whatsoever."

"Knowing that will help me sleep better at night." Guy didn't bother to hide his sarcasm. "Although I might lie awake wondering what agreement we had."

"You were courting our Matilda."

"I was?"

"Why, the day you arrived, you told me you were here to choose a bride."

"And behold, I did choose a bride."

Guy gestured broadly toward Arabella. Although ostensibly in conversation with Mrs. DeWitt and Miss Bell, she was no doubt eavesdropping on every word.

Sir Walter did not spare her a glance. "Of course, of course, and how delighted I am by that choice. But you appreciate my concern, as it is time for our sweet Matilda to marry."

"Freddie too," Guy said, with affected casualness. "Have you given any thought to whom she might marry?"

Sir Walter scratched his chin thoughtfully. "Indeed. A very important responsibility for a guardian. Your sister should marry a peer. I have long held that opinion."

"Have you, Sir Walter? Have you, indeed?"

"Sensible men, such as ourselves, understand that marriage is about improving the whole family. Consider your own example: You had refused to marry Miss Larke, but one glimpse of Vindale Court and you stole her from Lord Sculthorpe. His lordship was not happy about that!"

"Sculthorpe!" The name came out louder than Guy had intended. Arabella's head swiveled. She was listening openly now. "When did you speak to Lord Sculthorpe?"

"What? Speak? Never! Not seen him since he left. Purely my supposition, my lord. My assumption. My presumption." Sir Walter accepted a glass of port. "Although you did have a score to settle with him, did you not? Years ago, he stole your sweetheart, and you returned the favor. Of course, your first betrothed ended up as a courtesan. Let's hope that doesn't happen again!"

He smiled broadly and sipped his drink.

"My dear Sir Walter, I do believe you have impugned the honor of my betrothed. What a dilemma this poses. Honor says I must defend her, yet the law says I must not shoot you. Which course would you recommend I take?"

He gulped and was spluttering, "It was a jest, I mean, my lord," when Arabella drifted over to them.

"You are looking decidedly warm, Sir Walter. Perhaps you ought not stand so close to the fire." She turned to Guy. "Are you two enjoying your conversation?"

"Not really," Guy said, although in truth he was enjoying himself immensely. "I am debating whether or not to shoot Sir Walter."

That man emitted a squeaky laugh. "His lordship jests."

"I should hope so," Arabella said. "It's terribly inconvenient when guests shoot each other, plays havoc with the seating arrangements. It would be especially unsporting with Sir Walter's son arriving next week. Which day will the much-acclaimed Mr. Humphrey Treadgold be joining us, Sir Walter?"

Sir Walter's brow accumulated a few more beads of sweat. "I'm afraid our Humphrey has been unavoidably detained."

"What a shame," Arabella said serenely. "I was so looking forward to meeting him. Weren't you, Hardbury?"

"Very much."

Their eyes met. Again, Guy felt that sense of understanding.

"I do feel a trifle warm," Sir Walter said. "If you'll excuse me, my lord, Miss Larke."

As Sir Walter scuttled across the room, Arabella flicked a glance to the door. Guy caught her meaning, and together they casually drifted out into the deserted hallway.

"He knows the marriage license is gone but he means to brazen it out," Guy said, standing close and speaking softly, though no one was there to overhear.

"Yet they have given Mama no indication that they intend to leave."

"And he was in a very jovial mood. Until we ruined it."

"Suspicious, isn't it?" A smile danced in Arabella's eyes. "No one who is that cheerful can possibly be up to any good."

"I say, you make a useful sort of ally," Guy said. "I like having you on my side."

She opened her mouth to reply, when Miss Bell slipped out of the drawing room into the hallway.

"I'm glad I caught you two alone," Miss Bell said. "At dinner, Sir Walter was insisting there is something odd about your engagement and that his lordship actually means to marry Miss Treadgold. It might be nothing, but Cassandra and I thought you should know."

"Thank you, Juno," Arabella said, exchanging a look with Guy. "Sir Walter appears to be scheming something, but it remains to be seen what."

Miss Bell's eyes darted back and forth between the two of them. Then, with a mischievous smile, she said, "Carry on," and skipped back into the drawing room, blonde ringlets bouncing.

"Well, well, well," Guy said, once they were alone again. "We shall have to improve our game, if Sir Walter is running around saying our engagement isn't real."

"It isn't real," Arabella murmured.

"But he mustn't know that."

She stood against the wall, head high, back straight, as flawlessly elegant as ever, the rose silk-net of her gown drawing out the soft pink in her complexion.

Quick glances confirmed they had no witnesses. He edged closer to her.

"Guy. What are you doing?"

"Circumstances demand that I kiss you. Stop being obtuse."

"Someone could see."

"My point exactly." He traced the embroidered flowers, sliding his finger along the edge of her bodice. "After all, if we were to kiss, no one would doubt our commitment."

It would be a mistake to kiss her again, especially here and now, but Guy could not step back. Perhaps Arabella would be sensible and stop this—but she only cast a glance down the empty hallway, before straightening his lapel.

"I suppose that does make sense," she said slowly.

"Very rational, I thought."

"It's important to be rational about these matters."

"I've always thought so."

"So I expect this to be a rational kiss," she said.

"It will be the most rational kiss in the world."

He trailed his wayward hand up her throat to cup her cheek, and her fingers fluttered onto his jaw. As she closed her eyes, he breathed in her scent, basked in her warmth, and touched his lips to hers, in a lingering caress, potent with promise. It reminded him of their very first kiss in London. Everything had been wrong that night, but this, now, felt as if they were finally getting it right.

When he lifted his head, his eyes searched hers, though he could not have said what he sought.

"Well?" he asked.

Her tongue darted out to touch her lips, and she swallowed visibly. "Well what?"

"How does that compare to the other kisses?"

"I…" Her eyes shifted past him, widened slightly. Damn. They had developed a witness. A servant, no doubt, who would be smart enough to vanish like smoke. But that servant's presence was enough to make Arabella retreat into her usual poise.

"Of all the kisses I have ever received…"

"Yes?" he prompted, not turning.

"That was the most…"

"Yes?"

"Recent."

Guy chuckled. "For someone who claims not to know how to flirt, you are very good at it." He brushed a knuckle against her throat. "I'd like to point out that your pulse is racing."

"And I'd like to point out that my mother is watching."

"Ah."

Her eyes danced with laughter. Fighting his own smile, Guy backed away from her and turned to face the intruder. Lady Belinda stood with her hands clasped, chastening him with her serene, direct gaze.

He bowed. "Lady Belinda."

"Lord Hardbury."

He pivoted and strode away. The door to the drawing room gaped open, but his senses still burned with Arabella's closeness, so he kept on walking, seeking the respite and release of his room.

CHAPTER 17

"Oh, what a work of art!"

Juno's voice was threaded with awe, and she burst into activity, swiftly moving her charcoal across a leaf of paper.

Arabella did not need to look at that page to know what Juno was drawing.

Or whom, rather.

Arabella, Juno, and Cassandra had rounded a corner of the abbey ruins just in time to see Guy leap onto a four-foot-high crumbling wall, in a single bound like a cat. He paused, swaying in the sunlight, finding his balance, his face bright with simple, boyish fun. He was picturesquely framed by a high, distant arch, and a cluster of purple Michaelmas daisies rioted at his feet.

One gave Michaelmas daisies to say farewell.

"Beware distractions, Juno," Arabella managed to say, though she might as well have been warning herself. That morning, she had thrown herself into organizing an impromptu outing for the small party of remaining guests in a vain effort to keep her mind off that oh-so-irrational kiss of the evening before. "Perhaps you had forgotten that your assignment today is to draw the abbey ruins."

"I *am* drawing the ruins." Juno's swift, confident strokes did not pause, as Guy's image appeared under her hand. "I just happen to be drawing that portion of the ruins that have an athletic man prancing about on them. I would just as likely draw a bird or a cat had one landed on that spot, but since Lord Hardbury has been so obliging as to make a spectacle of himself, well, who am I to ignore Nature's bounty? *These beauteous forms...*" She glanced sideways at Arabella. "Poetry. Sorry."

"So you should be."

Guy was moving nimbly along the wall now, testing the stone, choosing his next move. A sky lark landed on a high wall nearby and he paused to admire it.

Breathtaking.

Good grief. More wretched poetry, and a nonsensical phrase to boot, but how else to describe this tightness in her chest? This bittersweet ache, as if all her breath had indeed been stolen, leaving her limbs light with a desperate need for air.

He could have been mine.

The thought jolted through her, with a sensation as physical as if she were falling.

A life with Guy could have been hers. A potentially beautiful gift had been bestowed upon her, but she had failed to see its worth, amidst her struggle to understand and control her own life. This breathtaking man and the life of joy he seemed to promise— they were as far out of her reach as that sky lark, and that was nobody's fault but her own.

If she had gone about life differently? Become the amiable lady her father demanded, the lady of Guy's dreams, less complicated, less combative, less herself?

But she didn't want to be different. She didn't want to change herself to please others. What she wanted was—oh, heaven help her, she was turning into a ninny!—but she wanted to be special to him. In truth, and not as a game.

"I wish I could do that," came a voice from her side.

It was Freddie, watching Guy wistfully, her fingers absently tearing a Michaelmas daisy to shreds. Glancing around, Arabella saw that she had unconsciously drifted nearer to Guy, leaving Juno and Cassandra behind.

"Climb the walls," Freddie clarified. "We went to see some acrobats and I've been practicing at home. I can leap and pivot mid-air, and even do somersaults and land safely."

"If you had thought to wear your Turkish trousers today, you could have impressed us all."

With a sigh, Freddie flicked away the dregs of destroyed daisy. "Lady Treadgold found them before I finished sewing them and took them away."

"You ought to take them back again." At Arabella's meaningfully raised brows, Freddie's expression brightened. "I'll speak to Holly about arranging that. And if you can spare a few coins, I daresay Holly can find a maid willing to finish sewing them somewhere Lady Treadgold cannot see."

A grin spread over Freddie's face as they turned back to study the walls. Guy leaped across a gap and landed effortlessly. How lovely it would be to take an action with such easy confidence and without first having to consider the forty-seven different ways it might be done. How lovely if she had the right to explore his body again. How lovely if he searched for her, smiled at her, acknowledged her as special to him.

"It's like doing a puzzle, choosing where to put one's feet, calculating the leap," Freddie said. "But it's better than a puzzle, because one's whole body is involved, and the risk of falling makes it more fun."

"That's the kind of thing Guy says," Arabella pointed out. "The two of you are very similar, you know."

Freddie didn't respond, behaving as if she wasn't listening. Arabella suspected Freddie heard everything and only pretended not to.

"You would know that about Guy if you spent more time with him, instead of riding off alone," Arabella added. "And he wants to spend more time with you."

Freddie shrugged. "What's the point? I'll hardly see him."

"He'll make time for you. He is trying to win custody."

"He's only trying to defeat Father. He doesn't really care."

"But he does. It matters to him, Freddie. Truly. For so many years, he has been horribly alone." She sought the words, needing Freddie to understand, needing to give Guy this one gift: the happiness he sought from family. "He's all heart, you know. Heart and muscle. He believes in things. He believes in them so fully he doesn't have to think about them first. He already knows what to do."

Her eyes followed him as he trod the wall. He would never be hers. How long would she be haunted by this strange nostalgia for a future she could never have?

She turned back to Freddie. "He believes in you like that. In family, in looking after other people. He'll fight for you, with all his heart and muscle. He'll fight for you to be happy."

Freddie was looking at her oddly. "He doesn't know what makes me happy."

"Then tell him."

What a hypocrite she was! Easy advice, when she had no idea how to speak her own truths to Guy, when she wasn't even sure what they were. But if only she could touch him, as he had touched her last night, and then...

Seduce him. There was an idea. Would it be such a terrible

thing to do? In less than a week, he would be gone, and they both understood the rules of honor no longer applied; he would feel no obligation to her, and she would feel no shame. A passing pleasure. A souvenir. To let herself pretend that he was hers, if only for one more hour. Of course, if he rejected her, that *would* be terrible.

Freddie beheaded another hapless daisy and set about shredding this one too. "I told him I don't want to marry, but he just said of course I want to marry, but that I could choose to whom."

Arabella considered. "You're wealthy enough not to marry if you don't want to, but you don't have to decide yet. Married women have more freedom, and you might yet find a man you like. You said no one has even tried to court you."

"It wasn't that great."

Arabella looked at her sharply. "Who was it?"

"Who was what?"

"Who courted you?"

"No one. It's nothing. I'm fairly sure I don't want to marry."

Guy bounded off the wall, landing easily on the grass and exchanging a friendly word with one of the other men.

"You know yourself best," Arabella said to Freddie, as Guy rounded the wall and disappeared from view. "Only... Don't be so sure that you miss a wonderful opportunity, or say the wrong thing at the wrong time, and ruin something that might have been precious."

GUY WAS NOT ENTIRELY sure how he came to be traipsing down the worn, uneven stone steps into the abbey crypt, with a lantern held aloft and four ladies in his wake.

"I do hope there are no ghosts!" he heard Miss Treadgold call from somewhere further up the stairs, her voice tremulous.

"If there are, they are very friendly," came the amiable assurance of Mrs. DeWitt, who carried the other lantern. Guy had met her husband in London, a magnetically energetic man who had deftly managed to offend everyone in the room. Odd pair, Mr. and Mrs. DeWitt. No wonder they lived apart.

"We are safe with Lord Hardbury to protect us," Miss Bell chimed in. "His lordship will not hesitate to battle the dead should they decide to rise from their graves."

"Not sure that's helping," Guy muttered.

Immediately behind him, Arabella laughed softly, and Guy resisted the urge to twist around and share in that laughter. He had vowed to ignore her today, to stop his foolish, flirtatious games, but still he always seemed to know where she was. He was helplessly aware of her presence, as if she had become some kind of necessary function, the way one knew that one's heart was beating or that one's stomach required food.

This infatuation will pass, he had told himself. *This game will end*, he had said.

Well, the infatuation hadn't passed, and the game did not feel like a game anymore.

"You have nothing to fear, Miss Treadgold," Arabella called. "The dead are more frightened of us than we are of them. Are you still with us?"

"Oh yes, I am determined to be brave."

"Your courage is admirable."

At the last few stairs, the air grew noticeably colder and the smell of ancient stone washed over him. Guy held the lantern higher as they filed into the dark cavern, the light outlining the sarcophagi and statues of the women whose bones lay within. Guy's boots echoed on the stone floor as he wandered into the darkness, sensing Arabella's presence beside him. Mrs. DeWitt headed in the other direction, leading the other two under the arches, their heads swathed in the lantern's glow, every footstep, murmur, and rustle of fabric amplified.

"Are you frightened?" he murmured to Arabella. "Will you faint? Shall I hold your hand?"

"I assure you, I am quite all right."

"But I am not. If you don't hold my hand, I shall swoon with fear, and you'll have to carry me out."

"Nonsense. I would have no qualms about leaving you here."

So Guy did the obvious thing: He shut the flap on the lantern, sinking their part of the crypt into darkness. A glow revealed the location of the others.

"You cannot be serious," Arabella said.

He laughed softly, and remembered too late he had vowed to stop these games. But neither could he move. In the darkness, robbed of sight, all his other senses sharpened with awareness of Arabella. He knew when she breathed, when she shifted, when she drew ever so slightly closer.

Something touched his neck. Warm fingers, teasing the hair at his nape. Heat shivered down his spine. A strangled sound escaped him.

"Oh! What was that noise?" came Miss Treadgold's cry.

The lantern glow showed the others moving back toward them. Arabella shifted again. Her hand landed on his stomach. Inched downward. Oh, so help him, she was going to master him at his own game!

Now her fingers nudged his waistband. He emitted another strangled sound; she responded with a muffled laugh.

"Was that a ghost?" whimpered Miss Treadgold. "Oh, there are dead people everywhere!"

In the dim light of the other lantern, Guy could make out the shape of Miss Treadgold, hugging herself, eyes fixed on a statue of a long-dead abbess.

Arabella's hand disappeared. Guy opened his lantern to increase the light.

"Miss Treadgold, are you all right?" Mrs. DeWitt asked. "It can be a bit overwhelming, can't it? We're all used to it, as we played here as children."

"If you are frightened, we can go back upstairs," Arabella said.

Miss Treadgold didn't move. "All those bones..."

"Stars above, she's frozen with fear," Guy muttered.

He lunged across the space toward her, took her elbow, and guided her up the stairs. Absently, he murmured encouraging words but his mind was on Arabella, teasing him in the dark, taking her playful revenge for his games under the table the night before.

Back in the sunlight, he handed off the lantern to a footman and turned back to Miss Treadgold, who, it turned out, was neither pale nor trembling.

"You must think me silly," she said with a pretty smile.

"Not at all. It's very becoming," he said automatically, at which she launched into a monologue about butterflies or flowers or something. Guy hardly heard a word. How easy she was. She made no trouble and demanded nothing, apart from the occasional rescue from nonexistent ghosts. She was precisely the kind of lady he had dreamed about these past lonely years, as he lay awake on hard beds or in rough tents and wove visions of his ideal life back home. He had been so sure that was what he wanted, so why could Miss Treadgold not stir up his blood and hold him in her thrall? Why could she not possess his mind and brighten his world and pull him in a hundred different directions all at once?

The monologue cut off abruptly. "Oh, do excuse me, my lord. My aunt needs me," Miss Treadgold said and darted away.

Miss Treadgold apparently had magical powers, for Lady Treadgold and her needs were nowhere to be seen. But there were Arabella and her friends, emerging from the crypt.

Once more, Guy reminded himself to put distance between them, but she looked right at him, as if she was as aware of him as he was of her.

Guy waited, as still as one of those statues in the crypt. Once her friends had gone and they were alone, his limbs unfroze. They advanced toward each other, pacing as carefully as duelists on the field. Her expression was remote. She was shutting him out again. He should welcome that, but instead he felt a peculiar ache in his chest.

He had discovered so much of her true character. He had unleashed her passion, unlocked her smiles. But he was not satisfied; he wanted to know her more.

They stopped a yard apart.

"Pleased with yourself, Hardbury?" she drawled. "For saving the damsel in distress?"

"Are you not impressed with my heroics?"

"You played right into her hands."

"The poor girl was terrified."

"And I suppose you find that very becoming."

Her tone was sharp. Her shoulders were stiff, her eyebrows issuing a challenge.

"Well, well, well." Guy clapped his hands once. "You are jealous."

Her eyes narrowed. "Don't be absurd. I never get jealous. I simply have limited patience when otherwise sensible men turn into fools over a woman."

Indeed, Guy was turning into a fool over a woman, but that woman was not Matilda Treadgold.

"But I suppose you cannot help yourself," she added. "What with her trembling need and her smiles and her *blushes*..."

"You *are* jealous."

"Good grief, Guy, I'd hardly be jealous of a few blushes. But do try to recall that we are meant to be engaged, and it hardly helps appearances if you insist on flirting with another lady."

Her tone was icy, but in her eyes lurked that bleak vulnerability, undermining her proud façade.

Tenderness pierced him. Curse him for his blather, when it was neither blushes nor jealousy he sought.

He wanted Arabella to trust him enough to let him inside her walls. To reveal herself to him of her own free will, to lower the drawbridge and invite him in.

"I don't care whether or not you blush," he said gently. "All I want is to know you."

Her chin jerked up. Her brow creased with confusion. She opened her mouth to speak, but all that emerged was a huff of breath. She tried again; again, no words. Finally, with an impatient shake of her head, she whirled around and marched away.

Guy stared at her stiff, retreating back, resisting the urge to run after her. He didn't fully understand what had just happened, but he understood this: If he wasn't careful, Arabella was going to break his heart.

CHAPTER 18

Later that evening, when Arabella was dressing for dinner, Holly warned her that the Treadgold family appeared to be brewing a plot.

The maid's suspicions made for a happy distraction. Hours after that scene outside the crypt, Arabella was still mortified over her outburst.

"All I want is to know you," Guy had said. Well, he knew now, didn't he? He knew that proud, perfect Arabella Larke was turning pathetic over a man. How embarrassing!

"'Twas something that Eliza said," Holly explained, as she pinned up Arabella's hair. "Eliza said that Tabitha said that she heard Lady Treadgold say something to Miss Treadgold about biding their time and acting at night."

And then, Holly reported, she'd heard from Ernest that Sir Walter's man had asked Lord Hardbury's man about his lordship's habits at night. "That is," Holly said that Ernest said that Sir Walter's man said, "if Sir Walter wanted to find his lordship at night, where might be a good place to look?"

And then the other Eliza—the Treadgolds' Eliza, that was, not the Larkes' Eliza—well, Mrs. Ramsay said that the Treadgolds' Eliza said that Lady Treadgold said that Miss Treadgold would not need her that night, and, as Holly said that Mrs. Ramsay said, "Whoever heard of a young lady not needing her maid at night?"

Who indeed.

Arabella praised Holly for the intelligence gleaned through the remarkable network. "I shall petition Mama to give the whole household an extra bonus," she added.

Holly thanked her. "We won't say no to that, but... We like Miss Treadgold, she's always pleasant and polite, but it's just not right, is it?"

No, indeed.

So it wasn't *jealousy* but perfectly justifiable suspicion that made Arabella pay special attention to Miss Treadgold that evening, as their much-reduced party sat in the drawing room. Miss Treadgold was reading, and Lady Treadgold and Mama talked quietly as they sewed. Guy was writing a letter, Sir Walter and Freddie played cards with Mr. Larke and the last of the ornithologists, and Arabella played pianoforte, a simple piece she knew so well that she didn't need to think. From this excellent position, she could see everyone else.

Then Guy finished his letter, stood, and started across the room.

Arabella looked at Lady Treadgold, who shot a look at Miss Treadgold, and Miss Treadgold rearranged her shawl. The movement dislodged something in her lap, something shiny and green, which slithered onto the floor.

A ribbon.

A ribbon falling right at Guy's feet.

Guy stopped walking. Miss Treadgold kept reading. Lady Treadgold shot a look at Mama.

But Mama was studying her sewing and did not see.

Arabella glanced back just as Guy scooped up the shiny, green ribbon.

Of course he did.

He twirled it in his fingers, shot a glance at Arabella, and dangled the ribbon in front of Miss Treadgold like she was a kitten and he wanted to play.

"Miss Treadgold," he said. "I do believe you have dropped a ribbon."

"Oh, did I? Thank you for picking it up, my lord."

"I am honored to do you a service."

Oh, good grief.

Miss Treadgold reached for the ribbon and Guy jerked it away as though she really were a kitten, and he grinned, and she smiled and said, "Oh, Lord Hardbury, you are too wicked!"

Still grinning, Guy flicked another glance at Arabella, but Arabella looked away, which was why she saw Miss Treadgold shoot a look at Lady Treadgold, who passed the look on to Mama.

But Mama was studying her hands and did not see.

"This is a very pretty ribbon." This time, Guy let her have it. "But the color does not match your gown. What is it for?"

Arabella hit the wrong key. If he was that interested in the girl's ribbons, he should just jolly well marry her!

"I am using it to mark my place in my book."

"And what is your book?"

Arabella hit another wrong key but no one seemed to notice. Miss Treadgold kept her eyes lowered, and yet again Guy glanced at Arabella, so Arabella looked away. Which was why she saw that Lady Treadgold seemed set to have a fit, her gaze was shifting so rapidly between Guy and Matilda and Mama, and then Lady Treadgold saw Arabella looking and turned away, and Arabella looked at Mama.

But Mama was studying a teacup and did not see.

"It is a book on Italy, my lord," Miss Treadgold said.

"Why, so it is! Are you interested in Italy?"

"I think it is the most fascinating place in the world. I have heard that you spent some time in Italy, my lord. Perhaps you could entertain me with your experiences."

"Miss Treadgold, it would be my immense pleasure to tell you all about it."

Again, Guy looked straight at Arabella, who again looked away, so again saw Miss Treadgold look at Lady Treadgold, who again looked at Mama, who again was looking absolutely anywhere else at all and so, of course, did not see.

"Perhaps we could do that later this evening, my lord."

"Of course." Guy strolled over to Arabella, who kept playing the pianoforte determinedly. "You are not reading tonight, Miss Larke?"

"Why on earth would I read? I already know everything worth knowing."

He chuckled and sauntered off. She did not look at him, nor at anyone else either, because she did not care who looked at whom.

If there was a plot to trap him into marrying Matilda, she ought to let him be jolly well trapped, and it would serve him right for being cabbage-headed enough to pick up ribbons in the first place.

But later that night, when the house was settling, Holly gave her a nudge, and Arabella discovered a need to loiter in the hallway outside Matilda Treadgold's chamber, with her ear very close to the door. And so she heard a short conversation that sounded something like:

"Hurry up, Matilda! His lordship is alone in the Reading Room right now."

"But Aunt Frances, I don't think this is right. Lord Hardbury is already engaged—"

"Hush. You will thank me for it when you're wed."

If the conversation continued, Arabella didn't hear it, for she was running along the hallway and leaping down the steps and skidding around the corner and hurtling down more hallways and through the music room and around another corner—and, good grief, was Vindale Court always this large?—until she reached the hallway door to the Reading Room.

At which point, she stopped, smoothed her skirts, patted her hair, breathed in, breathed out, and calmly stepped inside.

Guy was sitting by the fire, reading and sipping a brandy, with a green-and-gold banyan thrown over his shirt, his hair tousled, and his stockinged feet stretched out before him. He managed to look both dignified and rumpled, both potent and harmless, and the sight of him made Arabella think of domestic comforts, and long winter nights, and kisses and smiles and the hollow in her heart.

He looked up. The sight of her still did not make him smile.

"Are you coming in or guarding the doorway forever?" he said.

Which reminded her why she was there.

"You have to get out," she hissed. "Get out, get out!"

She shut the door to the hall and dashed over to shoo him out like a troublesome cat. Like a troublesome cat, he resisted.

"What have I done now?" he said.

She tugged his book and drink out of his hands and dropped them onto the table, then opened the connecting door to the library and peered in. It was empty and dark but for the last coals glowing in the hearth.

"Go in there." He had not moved. "Guy, for heaven's sake. Hide in the library. It's not safe here."

He stood. "Safe? What—"

"Matilda Treadgold is coming to get you."

"Is she coming with guns or knives?"

"Worse. I wager you a thousand pounds that in less than two minutes, Matilda Treadgold will come sailing through that other door, wearing nothing but a nightgown and a pretty smile, and she will draw you into a conversation about Italy, and who knows what else besides, and at a pertinent moment, the door will open again and every matron in the west of England will come flying in!"

He wandered toward the library, lazily amused. "I don't need a thousand pounds. Can we wager something else?"

"Do you *want* to marry Matilda Treadgold? Is that it? Do you want to be caught in a compromising position with her and be marched to the altar?"

"Of course not. But—"

"Shush. Now go."

She pushed him into the library, shut the door, and threw herself into the still-warm cushions of his chair. She picked up his brandy glass and arranged his book on her lap.

The door to the hallway eased open.

For the sake of her performance, Arabella focused on the words on the page, and almost dropped the book. Oh good grief, what *was* he reading?

A click: She looked up to see Matilda Treadgold turning around from closing the door, Matilda Treadgold wearing nothing but a nightgown and a grimace of horror.

"Good evening, Miss Treadgold," Arabella said calmly.

"Miss Larke! What—" Miss Treadgold looked around. "What are you doing here?"

"This is the Reading Room and I am reading."

Her eyes narrowed. "And you are drinking brandy?"

"Aren't you cold, wandering around in only your nightgown?" Arabella said, dodging her question. "Who knew whom you might have encountered?"

"I could not sleep, so I came downstairs looking for a book. I did not expect to encounter anyone."

Arabella raised an eyebrow.

"What?" Miss Treadgold sounded almost belligerent. "Don't you believe me?"

"Of course I believe you. It happens all the time." Arabella put down the book and glass and crossed to join her at the shelves. "You could have tried the library. Why the Reading Room?"

Miss Treadgold's eyes darted every which way. "I wanted a book I could read."

"A book you can read. Those are my favorite too."

"I mean, there are two kinds of book, aren't there? There are the books that one reads and the books that one doesn't. And it seemed to me that the books that find their way into the Reading Room must be the kind of books that one reads."

Even Arabella could not argue with this impeccable logic.

With a tight smile, Miss Treadgold turned to peruse the shelves. On one shelf perched a stuffed canary that had somehow wandered out of Papa's study. Oh dear: The poor girl had said how much she loathed and feared the dead birds! To spare her, Arabella went to move the canary out of sight.

But Miss Treadgold saw the canary first. She paused, staring at it—and then touched a finger to the bird's little yellow head. Her expression rapt, she stroked the feathers down its back and caressed the scaly feet and talons, which only a week ago she had described as hideous.

"The truth is, I like the birds. The dead ones, I mean," Miss

Treadgold said abruptly, her bright eyes on the canary as she petted its cold, feathered head. "*Especially* the dead ones."

"The dead ones. I see."

"And the crypt too. I was only pretending to be scared earlier. The truth is, I go down there by myself. I like looking at the sarcophagi and thinking about their bones."

"Their bones. I see."

"But Aunt Frances says I ought not like dead things, like stuffed birds and bones in the crypt," Miss Treadgold went on in uneasy tones. "She says it is not becoming and that men don't like women who like dead things. But it isn't as though I like *all* dead things."

Arabella studied her. Miss Treadgold was still undeniably amiable and likable—yet rendered interesting and new, with her surprisingly Gothic taste for the macabre so at odds with her ribbons and blushes. To think: All this time, Matilda Treadgold had been performing too. And one day, Matilda would perform her way to the altar, where she would marry a man who did not know her, and she would perform for the rest of her life.

"If you like dead things, you should say so," Arabella said. "That is who you are, Matilda, and you ought not conceal your nature to please others."

"I couldn't! A young lady must not express opinions or disagree with anyone, Aunt Frances says."

"You don't have to do everything they say."

An anxious look entered her brown eyes. "They took me in as a child and have looked after me; I would have nothing without them. My best way of repaying them is to marry well. That's why I... You understand."

Arabella understood: It was an apology for this plot to trap Guy. "I understand. It's all right. But you owe them nothing. They should have looked after you simply because it was the right thing to do. You must—"

The door to the hallway flew open. Lady Treadgold hurtled into the room, Mama drifting along in her wake.

"Matilda, I— Miss Larke, you—" Lady Treadgold stared at them both. "What is going on here?"

Arabella gave her haughtiest stare. "It's not what you think. I never touched the girl!"

A startled expression crossed Lady Treadgold's face and Mama pressed two fingers to her temple, as though she had a headache coming on. Matilda was fighting a smile.

"Is that—" Lady Treadgold's eagle eyes snagged on the table. "*Brandy*? There has been a *man* here!"

Arabella could only pray Lady Treadgold did not read the title of Guy's book, but Mama moved more quickly, casually drifting across the room to shake her head at the glass.

"Arabella, darling, really. I have told you before not to drink that." She picked up Guy's book and glanced at the page. Her eyes widened and she hastily dropped it, then turned back to the other women. "I hope I can count on your discretion in this matter."

They promised to be discreet.

"Now, Lady Treadgold," Mama went on. "What was it you wanted me to see?"

"I must have the wrong room."

"You said the Reading Room. This is the Reading Room."

"I meant the room with the peacocks. Isn't that the Reading Room?"

"No. The room with the peacocks is the Peacock Room." Mama's eyes met Arabella's and skated on without giving away a thing. "My dear child, look at you in only your nightgown. You must be freezing. And who knew whom you might have encountered."

"I couldn't sleep," Matilda recited doggedly. "I came down for a book. I did not expect to encounter anyone."

Lady Treadgold stepped forward. "Don't you believe her?"

"Of course I believe her. It happens *all* the time." Mama smiled. "Perhaps this excitement has made you sleepy."

"Yes, come along, Matilda," Lady Treadgold said and ushered her niece out.

Arabella folded her hands and waited for her scolding.

"Are you heading for bed, Arabella?"

"I thought I might sit a little longer. In the quiet. Alone. Reading my book. And...drinking my brandy."

Mama shook her head. "Take care, my dear."

"Yes, Mama."

"Take very good care."

And the door clicked shut behind her.

CHAPTER 19

Arabella counted out two minutes on the ticking clock before she opened the door connecting the Reading Room to the library.

"Guy?" she whispered.

A shadow detached itself from a nearby chair. Guy sauntered back in and leaned against the door to study her. In another world, she would have the courage to go to him. In this world, she did not move.

"You never touched the girl?" he repeated.

She laughed. "That whole situation was ludicrous. And you owe me a thousand pounds."

"I owe you something." He peered at his nearly empty glass. "I hear you have a drinking problem."

"Mama was covering for you. Ladies don't drink brandy. Besides, it's vile."

"Have a drink with me anyway, to celebrate my near escape from a life of Sir Walter Treadgold."

"Not escape Matilda?"

Shooting her a glance, he went to pour drinks. "I like Matilda. A man could do worse. Her main drawback is her dreadful family."

"Hm."

Enough said. She would not embarrass herself with another outburst he might misinterpret as jealousy.

She should leave. But it was warm here in the Reading Room. And intimate, when the house was asleep and the firelight was bright. Guy was in a good mood, and that escapade had left Arabella enlivened.

She lowered herself to the settee.

"So that was Sir Walter's scheme," Guy mused, with a rattle of the brandy decanter. "Why he was so pleased with himself."

"It wasn't a very good scheme," Arabella said. "It is risky, hackneyed, and difficult to execute."

"Tried and true."

Guy didn't seem bothered. But then he was not a schemer, so he had no talent for spotting others' schemes, or the flaws in their schemes.

Neither did he admire clever schemers, such as herself.

"Sir Walter could be in serious trouble when you reveal his intentions for Freddie," Arabella explained. "Yet all he was banking on was a pretty girl in a nightgown? And what about Freddie? I cannot believe he would so easily abandon his attempts to take advantage of his guardianship."

Guy shrugged. "If I had to marry Matilda, he would be safe, as I wouldn't press charges against my wife's nearest relative. Or maybe he thinks I would agree to marry Freddie off to his son."

"Either way, it was poorly planned and executed. I am disappointed in them. This charade would be more stimulating if we had worthier adversaries."

"We have each other." Handing her a brandy, which she took

without thinking, he dropped onto the cushions beside her. "If you were any worthier or more adversarial, I'm not sure I'd survive the experience."

"I'm not sure I can survive such flattery." She laughed, but something still niggled. "I thought he would be more sophisticated than that."

"You give the man too much credit. He is nothing more than a rank opportunist. Not a mastermind like you."

He sprawled back and studied her thoughtfully over his drink. Avoiding his gaze, she ran her finger around the rim of the cut-crystal glass, achingly aware of his legs, long and strong and close. They might never have a moment like this again. What if she... No, she would not attempt to seduce him again, not after her embarrassingly clumsy effort in the crypt.

"And so you rescued me from her," he said. "Are you determined that I do not marry anyone else?"

"Didn't you wish to be completely free to choose your own bride? By all means, if Matilda Treadgold is your choice, I'll merrily plan the wedding myself."

"She's very pleasant. Easy."

Arabella studied the reflected firelight dueling in her glass. He was after another reaction. Not a chance.

"Exactly what you claimed to want," she said.

"And you claimed to have a high opinion of her."

"I do." She cast him a cool look. "In particular, I admire the way she makes you men fall over yourselves to do her bidding."

"You would like that. But at least she only makes us pick up ribbons. If we were to do your bidding, the streets would be running with blood."

It was only a jest, of course, the sort she had never minded before, but now it stung. Guy had said he wanted to know her; odds were, he wouldn't like what he saw. What a strange turn! People often didn't like her; it had never bothered her before. Soon, he would be gone, still thinking poorly of her.

"Guy, I have to tell you... That I..."

"That you?"

"That I'm really rather harmless."

He fired off a rough round of laughter. Frustrated, she rapped her fingernail against her glass, as if its hollow ring might embolden her like a war drum.

"You persist in thinking the worst of me," she said. "But you see I... I never..."

I never meant to hurt anyone. But sometimes I get frightened and my pride takes over and I say things I do not mean.

"You never what?"

"I've never stabbed anyone. Or poisoned them. Or shot them," she said.

"How very restrained of you."

"I've never tried to trap anyone into marriage by running around in my nightgown. I know you think I did, but I didn't. And I've never..."

His glass hovered at his lips, but his eyes did not leave hers. Nervousness—*that* was this unfamiliar sensation! How horrid it felt, to want someone's good opinion, to care so much what another person thought that she had to say these things. How did people live like this?

"Go on," he said softly.

Again, she tried to shoot out the words, but all she said was, "And I've never dropped a ribbon in my life."

GUY SIPPED HIS BRANDY, not taking his eyes off Arabella. She perched on the edge of the settee like a hawk about to take flight, gripping her glass so tightly it might crack.

Her words were nonsense, but Arabella never talked nonsense.

For all his flippancy, Guy was fascinated by her keen intelligence, bright and sharp and multifaceted like a diamond. He admired her gift for seeing several moves ahead, whereas he could only react to the now.

If she was talking about dropping ribbons, the topic must have some meaning for her.

She was trusting him, after all. With something she could not express but that mattered so much she betrayed her nervousness. He simply had to listen.

"But I suppose that's why you like Matilda Treadgold," Arabella went on. "Because she makes men feel strong and important and necessary."

"Men are strong and important and necessary."

"Well, good. Who wants a man who is weak and insignificant and useless? But I don't see why a man cannot feel strong and important and necessary all by himself, without running around picking up a lady's ribbons."

Arabella scowled at her brandy, as though something had gone terribly wrong and it was all the spirit's fault.

Guy had picked up Miss Treadgold's ribbon that evening with no illusions about why that ribbon had fallen at his feet, but he had done it to tease Arabella. It seemed his every action concerned Arabella these days, driven by this intemperate longing that simmered beneath his skin.

"So Matilda..." he prompted.

"Exactly. *Matilda*." Arabella's hands twitched as if she meant to hurl her glass. "She's so very good at dropping ribbons. But whereas I am good at most things I attempt, dropping ribbons is one thing I simply cannot do."

This conversation was fast reminding him of a youthful effort to cross the Yorkshire moors in the middle of a fog, when he had to take great care where he put his feet, to avoid being sucked into a bog. Well, he always had enjoyed a challenge.

"Why would you even want to drop a ribbon?" he ventured.

"So that a man would pick it up."

"But you can pick up your own ribbons."

"Of course I jolly well can."

"And you would never drop one in the first place."

"Precisely! Which is why men like Matilda Treadgold."

"Because she makes them feel strong and important and necessary."

"Just because a man wants to feel strong and important and necessary does not mean I cannot be those things too." She sipped her brandy and recoiled. "Good grief, that is vile."

And Guy understood.

Arabella was unapologetically strong-willed and independent —traits rarely admired in ladies. But that same proud independence was isolating too; she realized that, perhaps, but did not know how to change.

Now, she wanted something from him, and she didn't know how to ask for it, and so he could only guess what it was. But Arabella was asking. Not demanding or bribing or coercing —*asking*. She was doing a very poor job of it, but then, as she said, she didn't know how.

Arabella, who knew everything, did not know how to ask for affection or help.

His heart ached for her, this woman so accustomed to raising her walls that she had forgotten how lonely it could be behind them, so determined not to seem helpless that she refused to make any requests.

"You are strong and important and necessary, whether you drop ribbons or not," he said, hoping those were the right words. "And sometimes to get what you want, you have to take a risk and ask for it."

"But it—you—I— When it matters— Oh."

She dumped her glass on the table, folded her arms, and frowned at the wall. Not the right words, then. What the devil was going on in that complex mind of hers? He could spend a thousand evenings with her—a hundred thousand—and still not fully know her, but enjoy every minute of trying.

"You could start by asking for something small, and work your way up," he suggested.

She glanced at him, thoughtful now.

Ah, that was encouraging. "You may improve with practice," he went on. "Why don't we try it now? Drop a ribbon and we'll see if I pick it up."

"I haven't any ribbons."

"You have a gown. Why don't you try dropping that? Although, I confess, I would not make the slightest effort to pick it up."

Something flashed in her eyes—Desire? Fury?—then she looked away. Damn. His flippancy was misplaced. In a moment, she would call him absurd and stalk out.

Well, good.

If he got any closer to her, he feared he would not be able to disentangle himself, until she cut him loose and he'd fall. And how very unwise to provoke her when they were alone in a warm room at night. So—good! It was good that he said the wrong thing. Good if she walked away.

He leaped to his feet and carried their glasses back to the sideboard, where, he vowed, he would remain until she left.

From the corner of his eye, he saw her move. But she did not leave. She sighed. Not a delicate, romantic sigh, of course. More an exasperated, impatient one.

Impatient for what?

He stilled, his hands on the glasses, his attention on her. Seeing her, not quite seeing her.

Again her arms moved. Again that sigh.

He turned to look.

Her glare told him she wished him dead and gone. He did not understand, until he saw what she had done.

She had removed two hairpins and dropped them onto the carpet. Her careful coiffure was coming loose.

Guy's fingers fumbled to grip the carved wood of the sideboard behind him.

Again, she tugged out a pin and dropped it on the floor. More hair tumbled free, and from her eyes came another killing look.

That glare! A lesser man would quail and quiver, and hide under the furniture like a dog in a thunderstorm. Guy was not a lesser man. Guy was a man who wanted to see Arabella Larke's hair, and would weather any number of storms to do so.

"A few more," he said, his voice rough and raw, "and it might be worth my while to get down on my knees to pick them up."

Not a glare this time, but something...inviting? He yearned to touch her for his own pleasure, because he was selfish and greedy that way. But he also yearned to give her whatever she wanted, to show her that she could ask and someone would give.

He wanted her to know that she could ask *him*, and *he* would give.

So he gripped the sideboard and waited. He could wait. At least three more heartbeats he could wait, but his heart was racing, so three heartbeats came too fast, and another pin dropped. Then another and another and the last.

249

Arabella kept her eyes on him as she ran her fingers over her scalp, lifting her hair, shaking it out, letting it tumble haphazardly over her shoulders and past her ribs. Her features looked softer when framed by all that hair, or maybe she just seemed softer, in the firelight, with that uncertainty in her expression and her lips parted. Her hair would be silken and fragrant, and he would bury his face in it and let it pour over his naked skin…

Their eyes held. His heart pounded. His hands released the wood. His legs carried him across the room. His knees buckled and landed on the rug. The hairpins hid amid the patterns and evaded his suddenly clumsy fingers. He did not mind. He made them both wait, while he gathered up those pins, one by one, and dropped them on the table with a little clatter, one by one. With each pin, he shot her a look; with each look, her eyes grew heavier.

When there were no more pins, he swiveled to where she perched over him, gripping the cushions at her sides. He planted his hands on her knees. Her gaze did not waver. She did not resist when he parted her legs as much as her skirts would allow, and rose as close and tall as he could with his knees still on the rug. Her face was above his, her palms on his shoulders, and he boldly buried his hands in her hair. The scent of orange blossom floated over him, and he raked his fingers through that heavy, silken mass, catching on tangles and sliding on again, bumping carelessly, exquisitely, over her shoulders and breasts.

Her lips were already parted when he touched them with his own.

The tenderness of the caress was startling: the first honest kiss they had shared.

Their mouths touched, parted, hovered a hair's width apart. Her knuckles were sharp as she twisted her fingers in his dressing gown, and his own hands formed fists in her hair, but by tacit agreement they kept their fury at bay, as they breathed each other in. She pressed her open lips to his and touched his tongue with her own; a sound leaped in his throat. He tugged her bottom lip between his teeth; she answered in kind.

Pulling away, Guy pressed his impatient hands into the top of her thighs. Here, her leg muscles were firm and strong, but her inner thighs would be soft, and how beguiling it was, her mix of strong and soft.

How could she look both uncertain and fierce? How could he feel both tender and rough?

"What is it you want?" he murmured.

"I want... I mean, we can't, we mustn't... But I..." She made a sound of frustration at her own intractable mouth.

"We won't do anything you don't want to," he said. "You can leave. Or tell me to leave. We could read a book, or play whist, or simply sit here until we burst into flames. We can do whatever you want, no more, no less. Tell me what you want."

She said nothing. She pursed her lips. She blinked too fast.

"Arabella? Tell me."

"I don't know how to."

A pained confession, frightened and lost. Oh, Arabella, so commanding and clever, who understood everything except her own self. She terrified men, she had said. The notion seemed to puzzle her, as if she genuinely did not realize that she glared and hissed, which was why men turned tail and ran. Sensible men, anyway.

That confession had cost her something; her demeanor turned cool. If she hid behind her pride, he would lose her as surely as if he walked out the door.

"I remember how you liked to be touched," he murmured.

She closed her eyes and took a deep, shuddering breath. Guy clenched his fists so tightly his fingers ached.

"Yes." She released the word on a sigh. "Yes." Her eyes snapped open, stormy with longing and fear, passion and hope. "But the risks of... We can't..."

"We won't."

He waited. She said nothing.

"Talk to me, Arabella," he urged. "Tell me what you would like."

When finally she spoke, her soft words flickered between them like a flame.

"I would like to be touched."

CHAPTER 20

Arabella had no idea what to do next, but Guy seemed to know.

Without another word, he led her to the hearth, where he stoked up the fire, then he slipped off his banyan and spread it over the carpet.

"That's silk and velvet," he said, answering her unspoken question. "The rug might burn your skin."

He is taking care of me, she thought, and let him strip off her clothes. He took his time, slowly releasing buttons, sensuously sliding the fabric off her limbs, skimming his fingers over her with taunting carelessness.

Those fingers stilled at her side. "What the devil happened to you here?"

She froze, belatedly remembering the tea-colored bruise. The marks on her arms were faint yellow smudges, invisible in the firelight.

"A horse," she said. "It's nothing. Don't stop."

He tugged her to her knees and knelt behind her, bracketing

her hips, his scent engulfing her. Arabella fixed her gaze on the flames, every inch of her suddenly sensitive to the air on her skin, the heavy silk of her hair caressing her bare back. She had never given her hair much thought before, but now it was the center of her world. No—*he* was, burying his hands in it, lifting its weight, letting it tumble back down like a waterfall.

"It's marvelous the way you aren't shy," he murmured.

"Oh. I suppose I ought to be."

"You ought to be exactly as you are."

As he draped her hair over her shoulders and breasts, his hands brushed her nipples and his lips nibbled her neck. Her body roared to sensual life, demanding to be touched, demanding more of these hot sensations swirling inside. Her hands floated in front of her, useless and awkward because he was behind her and she was meant to— What?

"I don't know what to do," she cried, in a voice unlike her own.

Guy's hands landed on her bare shoulders, warm and strong, with that luxurious roughness. Slowly, he trailed his palms down her arms, to her wrists, to her hands. He laced his fingers with hers.

"You don't have to do anything," he murmured, his breath caressing her temple with erotic promise. "You only have to feel. Feel everything I do, feel the way I touch you, feel the way your body responds to my touch."

She closed her eyes, yielded to sensation. This was what she felt: his linen shirt teasing her, his warmth enveloping her, his lips against her ear, goosebumps rippling over her skin. The heat from the fire, the silk of the banyan, the peace in his arms, the fury of her lust.

"Feel everything," he continued. "And if that splendid brain of yours starts thinking, ignore it and feel the sensations. That's all you need to do. Just feel. Let yourself feel, and you cannot get this wrong."

He freed his fingers and dragged them back up her thighs, over her hips. He must have leaned away from her, for cold air washed between them, and with the next pulse of her exasperated quim, she was arching, thrills racing through her, as his fingers burned a path up her spine.

"When I touch you," he said, hypnotic and heavy, "I imagine leaving a trail of stars, all the colors in the world, exploding from my touch, like a thousand fireworks flying up from your skin."

As he spoke, his fingertips roamed over her, sparking sensations, sparking light. She saw her own back through the dance of his fingers, saw his touch as fire and color and beauty, orange and blue and pink and green. Then all that color and light and heat were deep inside her too, swirling and rising, thousands of sparks igniting within, so her blood became a sizzling, colorful river of stars.

Those hands of his mapped her, like he was discovering her, remembering her. Skating down her back, shaping her waist, gliding over her hips and up her belly to cup her breasts and pinch her nipples and toss her hair.

Somehow she was lying down—she did not know when that happened—and his mouth joined the dance, his burning kisses sliding over her, those hands roving wildly, now fast, now slow, now firm, now soft, so much to feel that her mind could not keep up. He was everywhere: a callused hand on her shoulder, hot tongue at her navel, fingers whirling over her buttocks and her thighs, until she forgot about mouths and hands and thighs, until there was only sensation. Delicious, intense sensations tossing her about like a ship in a storm, the air alive with the crackle of the fire and the sounds from her throat, and his sounds too, soft growls and sighs.

Everywhere he touched her—but no, not everywhere! What was he doing, not touching her quim, when it was throbbing so hard it must make the house shake? He laughed and she grabbed him, but she caught only linen. Furiously, she yanked at his hateful shirt, and he bowed and shifted so it came off in her hands. She tossed it aside— What use was a shirt with no man inside? Again she tried to wrestle him, her hands frantic on his scorching skin, but one strong leg pinned her down. Again his palms roved over her stomach. Why on earth was he touching her stomach when she had more worthy places to touch?

A growl sounded in her throat. She met his eyes, green and glazed. The scoundrel was enjoying himself far too much.

"Something wrong?" he murmured.

"Curse you," she hissed. "You're not doing it right."

"Oh, I'm doing it exactly right."

"Do you need me to draw you a map? Can you not find my...?"

He flicked his tongue over her nipple; as if on command, she arched. "Find your what, sweetheart?"

"So help me, I'm going to kill you for this."

But he only laughed, saying, "That's right, just like that," and dragged his traitorous lips over her ribcage, over her stomach. She parted her thighs to give the blockhead a clue, but he ignored her, his mouth lazily exploring her stomach and the crests of her hips.

"You villain," she muttered. "You cad, you devil, you blackguard, you scoundrel, you... Oh."

Oh.

He had finally found her quim. With his mouth.

Dazed, she lifted her head to stare at him. He lay between her thighs, caressing her with his tongue, and then he pressed his thumb—

Oh.

Her hips rose; he pushed them down, so she looped a leg over his shoulder and pounded him with her heel.

Flashing her a smile, his eyes held hers as he lowered his mouth to do it again. How contented he looked! And so infuriatingly pleased with himself! Oh dear heaven, she wanted to strangle him and kiss him and love him and kick him. A different pleasure arose, a new pleasure, deep inside where even his touch could not reach.

"Still want to draw me that map, sweetheart?" he said.

He nipped the inside of her thigh. Need rushed through her, and with an alien yelp, she fell back, her hands helplessly curling in the silk and velvet of his robe, as the firm warmth of his mouth continued the exquisite work that his masterful fingers had begun.

She closed her eyes and followed his advice: to feel, only feel. Sensation coursed through her veins like hot liquid gold, drawn toward her center by his insistent, commanding mouth. Sensation flowed from her toes and her fingertips, from her back and her breasts, flowed to her center, pooling, swelling, building, a hot heavy whirlpool of sensation, swirling in her core, right above where his mouth—

Stopped.

Everything stopped. The torrent of sensations swirled in place, neither rising nor subsiding. She raised her head and glared at him, meeting his wild eyes.

"Curse you," she managed to say, the words a mangled cry of breath and torment. "What on earth are you doing? You can't stop! You must... You have to..."

His eyes burned into hers. She watched, mesmerized, as her world narrowed down to his hand, to the touch of his tongue on his own thumb. That thumb became the center of her universe, as he pressed it firmly against her; she bucked, crying out with pleasure and need, and then his mouth was on her again, continuing his call. She had no idea what he was doing, but she didn't care; what mattered was the insistent, swirling sensation, rising under his command, rising until it burst into hot waves that rippled back through every inch of her skin.

Arabella collapsed onto the rug, pleasure still pulsing through her with each thundering beat of her heart. Vaguely, she was aware of Guy extricating himself from her boneless legs. He stretched out beside her. She found enough strength to shift and flop against him like a cat.

Neither spoke or moved. The fire crackled and the clock ticked. Arabella's heart calmed, the sensations subsided, and her brain began to work.

Just enough to note that she had asked, and he had given. *Start with something small*, he had said. So she had, with success, and already she felt stronger, the way taking action always made her feel stronger. Perhaps it was the dizzying thrill that came with knowing she had faced a fear, that he had been generous and caring and undeterred by her fury, that made her feel more like herself than she ever had.

Perhaps it was that same thrill that made her rise and study him, as he lay with his arm thrown over his eyes, that feeling of strength that made her press her hand to his heaving chest, like she was staking a claim.

Guy kept his arm over his eyes and tried to breathe. Arabella's palm was exultant on his chest, and her lingering taste on his tongue clouded his last scrap of judgment.

"Now it's my turn to touch you," she said, her voice husky and unexpectedly playful.

"I promised we wouldn't." He flung his arm away from his face.

Her hair was a wild dark cloud, her lips swollen, her eyes languorous with erotic promise. "You asked to be touched; I touched you. That is all."

"You're being honorable again."

"It's a curse," he agreed.

"Not for me." She tightened her hand into a claw, scratched a tormenting trail over his sternum. "I don't have to be honorable."

"You…" It was a wonder he had sufficient wit left to form words. "You are a wicked seductress, a dangerous temptress."

Her hand stilled. Her nails dug in ever so slightly. "No man has ever called me that before."

"Because every man in the world is a fool."

"Except you."

"Obviously."

Obviously, he was the greatest fool of all.

A new, deeper pleasure flooded him, while Arabella, supple and smiling and mischievous, let her hands roam over his belly to the waistband of his breeches. She could not have missed the bulge of his cock but she ignored it. He should have been more careful with what he taught her.

"I have you at my mercy now," she crooned. "Wicked seductress that I am. I shall use you for my pleasure."

Her nimble fingers tackled his falls. Guy closed his eyes, lifted his hips on command, and tensed every one of his tortured muscles as she dispensed with his clothing. Groaned as she moved back up his body, her fingers teasing and exploring, the heavy silk of her unbound hair sweeping over his naked skin.

It felt even better than he had imagined.

"It is delicious to be touched, but delicious to touch too. It is good that you like games."

"Why so?"

"Because you make an excellent plaything."

He opened his eyes to see her smile broaden, and then she gripped his cock firmly. Nothing tentative with her; no half measures. She had decided to do this, and do it she would, and all Guy could do was submit.

"Careful," he groaned.

"Do you like this?"

She was studying him, stroking him, with almost scientific curiosity. Then she bent her head, brushed her lips over his belly, his hip, ignoring his cock against her cheek. Stars above, when had poised, prickly Arabella become this... this...

"Dangerous temptress," she murmured, as if she had heard his thoughts. "Wicked seductress."

"You're going to torment me, aren't you?" He was mesmerized by the sight of her perfect face so close to his cock.

Her eyes widened. "Is that an option? Oh. That's an option."

"What are you going to do to me?"

"Whatever I please." Her heavy-lidded gaze roamed over him. "If I am a dangerous temptress and wicked seductress, what would I do to you next?" Her eyes lingered on his cock, gripped in her hand. "This, I should think."

She bent her head and took him in her mouth. No hesitation, no half measures.

Closing his eyes, Guy let his head thud back onto the floor. Followed his own advice and let himself feel.

She had no idea what she was doing, and he was in no state to teach her. But her ineptitude didn't matter. He was so aroused that she could have done damn near anything and still the pleasure would come.

He grappled for air, for something to hold onto, as pleasure and pressure dueled and danced in his loins. His desperate hands found his shirt, tossed it at her. Surprise made her lift her head, grip him harder. He fumbled for the shirt. Pleasure shuddered through him and he came, groaning, into the soft linen folds.

"Oh," she said. "We keep ruining your shirts."

The shirts were the least of his problems. She kept ruining him.

Collapsing, he closed his eyes while she dealt with the shirt, then she shifted to sit against him. Her hand returned to rest on his belly, as though helping him heal. Heal from the sweet-hot fire of release, as if an earthquake had ripped through him and his organs were still adjusting to the newly shaken-up world.

In this new world, he was not in charge of himself. He was sapped of energy, sprawled helplessly on the floor, feeling more naked than ever before in his life. How easy, how right, how natural it was, to surrender completely to her call, to the way she enthralled him, thrilled him, humbled him, magnified him.

And best of all: Arabella, naked too, comfortable by his side.

He reached for her and she fell half on top of him, skin to skin, pulse to pulse. He wrapped an arm around her, held her tight, basking in the mix of decadence and intimacy as they lay amid silk and fire.

"I do see you differently now," he murmured, his hand tracing lazy lines over her back. She tensed ever so slightly, then once more became supple. Lowering her walls, or at least opening a door for him to find his way in. "But I still don't understand London," he added. "Explain to me. How did we get here?"

He felt her stiffen, come alert and wary, like a guard listening for bandits in the night.

He had misjudged. No. He had judged exactly right. Whatever lay behind London mattered to her—which meant it mattered to him. He needed to know.

He needed her to trust him enough to confide in him.

She pulled away and he let her go. She sat up and hugged her knees, her hair falling around her.

Guy sat up too. "Arabella?"

"Sculthorpe... He had an obsession, one might say. With my virginity. He prized it above all else, talked about claiming it. Claiming *me*. It repelled me."

Immediately, he understood. "So you decided to claim yourself first. That's what you wanted from me that night."

"But Sculthorpe guessed," she said softly. "Not you, specifically, but he learned I was no longer a virgin and he... He was angry."

"Yet he left without saying a word. Maybe I misjudged the man but I would expect him to be so outraged he would make sure the whole world knew."

"You didn't misjudge him. That was his intention."

He waited, but she added nothing. She merely rested her chin on her knees, studying him with unreadable eyes.

"Why didn't he tell everyone, if he knew that about you?" he finally prompted.

"Because I knew something about him too." Her voice was flat. "I told him that if he shared my secret with the world, I would share his."

Her words caught him off-guard. His spine straightened with abrupt tension. In a single, swift movement, Arabella pivoted around to face the fire, still hugging her knees. Her hair washed over her back, parting to reveal the bumps of her curved spine.

"That sounds like..." He groped for words amid the confusing clamor in his head. "The way you phrase that, it sounds as if you blackmailed him into silence."

For long moments she said nothing, the silence punctuated only by a crumbling log, breaking apart in a shower of sparks.

When she finally spoke, it was with her typical hauteur. "I suppose I did."

"Why?"

"Because I could. Because it achieved the desired effect. Because I wanted to defeat Sculthorpe and I did." She twisted and straightened to look at him directly, brows raised in a challenge. "That must appall you, learning I am a blackmailer, in addition to all my other sins."

True: Blackmail was appalling. Yet all those other sins she had committed for a good reason. At least, he believed she had—unless she had indeed been manipulating him. After all, his father had been the most unprincipled person Guy had ever met, and his explanations always sounded reasonable too.

She was eyeing him defiantly, as if wanting him to agree that she was appalling. Using her sins to shut him out.

"But what did he do?" he insisted. "You're not telling me everything."

Her gaze veered away. "It's enough."

It wasn't enough, and it never would be. *Talk to me*, he wanted to plead, but he had tried that and it had not been enough.

Perhaps she refused to confide because she truly had done something unpardonable this time. How could he know? If Arabella wouldn't confide in him, if she wouldn't trust him, how could he trust her?

Neither wore any clothes, but their intimacy had dissolved like mist, and suddenly Guy felt that he was the much more naked of the two.

Why did he even bother?

Whatever she had wanted from him earlier, apparently she had received it, and now she wanted nothing more. Certainly, she wanted no future with him; *that would be the worst thing in the world*, she had said, that day by the lake.

Already he missed her, even as she sat nearby, so cool and defiant that he did not know if she was hiding herself or revealing herself, and the confusion tore at his heart. If only he could recapture their ease and camaraderie, their passion and intimacy —but there was a solid great bloody wall between them, and she had put it there, and if he kept beating his head against it, the only person he would hurt was himself.

He bounded to his feet, found his drawers and breeches, dragged them up over his legs. In silence, she watched him dress. She still sat on his banyan but he didn't want to ask her to move, so he bundled up his stockings and the soiled shirt, prepared to walk bare-chested to his room. He paused, staring down at her, willing her to say something, anything, to put things right.

She said nothing.

He took a ragged breath, let it out. "This has to stop. I'll leave tomorrow. I'll write. Your scheme will continue as planned."

The hollow inside threatened to overwhelm him. Without waiting for her response, he turned and stumbled out, into the cold, dark hall.

ARABELLA STARED into the dying fire. Warm air caressed her bare skin, but still she shivered.

Barely minutes ago, she had lain against Guy, feeling warm, full, right. But of course, it could never have lasted. In all her efforts to fool the world into believing she was perfect, she had never fooled herself. When Guy listened to her, praised her, touched her, teased her, when she felt strong and desirable and accepted, alive and happy and free— She had known that would end, sooner or later, one way or another.

And it had.

Dressing seemed too much trouble, so she pulled Guy's banyan over her numb limbs. It smelled of him, felt like him, the soft, warm fabric cascading around her like the effect of his touch. Since she was on her feet anyway, she tidied the glasses, bundled up her clothes, gathered her hairpins from the table. Clearing away all evidence of their time together.

Back in her room, a single candle burned and red coals glowed. Arabella went through her nightly ritual, washing her newly sensitive skin, brushing and plaiting her newly discovered hair. She was brisker than usual, as if that might prove an antidote to Guy's gentle, reverent touch.

In the drawer, her fingers fell once more on the miniature of Oliver. She tugged it out, traced the carved frame.

"I made a spectacular mess of that, didn't I?" she whispered.

You just couldn't find the right words, could you?

Why had she refused to tell Guy the whole story? Why had her pride intervened, yet again, and with such terrible timing?

"He said he wanted to know me."

If he truly knew you, he definitely wouldn't want you.

"Oh, Oliver, what is *wrong* with me?"

Maybe none of her sinful deeds had even been necessary. Oh, everything seemed necessary at the time, but perhaps there had been other ways to deal with her problems. Perhaps, if she were different, she'd have found those other ways. Perhaps it was some deep flaw within her mind that made it take such twisted turns.

But this was how she was. She didn't know how else to be.

Which was why she was alone, in a stolen dressing gown, talking to the portrait of a dead boy.

She squeezed the frame so its carved wood dug indents into her flesh. "Why did you have to leave us, Oliver? We were happy, before. None of this would have happened if you had not gone."

No response was forthcoming, and anyway, she hadn't the

heart for a squabble. A droplet of water fell onto Oliver's frame. She blinked rapidly, wiped her face and his, and replaced him in the drawer.

She let the banyan drop to the floor and pulled on her nightgown. Immediately, the cold slammed into her, so she swept Guy's dressing gown back over her, pressing the silk to her face.

Thus embraced by his scent and warmth, she crawled into bed, alone.

CHAPTER 21

Ursula yelled Guy's name and trotted toward him across the lawn the following morning. He scooped her up before she fell and whirled her around, until she squealed and demanded more.

"I have to go to London today, Little Bear," he said, poking her belly so she giggled. "But I'll come back for you. You'll come and live with me, I promise. I love you."

She said something that sounded like "I love you," and Guy decided that was exactly what she meant.

Dropping into a crouch, he set her on her feet and she threw her arms around this neck. He hugged her, trying to find in his baby sister's embrace something to soothe the ragged hollow in his chest.

All night he had ached with longing, tempted to go to Arabella's bed, take her in his arms, and sleep by her side. He awoke still haunted by a feeling of loss, even as he insisted he had lost nothing.

"We'll have a home together soon, I promise," Guy said to Ursula. "We'll be a happy family."

She patted his cheek. "I want a nice home with cake every day," she might have said, and he decided he'd take that too.

Of course, his household would be nothing like the harmonious place—or dollhouse, according to Freddie—he had imagined. Ursula was a rambunctious child, and Freddie was downright unruly.

He wouldn't have them any other way.

He went in search of Freddie, hoping to find her before Arabella returned from her ride, but instead, in the music room, he found Lady Treadgold distressed and Matilda Treadgold confused.

"She needs to be here." Lady Treadgold was wringing her hands. "Of all the times for Lady Frederica to be running off. She knew we needed her here."

"What for?" Miss Treadgold asked. "No activities are planned, and you never minded when she went off alone before."

"Yes but today…"

"What's happening today?"

Guy had no patience for their family squabbles. "I need to see Freddie now," he interrupted.

"You see?" Lady Treadgold said to her niece. "His lordship needs to see her. But she went… Oh, and she's wearing those dreadful trousers. Though I've no idea how she found them again. Whatever will he think?"

"I think they look regal," Miss Treadgold said loyally.

"I'll find her," Guy said.

Better to run around the estate seeking Freddie than to chance a meeting with Arabella.

Sheer luck had him heading toward the abbey ruins first, where he spotted Freddie riding ahead. By the time he dismounted, Freddie's horse was already tethered, and she had just started climbing the ruins. The Turkish trousers were paired with a man's shirt, waistcoat, and boots—an eccentric, mismatched ensemble, but she likely had few options. She climbed higher than he ever had, apparently indifferent to any danger. Nimble and sure-footed, she traipsed along a broken wall to reach what had once been a long hallway, now an exposed platform.

Guy climbed and found her sitting cross-legged like a tailor under the arch of an ancient window.

He dropped onto the sill beside her. The ground was far beneath them, but the view was magnificent: a rolling patchwork of fields and woodlands, punctuated by villages and manors and rivers.

"You're good at climbing," he remarked. "Those Turkish trousers are perfect for it. Lady Treadgold doesn't approve."

"She took them away, but Arabella arranged to get them back for me."

A pang struck him. Yet again, Arabella had done a kindness for someone else.

"How do you know where to put your feet?" he asked Freddie.

"I just do what feels right."

"A philosophy to live by."

Freddie picked the moss off the stones. "Everyone's always telling me what to do and how to be and what I want. If I listened to all of them, my head would explode."

"You don't seem to listen to any of us."

Freddie sighed and shifted. "Arabella told me to give you another chance."

"Arabella said that?"

"She said I should get to know you again. That you are all heart and muscle and you fight for what you believe in."

Guy dug up some moss too. "What else did she say?"

"She told me I should tell you. That you would listen."

He shoved away the memory of Arabella: remote, defiant, and refusing to confide in him.

"Listen to what?" he said. "Tell me."

"I'm nineteen, and they say I must marry or I could end up on the shelf. But I don't mind. I think the shelf would suit me nicely."

Guy opened his mouth to argue, remembered that Arabella had promised he would listen, and paused as he tried to understand.

"But don't you want a family?" he said. "I enjoyed the freedom of my adventures, but the last few years, I came to crave a proper home, a companion, a family..."

Freddie flicked the moss into the air. "In my experience, a family is nothing but a group of people telling me what to do. When I reach my majority, I'll have enough money to do whatever I like."

"The difference," he ventured, "is that, when we reach our majority, we can shape our own family to fit with what we want."

Her expression grew thoughtful, as she tilted her head to consider the sky. Guy wondered if he had actually managed to say the right thing.

As he had with Arabella the previous night. Yet with Arabella, it had not been enough.

"I'm leaving today," he said. "Back to London and then to Roth Hall. Would you like to come with me?"

Freddie twisted so suddenly, he feared she might fall. "Yes! Please! I must get away from here."

"Why? What have the Treadgolds done?"

"Oh, the Treadgolds are fine. I think I did something silly."

"What did you do?"

"Nothing."

Guy bit back his impatient reply. Freddie would talk when she was ready.

Then she slumped back against the window frame. "Sir Walter won't let me go with you."

Ah, but Sir Walter had been naughty and would face some trouble in Chancery, so...

"I think I'll be able to persuade him," Guy said.

"What about your wedding?"

"Everything is under control."

Nothing was under control. Not for him, anyway. Arabella had everything under control. She had a plan. She had Hadrian Bell. She didn't need him.

"Do you mean, I could live with you?" Freddie asked.

"If you want. Ursula too, if I can arrange it."

She considered. "I'd miss Matilda. Perhaps she could live with us too."

Perhaps Guy would give in and just marry Miss Treadgold. She was pleasant and undemanding. He wouldn't get bored. He *wouldn't*. It would be peaceful. Peaceful was good. Life with Arabella would never be peaceful.

It would never be boring either.

He stood and extended a hand to Freddie. "Come on, then," he said, and she put her hand in his and said, "Let's go."

Sir Walter was entertaining a guest in the drawing room, Ramsay the butler told Guy, when he and Freddie arrived back at the house. His mouth was tight and he was fidgeting with his buttons in a most un-butler-like manner.

"Lady Belinda is not in the house," Ramsay continued.

"Perhaps, Lord Hardbury, you would be so kind as to offer your assistance."

"With what?"

"With removing the guest. His lordship is not welcome. But he will not leave, and Lady Belinda is not here, and Mr. Larke does not wish to be disturbed. If... If you would be so kind, Lord Hardbury."

Guy charged into the drawing room. He had no intention of being kind.

Because the unwanted guest was Lord Sculthorpe.

He sat at his leisure, the very image of the ideal gentleman, across from where the Treadgold family were lined up in a row: Sir Walter beaming with self-satisfaction, Lady Treadgold looking ill at ease, Miss Treadgold studying her fingernails, her cheeks pink.

No need to ask why Sculthorpe was here. Another match. Poor Miss Treadgold.

"You're not welcome," Guy said by way of greeting. "Get out."

Sculthorpe rose lazily, offered Guy a mocking half bow, followed by a smile. "Here is my beloved betrothed now."

Miss Treadgold's eyes were firmly on her fingernails. Guy spun around, seeing only Freddie, her strawberry-blonde hair disheveled, her dress eccentric, her complexion deathly pale.

Guy looked back at Sculthorpe, who was looking at Freddie. Guy looked at Freddie, who was looking at the floor.

Guy looked at Sir Walter, who was beaming broadly.

"Felicitations are in order," Sir Walter said.

"Freddie?" Guy said. "You told me you don't want to marry."

Her tight smile made her face appear even more elfin. "I also told you I did something silly."

Sculthorpe sauntered across the room, a hand extended. "Come now, my little dove. That's no—"

Knocking his arm aside, Guy planted himself between his

sister and the baron. "Don't touch her. Don't even speak to her or look at her."

Sculthorpe smiled. "I say, that will make our wedding night awkward. Won't it, Frederica, my dreamy little...dove."

"My sister will not marry you."

"She seemed willing enough."

"I'm not!" Freddie said from behind him. "I was merely curious."

Sculthorpe laughed. "I promise to satisfy your curiosity."

Guy shoved him. "Stars above, man, do you *want* me to beat you up?"

"Not in the drawing room, Hardbury." He straightened his coat. "Besides, let's not forget what happened last time you challenged me. I left you as a sniveling, whimpering mess curled up in the dust. Do you remember that?"

"I do. I do remember that."

"I should do it again, in the circumstances. But I prefer this solution: You took my betrothed, so I shall take your sister. You see how it works?"

Guy stared. "That is the most distorted piece of logic I have ever heard."

"I learned a bitter lesson about the perfidy of women when I was young," Sculthorpe carried on, oblivious. "I have waited for a woman to prove me wrong, but it seems they're all the same. Maybe your sister will put me right."

Freddie was hunched against a wall, gripping the blue brocade curtain. She was scowling at Sculthorpe, her expression more furious than scared. The Treadgold family were watching the scene like spectators at a game of shuttlecock.

"What a conundrum," Guy said to Sculthorpe, trying to affect a light tone to conceal the tension coursing through his muscles. "I am experiencing a very intense desire to turn your face into pulp with my fists and then rip off your arms and use them to beat you around what is left of your head."

"Your ire is admirable but misplaced," Sculthorpe said. "The fact is: You took what is mine, and I am entitled to a replacement."

"Bloody hell, they are not dolls for us to fight over or to *claim*. Freddie, let us be very clear about what you want."

"I don't want to marry him."

"That isn't what you said to me," Sculthorpe broke in.

Freddie glared at him. "I didn't say anything to you. You assumed."

"Freddie, what the devil?"

"Lady Treadgold said no men wanted to court me so I would find it less distressing to marry whomever they chose. Then Lord Sculthorpe sent me a note, saying he'd broken off his engagement with Arabella because he had fallen madly in love with me and wanted to meet."

"You were off meeting him?" He whirled back to the Treadgolds. "And you knew about this? Freddie?"

"I just wanted to know what it was like, to be courted."

"And how was it?" Miss Treadgold piped up.

"Really dull. He kept saying things that made no sense, and talked about himself a lot."

Guy clenched his fists. "Did he...touch you?"

"No. Well, he did kiss my hand. It was... You know."

"No, Freddie, I don't know. It was what?"

"Wet." She shrugged. "I don't know why everyone makes such a fuss about being courted. Why marry someone who's boring and talks about himself all the time?"

The outrage on Sculthorpe's face made Guy laugh. He wrapped an arm around his sister's shoulders and planted a kiss on her temple. "Freddie, you are glorious. The poor bloke never stood a chance."

Sculthorpe did not share his amusement. "As perfidious as the rest of them. But no matter, my lady. You'll marry me anyway."

"I will not."

"She will not."

Sir Walter jumped to his feet. "With all respect, Lord Hardbury, it isn't your decision. As Lady Frederica's guardian, I decide whom she will marry, a very solemn duty entrusted to me by your dear father."

"Ah, so that's what you got your knighthood for, Sir Walter: being a complete and utter weasel." Guy wished Arabella were here; she would know how to navigate this. Guy was no diplomat, and he could not be bothered trying. "Enough with the pretense, man. First, you intended to marry Freddie off to your son, and now you try this little trick. Once we have a hearing in Chancery, you will no longer be Freddie's guardian."

Sir Walter spread his hands in a show of indignant innocence. "Whatever can you mean, my lord? Our darling Lady Frederica has no facility for making conversation with young gentlemen. Why, it would be cruel to expect her to endure the social rituals of a young lady's Season. Besides, you must admit she does not exercise good judgment. Consider her trysts with Lord Sculthorpe! That special license was procured merely as insurance, in case she got herself into trouble and we needed to salvage her reputation. But now, here is Lord Sculthorpe, undeniably a suitable match for a marquess's sister. How could you possibly argue that I am neglecting my duty?"

"Freddie doesn't want to marry him."

"Lady Frederica is too young to know what she wants. That's why they have guardians. And Lord Sculthorpe has done the right thing in approaching me to ask for her hand. It isn't as though he kidnapped her and whisked her off to Scotland, now, is it?"

"Don't give him any ideas," Guy muttered.

Sir Walter was lying through his teeth. Guy would wager that Sculthorpe's reappearance was the reason for Sir Walter's good cheer, once he'd noticed the special license was missing. They must have met at the village tavern. The question was whether anyone else would see it, and if Freddie's reputation would survive, should this matter be dragged through the courts.

Sculthorpe was smirking. Because Sir Walter was right: On paper, the baron was a good match for Freddie. If Arabella were here, she'd find a way to resolve this. In the meantime, Guy could borrow her methods.

"Have you told Sir Walter your secrets, Sculthorpe?" he ventured. "The one Miss Larke knows, for example."

Sculthorpe tensed and his eyes darted nervously to Sir Walter. Why the devil would Sculthorpe be scared of Sir Walter, of all people?

Whatever Arabella knew about him, it was not trivial.

Bloody hell. Guy should never have walked out of that room without making her tell him the full story. He should have found a way to assure her that whatever Sculthorpe had done, whatever anyone did, Guy would always be there to help.

I just do what feels right, Freddie had said.

Ah, Freddie. Terrible judgment in some respects, but wise in others. And what felt right...

What felt right was to trust Arabella.

Guy crossed to where the butler was hovering in the doorway. "We need Miss Larke here as soon as possible," he said softly. "She'll know what to do."

"I believe she is out riding."

"I'll have to keep them talking," he said. "We need Lady Belinda too. And if—"

"I say, Lord Hardbury," came Sir Walter's voice.

Guy excused himself to Ramsay and turned around. "Are you still talking?"

Sir Walter shot a shifty look to where Sculthorpe was lounging against the mantelpiece. "It occurs to me we could find another solution. I refer to our previous agreement."

"What agreement?"

"Whereby you marry our Matilda and custody of your sisters passes to you."

Guy glanced at the butler. "And if you would be so kind, Ramsay, it seems I'll require a gun."

Ramsay's mouth twitched. "Yes, my lord."

Across the room, Sir Walter looked earnest.

Guy shook his head. "It continues to astound me how my father's will is a powerful legal document when it suits you, and easily overruled when it does not."

"I speak of a gentleman's agreement, my lord."

"For that, we would both need to be gentlemen."

Sculthorpe chuckled, as he turned his silver cigar case in his hands.

"We had an agreement too, Sir Walter," he said. "Don't wriggle out of it now."

"Agreement?" Guy repeated. "What did Lord Sculthorpe offer you, Sir Walter, in exchange for giving him my sister?"

"Why, my lord, you offend me! I do this not for my own benefit but—"

"Oh, let up, Treadgold," Sculthorpe interrupted. "We all see you for the weasel you are. If you must know, Hardbury, I offered to create a sinecure for him, worth two thousand pounds a year, and another for his son, whatever his name is. It's what your father used to do."

"Yes, I recall. The Old Corruption is alive and well. Well played, Sir Walter. Let me get this straight." Guy glanced out the window, wishing Arabella would arrive. He wasn't sure how much longer he could restrain himself from beating these men's heads together. "If I play by your rules, the only way to save Freddie from Sculthorpe is to marry Matilda, to do which, I would have to jilt Miss Larke."

Sculthorpe slipped the cigar case back into his pocket. "No more than she deserves. Come, Hardbury, you cannot still be so naive about women. You must know what kind of woman Miss Larke is."

"I know exactly what kind of lady she is."

Guy met the other man's eyes steadily. Sculthorpe's features tightened, and there might indeed have been a brawl in Lady Belinda's drawing room had Sir Walter not interrupted.

"What is your decision, my lord?"

Guy took his time ending the staring match. "I refuse to play your repugnant game of brides. Sculthorpe, you are not marrying my sister. Sir Walter, I am not marrying Miss Treadgold."

Sculthorpe shrugged. "Very well. I'll marry Miss Treadgold instead. She was equally amenable to my advances."

Sir Walter's eyes widened. "What do you mean?"

"You and your wife were happy to facilitate my trysts with Lady Frederica. But you failed to realize how enterprising your niece is. We also had some lovely trysts."

"You met him too?" Freddie said to Miss Treadgold.

Miss Treadgold, looking very pink now, crossed to Freddie's side. "I was visiting the abbey ruins when he showed up and professed his love. I had no idea he was meeting you."

"Now, now, my little doves, no need to fight over me. I enjoyed meeting you both." Sculthorpe looked around the room. "Oh, put away those judgmental faces. I did not compromise either of them in any way. I didn't need to. A few sweet nothings and they were mine." He smiled broadly. "Each has her own appeal, so long as they, at least, are chaste. Now, Miss Treadgold, Lady Frederica: Which of you will marry me?"

"Neither."

The word came, hard and low, from the doorway.

Arabella had arrived.

She stood tall and proud, still in her red riding habit, hat, and gloves, riding crop in her hand. Her eyes blazed as she slapped the end of her crop into one gloved palm.

Those blazing eyes were directed at Sculthorpe. With a slow, deliberate movement, she pointed her crop at him like an avenging angel brandishing a flaming sword.

"No one is marrying that man."

CHAPTER 22

Arabella dragged her eyes off Sculthorpe's smirk to study the other faces, so she would not cross the room and take to the blackguard with her crop.

Lady Treadgold looked shocked. Sir Walter looked outraged. Matilda and Freddie, huddled together by the window, looked thrilled.

And Guy... She could not bear to look at him, but she saw him nonetheless. He had positioned himself between Sculthorpe and the young ladies, with that alert air, as if ready to strike.

"Arabella," Guy said. "Exactly the person we need."

She had to look at him then. He held her gaze steadily, and she was still puzzling out his meaning when Sir Walter's voice intruded.

"This does not concern you, Miss Larke," he said. "You lost your chance to marry Lord Sculthorpe. Now he will marry—"

"Enough." Arabella slapped her crop into her palm. Sir Walter shut up. "Allow me to repeat myself for those who did not understand the first time. No one is marrying that man."

And so it would unravel. Sculthorpe would assert his right to marry Freddie, and Arabella's accusation would end up in court, in support of Guy's petition. In arguing that Sir Walter was benefiting himself by marrying his ward to a violent man, she would have to reveal that violence. The whole country would read how she had lain weak and helpless on the grass. In retaliation, Sculthorpe's barrister would eloquently argue the defense: The poor, heartbroken baron had merely reacted with passion to the news that his betrothed had cuckolded him.

She would do it, of course, for Freddie and Matilda, and any other young woman unfortunate enough to catch Sculthorpe's eye. She would do it and end up completely ruined.

It would ruin Guy too, although in a different way. If he admitted to his part, he would have to marry her, or be denounced a cad in turn. But why should he confess? After all, she was the cad who had seduced him; she was the scoundrel who had blackmailed Sculthorpe.

She was the one brandishing a crop, and sorely tempted to put it to use.

Why would a decent, honorable man want a lady like that?

She continued: "Lord Sculthorpe is a violent man."

Guy shot to attention, while Sir Walter spluttered. "Mind what you say, Miss Larke. His lordship is a war hero."

"And I'll marry whom I please," Sculthorpe said.

He extended a defiant hand toward the young ladies. Without a thought, Arabella whipped the crop down onto his wrist.

With a yelp, he jerked it back. "You dare!" he snarled, rubbing the welt.

She ignored him. "This man must never be entrusted with a wife. He threw me to the ground and kicked me, and he—"

Her next words were lost in Guy's roar, as he charged at Sculthorpe.

"Guy, you don't have to..."

Sculthorpe ducked and spun, but Guy, faster, seized him.

"But if you were to..."

He hauled a struggling Sculthorpe in front of her; the baron grunted as Guy twisted one of his arms behind his back.

"Be careful not to..."

A well-aimed kick made Sculthorpe's legs collapse; he cried out and his kneecaps cracked as they hit the floor. Guy held him in place.

Sculthorpe was on his knees before her, put there by Guy.

"Oh yes," she said faintly. "I see."

Sculthorpe had likely been in worse situations while at war. He merely sneered up at her. "You must be better than I dared dream, if Hardbury comes over all manly like this. Now I *will* take his sister, and—"

"Now you will be silent."

"Because obviously he was the one who..."

Sculthorpe's words trailed off, and his eyes were watching her arm. Watching as she raised it, ever so slowly, with the crop gripped in her hand.

Then he looked in her eyes, and she looked in his, and those minutes whirled between them, when he had bruised her and cursed her, when he had thrown her down and kicked her. When he had cried like a little boy because he saw her as his and someone had taken her away, just as his brother had taken another woman he saw as his, and he did not see her as someone like himself, but something for him to use, to possess, to parade.

That face. How she loathed that face, those repellent eyes, quivering now, following the arc of the crop in her raised hand. Let him bear her marks! Let him know how it felt! Look at him, on his knees, held there by someone stronger, because he was nothing. He was weak.

Guy called her name; she ignored him. How she must repel him right now. She didn't care. He had wanted to know her? Let him see!

Releasing Sculthorpe, Guy stepped away, but Sculthorpe didn't move. He sneered up at her defiantly.

"Do you mean to horse-whip me, Miss Larke?" he taunted her.

"If I did, sir, it would be the only joy I ever got from you."

The silence was stark. Even the air dared not stir. In the stillness, rage surged through her, engulfed her, conquered her, and she whipped her arm downward, watched Sculthorpe's expression change as he realized her intent. She felt a momentary triumph, a surge of satisfaction, as he cowered, flinched away, cried out in fear...at the blow that never came.

Because her crop was no longer in her hand.

Sculthorpe opened his eyes. Arabella stared at her empty hand. She turned.

Mama stood right behind her, still in her bonnet and cloak. The crop was in her gloved hands and she was rapidly blinking away tears.

"Take care, my dear," Mama said mildly.

"Listen to your mama," Sculthorpe jeered. "You should have listened to your mama before you—"

Arabella never heard his wise advice, because Guy shoved him forward and forced his face to the floor. Sculthorpe yelled and struggled, but once more Guy had the baron's arm twisted and his foot on his shoulder.

She looked up to meet Guy's steady gaze. He was on her side. Her violence had not revolted him. Her weakness had not filled him with disgust.

Her rage dissipated, replaced by a peculiar peace.

"That works rather nicely, actually, doesn't it?" she said.

"I thought you might like that."

Like an exhausted lamb, Sculthorpe had stopped struggling under Guy's boot.

"I say, that's a fine-looking boot you have," she said to Guy.

"They're very comfortable."

"I'm glad to hear it. A man needs a pair of comfortable boots."

In the engulfing silence, Arabella could hear everyone's confusion, but her world consisted of nothing but a pair of summer-like eyes.

"You lied," he said.

"Yes. Lying is one of my more notable accomplishments, along with archery and needlework."

Mama stepped forward and put her hand on Arabella's arm. "Thank you, Lord Hardbury, but you have impressed us long enough. You may assist Lord Sculthorpe to leave my house."

"But Lady Belinda, this is outrageous," spluttered Sir Walter. "His lordship is here as my guest."

"Then you may leave too, Sir Walter. Lord Hardbury, please escort Lord Sculthorpe outside. If he is unable to find his way to his horse, perhaps you would be so kind as to show him."

Guy hauled Sculthorpe to his feet. "Your wish is my command, my lady. My only concern is that in escorting him, I might trip and accidentally plant my fist in his face."

"There are many holes and stones upon which a man may trip," she returned blandly. "I do hope you take care, but I understand if that is not the case."

Guy released Sculthorpe, who took his time adjusting his sleeves and wiping his face.

"Let me explain again, Lord Sculthorpe," Arabella said. "If you ever try to marry any woman, I will stand before the Chancellor or the Chief Lord Justice or the journalists or on a soapbox in Hyde Park, to tell the world of your violence."

Sir Walter broke in. "No one will believe that of such a noble man."

"Perhaps they'll believe the testimony of my mother and my maid, who saw the marks left on my body."

"I believe her," Guy said.

"Good, because it is true," said Mama. "Lord Sculthorpe, I advise you to leave, before I run out of patience and shoot you myself."

SCULTHORPE WOULD NOT BE HURRIED, even though Guy occasionally shoved his shoulder, furious at him for harming Arabella. And why the hell had she not just *told* him? That bruise! He had asked her and she had lied and at any bloody moment she could have bloody well said.

"It *was* you, wasn't it?" Sculthorpe said. "It's the obvious explanation. I knew it had to be you, when I heard of the engagement. That's why I came back."

"You should never have shown your face here again."

"You self-righteous hypocrite!" Sculthorpe whirled to a stop, square features hard as he advanced one threatening step. "You're the villain here, Hardbury, not me. I did nothing wrong."

Guy shoved him. "You kicked her! You bloody—"

"I was good to her and she betrayed me! With you! She was *mine*."

Sculthorpe had wanted to claim Arabella, she had said. Guy shook his head, stepped away before he was tempted into more violence. "You never even made an effort to know her."

"We understood each other perfectly." Sculthorpe's expression was bitter as he smoothed out his lapels. "She knew and shared my desires. She was mine and you stole her."

"Arabella makes her own choices."

That earned him a jeering laugh. "Not yet wed and already hen-pecked! After all those years doing whatever your papa told you, now you need your wife to tell you what to do."

Sculthorpe's contemptuous sneer was intended to provoke him, but it merely struck Guy as pathetic. With such a controlling father, Guy had indeed feared being made to do anyone else's bidding. But no longer. He knew himself. He knew his values. And he knew Arabella.

"Your problem, Sculthorpe, is deep inside you like a worm, and it will never go away. After hurting Arabella, you could have seen how you were wrong and changed your ways. But you didn't. Another day will come when a woman says something you don't like, and you'll strike her and convince yourself that was your right."

"She was mine, damn you," Sculthorpe hissed, and swung for Guy's face.

Guy stepped aside.

Sculthorpe quickly recovered his balance and sneered. "Take it like a man."

This bit of nonsense made Guy snort. "If you say so, my lord," he said, and smashed his fist into the other man's jaw.

By the time Guy had finished with Sculthorpe, the man was in no state to ride. So he hauled him to the far stables, which were old and empty, and tossed him onto a pile of hay.

"You have one hour to get yourself out of here," he said.

"You grew up, Hardbury." Sculthorpe laughed wheezily and swiped at the blood on his face. "Little whiner grew up to defend another whore."

Rubbing his knuckles, Guy left the other man sprawled on the straw. The fight had left him both energized and exhausted. At the main stables, he found a pair of grooms, told them to take water and linens to Sculthorpe, and to fetch him in an hour if the baron hadn't left.

Back in the house, Freddie and Miss Treadgold were cluttering up the foyer, eyes wide and faces pale.

"What were you thinking, Freddie? Miss Treadgold?" Guy looked from one to the other. "Why would you think it was a good idea to meet any man secretly, let alone that one? Let's hope your guardians hush this up, but what the *hell* were you thinking?"

"I was thinking I wanted to know what it was like to be courted," Freddie said.

"That was a rhetorical question," he bit out.

"I was thinking I must repay a debt of gratitude to my guardians by marrying well," Miss Treadgold said.

Guy gritted his teeth. "The point is, you weren't thinking. Those are dreadful reasons."

"Easy for you to say," Freddie sniped.

"You're not us," Miss Treadgold agreed.

"Stars above, Miss Treadgold. When did you become so defiant?"

"Miss Larke told me I should express myself. She's right. It feels good."

"Express yourself? She said that? Ha!"

The hypocrite! Arabella would not be able to express herself if the Spanish Inquisition had her stretched out on the rack under a vat of boiling oil.

Lady Belinda appeared in the doorway, as unflappable as ever. "Is he gone?" she asked.

Guy rubbed his aching jaw. "He's resting in the far stables and will leave when he is able to ride." He turned back to Freddie and

Miss Treadgold. "You will not leave this house tonight. You will go nowhere alone, not until we know what he's planning. His is a vengeful nature and he does not like to lose."

"Lord Hardbury! Please!" cried Lady Treadgold, bustling in. "You are frightening the girls."

"They should be frightened. That man is a menace, and you, Lady Treadgold, wanted one of them to marry him."

"It would be a good match for either one. You cannot argue with that."

Guy held up his hand. "I already have."

"My lord?"

Miss Treadgold was staring at his bloody fingers. He clasped his hands behind his back. "Miss Treadgold?"

"I like dead things."

"Matilda! Hush!"

"Lady Frederica likes to ride astride and I like dead things. There, I said it. Now you know."

Guy blinked at her. "Yes. Now I know. Ah... Thank you for telling me?"

With an exchange of grins, the two young ladies dashed away.

"I think I caught a few too many blows to the head," Guy muttered, as he headed for the stairs.

Lady Belinda sidestepped to block his way.

"Excuse me, my lady," he said shortly. "I wish to speak with my betrothed."

"Arabella has retired to her private chamber. Please join me in my sitting room, my lord."

"I need to see Arabella."

Lady Belinda did not move an inch. "You will not see my daughter in this agitated state and with another man's blood on your hands."

"To be fair, some of this blood might be mine."

"Why do I not find myself comforted?"

With a swish of her skirts, she walked away, leaving Guy little choice but to follow.

Lady Belinda's sitting room was a cozy, elegant parlor, decorated in cream and lavender, with a neatly organized workbasket and an array of books.

As he shut the door behind them, she said, "Let me wash your hands," and set about pouring water into a basin.

"I appreciate your care, my lady, but I really need to speak to Arabella."

"You really need to calm down."

She gestured at the basin. Guy gave up and obeyed. The water stung his torn skin, but her hands were cool and efficient, keeping him prisoner under the guise of washing his hands.

"I always liked you as a boy," she said, her eyes on her task. "I paid attention, obviously, as my husband and your father had decided the two of you would marry. I approved of your essential character: You were fair, good humored, and a natural leader. Your behavior worsened in your youth, but I have noted that a young adult who displayed a good character as a child will likely return to that good character upon maturity. It seems that you have made good decisions and become a man I admire."

"I confess I have made some poor decisions as well, where Arabella is concerned."

"Did you know what Lord Sculthorpe did to her?"

"No. But I knew there was something and I saw—"

He stopped short.

I saw her naked, I saw that bruise, and she lied and said it was a horse, and you are her mother and I cannot tell you any of that.

"You saw?" Lady Belinda prompted.

"I saw...the error of my ways." He remembered that night, when she had loitered outside his room, right after Sculthorpe had left. The bruises must have been new and tender then, her mistreatment still fresh in her mind. She had slipped her arms around him. She had been seeking comfort and he—

"Why won't she talk to me?" he asked. "I saw her the night after it happened. I asked if she needed help and she…"

Because when Arabella was frightened, she hid behind her walls and attacked everyone, even her friends. Consider that moment in London, when she had gripped the table, eyes turned upward as though begging the heavens, and when Guy had offered help, she had attacked him, hurting herself.

"Why won't she *say* these things?" He thumped a fist against the side of the basin, nearly upsetting it. "Just *tell* me. Ask me for help."

With a sigh, Lady Belinda lifted his hands from the water and wrapped them in a dry linen. "I was always too hard on her, I'm afraid. I thought that if she was the best she could be, her father would see how wonderful she is, and he would… But he never saw her. He never saw what he had; he only ever saw what he didn't have. He would never be satisfied. And Arabella is rather proud and independent, you know."

"Yes," Guy said on a desperate laugh. "Yes, I know."

"The last time I heard Arabella ask anyone for help, she was ten," Lady Belinda added. "It was her father she asked. He told her to go away. Called her a useless burden and a worthless parasite."

"Bloody hell."

"Mr. Larke never spoke so harshly to her again, but I think she never forgot it."

Over the fireplace was yet another portrait of little Oliver, but in this one, Oliver held hands with a dark-haired girl. It was the only portrait of Arabella that Guy had seen in the house.

"She was only a child too," he said. "Your son died from an illness. It was not her fault."

290

Lady Belinda followed his gaze. "She asked me once if it was her fault, because she was always the more robust of the two. She asked if she had been selfish and greedy in my stomach, which made her stronger than Oliver, and if that was why he did not survive the illness whereas she did. I did my best to tell her otherwise, but one is never too sure what a child believes deep down to be true."

"And Mr. Larke?"

"Oliver was growing up to be a scientist just like him; he could see himself in Oliver, see his legacy passed on. Arabella never had the patience. Whereas Oliver wished to observe the world, she wished to fix it. Not a quality much admired in a lady, but it is not in her nature to change to please others."

"And I am glad for it," Guy said.

"As am I."

She whipped away the cloth. "You wondered why she does not confide in you. Now you know."

Yes. Now he knew that Arabella was a woman who needed love. His love. And he was there to love her. It was a powerful responsibility, a daunting, exacting, thrilling honor. One that he alone was qualified to fulfill.

What a stubborn fool he had been, letting his resistance to his father's commands blinker him like a horse, even when that man had been dead more than a year. Now he had flung off those blinkers and could see Arabella simply as she was: a woman who loved and fought, who made mistakes and fell down, then got back up to love and fight another day. A woman whose very existence made him thrill with the glory of life, made him feel both as magnificent as the heavens and as inconsequential as a pinprick of light in the sky.

Suddenly, Guy was grateful for his years of exile. Grateful for his controlling father, for Sculthorpe and Clare, for his impulsive decision that long-ago day to sail away from England. Only by leaving had he discovered himself, had he learned what he was capable of, had he become the man who could love Arabella Larke.

And to think of her cruelly misguided father, and all the world's cowards and fools, holding her back, no doubt scared of what she might do given her full potential.

Stars above, how he wanted to see that! If Arabella was this remarkable now, when wasting herself trying to please her father and behave, imagine how she'd be when unleashed!

"She is in her private chamber now, where you must not visit," Lady Belinda said. "The house is in an uproar and I have much to do, so there will be no one to check that you do not go to my daughter's room and stay there for a length of time." She opened the door. "My lord."

"My lady."

In the hallway, Guy paused to consider Lady Belinda's odd parting speech. He did not possess the subtlety of thought displayed by Arabella and her mother. But he suspected he was learning fast.

He skipped around and raced toward Arabella's room.

CHAPTER 23

The footsteps coming down the hallway belonged to Guy. Arabella could not have said how she knew that from the sound alone—the assuredness of the steps, perhaps, their speed, their boldness—but she was on her feet, chest tight and trembling hands clasped, when the bedroom door flew open.

He paused in the doorway, their eyes meeting with a jolt. His cravat was askew and a shadowy bruise was forming on his jaw. She longed to go to him, soothe him. She clasped her hands more tightly and didn't move.

"You're hurt," she said.

With a rough bark of laughter, he stepped inside, kicked the door shut, and fell back against it so heavily a picture toppled sideways on its hook. Following her gaze, he shoved off the door to straighten the painting, then turned back to her, his tension filling the room like steam.

"I wish you had just told me," he said. "You announced it to everyone in there, but you could not tell me in private."

"I had to say it, for Freddie and Matilda. Mama started

whispers at the ball, so word would have spread and thwarted him, but so long as it was only whispers, I could pretend no one knew."

"I wish you had trusted me with the truth, rather than try to convince me you're a cold-hearted, amoral blackmailer."

"Better than you sneer at me for being helpless and weak."

The words had a surprising effect: They seemed to wash away his heated tension like summer rain. His eyes were intent, uncomfortably so, but thankfully, the sash on the curtain was crooked: a reason to look away, to busy herself with setting it straight.

"So that's it," he finally said. "You sneer at me."

She spun around. "I what?"

He advanced a couple of steps. "You know Sculthorpe beat me when I was younger. He had me curled up in a ball on the ground, whimpering like a lost puppy. How you must disdain me for that."

"Of course I don't."

"Then why is it any different for you?"

Oh. That was a trap, and she had stumbled right into it. How shaken she must be, to fall for such a trick! She turned away, but she heard him approach. He stopped behind her, close enough for her to feel his warmth.

Already he knew her body so well that when he rested his hand on her side, he unerringly found her bruise. The pain was long since gone; all that remained was a stain like spilt tea. It would be no surprise if his touch healed her even further, so she would undress that night to find even the last discoloration of the bruise gone.

"These impossible standards you hold yourself to," he murmured.

"It was not severe," she said. "I've been hurt worse."

Something brushed her hair: his cheek or his chin. He stood closer now, his scent sliding over her, his heat engulfing her.

"The pain is not merely physical," he said. "It is an additional shock, to be confronted with one's own weakness, especially for those of us accustomed to thinking ourselves strong. When he first beat me, I had never lost a fight. It never occurred to me I might not win. When our bodies are overpowered so swiftly our mind can hardly comprehend it... The shock is not that our body has been battered, but that our whole view of the world has changed. Then we recall that we survived and they did not diminish us, and that knowledge alone makes us stronger."

Arabella closed her eyes and listened for the beat of his heart. "He wanted to own me."

"The fool. One could as easily own the stars."

She eased back against his chest. He held her against his sure, solid strength, strong despite a hundred beatings, strong even after confessing to be weak. None of it had diminished him; none of it need diminish her.

In halting words, she told him everything: about Clare's advice, her victory, those minutes in the garden, how Sculthorpe had wept, and the command she had issued.

"Oh stars above, that night outside my room." His arms tightened around her. "I was playing with Ursula and wondering where you were, and the whole time... You came to me for comfort and I accused you. Arabella, if only you'd told me then!"

"And have you haring off to attack him."

"He deserved it."

"Then I'd have that on my conscience too. I do have a conscience, you know."

"I know."

"We must work out what to do with him, so he does not hurt anyone else," she added. "As a peer, he will not be held accountable, and there will always be those willing to overlook his violence for their own advancement."

We. How presumptuous of her, to speak as if they were still allies. Maybe they were. She no longer knew. Experience had only taught her how to issue commands and solve problems alone. Yet after embrangling him in her mess, after all he had given, she had no right to ask for anything more.

She tugged away from him; he dropped his arms and let her go. She drifted to the window and waited for him to speak. To announce his next move.

But he said nothing. He simply studied her.

When other men looked at her, she wanted to deflect their gaze. Even without meaning to, she had. So they had found easier, more soothing places to rest their eyes, more willing recipients for their smiles and wit. It was a triumph of sorts, for if they did not look at her, they would not see her, and if they did not see her, they would not notice her flaws. It was difficult to maintain a charade of perfection; if anyone examined her too closely, they might see the cracks.

Yet she wanted Guy to see her, with all her terrible flaws. To see her, and still want her.

But as the silence stretched on, a familiar discomfort blossomed and grew. Perhaps he was, indeed, seeing the cracks and flaws. He would remark on them, and hurt her. He would confirm he did not truly want her, and free her from this fierce longing for him.

"How is the light?" she asked, her tone sharper than she intended. "Shall I turn so you can study me from another angle?"

"There aren't enough angles in the world to see all of you," he said easily, undeterred.

"I don't even know what that means. Are you attempting poetry again?"

His voice was warm as velvet. "Looking at you is like looking at the night sky. So vast and varied and infinite, the view changing depending on where one stands, or the hour or the season. One can only ever see a tiny bit of it at a time, unbearably, voraciously, insatiably aware that however wondrous the view, there is always so much more."

Arabella tried to tell herself that his words made no sense—he was spouting poetry, and poetry never made sense—but this valiant voice of rationality grew fainter and fainter, until finally there were no words, there was no voice.

Wondrously, under the spell of his words, under the warmth of his gaze, she became the night sky. Her soul expanded to embrace it, her mind became deep and infinite and unfathomable, her body became a star, a thousand stars, all shining for him.

This was love, she realized. This was how it felt to love. To love him.

"Then you are the mountains," she said softly. Her voice came from an unfamiliar place. Perhaps that was her heart, finally making itself heard. "Strong, enduring, sure."

She had to turn away from him to say this. Her heart, it seemed, was shy. Through the window, the world was dissolving into the fading evening light, but all she saw was his reflection in the glass. "And when you..."

In the distance, something caught her eye. For long seconds, she stared, puzzled, until an alarm sounded in her mind and her thoughts cleared.

"There's a fire," she said. "In the far stables."

"What?!"

"They're empty but—"

But Guy was already moving. "Sculthorpe. If he's still in there..."

He whirled about and ran.

CHAPTER 24

Guy ran, yelling "Fire!", stirring up the household, not pausing as he raced outside. He passed a frantic messenger sprinting toward the house and ran on.

Too late. By the time he reached the far stables, the building was ablaze. Grooms and other workers circled it, clutching buckets of water, but no longer trying to extinguish the flames.

Horrified, ash-smeared faces greeted him, and he searched through them for the grooms he'd sent to tend to Sculthorpe, identifying one through his smoke-stung eyes. He put a hand on the man's shoulder.

"Did he get out?"

The groom looked close to tears, his mouth working hopelessly, his head shaking.

The stable master arrived at Guy's side. "My lord. I'm sorry. We were too late. We saw him try but... He must have been asleep and by the time we noticed the fire... We sent a message up to the house."

"Bloody hell." Guy raked his hands through his hair, stared at the flames engulfing the old, wooden frame and the man Guy had left inside. "What happened?"

The groom gulped. "We took him water and linens, like you asked, and he wanted whiskey too, so we got it, and then he told us to bugger off. He threw an old horseshoe that hit Roger, so we buggered off and we were all off in the other stables and...and then we smelled the smoke."

The smoke now swirled around them, tickling throats, inducing coughs.

"Sculthorpe was always smoking," Guy said. "If he had drunk whiskey, lit a cigar, and gone to sleep..."

Guy cursed again. He had never meant for the man to die. But then, neither would he have expected someone as practical and experienced as Sculthorpe to be so foolish as to smoke in a stable.

No one had anything to add. They stared somberly at the roaring blaze, until the old stable's wooden walls cracked and shuddered. Yelling, everyone hastily backed away to safety, as the entire structure collapsed.

NEARLY TWO HOURS LATER, Guy joined the family and guests in the drawing room. He had washed his face and hands and removed his soot-smeared coat, but ash streaked his breeches and he stank of sweat and smoke. Guy had stayed with the workers until the fire was extinguished, while a messenger went for the magistrate and doctor, and everyone else sat inside to wait.

They made a stunned, somber group, scattered about the room like ornaments. Arabella was perched on the window seat, the blue velvet curtains closed at her back. Her father frowned at the fire. Freddie and Matilda huddled together on the settee. Sir Walter was pacing, agitated; Lady Treadgold was completely still.

Every face turned as Guy entered with Lady Belinda.

"Sir Gordon Bell has inspected the site and wishes to interview everyone in his position as magistrate," Guy announced. "Lady Belinda has gathered the staff in another room. The doctor has left and the—" Guy stopped at a sound like a mirthless laugh. "You wish to speak, Sir Walter?"

"Doctor," that man repeated. "Not much use for one of those."

Lady Belinda inhaled on a hiss. "Thank you for that insight, Sir Walter."

She crossed to sit at her husband's side, squeezing Arabella's shoulder as she passed. Aware of his dirty clothes, Guy stayed off the furniture. He found it hard to be sorry that Sculthorpe had left the world, but stars above, what a godawful way to go.

Sir Gordon entered and addressed the room with the practiced eloquence of a former barrister, requesting everyone's patience.

"There must be a formal inquest," he finished, "especially as this concerns the death of a peer, though the circumstances seem clear."

Sir Walter threw up his hands. "Clear case of arson. And clear who started the fire."

Sir Gordon barely spared him a glance. "Lord Sculthorpe was a frequent smoker of cigars. Furthermore, the grooms had brought him whiskey and he was drinking. The most likely scenario is that he fell asleep while smoking and dropped his cigar on the hay."

"But how did he light the cigar? Hm?" Sir Walter said. "I never saw him light a cigar himself."

To be fair, Guy had never seen Sculthorpe light a cigar either.

"He liked having people serve him." Arabella did not try to conceal her impatience. "Lord Sculthorpe picked up the habit when fighting in Spain. It is impossible that a soldier could not light his own cigar."

"You would say that, wouldn't you?" Sir Walter's hand was

shaking as he pointed an accusing finger. "When I said it's clear who started that fire, I mean it's clear it was she. Miss Larke."

Stunned silence fell, all wide eyes and dropped jaws. Arabella looked so startled, Guy had to laugh.

Sir Walter turned on him. "Find this amusing, do you? You won't want to marry her now."

"The shock has addled your senses, old friend," Guy said.

Sir Gordon looked uninterested. "That's quite an accusation, Sir Walter."

"An innocent man has died!" Sir Walter seemed truly distraught. "If you had witnessed her appalling behavior, sir! She meant to strike him. We all saw the violence in her face. It was shocking! Horrific! Unnatural!"

"Enough of this nonsense," Mr. Larke snapped. "My daughter is a harridan, but I'll not suffer you to accuse her of murder. It's impossible. She was in her bedchamber with Lord Hardbury at the time. I was in the corridor when Hardbury came tearing out of her room, yelling up a storm. Followed by the girl."

"They were in her *bedchamber*? *Alone*?" Lady Treadgold's scandalized tones flew across the room, her words tumbling through air that crackled with embarrassment. Everyone's eyes hastened to study something—anything—that wasn't Guy or Arabella.

"No one else came out after them," Mr. Larke said thoughtlessly.

Well done, Larke. Nice touch that, completely ruining your daughter's reputation.

Lady Treadgold kept fulminating about disgrace and scandal and corrupting influences on young ladies, but she might as well have sung an aria for all Guy heard.

All he knew was Arabella, framed like a portrait against the backdrop of blue velvet curtains. Like a painting, she was completely motionless. Even her gaze was unwavering as it met his.

It was over.

The knowledge flared between them, like a thread of lightning connecting them across the room. No hope for discretion, not from Sir Walter and Lady Treadgold. Not from anyone. Word would spread.

Before this, Arabella might have managed to end their engagement with her reputation intact; a trifle tattered, perhaps, but wealth, connections, and demeanor could paper over a multitude of sins. But not with this fresh evidence of their intimacy. Not with her engagement to Guy so soon after Sculthorpe's hasty departure. Not after Sculthorpe's accusations, after her violence, after Guy had beaten him. Not with Sculthorpe lying dead somewhere on her father's estate.

Only two options remained to her: marry Guy or experience complete ruin.

Mr. Larke remained unbothered. "Enough with that nonsense," he grumbled at Lady Treadgold. "They'll be married shortly. Won't you, Hardbury?" he added sharply.

Guy's eyes did not leave his betrothed. Sweet peace flooded through him, for the first time in years.

"No need to clean your guns, Larke," he said. "I have every intention of marrying your daughter as planned."

Almost immediately, Lady Belinda took control and herded everyone out. Everyone but Arabella and Guy, neither of whom had moved. In the doorway, she paused. "Five minutes," she said, "and the door stays open."

"Stable door," Arabella muttered. "Horse bolted."

"The door stays open," Lady Belinda repeated.

"Yes, my lady," Guy said, and closed the door as soon as she was gone.

He lounged back against it to study Arabella.

"This was never my intention," she said.

"I know."

She stood, her fingers steepled, her narrowed eyes boring a hole in the ceiling. The wheels of her brain were spinning; he could hear them whirring from across the room. She was still fighting. It was over, and still she fought.

"By the lake that day," he ventured through his tight throat. "You said that marrying me would be the worst thing in the world."

A terse shake of her head suggested she was irritated by his intrusion. "I cannot think of a way out of this. I have always prided myself on being able to solve any problem and being good at making plans. But I am *bad* at it." The notion appeared to astound her. "I won't even find a position as a governess after this."

"Why the devil would you need to? You'll be a marchioness."

She blinked at him, as if that notion astounded her too. "You're very sanguine, considering you've spent your entire life avoiding precisely this. Your wretched honor and sense of duty, I suppose. Admirable as they are, they have landed you in such a mess. I arrived here through terrible planning. You're so impulsive you simply waded right in."

Oh so help him, but she was struggling like an animal in a snare; if she kept this up, she might just chew off a limb. She had never wanted to marry him either. She still didn't; only he had made that leap. He could tell her that— But no. Unbidden, Clare's words clouded his brain: *The more you told me you loved me, the more trapped I felt.*

Arabella's choices had been stolen too. And Arabella needed time and space to think. Rational thought would help calm her. Rational reasons would make her feel safe. He had to tread carefully, and not scare her away.

He navigated the furniture to reach her side and took one chilled hand in his.

"Don't," he said.

"Don't what?"

"Don't hide behind your walls."

How charming was her confusion, when he observed a truth about her. He knew such things now, knew them like he knew that tiny mole on her left cheek. He brushed it with a knuckle.

"All things considered," he said softly, "I think you'll find I'm not quite the worst thing that could happen to you."

Mercifully, she did not retreat fully into her haughty aloofness, but neither was she melting in a puddle of smiles and sighs. A perfect future stretched out in front of them; Guy was indeed eager to wade right into it, but Arabella would need time to think.

He entwined his fingers with hers. "If this charade has taught us anything, it's that we can rub along quite well," he continued with a lightness he did not feel. "We'll quarrel like two devils, of course, but we're used to that now. You will help me navigate society and politics, and I'll temper your more Machiavellian tendencies. And the marital bed will be satisfying, to say the least."

She studied their joined hands. "You wanted to marry someone amiable, pleasant."

"You were right: I'd be bored. You will never be boring."

She looked back up at him. A triumph: Her bleakness was gone, her face aglow with humor.

"You're saying I was right?" she said.

"That's precisely what I'm saying. How insufferable do you intend to be?"

"I shall be exactly the right amount of insufferable."

Laughing, he lifted her hand and pressed his mouth into her palm. She responded by feathering her fingertips over his eyebrow and down his cheek. He released her, rested his hands on her waist.

"You truly don't mind?" she whispered. "About having to marry me?"

"I mind that our wedding is not for several days, and I shan't be allowed to touch you before then."

Her fingertips continued their feather-light dance over his cheek, to his lips. He still didn't know everything going on in that mind of hers, but finding out would be the most splendid, enduring adventure of his life.

Then she slipped away from him, escaping his hands to cross to the door. She reached out, as if she meant to open it and walk away from him forever.

Guy started to call her name, to stop her from opening that door.

But she didn't open it.

She turned the key.

Locked.

And her expression when she faced him again: deliciously brazen and bold.

"Arabella, what are you doing?" he asked, though he and his happy body already knew.

She lifted one eyebrow, favored him with her most imperious stare. "Why, I'm seducing you, of course."

THE WOODEN DOOR at Arabella's back seemed to thud with the pounding of her heart.

Across the room, Guy didn't move. A wickedly welcome smile teased his lips, and that familiar intensity smoldered in his gaze.

She launched herself toward him, her skirts swishing

obstructively around her legs, the devious carpet threatening to trip her up.

"In the drawing room?" he said.

"I have a fondness for drawing rooms. I've done some of my best seducing in them."

"As I recall from the last drawing room, your seduction technique is dreadful."

"I've been taking lessons. I'm a very fast learner."

She docked before him, basking in his warmth, his scent, his intoxicating vigor. He remained still, awaiting her next move. She faltered, and concealed her nervousness by studying him. A smear of soot marked his cravat. His shirt was spotless, the linen cruelly concealing his arms. Also unmarked was his waistcoat: an olive green, with regiments of tiny taupe tulips marching in exquisitely straight rows. Each tulip was a marvel of needlework: a hundred tiny tight stitches that would take longer to unpick than they had taken to sew.

With one unsteady finger, Arabella traced a column of tulips from his collarbone to his waist. Her motives for this seduction were suspect. Oh, she wanted him; no deception there. But honesty—it was new, this honesty, a result of discovering those hidden parts of herself—this novel honesty compelled her to admit she was driven by more than pure lust. At her core was a deeper desire: to stitch him to her even more tightly than those tulips were stitched into the silk.

To know, without a doubt, that he, too, wished them to be so bound.

She flattened both palms over those tulips, soaking up the feel of his broad chest.

"Careful," he warned. "There's soot all over my breeches."

"And you smell of smoke and sweat."

"How charming of you to mention it."

"I'm being romantic."

She pressed one of his hands, deliberately, meaningfully, to her waist. He used it to yank her against him, and she kissed him. *Want me*, that kiss both commanded and begged. *Want me now and forever.* Her hand trailed over his throat, kept from her by a mile of linen. She hooked her fingertips in the folds of his neckcloth, willing it gone.

It ignored her.

"What's wrong?" Guy murmured. "Have you forgotten what comes next? Will you require instructions?"

"Your cravat. You did not wear one on previous occasions. I don't like it." She stopped pestering his neckcloth and grabbed a handful of linen. "And as for this bothersome shirt..."

"Do you mean for us to ruin another of my shirts?"

She looked him right in the eye. "I mean for us to ruin me."

He caught her meaning. His eyes darkened; his breath hitched. He wanted this. He wanted *her*. He must. A man as honorable as he would never take that step if he was not truly willing to marry her.

"My last chance to ruin you, and I do hate to waste an opportunity," he murmured. "It won't be ruination once we're married."

Arabella's palm drifted to rest on the hollow of his cheek, his sharp jaw, where his skin was intriguingly rough with stubble. On previous occasions, he'd been freshly shaved. She would know such things about him once they were married, little intimacies such as the feel of his beard at different times of the day. Did he wake quickly or slowly, cheerfully or not? How did he sleep? What were his moods? So much of him to discover. A lifetime of it. Hers to take, starting now.

"We don't have much time," she said. "Sit on the settee."

At first, he didn't move, his hand still burning her through her gown. Uncertainty threaded through her: She had miscalculated yet again. He did not want a quick seduction in the drawing room. He did not truly mean to marry her. His taste for dangerous games did not run to this.

But then his palm skittered upward, over her waist to her ribcage to the underside of her breasts, carelessly dragging the fabric of her gown with it, so the air weaved around her ankles.

"The settee, Guy. This is no time for a crisis of principles."

"Firstly, my breeches are dirty," he said, the rough promise in his voice at odds with his mundane words. "While my principles permit me to debauch a willing young lady in the drawing room, they forbid me from dirtying the furniture. I would have thought you'd appreciate that."

"I do, rather."

"And secondly..."

He moved swiftly, stooping to loop one arm around her buttocks. Her feet left the ground and she gripped his shoulders as he barreled her backward across the room to the table. A sweep of his arm sent a workbasket flying and she landed on the sturdy oak. Before she could find her balance, he flipped up her skirts, so she was staring down at her own pale, naked thighs above the royal-blue ribbons of her stockings. Brazenly, he shoved up her skirts further, exposing the dark curls of her quim to the velvet air.

He laughed, a wicked, triumphant laugh. Dazed, aroused, breathless, Arabella locked her hands around his neck, and let herself fall backward as he loomed over her, eyes smoldering.

One hot, rough hand landed on her thigh, and began a slow, relentless march upward; her quim, rather pleased with this change in circumstances, pulsed in readiness for his touch.

"This isn't the settee, Guy," she said, her tone miraculously resembling hauteur. "Will you always have such difficulty with taking direction?"

"And secondly," he repeated, as calmly as if he had not exerted himself at all; it was rather humbling to realize he had not. "Let us agree, right now, that you will not spend all our marriage ordering me about."

His fingers were advancing up her thigh in inflammatory circles. No mistaking her own scent now, mingling with his. Earthy, messy, awkward— Perfect.

"Of course not," she retorted, with treacherous huskiness. "I had not thought to order you about more than three quarters of the time."

"Is that so?" His infernal touch danced in place at the uppermost inch of her inner thigh. "I do believe there is scope for further negotiation."

"You mean to haggle at a time like this?"

"Seems the ideal time to haggle."

His fingers broached that final inch, slipped between the folds of her quim, slid inside her. With a desperate gasp, she reared up to kiss him, but his teasing lips hovered out of reach. His intrepid fingers continued their exploration. They found the sensitive spot they were seeking; rampant pleasure made her arch and gasp.

"As I shall be a reasonable and lenient husband, I shall allow you to order me around one-third of the time."

"What you think you will allow me is of little interest," she retorted. His exquisite strokes did not pause. "My final offer: I shall order you around only one-half of the time. The other half, I shall allow you to *think* you are ordering me around."

Again, she reared up to kiss him; this time, he let her catch him, their lips meeting and moving in time with his rhythmic touch. He straightened, bringing her with him, their mouths not parting for a moment, as she grappled with his breeches and released his hot, hard length into her hands.

He gripped her hips, yanked her to the edge of the table, her naked thighs wide around him. Finally, his breathing was ragged.

"Now," she murmured. "And that's an order."

He didn't move.

"If you don't do this right now, so help me, I'll—"

"You'll what, sweetheart?"

She glared at him.

"Oh, you'll *glare* at me. It'll take more than that to scare me away."

But he required no further instruction: He pushed firmly, unhesitatingly, into her.

Arabella wrapped her legs around him, squeezing him to her as tightly as she could. She forced her eyes open, held his. She longed to throw back her head and surrender to sensation, but she needed to look at him, to show him what he did to her, what he meant to her, how intensely she wanted to hold onto this. That she offered her body in a vow to him; that she received his touch as his vow to her.

With one arm, he held her off the table, taking her weight, moving inside her. She moved with him, passion guiding her, reveling in each sensation, in the powerful movement of her hips and thighs. Taking her own pleasure, heightening his. No thoughts now, no breath, her face pressed into his neck, smothering her gasps, as glorious pleasure shuddered through her, holding him tight as he shuddered too, their bodies still joined.

Guy's shoulders heaved under her airless limbs, and he released a long, slow groan into her hair. His arms tightened around her, gathering her together, gently lowering her to the table. His eyes were glazed and sleepy. He smoothed a hand over her cheek. Holding his gaze, she pressed a kiss to his palm.

"I didn't hurt you, did I?" he said.

"No. That was..." She sighed.

"It was, wasn't it? One day, I'll tup you very slowly, and then you'll be sorry."

He leaned toward her and—

A quiet knock sounded at the door. His eyes widened; no doubt hers did too. A heartbeat of stillness, until they leaped into action, smothering their laughter as he pressed a kerchief into her hand and they tidied themselves as best they could.

Taking his time, Guy sauntered across the room. He unlocked the door and lounged with one shoulder against the wall.

Mama stood in the doorway. Her expression remained bland as she looked them over, first one, then the other. Her gaze came to rest on the workbasket sprawled sideways on the floor. An unfamiliar heat flooded Arabella's cheeks and throat.

Guy's laughter shattered the fragile air.

"You're blushing," he said. *Gloated*, the fiend. "Arabella Larke is actually blushing."

Mama ignored them both, her eyes on the fallen basket. "There is enough time for you two to clean up before Sir Gordon speaks to you," she said mildly. "And Lord Hardbury?" She faced him with such scolding serenity that he straightened. "It might be advisable for you to remove yourself from Vindale Court until the wedding, for the sake of...appearances. I am sure Sir Gordon and Lady Bell will have a room for you at the Grange."

"Of course, my lady."

He sketched a bow. Mama stood aside that he might exit, but once past her, he turned and caught Arabella's eye.

"Blushing," he mouthed over Mama's head, winked, and left.

Arabella stared into the empty hallway, then darted after him, brushing past her mother.

"Guy!" she called.

He pivoted, waited, as she reached his side.

"I agree," she said quietly. "You are not quite the worst thing that could happen to me."

He grinned. "It is just as well your seduction technique has improved, because you are still dreadful at flirting."

Whistling, he sauntered off.

Mama raised an eyebrow.

"Yes, Mama," Arabella said, and with as much dignity as she could muster, headed to her room.

CHAPTER 25

C arrying the portfolio containing the manuscript, Arabella knocked on the door to her father's study. Behind it, she heard Queenie cry, "What a day! What a day!" and then Papa's voice, inviting her in.

Inside, she ignored Oliver. He ignored her.

"'Tis a lovely day, you beautiful bird," Arabella said to the parrot, who nodded sagely and said, "Yes, yes, indeed."

"Good timing," Papa said from behind his desk. He stood, waving the page in his hand. "One of my colleagues recommends a former student to take over your work editing the journals. Have a read."

Arabella exchanged the letter for the portfolio.

"That's the final manuscript for the guide to your aviaries. It wants only your foreword," she said. "If you could complete it before the wedding, I can take the whole thing to London when Hardbury and I go."

That they would go first to London was one of the few details Guy and Arabella had decided on so far. It was not for want of trying. Every time he had called in the days since he left Vindale Court to stay with Sir Gordon Bell, they had not managed a minute alone.

No sooner would he enter the house than someone would intrude: a dressmaker insisting Arabella attend an unnecessary last-minute fitting; Ramsay asking questions on matters he had dealt with for years; and, on the third day, Ursula, bursting into the room out of nowhere, toddling along with a stream of urgent chatter.

"This is a bloody conspiracy," Guy had said, scooping his laughing sister into his arms. "Isn't it, Little Bear? Lady Belinda will not give us a minute alone." He had lowered Ursula to the floor and shaken his head at Arabella. "There are things I wish to say to you."

"I daresay even Mama will leave us in peace on our wedding night."

Under this persistent surveillance, they managed only practical, sensible conversations.

"We'll go straight to London, if you don't mind," Guy had said. "Then on to Roth Hall once this matter in Chancery is settled. Sir Walter has agreed that Freddie and Ursula can come with me in the meantime, with their maids and nanny, if you approve of her. An instant household for you to manage, which you'll do easily. You'll be a brilliant marchioness, you know. Society will be shocked and the lawmakers will be scared."

Then he had announced an impromptu trip to Birmingham, to keep him busy until their wedding, muttering something cryptic about jewelry makers and diamonds.

Arabella had plenty to keep her busy during his absence, as she prepared to leave her childhood home. Cassandra and Juno called several times, eager to discuss the inquest into Sculthorpe's death.

Evidence indicated that many people in the household had known Sculthorpe was in the far stables, and the grooms testified that the baron had been conscious and active after his fight with Guy. Yet still Sir Walter grumbled that no one had yet confirmed whence Sculthorpe procured the flame.

Juno had laughed over her teacup. "Yesterday, Sir Walter called on Uncle Gordon to insist that Lady Belinda could have lit the fire. Apparently, Lady Treadgold's maid claimed to have seen her heading for the stables at the pertinent time."

"No!" Cassandra said. "I refuse to believe it."

"As did Uncle Gordon. Ramsay and Mrs. Ramsay immediately said they were with Lady Belinda, so the maid must have been mistaken. You should have heard Uncle Gordon saying, in that lawyerly way of his, 'We are dealing with evidence, Sir Walter. We do not randomly accuse people of murder without evidence.'"

In the meantime, the dressmakers had finished Arabella's gown for her wedding and the rest of her trousseau. Her trunks were packed and nearly ready, and she had written to Hadrian Bell about her marriage.

Finalizing the manuscript was the last item on her list of tasks.

Papa opened the folio on his desk and turned over a page. "I hear Hardbury has gone to Birmingham."

"Yes."

"He had better come back."

Arabella unfolded the letter and stared unseeingly at the words. Of course Guy would come back. Unless he didn't. Unless he fell back on their old scheme, wrote letters full of detailed, regretful excuses, stayed away until the banns were no longer valid.

Don't be silly, she scolded herself. He had days, yet, to get back before their wedding. He would not have made love to her like that if he didn't intend to marry her.

But perhaps he had changed his mind.

She pressed a palm to the familiar dull ache in her abdomen. Their passion in the drawing room would not lead to any babies; the signs had come that morning. If Guy didn't return, there would be no consequences. He could run free if he pleased.

She would be ruined, but he would be free.

"He will come back," she said firmly.

"You see, my girl, I chose the right husband for you decades ago." Papa's hands faltered. When he looked back up, his expression was sincere. "I am sorry about Sculthorpe. I never imagined... I was impatient, after my illness. You understand."

"All I wanted was to choose my own husband." She paused. "I had considered Hadrian Bell as an option. I tried to tell you."

Papa cocked his head, considering. "That would have worked, actually. But you've done even better, and we agree on this one too."

Arabella let it drop. It didn't matter anymore. She scanned the letter about the potential new journal editor. Papa had wasted no time in replacing her.

"These illustrations are good," he said, nodding at the peacock. "Quite talented, that Bell girl. Not bad for a woman. Not bad at all."

"A woman can have as much talent as a man, Papa."

"You were never one for drawing. Adequate, of course, but your lines were too straight. I say, take a look at these."

His tone was suddenly jaunty. Bright-eyed, he opened the bottom drawer of his desk and pulled out a thin folio, tied with a yellow ribbon. Arabella came to his side as he opened it, letting a dozen drawings spill out. They were done by a child, clumsy and out of proportion, but already they captured an impressive level of careful detail. The feathers on an owl. The veins in a leaf. The name on every page: Oliver.

Not one of these drawings was hers. But, as Papa had said, she never had been one for drawing.

She curled the corner of one page between her fingers. "You kept these, all these years."

Papa traced the owl's lumpy head. "This house will have children again. Your boys will love it here."

Helplessly, Arabella found her brother's portrait, looked away, to Pirate the falcon with his single, knowing eye.

"You don't have to name the boy Oliver, of course. Name him whatever you please, but he'll come here and learn everything there is to know." Papa gathered up the drawings, neatly, reverently. Closed the folio on them. Tied that little yellow ribbon. "That's how my interest grew, you know. When my book lessons were finished, my father used to take me around, teach me things. He found my fascination with birds amusing, given our name, but that was only ever a coincidence. I liked it when my father took me around, just as I did with you two. It'll be wonderful to do that again."

"With us two," Arabella repeated.

Yes, Papa had always been there, when they were two. But when there was only one...

"I came to tell you about a nest I had found," she said. "You scolded me for the dirt on my gown. I brought you a butterfly I had caught. You complained that my hair was a mess. I tried to learn about farming. You sent me away to help Mama plan the menu."

Papa busied himself with replacing the folio. "Yes, I remember you barging in here, all of twelve, lecturing me about drainage or timber or something else you'd read in some outdated book. Telling me this would be your estate as you had no brothers and demanding I teach you." He looked up, his knuckles on the desk.

"It'll be your son's estate, not yours. That's the natural order of things."

Arabella caught herself crumpling the letter and dropped it as if scalded. She had to speak. Guy had taught her that. He had shown her it was safe to say what she felt, to ask and not demand.

"I only wanted to spend time with you again. As we used to. I wanted a home. I wanted..."

She had wanted her home to go back to how it had been before Oliver died. Fifteen years had passed, and still she wanted that.

"If you wanted a home, you should have married years ago. But no matter now. You'll marry, have children, and your second boy will live here with us."

"So I exist only to bear children, which you will take away."

"Don't turn it into a drama, girl. You know what I mean. This estate is your son's birthright. Don't deny him that. Don't deny *me* that."

Swallowing away the bitterness in her throat, Arabella let her eyes wander over the pages on his desk: the text and illustrations she had commissioned to make this book. A silly little guidebook! And those journals, bound and lined up in a neat matching row on Papa's bookshelf. How enterprising she had fancied herself, at the age of sixteen. It had been during one of the ornithology conventions, not long after Guy's departure. She had overheard Papa saying that his daughter should have been getting married, but her bridegroom had run away. But she had distracted him, all of them, with her brilliant idea of turning the conference papers into a regular journal.

What a waste of her time. What a waste of her talent! What else might she have been doing, all these years?

Their quarrel must have upset Queenie, for suddenly she flapped her wings and again cried, "What a day! What a day!"

Immediately Papa went to soothe her. Of course he did. He spent more time with that parrot than he did with his daughter. He spent more time with two dozen dead birds.

Do you even like birds? Guy had asked her. She had never thought to query it, because it had never been about the birds, or the journals, or the books, or even her inheritance. It had only ever been about getting her family back.

Truth was, she didn't like birds, much.

She looked at Papa. "If you could have had a choice, you would not have chosen me, would you?"

He needed no explanation. His eyes went straight to the portrait and back to Queenie. "You know that's not it," he said, his hand resting on the parrot. "I would have chosen you both."

"But you lost only one, not two. Yet you could not be pleased with the child that remained."

He said nothing.

"I loved him too," she said. "He was part of me, my twin. Always at my side."

Silence filled the room, so dense even the parrot dared not break it.

Finally, Papa dropped his hands and took a deep breath.

"He still is," he said quietly. "Every time I look at you, I see him. Right there."

Now she knew why Papa could hardly bear to look at her.

"Maybe if you had not been twins, maybe it would have been different. I know it was not your fault, it was never your fault. But... When I look at you, I see what I could have had. What could have been and never was."

The jury of dead birds stared at her, their glass eyes as cold and judgmental as ever.

"So you found fault with me," she said. "I would never have pleased you. I worked hard to excel, and the world sang my praises, but not you. Never you. It wasn't about whether my hair was messy or my dress was flawed, or my fingers were stained from blackberries or my tongue too sharp. It was because I was a living reminder of your loss. I didn't only lose my twin brother. I lost my father too."

He closed his eyes and pinched the bridge of his nose. "It'll be different now. You'll see. Everything will be fine."

All these years she had been fighting, and the whole time it had been in vain. She had lost before she'd even understood what the battle was about.

"You are not taking my children from me, Papa. Any child I have, I will keep with me for as long as I am fortunate to have them. You have taken too much from me already."

THE WIND SLICED Arabella's cheeks as her horse galloped along with bone-jolting speed, but the effort to keep her seat meant she could not think, not until she reached the abbey ruins and toppled out of the saddle onto unsteady legs.

But even up here, even a good hour since her quarrel with her father, she found no peace, no escape from the eruption of messy, hot, stinking emotions. In the dull light, these abbey walls, too, were haunted by memories. Here she had played at knights with Oliver. There, they had picked blackberries. And that wall there— that was where Guy had walked, traipsing along carelessly on a sunlit day.

Curse him for going to Birmingham. She needed him. She needed his arms, his comfort.

She needed to grow up.

Yes, Oliver was always by her side, the little boy who never grew up. And here stood proud, arrogant Arabella Larke: the little girl who never grew up, still eight years old, trying to bend the world to her will, waiting for her life to go back to how it was, when their family was happy and she was always welcome, Oliver's sister and protector.

What a tragic pair they made, she and Papa, so terribly alike, both trying and failing to fill the hollow left behind, in their own pointless, useless ways.

Thus had begun her struggle with her father. Poor Mama, caught in the middle. Even Sculthorpe had been a casualty of it. And now Guy was swept up in it too.

If it wasn't for this futile fifteen-year struggle with Papa, she would never have become engaged to Sculthorpe, never have devised her scheme, never have chosen Guy, never have gone to his house that night in London.

And she and Guy would never have ended up here: due to be married in a few days. Instead, she would likely have married someone else years ago, and Guy would have been free to choose the life he wanted after all, with the amiable, pleasant wife of his dreams.

In the end, they had wanted the same thing, she and Guy: a warm, safe, loving home.

He wouldn't get what he wanted, not with her.

"No," she said out loud, to the stone, to the blackberries, to the cluster of Michaelmas daisies by the wall. "No. He will come back from Birmingham. He will marry me."

Papa might not have wanted her, but Guy did. Papa had resented her all these years, but Guy had chosen her.

In a way.

He was happy to be marrying her. For now.

He was content with the decision. For now.

He enjoyed their arguments. He looked past her flaws and mistakes. He indulged her prideful nature and her foibles.

For now.

But marriage was not just for now. It was for years. Decades, if they were lucky. Guy's reality would not meet his dreams: the pleasant, amiable bride, the peaceful home. Arabella was not his first choice.

Every time I look at you, I see what I could have had. What could have been and never was.

Guy got himself into these situations and then he made the most of them. He didn't waste time and energy considering future possibilities, not the way she did. He was spared the curse of seeing seventeen moves ahead. Seventeen years ahead. Would he still be content with his decision a decade from now? Or would she start one quarrel too many? Issue one too many commands? Devise one too many insupportable schemes? Offend the wrong person one too many times?

Until the day came when Guy did not see her, but instead saw what he could have had. What could have been and never was.

Arabella climbed onto a low section of wall and hauled herself back into the saddle. On she rode, her thoughts and feelings swirling into a fierce, tangled mess.

Never again. She could not bear to feel like this again. She could not bear to see Guy turn remote, find interests that separated him from her, hide his resentment under smiles and false cheer.

Arabella kept riding, across her father's estate to the neighboring estate of Sunne Park, with the old Tudor pile that was Cassandra's home. By the time she dismounted, her roiling emotions had settled. She had a plan. Arabella liked having plans. Having plans gave her the illusion of having control.

Cassandra was in her garden, singing to herself as she tended a flowerbed, an old bonnet sitting lopsided on her head.

"Arabella?" Her smile faded. "Whatever brings you here? You look distressed. What is the matter?"

"You said if I ever needed help, I should come to you."

"Of course. What is it?"

Arabella briefly squeezed her eyes shut. This was the right decision. Guy would be happy this way, and his happiness mattered more than anything else in the world. That knowledge helped her utter words she had not spoken in more than a decade.

"Cassandra," she said. "I need your help."

CHAPTER 26

Guy's errand in Birmingham took longer than he had anticipated, for while the city boasted some of the country's best jewelry makers, it took time to perfect the piece for Arabella.

As he arrived back in Longhope Abbey, he pictured giving it to her: the firelight caressing her skin and catching in the diamonds, her hair tumbling around her face, her eyes darkening as he told her of his love, her lips parting to tell him of hers.

And perhaps he would also tell her of this odd sense he had, that this was where his long journey finally came to an end.

It had not ended in Rome, when he had learned of his father's death. Nor when he arrived back in England. Nor when he entered the house in London, or even Roth Hall, the place where he was born.

Now, today, that restlessness vanished. *Zugunruhe*, the Germans called it. The restless need to move, to fly home. This was the end of his journey, and the years of travel had prepared him only for this. Coming back to Arabella—that was what it meant for Guy to come home.

The light was fading when he arrived at Sir Gordon's house; the first evening stars had appeared. The days were already getting short. The years were long. Good. Long years and lots of them. Guy was thrilled at the thought.

Indeed, the thought of seeing Arabella again, of their wedding night, and provoking her and loving her for decades to come had him in such a good mood that he was whistling when he strode through the Bells' front door.

Servants ran into the foyer. Stared at him nervously.

A moment later, Sir Gordon came racing in.

Guy's heart lurched and thudded. "What's going on? What happened?"

Sir Gordon said, "You haven't heard yet."

"Heard what? Is she harmed?"

"No. She's gone. We don't know where."

The world tilted. Gone. Arabella was gone.

"What do you know?" he asked.

Sir Gordon shook his head. "Two days ago. She left a sealed note for you. It is with Lady Belinda."

Guy spun around and went back out the door. It was still open. They had not even had a chance to close it behind him. On the steps, he had to stop and stand, to keep from falling over.

You're not quite the worst thing that could happen to me, she had said.

Yet she was gone.

She had left everything: family, money, reputation, name. Her father would cut her off, her reputation would be in tatters, her family members would not receive her.

Why would she do this? Why would she give up everything rather than marry him?

Curse you, I am no one's martyr, she had said. True: If Arabella wanted him, she would have held on with both hands and her teeth. But she had chosen to leave. She had chosen to be homeless, friendless, destitute, because that was better than being married to him.

It seemed he was the worst thing that could happen to her after all.

Humbling, that.

Above him, the night sky persisted, the first stars appearing, cold, splendid, indifferent.

She was somewhere under this sky too. Was she looking at these same stars? Was she frightened? Relieved? Did she think of him at all? Now he was getting pathetic. It was almost their wedding and she had run away. Of course she must spare him a passing thought.

He stood by his horse, but suddenly his limbs were too weak to mount. The horse shied away. Guy rested his hands on the saddle and breathed.

She had chosen ruin over him.

As SOON AS Guy's feet hit the gravel outside Vindale Court, Lady Belinda emerged, a taut, tired thunderstorm in a dress.

"What did you do to her?" she demanded, advancing on him. "She would never have given up everything unless she was frightened. What did you do? You will tell me, my lord, and then you will stand still that I might shoot you in your rotten heart."

"I swear I do not know, my lady. But if I have indeed harmed her, I will load the gun and hand it to you myself."

Lady Belinda was not appeased. "I thought you would be the one to love her, the way she deserves to be loved, the way she *needs* to be loved. I thought you were strong enough for her. I entrusted her to you, tried to help you, and you— You must have hurt her too, and you know what happened to the last man who harmed my daughter."

The implications chilled him, but Guy swallowed his questions. Now was not the time. Never was the time. If Lady Belinda had been involved in Sculthorpe's death, he did not want to know.

"I will give her what she needs," he said shortly. "So perhaps, madam, you would kindly resist shooting me until I have had a chance to do that. Her note, if you will."

Without another word, she whirled around. He followed her through the house and into Larke's study. There, among the dead birds, witnessed by a dead boy, Lady Belinda handed him the sealed note.

It trembled in his hands; they were shaking. His courage faltered. He stared at the lump of wax and tried to imagine what Arabella might have written. She would have argued, naturally, which would give him a reason to argue back. Or perhaps she had made a demand, which he would race to meet. Or she had sent him on a quest, and he would defeat the ogre and seize the gold and she would consent to marry him again.

He fumbled with the paper, but he still wore his gloves. He took his time removing them. Delaying the moment.

The note was his last chance. The note was his only hope.

The note said:

Hardbury—

I release you from our engagement. You owe me no debt or duty. There is nothing else to say.

A.

What the devil?

He turned it over, held it up to the light, waved it over a flame in case she had written in lemon juice. He felt like a fool, but surely, there had to be more.

Before his eyes, the note turned into a blur of black marks. No matter: Those words were already seared onto his eyeballs like a nightmare.

"She did not write this," he said witlessly.

Lady Belinda came to his side, peered at it over his shoulder. He felt her taut anger soften into pity. "It is her hand."

So he scoured those twenty words, those three empty, succinct sentences. He searched them for a way in. He found nothing. He could not argue with this. She had made no demands, placed no blame, sent him on no quests.

Here he was, one of the most powerful men in the land, willing to do anything for her, and she had asked him for nothing.

She did not even want to try.

The simple finality of it ruined him.

If only he had told her of his love. But he had held his tongue. He had not wanted her to feel pressured or trapped. He had not wanted to scare her away. She needed time and space to think, he had told himself, after which he had made love to her on the table, to prove to them both that he wanted her forever. But he had not uttered those words of love.

Maybe it would have made no difference, but he could not bear the thought of her, so proud and alone, going out to do battle with the world, without knowing someone loved her so much he would fight any battle by her side.

And maybe the day would come when she would turn to him and smile with the splendor of a thousand stars and find that, by some miracle, she loved him too.

Crouching, Guy fed the letter to the fire, let the flames engulf it, watched it crumble into ash.

"Hardbury? My lord?"

The smoke had stung Guy's eyes. He blinked away the tears and stood to face Mr. Larke, holding his wife's hand. Guy had not heard him come in.

"I fear..." Mr. Larke's mouth worked. His parrot began to mutter and he crossed to stroke her neck. "This is my doing. We quarreled."

"Why?"

"Over...the education of your sons and this estate. Because..." The man looked distraught. The parrot rubbed her head against his arm as if to comfort him. "I vow, I never imagined she'd leave. She's so stubborn, so certain, so proud. I never thought..." Shooting a glance at the portrait on the wall, he took a few steps and sank into a chair, head in his hands. "She's always been so damnably strong-willed, so difficult to control. Using this estate seemed the only way. I was so sure she'd never give this up."

"Oh, Mr. Larke, you selfish, stubborn sod." Guy pressed his fingers into his eyes, furious at the waste and the heartache and the loss. He dropped his hands and shook his head at the other man. "It was never the estate she wanted. It was a family. A family to love her. A home."

"She had that."

"Did she? Or were you scared to love her in case you lost her too?"

"Lord Hardbury," Lady Belinda admonished softly. "Please."

He turned away, mind racing, seeing only Arabella, that first time she smiled. He was the one who had done that. He was the one she needed, even if she was too bloody proud to admit it.

"We've sent word to our house in London, to see if she's there," Lady Belinda added. "And written to my family."

Larke clenched the arms of his chair. "You'll find her, Hardbury. You'll not rest until you bring her home."

"And if she doesn't want me?"

"Find her anyway. It's your duty."

Duty. Her note had mentioned duty. And that day in the drawing room, when their marriage had seemed inevitable, she had spoken of his sense of duty then too.

He regretted burning the note, but he knew it well enough to recite in his sleep. *You owe me no debt or duty.*

Thank the stars. She had given him a clue, after all.

CHAPTER 27

Arabella made no effort to hide, because she knew Guy would not come after her. And if he did come after her, why make it difficult? But he would not come after her. She knew he would not.

And he didn't.

It was two days' travel to London, and she was thankful for Cassandra's help in providing her comfortable carriage. She avoided her family's house; the humiliation if Papa wrote to cast her out would be unbearable. Instead, she traveled two extra streets to the London house of her friends, Lord and Lady Luxborough. The earl and countess were at their home in the county of Somerset, but their retainers knew her well. They opened the house and let her in.

Like all her other oh-so-brilliant solutions, it turned out to be a mistake.

Because the Luxborough house formed part of a square, and in the middle of that square was a small, leafy park, and on the other side of that park was Lord Hardbury's house.

Several days after Arabella arrived, Guy did too.

She knew from the bustle of carriages. She knew from the chatter of servants. She knew because she saw him, day after day after day, playing with Ursula in the park.

She knew because he looked right at her each time, his expression unreadable as he held her gaze.

As always, she was the first to look away; as always, he continued as if she were not there.

"What did you expect?" she muttered to the window. "A bunch of flowers and a thank-you note?"

"Did you say something?" Juno asked from behind her.

Good grief. Arabella had forgotten her friend was even there. She had expected heartbreak to hurt; she had not expected it to be so all-consuming she could concentrate on little else.

"No. Nothing," she said.

With a whisper of skirts, Juno crossed the room to join her, and side by side they watched Guy and his little sister play. Ursula had spotted the robin redbreast that frequented the park. Guy crouched, with his arm looped around her, as she pointed out the little bird.

"Lord Hardbury came by the studio, with Leo," Juno said.

As a professional artist, one of the very few women in London with her own studio, Juno inhabited a space parallel to society's usual rules. While she would never be received in respectable places, it was perfectly acceptable for respectable people to mingle in art studios. Leopold Halton, the Duke of Dammerton, was known to mingle in Juno's studio quite often.

Perhaps Arabella would learn to exist in a space like that, if she managed to start her publishing house. By jilting Guy, she had thrown herself out of society, but a publisher had little use for a good reputation. All she needed was money. And friends.

Abruptly, Juno bounded back across the room, grabbed her

charcoal and paper, and started sketching. Arabella leaned against the windowsill to watch her work.

"How is he?" Arabella asked.

"He didn't talk much. He seemed distracted."

"Was he poking and prodding things?"

"Oh dear me, yes."

Arabella smiled, remembering. "He does that. He gets restless."

Oh, but she missed him. She made her longing worse, she supposed, the way she kept taking out her memories of Guy and studying them like treasured pieces of art. But she welcomed the heartache; it came with love, and she refused to surrender her love.

"We could arrange a meeting," Juno said, not looking up from her work. "At my studio. It could appear purely incidental. You would be there visiting me, and Leo will bring Hardbury again. You could talk to him."

Arabella shook her head. "Talking won't help."

Cassandra had said something similar: *Don't make it more complicated than it needs to be.*

But they didn't understand. Suppose Arabella had expressed her fears that Guy was marrying her for honor and duty and nothing more? He would have denied it, of course. His honor and sense of duty demanded that he marry her, and his good character demanded that he pretend to be glad. He would have concealed his true thoughts behind bonhomie and jokes, but she would have felt his underlying tension. She would have felt it worsen over the years.

Besides, it was too late now anyway. A lady could not jilt a man, then wander back a few weeks later and say, "Actually, I've changed my mind."

Finishing her sketch, Juno hopped up and handed the page to

Arabella. The drawing was of Guy, but Guy looking solemn and stern. Arabella ran a fingertip along the charcoal line of his jaw, as if she could magically touch him, but all she got was a dark smudge on her skin.

"He should be smiling." Absently, she rubbed at the smudge. "Draw me one of him smiling."

"He wasn't smiling when he visited the studio with Leo," Juno countered, but she started a fresh sketch anyway.

"He has a lot on his mind." Arabella lowered the page and turned back to the window. In the park, Guy and Ursula were playing a game of chase. Guy was laughing. Once or twice, Arabella had made him laugh. "He is in the papers most days. Between us all, we've been keeping the news correspondents busy."

The inquest had ruled Sculthorpe's death accidental, and the newspapers overflowed with accolades for the heroic peer, tragically lost in his prime. Speculation buzzed as to why the baron had even been on the Larke estate, and why Hardbury was no longer engaged; few yet dared to explicitly name Arabella, but the implications were clear, if one read between the lines.

The papers had also reported that Chancery was hearing Lord Hardbury's petition to gain custody of his sisters, while observing that his sisters already lived in his house. Next, they announced his success: The late marquess's will had been overturned and the guardianship was his.

"They're going back inside now," she said. "Ursula has grown. I think Guy's hair has darkened. Or maybe that's the light."

"You could become a news correspondent yourself," Juno said. "I can imagine your reports: 'Today, Lord Hardbury wore a new blue coat and scratched his chin. It was very exciting.'"

"That's hardly exciting news."

"Exactly. You are becoming boring, Arabella."

Arabella whirled around with an imperious glare. "Don't be absurd. I am never boring. My reputation, certainly, is becoming much more interesting. Almost as interesting as yours," she added archly.

Juno responded with her merry laugh. "My reputation is only interesting because I am friendly with the Duke of Dammerton."

"Whenever the newspapers report that, they put 'friends' in italics."

"Because they are incapable of understanding that a man and a woman can enjoy each other's company without tupping each other. It's excellent for business. Wealthy bankers' wives commission portraits in the hope that if they sit in my studio, they'll meet a real live duke. Leo is very obliging about it. He says he ought to charge me a commission."

Helplessly, as if compelled by a stronger force, Arabella turned back to the window. Across the park, the front door was closed. In that house was Guy, creating the peaceful, loving home of his dreams. Already he had his sisters; soon he would find a bride, someone as unlike Arabella as possible, and she would read about his betrothal in the news.

Perhaps he'd send the flowers and a thank-you note then.

And she'd send them right back. It was not his gratitude she wanted.

She wanted to be in that house with him, sharing his troubles and triumphs. She wanted to be the one he came home to. The one he confided in and teased and quarreled with and kissed. She wanted to be the one on his arm when he entered a ballroom, exchanging looks down the table when they hosted a dinner. Riding beside him through Hyde Park, nestled against him in a cozy parlor at the end of the day.

She wanted to be the one he opened his arms for, the one who made him smile. The one he looked for when he had news. The one he held against him when he slept.

But more than that, she wanted him and that great big heart of his to be happy. She wanted him to create the warm, peaceful home he craved, to have the freedom to love whomever he wanted and marry as he pleased.

That, at least, she could do for him.

"Leo is leaving for Lincolnshire shortly to visit his mother and younger sister. Lord Hardbury will accompany him," Juno said. "Lady Gisela is making her come-out next year. Leo says she's very pretty. I wonder if Lord Hardbury will think so too."

"You are not subtle, Juno." She turned back. "Is Lady Gisela amiable and pleasant? That's what Guy wants in a wife."

"I thought what he wanted was you."

Juno handed her another finished sketch. This one showed an old woman, with sharp cheekbones and finely arched eyebrows. Her haggard face was creased with lines and frowns.

"That is a portrait of you," Juno said. "When you are old and miserable and lonely, all because you're too proud to talk to him."

"It isn't pride this time." On the paper, her miserable future self scowled at her. "He is going to Lincolnshire, you say?"

"Soon."

"Then it is time for me to stop dithering and leave London too."

CHAPTER 28

T he carriage was loaded, the coachman was fidgeting, and a groom held the door open, waiting for Arabella to climb in.

She would climb in. Of course she would. She had marched out of the house with every intention of jumping straight into that carriage and letting it carry her away west.

Yet, curiously, in the short distance between house and carriage, she had lost her way. As if compelled by an unseen power, she had walked around the horses in their clinking harnesses, and now stood in the middle of the street, turning her bonnet and gloves in her hand, staring at the park.

At Guy.

He was with Ursula and Freddie, the three of them watching the little robin redbreast again. They must know she was there, but they paid her no mind. Clearly, a robin was much more interesting than the comings and goings of proud, foolish Arabella Larke.

Perhaps she could draw near him, for one more moment. For one more word, one more smile. Her body would not turn away. It was as if a force of nature was pulling her toward him, the way migrating birds were pulled across the world.

How could she fly off to her friends in the countryside, when all she needed was right here?

Arabella shoved her bonnet and gloves onto a footman and was crossing the road before she even knew her own intention. She was dimly aware of Freddie taking Ursula away, but all she saw was Guy, straightening, turning, tensing, watching her approach.

Oh, to keep walking, right into his embrace, to press her face into his neck, and know that she had come home.

She stopped some six feet away from him. His hair was still golden. His complexion still tanned. She had seen that face laughing and sad and angry and passionate. Now it was inscrutable. Unwelcoming. A closed door to the home she sought.

He could have been mine.

Until he regretted his honorable actions, and resented her presence.

She had made the right decision, for both of them. She *had*. She had set him free to find the true happiness he deserved.

It was just that she had to break her own useless heart to do it.

His gaze flicked past her, to the abandoned carriage. "Running away again, Arabella?"

"I didn't—"

"You—ran—away."

"I set you free."

"Did you expect a thank-you note?"

Habit had her retreating. "Some flowers, also, would have been nice."

She stopped herself. *Not now, pride.*

How her heart ached to see him so close, his unsmiling,

untouchable face. He could never be hers, but perhaps she could salvage something from the debris.

"Let us put this behind us," she said. "We can be civil to one another, acquaintances who—"

"No. We cannot." He fairly scowled at her as he withdrew a letter from his pocket. "This is from my solicitor. It needed only my signature before he sent it, but since you're here, I might as well give it to you now."

The thick creamy paper was slightly crumpled as if it had been well handled. More interesting were his bare hands. Were his palms still rough, or were they already smooth? She had given up the right to know.

"What is this?" she asked.

"That thank-you note you wanted, I suppose." His voice was dry, mocking. "Thank you for setting me free."

He shoved the letter at her impatiently, so she took it and tore it open.

He began to explain, speaking faster than usual, as if he wanted this over with as quickly as possible. "In the breach of promise suit you brought against me, your solicitor argued—"

"I ended the engagement," she interrupted, baffled. "I never brought a suit against you."

"And highly annoying that was too. I had to do it on your behalf."

Confused, Arabella unfolded the letter and stared at the neat, indecipherable writing. The first words were in legal language. She was good at legal language. She read case law for fun. It was incomprehensible nonetheless.

"You sued yourself on my behalf," she repeated.

"Yes. Do keep up. Your solicitor's petition notes that—"

"I have a solicitor?"

"I had to hire one for you. He's good but expensive. I'll send you the bill."

"Guy, you are making no sense. I released you. You could have brought a breach of promise suit against me."

"In his will," he continued testily, "my father named three properties that would come to me if I married you, and to Sir Walter Treadgold if I did not. Your solicitor's petition successfully argued that, given our broken engagement, those properties should go to you."

"You gave me houses."

"Yes. It's all there in the letter."

She still couldn't make out a word of it. "Three houses."

"They have some land attached. Cows and crops and so forth."

In an effort to clear her head, Arabella looked past him, to where glossy ivy wound around the iron fence. She watched its leaves tremble in the breeze and still did not understand. Apparently, in breaking her own heart, she had also broken her brain.

"Why would you do this?" she asked. "I stated very clearly that you owe me nothing."

"Indeed, your note was exceedingly clear." His dry tone forced her eyes back onto him, but still his expression gave nothing away. "This settles it definitively. We are completely free. No debt, no duty, no honor, no obligation. I can't do much to salvage your reputation, but that's mostly your fault, so I refuse to feel responsible for that."

"Completely free," she repeated.

"Completely free," he agreed. A thread of tension hummed under his light tone. "I owe you nothing, you owe me nothing. I am now free to choose my own bride. Someone I love, someone who knows me, someone who makes me happy. I can choose whomever I wish. And you can too."

Arabella didn't feel free. She felt the tightness of her corset, and the breeze in her hair, and her silly, sorry heart breaking all over again. How eager he was to sever all ties! Yet he could have severed those ties without granting her financial independence. Why did he have to be so wretchedly *decent*?

"I entangled you in my problems, and nearly ruined your life, and you do this." Her fingers tightened on the page, tempted to tear it to shreds. "I gave you no end of trouble and you gave me three houses. Do you want nothing from me?"

"You have nothing," he said sharply. "You gave it all up."

"True, but—"

"But there is one thing you can give me."

Anything, she wanted to say. She waited.

"An explanation," he said. "Tell me why you ran away. Why you preferred to lose everything rather than marry me."

"I didn't run—"

"Tell me."

His features were implacable, his stance as welcoming as that of an enemy soldier at the gates. Nothing about him invited her to lower her guard and surrender her frightened heart.

"You want this finished with," she said.

He closed his eyes briefly. "So help me, but I want this finished with."

If he wanted an explanation, then that was what she owed him.

She let her eyes wander back to the ivy-wreathed fence. The robin redbreast was perched there now, a puffy ball of feathers on little legs. She might not like all birds, but she liked that one, she decided. She admired its gumption, the way it chirped so merrily, oblivious to cats and cages and the myriad other dangers that came with simply being alive.

"You fought against being forced to marry me," she said to the robin. "But suddenly, you were trapped. You put a cheerful face on it, because that is what you do, but we both know the day would have come when you tired of me. After all, you did not truly want me. You would look at me and see what you had lost, the life and home you had dreamed of and had to give up. I did it for you, because I want you to be happy. But I did it for myself too. Because there is something worse than losing everything."

The intensity of his silence called her gaze back to him. Once their eyes met, an earthquake could not have made her look away.

"I have spent my life amid resentment and hostility, all the while longing for love. I could not bear to spend my marriage that way too."

His eyes narrowed. "Why would you be longing for my love?"

"Good grief, Guy, you cannot possibly be that obtuse."

"Why not? You are." When she added nothing more, Guy raised his eyebrows. "Your explanation is not good enough. There's more."

There was more, but her words failed. Behind them, Freddie and Ursula went back inside. Guy twisted around to watch them go, then turned back.

"I know I have not always been good at listening to you," he said, "but I promise to listen to whatever else you have to say. But Arabella—" His gaze skewered her. "This time, you will actually have to say it."

"You aren't making this easy."

"You don't deserve for me to make this easy."

Fair enough. She did owe him. Because he had gone to the effort and expense of looking after her, despite everything being her fault.

So he could set himself free. Free to choose, he had said. Free to choose a wife whom he truly wanted.

Free to choose her.

Hope swelled within her, foolish, vain hope. He would never choose her, not with her mistakes and flaws, not after his efforts to sever all ties. If only she could command him to love her. If only she could buy or bribe or beg his love.

What a pity love did not work like that.

Love could not be bought or forced or demanded or taken. Love could only ever be given.

Then she would give him her love, whether he wanted it or not. It was the only thing she had left to give.

Do not tell him, her pride warned. *He will mock you, dismiss you.*

From somewhere deep inside came the whisper of her heart: *Don't be absurd. I would never love a man who mocked love.*

Leave now, her pride insisted. *He doesn't want you. Get in that carriage and go.*

Shut up, pride, said her heart. *I'm in charge now.*

And suddenly, it was not hard. The words were there, in her heart, where they had lain since before she was born, and all she had to do was speak them. This time, her mouth did not betray her, and the words emerged, pure and true.

"Because I love you," she said.

The robin fluttered past in a panic and a gust of wind rustled the leaves. But the sky did not collapse. The sun went on shining and Arabella went on breathing, albeit with a little more difficulty.

Guy said nothing.

"There is more," she said. "I accepted that I must surrender you to someone else, someone who can better give you what you want, and that I could only love you from a distance. Which is not ideal, because one does like to be near the object of one's affection. But also, I need you."

Still he said nothing.

"Of course, I would survive without you," she added.

Was that a smile? "Of course."

"I need you in order to...to be myself. I realized I have shut myself away for so long, holding onto my childhood, seeking the family and home I wanted but foolishly looking in the wrong place. It is thanks to you that I am able to grow up and start my life anew. My own life, my own way. I am making a dreadful hash of it so far but... I will never regret loving you, or being the way I am. I regret only that I am not what you want in a wife. Because you are everything I desire in a husband."

He closed his eyes and muttered something that sounded like a curse.

"There. That is your explanation," she said hoarsely. Her throat was achingly tight. "Now I owe you nothing either, and there really is nothing left for us to say. I'll not keep you."

She whirled around to leave, before she shattered at his feet. He seized her wrist with his bare hand. Heat jolted through her. Her limbs froze. She could not turn to face him. But she felt him, standing behind her. He touched only her wrist, but she felt him all the same.

She heard his deep, shuddering breath. Felt its warm release on her neck.

"Oh thank the stars, I had hoped that was it," he said, his voice shaky.

Blood rushed through her, blood and something else, something that coursed through her veins and made her muscles weak. Still she dared not turn. He laid his hand over hers and entwined their fingers. She closed her eyes, surrendering her senses to his presence, until he was all she knew.

"I cursed you, you know," came his low voice in her ear. "I cursed you so long and hard it's a wonder you don't have a cloud of locusts swarming around your head. Cursed you and your blasted pride. Debt and duty, you wrote: That's what you believed, isn't it? And anything else I said, you would have dismissed as a gallant lie." His other hand landed on her hip, as if they were ready to waltz, but she was facing the wrong way. "You started thinking, didn't you? You and that brilliant diamond mind of yours. But thinking is like walking: If you begin in the wrong place, facing the wrong way, you'll head in the wrong direction, and end up falling off the edge of the world."

He eased closer; his chest brushed her back. She could not have turned, he held her so firmly in their backward dance.

"I've been carrying that blasted letter around in the hope you would come to me first. I wanted you to come to me. I needed—" His voice broke. He breathed in sharply. "I needed you to come to me."

His grip relaxed. She pivoted in his arms, to stare into those eyes of his, eyes like summer rain.

"But you never wanted me," she recited, stunned. "You deserve to have the home you dream of. You deserve to have what you want."

"A home," he repeated. "A safe, welcoming place to come back to, a place where I feel comfort and passion, joy and delight." He cupped the back of her neck, as if to hold her in place. "Arabella, you proud, impossible fool. You *are* my home."

His words stole her breath, but it seemed she did not need air, for all her shakiness was gone. Her legs were strong and her arm steady, as she pressed one hand against his beloved face. He let his forehead drop to meet her own.

"It took me so long to see it," he continued softly, their breaths mingling. "My struggle against my father made my thoughts rigid. But finally I understood: I had to travel the world and become myself, so I could see that what I most needed was here the whole time."

"You mean..."

"I mean, I love you too. I meant to tell you, but I didn't get a chance."

She lifted her head to search his eyes, needing to believe it, to find a way through her fear.

"I'll make mistakes," she said. "I'll say the wrong thing. I'll—"

"Of course you bloody well will. As will I. Will you leave me when I make a mistake?"

"Of course not."

"Then why not grant me the same grace?" He smoothed back a tendril of her hair. "I know you, Arabella, and I am choosing you. This time, surely, you can have no doubt. I choose to share my life with you, because my life is better with you in it. I want you to choose me for the same reason. Stop fighting, for once in your life, and spare me this wretchedness."

Pain sliced her tender, battered heart. Oh so help her, what had she done?

"I hurt you," she said, tears pricking her eyes as she hurt with him. Urgently, she pressed her hand to his face, to his neck, to his shoulder, as if she could heal him. "Oh, Guy, I didn't realize. I never wanted to hurt you. I never realized I could. I only wanted you to be happy."

He shook his head with a short, mirthless laugh. "You were wrong. You were so—bloody—wrong."

"I am so sorry. Will you forgive me?"

He brushed her cheek. Cool air danced over the dampness left by her tear. "Everything was a mess between us. It took some untangling. Just promise me: Don't do it again."

I can fix this, she thought, as her hands rested on his chest. *I just need a plan.*

Guy laughed lightly. "Beautiful, brilliant Arabella," he murmured.

"Why are you laughing?"

"Because you are trying to make a plan, aren't you?" he said. "Very well: Tell me your clever plan. How do you mean to fix this?"

A thousand options flew through her head, but she ignored them all. She already knew what to do.

"I shall...talk to you," she said hesitatingly.

He nodded, smiling. "Good plan."

"I shall apologize for running away."

"You've done that."

"And seek your forgiveness for hurting you."

"You have that."

"And then..." This was new to her, but it was too important; she must not get this wrong. "I shall ask you... What do you need from me, so I never hurt you like that again?"

"One thing."

"Anything."

"Trust me. Trust me to love you. Trust me to know my own heart. Trust me to look after yours."

His eyes looked into hers, so deeply he must have seen all the way to her heart. She felt her heart open to him in sweet surrender. Blessed peace flooded through her.

"Yes," she said firmly. "Yes."

"I truly love you. You do see that."

"And I love you." She tilted her head. "Considering I had never uttered those words before today, I'm getting quite good at saying them, aren't I?"

"Do keep practicing, though."

"Every day."

Which reminded her: One thing remained undone.

She took one step away from him. Gripping both his hands, she looked into his beloved face. His fingers curled around hers.

"Guy," she said slowly, "now that we are completely free..."

"Yes?"

"Perhaps this might be a good time for me to ask you…"

"Yes?"

She inhaled deeply, and as her chest swelled with air and joy and love, she felt her mouth widen into a broad, helpless smile. "I was wondering, Guy Roth, if you would do me a great honor…and marry me?"

His smile matched hers. "I thought you'd never ask." He lifted her hands and pressed a light kiss to her knuckles. "Yes, Arabella Larke, I will marry you. Yes."

THE GOWN MADE for Arabella's wedding was no more beautiful than her other gowns, but it transformed her as no other outfit had ever done. She studied herself in the mirror, examining every inch of the white skirt and bodice, the profusion of bluebells bursting around the hem. She looked utterly like herself and yet like someone completely new.

It took her a moment to understand why.

Every day of her life she had dressed as if she was donning armor, readying to fight in the world she saw as a battlefield.

The world was not a battlefield today. She would find another battle another day; that was who she was and she was exactly as she ought to be. But today, after a lifetime of fighting, it occurred to Arabella that she had finally won. She hadn't even known what she was fighting for, and she still wasn't sure how she had earned this victory, but she would happily claim it as her own.

The carriage was ready, but Arabella was not. Mama had not yet appeared, so she picked up the skirts of her beautiful gown and dashed into Papa's study.

She ignored the birds, which, in the end, were only dead, stuffed birds, and looked up at the portrait of her twin brother.

Beautiful, beloved Oliver. The perpetual little boy who had always been part of her, and always would be. Who had left her too soon, but always walked at her side.

There you are, little brother, she thought.

His smile today was sweet, like the little boy she had loved, and fond, like the young man she had never known.

I'm getting married today. To someone I love who loves me too.

I'm happy for you, was his response. *You deserve it.*

"I miss you." Those words she spoke out loud. "I wish you were here. I'm sorry you died."

He was only a portrait and he could not speak, but she heard the words as surely as if he had spoken out loud too: "I miss you too, but I'm glad you lived."

The door opened and in came Mama.

"There you are. The carriage is waiting. What are you doing?"

"Talking to Oliver."

Her mother took her hand, and they stood together, looking at the portrait of the little boy, who had nothing left to say.

"I love you, Mama."

Her mother pressed a kiss to Arabella's temple. "I love you too, my dear."

Again the door opened. It was Papa this time, coming to stand at Arabella's other side. For a long moment, they didn't speak.

"I hope you'll be happy, my girl," he finally said. "And I'll say this for Hardbury: At least he can handle you."

"He can try."

Papa laughed. "Yes, I suppose he can. I..." His laughter faltered, and his eyes fled from her, up to the wall. When he turned back, he took her hand. "I've done badly by you, I know. But I'm proud to call you my daughter. You've grown up to be a fine woman, and that's despite me, not because of me. Yes, you're a fine woman indeed. If a little proud and stubborn."

On her other side, Mama laughed. "Proud and stubborn, is she, Peter?" she said archly. "Remind you of anyone?"

Arabella could not remember a time she had stood like this, flanked by her parents, the family connected, laughing together at their own folly.

"We will come to visit, Papa, as often as you please. You'll have plenty of time with the children here, if we are blessed with any. I truly hope that at least one of them will take after you."

"A little man of science?"

"Or a little woman."

He snorted. "Thank you. But even if you are not so blessed, I hope you will still sometimes visit your foolish old father. Now," he added more briskly. "We'd best get you to the church before Hardbury starts panicking you've run off again."

The little church was full, and as Arabella and her father entered, every head turned.

Every head but one: Guy's.

He was waiting at the altar, his broad back tall and straight. A beam of sunlight broke through the stained glass to paint his hair with gold and red and blue.

Their slow walk began. Arabella kept her eyes on Guy. Still he did not turn.

When they reached the altar, Papa kissed her cheek and stepped aside, leaving her next to her bridegroom. She looked at him, and perhaps he felt her gaze, because finally, he turned. His eyes traveled over her face.

And something wondrous happened.

Guy Roth smiled.

It was a warm smile, a joyous smile. A smile full of pleasure, simply because she was there.

Guy smiled at her because he was happy that she was alive.

And that was the most marvelous thing in the world.

ACKNOWLEDGMENTS

My thanks to May Peterson, Johanie Martinez-Cools of Tessera Editorial, and Melinda Utendorf, for their valuable feedback and editorial skills, which immensely benefited this book.

THE LONGHOPE ABBEY SERIES

Available Now

A Beastly Kind of Earl

A Dangerous Kind of Lady

A Wicked Kind of Husband

Coming Next

A Scandalous Kind of Duke

For news on release dates, future books, and more, sign up at miavincy.com/news or visit miavincy.com.

Each book in this series can be read as a standalone, and the books can be read in any order. As the characters move through the same world, they do appear in each other's stories, but without any overarching plot.

ABOUT THE AUTHOR

Mia Vincy holds degrees in English Literature and journalism, but she has managed to overcome the negative effects of this education and now writes historical romances.

Mia's studies and former work as a journalist, communications specialist, and copyeditor took her to more than sixty countries around the world. She is now settled in Victoria, Australia.

For more, visit miavincy.com.

 facebook.com/MiaVincyBooks

 twitter.com/miavincy

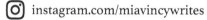 instagram.com/miavincywrites

Printed in Great Britain
by Amazon

46649096R00215